Murray Pura's first Harvest House novel
The Wings of Morning stole the heart of reviewers...

From Romantic Times...

"Pura has created one of the finest stories of Amish fiction I have ever read. The WWI-era Amish religious practices engage the reader, as does the dramatic love story...The reader will be applauding the exceptional writing, and the cast of characters demands an encore performance."

From Publishers Weekly....

"Pura has penned a meaty story dealing with complex issues as the impact of WWI and the Spanish influenza epidemic affect a Lapp Amish community in Lancaster, Pa., during 1917–1919...Pura, who has been a pastor and author in Canada for more than 25 years, masterfully balances depictions of simple Amish living with the harm that can be caused when religious ideology overrides compassion and understanding...Pura's nearness to historical and Amish accuracies makes for a plausible and intriguing tale. Pura's previous works have been shortlisted for several literary awards; this entry into historical fiction is noteworthy as well."

From Eugene H. Peterson, Professor Emeritus of Spiritual Theology, Regent College, Vancouver, B.C., and author of more than 30 books, including his Gold Medallion Book Award winner *The Message: The Bible in Contemporary Language*...

"Murray Pura's novel of an Amish community facing an unprecedented world war is accurate and winsome. But his portrayal of the two main characters, young people of integrity and maturity, is absolutely riveting. A book to be relished by any age, from young readers to their elders."

From Connie Cavanaugh, author of *Following God One Yes at a Time*...

"Murray Pura's first foray into Amish fiction does not disappoint. As a novelist of some distinction, Pura has already established himself in other genres, and his ability to tell a great story is as evident in this book as in his others. Pura weaves romance as well as spiritual depth into a challenging plot that will keep readers turning pages and leave them sweetly satisfied when all is said and done."

From Christian Manifesto reviewer Rachel Ropper…

"…I completely fell in love with Murray Pura's take on the Amish during the First World War. *The Wings of Morning* wasn't simply an attempt to break out of the typical mould of Amish romances by sticking the story in front of the backdrop of WWI. Murray's writing showed that he'd researched not only military camps and bases, the treatment of conscientious objectors and the role that aeroplanes played in WWI, but the actual flying of these planes…I never thought I'd enjoy reading flight sequences but Jude and Lyyndaya's descriptions of their experiences surprised me and made me think about what it would have been like to fly in one of the open-cockpit planes that were flown in this period…Murray Pura shows the beginnings of being a popular voice in inspirational fiction and I look forward to reading more emotionally stirring and well-researched depictions of history in the next volume in his *Snapshots in History* series."

From Amazon.com Hall of Fame reviewer Harriet Klausner…

"This excellent fresh WWI era Amish thriller provides wonderful unique perspective of the community at a time when aeroplanes and electricity are so new they have not been banned yet; even Bishop Zook demands a flight. The seemingly star-crossed romance between the shunned hero and the woman he cherishes enhances a great period piece that will have readers wanting more historical tales like this winner from Murray Pura."

THE
FACE
OF
HEAVEN

MURRAY PURA

HARVEST HOUSE PUBLISHERS
EUGENE, OREGON

Unless otherwise indicated, all Scripture quotations are from the King James Version of the Bible.

The Scripture quotation on page 8 is from The Bible in Basic English version.

Cover by Garborg Design Works, Savage, Minnesota

Cover photos © Chris Garborg; iStockphoto/Taylorhutchens, WilliamSherman, Jpecha

THE FACE OF HEAVEN

Copyright © 2012 by Murray Pura
Published by Harvest House Publishers
Eugene, Oregon 97402
www.harvesthousepublishers.com

Library of Congress Cataloging-in-Publication Data

Pura, Murray
   The face of heaven / Murray Pura.
      p. cm.— (Snapshots in history ; bk. 2)
   ISBN 978-0-7369-4949-1 (pbk.)
   ISBN 978-0-7369-4951-4 (eBook)
   1. Married people—Fiction. 2. Amish—Fiction. 3. United States—History—Civil War,
1861-1865—Fiction. I. Title.
PR9199.4.P87F33 2012
813'.6—dc23

2012002226

Printed in the United States of America

12 13 14 15 16 17 18 19 20 / LB-GLD / 10 9 8 7 6 5 4 3 2 1

For Lyyndae Levy Pura, RN, BN,
graduate of Dalhousie University School of Nursing, 1983,
and for all the nurses of America, Canada, and the world,
whose skill, dedication, and compassion have saved millions of lives.

And for the men of the Iron Brigade.

LIBERTAS SUPRA OMNIA

I prefer the tumult of liberty to the quiet of slavery.

THOMAS JEFFERSON

This is not a history of the American Civil War. Nor is it a history of one of the Union Army's most famous units in that conflict, the Iron Brigade, or of the 19th Indiana, one of several illustrious regiments that made up that brigade. It is instead a story of a young man and a young woman who sought love and God and forgiveness in the midst of America's greatest trial and its greatest tragedy.

But in answer he said to them,
At nightfall you say, The weather will be good, for the sky is red.
And in the morning, The weather will be bad
today, for the sky is red and angry.
You are able to see the face of heaven, but not the signs of the times.

Jesus, in Matthew 16:2-3

Whenever she thought back to that morning years later, or told friends about how life was before the whole world changed, it was the warm spring sunshine and the brightness of the sky Lyndel spoke of the most. That and the green scent of the grass over which a morning rain had just come and gone, the opening of red snapdragons, and the talk of the men on the porch being lost to her ears as robins and larks opened their throats on that second day of April, 1861, in Lancaster County, Pennsylvania.

The cows had already been milked and Lyndel's three younger sisters were hard at work with the butter churn in a room just off the kitchen. She was heading to the barn to open the doors and lead the dairy herd out to their spring pasture. A sudden pause in the birdsong allowed the men's voices to reach her as she crossed the yard.

"Jacob, they have seized the federal forts in South Carolina and Mississippi and Georgia. Their intent is clear. I see no hesitation on the part of the states that have left the Union. They mean to have their own country."

"Just wait. It's only a ploy to force President Lincoln to take their demands seriously. All will be right as rain by summer."

"I'm not so sure, Jacob. They mean to keep their slaves. They are afraid of Lincoln."

"So you don't think the president can stop the Southern states, Samuel?"

"I don't know. Only I don't think they're merely spinning tops and playing games. They will have their slaves and they will have their own country."

Lyndel was surprised to find the cows pushing against the barn doors, more eager than usual to make their way to the pasture. Once she opened them, the herd rushed out, almost knocking her to the ground. Without Lyndel having to say a thing, Old Missus rapidly led the way to the pasture gate so that the young woman had to run ahead and swing it wide.

The cows shouldered through side by side, a few of them bawling, and traveled at least a hundred yards before deciding to stop and crop grass. Latching the gate, Lyndel went back to the barn to see if she could find out what had disturbed them. Perhaps a snake had found its way in among the straw.

Picking up a pitchfork to chase away any pest she encountered, she began to walk through the barn, glancing often at her feet as she stepped through the dirty straw.

Looking into the first stalls, she found they were empty of anything like porcupines or skunks or badgers. She stopped and listened a moment but heard nothing.

Slowly she made her way to the back of the barn, holding the pitchfork at chest height. Sunlight trickled between cracks in the walls and through the dusty skylight so she could make out what was in the corners. But by the time she reached the end of the barn there was still nothing. She didn't bother taking a look at the last two stalls and turned to head back. Whatever had spooked the milk cows was long gone. But suddenly she heard a groan.

She whirled, fear pricking her chest. Brandishing the pitchfork she stepped toward the last stall on the left, expecting to see a wild dog or a coyote or fox. Instead, in the dim light she saw two sets of human eyes—then teeth as a face grimaced, struggling to breathe.

"We mean you no harm!" a voice cried and a hand shot up to ward off a blow.

Lyndel immediately lowered the pitchfork and stepped closer. "You're slaves!" she said in astonishment.

"We're men."

"How long have you been here? What has happened to you?"

One man was holding the other in his arms. He was the one who spoke to Lyndel, while his friend could only fight for air and wince. "We've been on the run from our plantation in Virginia for three weeks," he said, holding the wounded man close to his chest. "We made good time riding the boxcars. But we had to jump while the train was moving last night and Charlie got hurt pretty bad."

Lyndel was wearing a traditional Amish dress of navy blue over which she had tied a large black apron. Leaning the pitchfork against the wall, she knelt and took the apron off. The man named Charlie had a deep cut at the side of his chest, and she folded the apron twice and pressed it against the wound to slow the flow of blood. She used the apron strings to tie it tightly.

"Have you had anything to eat or drink?" she asked the man who was doing the talking.

"There's plenty of water in the streams and rain barrels. But we haven't had anything to eat. Not for two days."

"Let me fetch you something."

A hand grabbed her by the wrist. "Don't tell anyone. They're hunting us. This is the third time Charlie's tried to escape. They said they'd hang him if they caught him running again. They'll cross the state line and comb this county."

Lyndel, still kneeling, fixed her eyes on the frightened man. "I will only tell people I can trust. I won't tell anyone who would go to the sheriff in Elizabethtown. He would feel bound by law to tell the slave hunters if they showed up here."

"They'll show up here." For the first time a smile came over the man's face. "We may not look like it right now but we're worth a lot of money."

"And why is that?"

"Book learning, ma'am. I was taught to read and write by an elderly gentleman at the plantation. He had me read the Bible to him and all sorts of books written in America and England. Seven times I read the Bible through from beginning to end for that fine man."

Lyndel paused. Smiling back, she patted the man on the arm. "Then we must take good care of you."

He released his grip on her wrist and she stood up. "I will be a few minutes," she said. "Please don't worry. I will not betray you."

He was still smiling. "I believe you."

"What's your name?" she asked.

"My name is Moses Gunnison," he said.

She reached down and took his hand in hers. "I am pleased to meet you, Mr. Gunnison. I am Lyndel Keim."

"Pardon me for saying so, but you have large hands for a woman, ma'am. And some strength in them."

"I have been a farmer's daughter all my life, Mr. Gunnison."

"Do you have a husband, ma'am?"

"Oh, no. There's been no time for that. But I do have a brother. He's the one I will go to. He will help you. We will both help you."

"Thank you, ma'am. God bless you."

Lyndel straightened and brushed the straw off her dress. "Why, God bless you too, Mr. Gunnison." She adjusted the black prayer *kapp* on her head and looked down at Charlie. "You are going to be all right." He stared up at her, his eyes exhausted from fear and pain. "I will be right back with my brother Levi as well as food and drink."

She thought quickly as she walked through the barn and out into the morning sunlight. The men were still seated on the porch and still talking politics. Her father, the bishop of their Amish community, sat in the middle of them, tall and slender, his beard night-black, listening carefully to the different opinions, now and then leaning forward and interjecting. She loved her father—indeed, she cared for all the men seated with him, several of whom were the church's ministers. But she also knew how law-abiding they were. If she told them about Moses and Charlie they would offer as much assistance as they possibly could. Yet they would also feel bound to hitch up a wagon and drive into Elizabethtown and inform the law there were two runaways hiding out in the Keim barn. Instantly she decided against confiding in any of them, including Papa. She smiled as she walked past them toward the stable, where she knew her brother was doing the work of a farrier and trimming their horses' hooves now that it was spring.

Levi was wiping his face with a red handkerchief, sweat running down into the collar of his white work shirt. He was speaking to someone who was bent over and holding a horse's hoof between his legs and fighting to get the nipper in position to cut. Lyndel hesitated. Even though the man with the hoof nippers had his back to her she recognized his build, and when he answered her brother she knew for certain: Levi's good friend, Nathaniel King, was the one wrestling to trim Dancer's left front hoof. She had not expected to see him today but Levi must have asked him to come over and lend a hand with the horses.

Her brother glanced over and grinned as she came into the stable. "Hello, Ginger. You're just in time to help. Nathaniel can't get Dancer to cooperate and since she's your mare, can you reason with her?"

"I can try."

She walked over and stood in front of Dancer, who whinnied and allowed Lyndel to hold her head and scratch her between the ears.

"That's better," grunted Nathaniel. He moved quickly with the nippers and the mare was done. He released the leg and stood up, stretching his back and smiling at Lyndel. "*Danke.*"

"*Bitte.*"

"May I call you 'Ginger' too?"

"No, you may not. You both know I don't like it. Only Levi gets away with it."

"So just plain old Lyndel?"

"Yes, just plain old Lyndel. You make me sound like one of Levi's horses."

"My apologies. You certainly deserve better than that. Hair like fire. Eyes like sky."

Lyndel felt the heat in her cheeks.

Levi laughed. "Are you going to court my sister? I thought you came over to help me."

"I did," smiled Nathaniel. "But now we're finished."

"*Ja,* well, how about sitting down for a coffee before you ask her to go for a ride in your buggy?"

"Sure, a coffee would be good right about now."

Lyndel walked Dancer out of the stable and into a bright green paddock with two other horses. "You don't need to talk as if I'm not here, you two," she said over her shoulder. "And the older men are sitting on the porch."

"Still here?" groaned Levi. "What do they find to go on about for so long?"

"The South."

"Oh, the South. These things work themselves out." Levi glanced at Nathaniel. "If we want coffee we will have to run the gauntlet. They'll probably make us sit with them and offer up our opinions."

Nathaniel shrugged. "I don't have an opinion on the South. They live what they live and we live what we live."

Lyndel turned from closing the stable gate. "And what if others *can't* live, Nathaniel King? What is your opinion on that?"

The firm tone of her voice made Levi and Nathaniel stare at her.

"What do you mean?" Nathaniel finally responded, wiping his hands on a large blue rag.

"Would you favor slavery for yourself or your family?"

Nathaniel met her gaze. "No. I would not. I've read about these things and thought deeply about them. That is why I am still Amish and still a Northerner."

"How is it you have been coming to our house for years to visit my brother but I've never heard you express these thoughts?"

"Why, the occasion for it has never occurred in your presence."

She kept her eyes on him, turning over what he said. Ever since she had seen Nathaniel in the stable she had been debating with herself about what to do—should she tell him about the men in the barn or not? Now she made up her mind to find out what sort of person he really was behind his soft brown hair and shining green eyes. Besides, the two men in the barn were hungry and scared. She wouldn't keep them waiting longer.

"I need your help, both of you," she said. "Two men are in the barn. They have run away from a plantation in Virginia. One of them is wounded. I'm afraid to tell the elders. I don't want them to go to the law."

"Slaves?" asked Levi in shock.

"They don't like to be called that."

"What are they then?"

"What you are. What Nathaniel is. Men who are hungry and thirsty."

Nathaniel kept his eyes on her. She wondered if he was looking at her red hair and blue eyes or waiting to hear what she had to say. For a brief moment she realized she hoped it was both. Then her thoughts returned to the crisis at hand.

"Levi, can you get a sausage from the smokehouse? I don't dare go into the house for bread. Mama will ask what I'm doing."

"Why can't we tell her?" Levi asked.

"Because then everyone will find out and someone will speak with the sheriff. And if slave hunters come, the sheriff will tell them two men are in the Keim barn."

"Are they headed for Canada?" Nathaniel spoke up.

"I didn't ask," Lyndel replied, "but that would only make sense."

"All right." Nathaniel reached for a bottle on a shelf. "You said they had wounds? This alcohol will help with that. Can I draw some water from the well for you while Levi gets the sausage?"

She gave him a small smile, wanting to make up for some of her harshness. "That would help." Then she glanced around her. "My problem is bandages. I can't go into the house. And I already gave the man who is wounded my apron to stanch the blood."

Nathaniel nodded. "I have a clean shirt in my wagon to change into after helping your brother. It's just under the driver's seat."

She didn't mean to give him her full smile but it opened upon her face before she could stop it. "Thank you so much, Nathaniel."

"My pleasure. And an honor." He gave her a slight bow of the head and then walked out of the stable in the direction of the well.

Lyndel went out to Nathaniel's wagon parked near the house and was surprised to see that the porch was now empty and all the visitors' buggies gone. She patted Nathaniel's bay, Good Boy, who stood patiently in the shade of a crab-apple tree, and reached under the seat for the shirt. It was wrapped in a thin blanket to keep it clean. She ran her hand over it a moment and thought of Nathaniel wearing it, a young man so tall, so strong. Then she tucked the white shirt and blanket under her arm and walked toward the barn doors where Nathaniel and her brother were already waiting for her. They entered the barn together.

As soon as he saw them Moses said to Lyndel, "There are three of you."

"Yes, Moses. This is my brother Levi. He's brought you meat from our smokehouse. And this is his friend Nathaniel who has brought you a pail of water."

Moses stared at Nathaniel. "Can we trust him?"

Lyndel knelt and began to rip Nathaniel's good cotton shirt. "Well, he gave me this for Charlie's bandages. Let us give him an opportunity to prove himself, *ja*?"

Nathaniel set down his bucket. "I have some well water. And a tin cup. Can I give your friend a drink?"

"Give me the cup," growled Moses. "I'll give Charlie the drink."

Lyndel dipped a square of Nathaniel's shirt in the water and mopped Charlie's forehead and face. "How is he?"

"Now and then he starts to shake. The blood seems to have stopped coming out of his wound though." Moses put the tin cup to Charlie's lips. "Come on now. You got to take some of it in."

Lyndel gently lifted the folded apron from Charlie's side. It was thick with blood. She reached her hand toward Nathaniel. "May I have that bottle of alcohol now?" He tugged out the stopper and gave it to her. She poured some onto another cloth and pulled Charlie's shirt back from his wound. She began to clean the gash, and the sting made him cry out once and then clench his teeth. Sweat covered his forehead again.

"Levi?" Lyndel asked her brother. "Could you take another piece of Nathaniel's shirt and wipe Charlie's face?"

Levi had been standing there taking it all in. He squatted down and, not knowing where to put the two large rings of sausage, placed them on Charlie's lap. "Are you hungry? It's very good sausage. My mother's recipe and her mother's also." Then he splashed water over a cloth and patted Charlie's face and neck. "How is that? Is that all right for you?"

"Perhaps I should go back to my house," said Nathaniel, "and get some blankets and pillows. We need to make them comfortable here. They will need a few nights of rest before they move on."

Lyndel glanced up at him. "That sounds like a good idea."

Moses shook his head. "No. They're on our trail. The reason we jumped from the train was we could see a whole gang of them waiting on the station platform a quarter mile ahead of us—bloodhounds, rifles, and rope."

"But we have to get Charlie's wound closed up first," protested Lyndel. "He'll bleed to death if you run too soon."

"They'll hang him from the tallest tree on your farm if we run too late." Moses looked around at their faces. "I appreciate what you're trying to do. I'd heard there were good people hereabouts, good Christian people." He tightened his grip as Charlie let out a moan. "But they're going to hunt until they find us. One more night here and then we have to get up to New York and Ontario. I tell you, we've got to move on no matter how bad Charlie is."

Nathaniel nodded. "In that case we have to make sure you have a restful night. I'll fetch bed linen for you and Charlie from my home. And a poultice recipe of my mother's she swears can close any wound."

"No need to go all the way back to your home when there's a spare room here."

Lyndel jumped to her feet. Her father was standing behind them. His eyes cut dark and sharp right into her.

"You should have told me, daughter," he said. "You should have trusted me."

2

Moses and Charlie were lying in separate beds in the spare room of the Keim house. It was on the third floor and the window offered a long view of the hay fields just starting to sprout from the ground in the spring warmth. The sun was setting and an oil lamp was burning on a small table between the two men.

Lyndel finished the reading from the Bible with the words, "*Because he hath set his love upon me, therefore will I deliver him: I will set him on high, because he hath known my name. He shall call upon me, and I will answer him. I will be with him in trouble; I will deliver him, and honour him. With long life will I satisfy him, and show him my salvation.*" She looked up and smiled at Moses and Charlie. "Psalm 91. One of my favorite chapters in the holy Scriptures."

"Amen," grunted Moses.

Charlie smiled. He was only able to speak in a whisper. "Thank you, Miss Lyndel. I do enjoy hearing the Bible read to me and you have such a fine voice."

She stood up. "Why, thank you yourself, Charlie Preston. Now let's take a look at that cut of yours."

She pulled back the quilt and sheets from Charlie's left side and slowly untied the string fastening a thick square of cloth tightly to his body. Then she gently peeled back the poultice of Canada wild ginger. The angry red was gone from the lips of the wound and the skin seemed to be starting to bind together.

"Well?" asked Moses from the other bed, lifting himself up on his elbow.

Lyndel removed the old leaves of ginger and applied some fresh ones from a small bowl. She shook drops of water off before placing the heart-shaped green leaves in the poultice. "He is doing very well, Mr. Gunnison. You may thank God for that. But I wouldn't advise rushing out the door at midnight as if the hounds of the devil were after you."

Moses sank his head back on the pillow. "The hounds of the devil *are* after us. But I'm mighty weary myself and, devil or not, I need a powerful lot of sleep before I can lift another foot." He turned his head and looked at her, the slow smile completely altering his stern face. "I'm much obliged to your mother for all that good soup. I'm afraid that between Charlie and me we emptied a pot as large as your barn."

Lyndel laughed. "That's what food is for, Mr. Gunnison. And guests were made by God to be fed. And you, Charlie Preston," turning to the other man, "why, I'm proud of you. What a fighter you are! I suppose you're just about ready to outrun Moses all the way to the border."

He smiled and whispered. "Thank you, ma'am."

"Now I'll leave you alone and let you get that sleep you need so badly."

"Miss Lyndel. Would you read a bit more of the Scriptures to us?"

Lyndel looked at Charlie in surprise. "Why, Mr. Preston, you can hardly keep your eyes open. You need to rest."

"I will. I'll drift off as you're reading. I swear I will."

She glanced over at Moses. He had his eyes closed. "It's no never mind to me, Miss Lyndel. I can sleep in the middle of a thunderstorm and your voice isn't anything worse than a summer breeze."

She sat back down in her chair and picked up the big black Bible. "Well, all right. But this was your idea, Charlie Preston, so you have to tell me what you would like to hear."

"Read to us about Jesus. He gives me peace."

So she began to read from the Gospel of John. By the time she had reached the fourth chapter the snoring from Moses' bed made her pause and look at both of them. Ten minutes earlier Charlie's eyes had been locked onto her when she glanced up. Now they were shut and his head was turned to the side. She closed the Bible and prayed a silent prayer over them.

The jingle of harness made her go to the window. A carriage was pulling into their yard. It was Pastor Yoder. All three ministers would be coming to the house this evening to discuss what was to be done about Moses and Charlie. Levi and Nathaniel were required to join them. As another buggy rattled up the drive she quietly shut the window. Then she went to the table between the two beds and turned the knob on the lamp until the flame was gone. Returning to her seat she sat in the dark with her hands folded in her lap.

The men would be meeting in the kitchen. Mama would leave them with a large pot of coffee and a plate of fresh buttermilk biscuits. After prayer Levi and Nathaniel would be taken to task for not telling her father, the bishop, that two runaway slaves were hiding out on his property. Her hands twisted about one another—it was her fault they were going to be castigated. The fact that her father had spent a full hour reprimanding her earlier in the afternoon did nothing to assuage her guilt over being the cause of her brother's and Nathaniel's trouble. The small comfort she clung to was that the leadership of the church couldn't spend a long time raking the young men over the coals. The main point of the meeting was Charlie and Moses, and they would have to get to that sooner rather than later.

A half hour went by as she waited and thought and prayed. Then the door opened silently and her mother appeared, a candle lighting up her face. She smiled at her daughter, crossed to the beds, examined the two men, nodded, then came and stood by Lyndel.

"How long have they been asleep?" she asked in a whisper.

"Perhaps as much as an hour," Lyndel whispered back.

"And you've just been sitting here alone in the dark?"

"Not alone."

Her mother patted her shoulder. "There's no need for you to hide away. Your father has forgiven you. And he understands your concern for the men here. No one wants to see them return to a life of slavery. The sheriff has not been made aware of their presence on our farm."

"He soon will be."

"Not tonight, at any rate. By the time the meeting is over it will be too late for that. It will have to wait for the morning."

Lyndel looked up at her. "What time in the morning?"

"Not before lunch, my dear. So your father assured me."

Lyndel smiled and her eyebrows lifted. "Truly?"

"Yes." She placed a hand on her daughter's *kapp*. "Now if you're upset about getting your brother and Nathaniel in trouble I can tell you the tongue-lashing didn't last nearly so long as your own. The discussion has already begun. I thought you might wish to listen in."

"May I?" Then Lyndel frowned. "But I will not be permitted to sit in the kitchen."

"Go to the second-floor landing. You can hear them from there. Just make sure they don't notice you."

"What about the girls?"

"Long in bed."

Lyndel got to her feet. "And where will you be?"

Her mother promptly sat down in the empty chair. "Where you were. Thank you for keeping the seat warm."

"I don't wish to take your candle."

"Don't trouble yourself. You won't be taking it. The light would be far too noticeable to anyone glancing up at the staircase. You have the blue eyes of a Siamese cat, don't you? So your little sisters say. Make your way in the dark."

Lyndel bent down to kiss her mother on the cheek.

"Cat or no cat," her mother said, smiling, "mind you don't go tumbling down the stairs."

Lyndel used the banister to navigate the staircase from the third floor to the second. At that point, the light from below was sufficient for her to see where she was going. The men's voices were clear and she sat down on the landing where she couldn't be seen.

"There was slavery in our Lord's day," she heard one of the ministers argue. "He did nothing about it. Neither did Paul. We have verse after verse where Paul tells slaves to behave, to obey their masters, not to cause trouble, and by so doing set a good example as followers of Christ."

"True." It was her father's voice. "But Paul also said if a slave could obtain his freedom he should do so. Clearly he didn't consider slavery to be an ideal state for a human being."

"Nevertheless, he didn't tell Christians to go to war over it."

"Oh," her father said sharply, "who is talking about going to war, Samuel? We're discussing how we should help these two men."

So, Lyndel realized, the one arguing with her father was Samuel Eby. Samuel spoke up again. "You have fed them and bandaged their wounds. You have given them a room at the inn, so to speak. Fine. Now it's time to drive into Elizabethtown and tell Sheriff Jackson."

"Why is it time?" She recognized the voice of one of the other ministers, Abraham Yoder, whose carriage she had watched pull into their yard. "What's the hurry? We've scarcely begun to discuss this issue. Why is there a fire in your britches, Samuel?"

"I don't want the sheriff to think we've been keeping something like this from him. After all, these men are breaking the law—they belong to the owners of a plantation in Virginia. And they're breaking the Word of God as well—they are to be good slaves and carry out their duties in obedience to their masters. Not to engage in this act of rebellion."

"So you would like to be a slave, Samuel?" asked Pastor Yoder.

"No, I should not like to be a slave. But if I were a slave, I would carry out my duties with reverence and respect to my God and those he had placed in authority over me."

"If you feel that way perhaps you could trade places with them."

"*Vas?*"

"Sure. You go to the sheriff and tell him that when the slave hunters show up from Virginia you are substituting yourself for them. They wish to be free and that will secure their freedom. Meanwhile you can show us what a good slave looks like in the eyes of God."

"Do not talk such nonsense, Abraham," Lyndel heard Samuel fume. "God did not make me a slave. He made me Amish."

"He made you a man." Lyndel sat up. It was Nathaniel's voice, calm and clear. "He made these others men as well. Human beings fashioned in his image. It is for freedom Christ has set us free. How can you place them back in the yoke of slavery, Pastor Eby?"

"Paul is talking about spiritual freedom," came a new voice that Lyndel recognized as Solomon Miller's. "There is no talk in any of his letters about striving for physical freedom for slaves. It's their hearts that are to be free in Christ. Not their bodies."

"No talk in any of his letters?" Lyndel detected a slight rise in Nathaniel's voice. "So when was it you last read Philemon, Pastor?"

"Gently, Mr. King," interjected Lyndel's father.

"I have read Philemon," retorted Solomon Miller. "I read the Bible through twice every year."

"*Gut.* Then you will recall that Paul sent the slave back to Philemon a brother in Christ. And by so doing sent back a man who was his equal."

There was a moment of silence. Then Samuel Eby spoke up again. "Still, Paul sent him back a slave."

"No. That is precisely what Paul did not do. Under the inspiration of the Holy Spirit—we all agree on that, yes?" Nathaniel paged through his Bible, which he had set on the table during the discussion. Reaching his place, he continued, "Paul plainly said, *Receive him back not now as a slave but above a slave, a brother beloved specially to me, but how much more unto thee, both in the flesh, and in the Lord? If thou countest me a partner, receive him as myself.*

"Paul said no to slavery. He said it here, he said it when he declared a slave should try to win his freedom, and he said it when he told us there was neither slave nor free but all of us are one in Christ. How can we say we live the gospel of our Lord Jesus and keep men and women in bondage? How can we say we follow the Word of the living God and deny those made in his image the liberty to live as we here in Elizabethtown have the liberty to live? Did our forefathers not come to America from Europe so that they could have this liberty? Yet we will not give that same freedom to men like us sleeping in the room upstairs."

His voice was still not that loud but his words struck her heart with what seemed to her the very fervor of God. How was it possible that all these thoughts had been locked away inside him and she had never known about it? But how could she know? Nathaniel was just her brother's friend, it was all he had ever been, never anyone special to her or she to him. Yet now all sorts of feelings stormed through her, most of them to do with what he was saying to the Amish leaders, but others touching on feelings she had never experienced before for any man in the community. She closed her eyes and put her head in her hands. What was happening?

This time the silence after Nathaniel's words was even longer. Finally Samuel Eby spoke again. "Still, we are commanded to obey the law of the land. It is Paul himself who tells us that in Romans."

Lyndel lifted her head from her hands in surprise. Now it was her brother, quiet Levi Keim, who was talking. "Pastor Eby, we Amish do not obey the law when it comes to war, do we? The government tells us we must fight, but we say no, we will not fight. Why do we not obey the law then, Pastor Eby?"

The pastor didn't respond. Lyndel listened to her brother answer his own question. "The law of the land tells us to go to war but we do not go to war because we say God's law is higher and that he commands us not to kill. So do you not think God requires us to answer to a higher law when it comes to slavery? Do you not think we should obey God rather than man, as Peter and John argued in Acts? Do you not think we should treat slaves as fellow human beings in the eyes of God and grant them the same liberties we enjoy since they are made in his image just as we are?"

Nathaniel spoke up softly as Levi finished. "The Scriptures say that God 'hath made of one blood all nations of men.'"

"Not to mention," Lyndel's father said in the hush that followed Levi's and Nathaniel's words, "that Paul tells us in Timothy that the law is not made for the righteous but for the lawless and disobedient, for the ungodly and the sinner, for the unholy and profane. And he includes murderers among those who are lawless and unholy—he includes those who commit adultery, those who commit perversions, those who are liars and perjurers. He includes those who are slave traders—yes, slave traders. He reached for Nathaniel's open Bible, now setting again on the table. Reaching his place, he read, "*Knowing this, that the law is not made for a righteous man, but for the lawless and dis-obedient...for menstealers*—slave traders—*and if there be any other thing that is contrary to sound doctrine; according to the glorious gospel of the blessed God, which was committed to my trust."*

"Amen." Lyndel just made out Abraham Yoder's whisper.

Suddenly there was hammering at the door. Without thinking Lyndel shot to her feet. But none of the men saw her—they had all turned toward the door and several were out of their chairs. Lyndel's mother was rushing down the staircase without her candle and she cried, "The yard, it is full of men with torches and guns!"

Lyndel watched her father swing open the door to Sheriff Jackson. The sheriff had a grim look on his face. Behind him several men were clutching blazing torches in one hand and long rifles in the other.

"What is it?" Lyndel's father demanded. "Why do you come to my house at such an hour and in such a manner?"

"Bishop Keim," the sheriff replied in a dark voice, "it's my under-standing that you are harboring fugitives on your property. I must order you now, in the name of the law, to give them up to these men so they can be returned to their rightful owners in the Commonwealth of Virginia."

3

Lyndel's father stood firmly in the doorway and would not move. "This is a matter we have just been discussing among our leadership," he told the sheriff. "We will need a bit more time."

"A bit more time for what?" growled a man with a torch just behind Sheriff Jackson. "To make sure our slaves get clear to the border?"

"Are they in the house, Bishop Keim?" asked the sheriff.

Lyndel's father hesitated. "They are resting."

"Where are they resting?"

"In a room upstairs. They cannot be disturbed. One of them is wounded."

"Cannot be disturbed?" The man behind Sheriff Jackson mimicked the bishop's voice. "Who do you think they are? Lords and masters of a Virginia plantation?" He shouldered past the sheriff and shoved Lyndel's father to one side. "We're wasting time. And you're breaking the law."

Lyndel watched Nathaniel spring to the staircase, blocking the man's path. The man stopped, surprised. Then he handed his torch to one of his companions, all of whom were crowding into the house. He swung the stock of his rifle as hard as he could into Nathaniel's stomach. Lyndel cried out and rushed down the staircase as Nathaniel gasped and his knees bent. But he would not fall and he held his ground, glaring at the slave hunter, his green eyes on fire.

"Why, ain't you a tough one for a Yankee."

The man swung his rifle into Nathaniel's stomach two more times as fast as he could. This time Nathaniel groaned and collapsed. The slave hunter ran up the stairs followed by six of his companions. Once they reached the second floor they began throwing open doors and brandishing torches and pointing pistol and rifles. Lyndel's younger sisters began to scream. Their mother ran up the steps, calling out in Pennsylvania Dutch for the men to stop, and the bishop bolted up the steps behind his wife. Lyndel knelt by Nathaniel and lifted his head as the slave hunters charged to the third floor and one of them shouted, "Well, boys, look what we have here! What's the matter, Charlie? Ain't you happy to see me?"

The man tugged Charlie out of bed and pushed him roughly toward the stairway. When they arrived at the second landing, the man shoved him forward down the final set of stairs and the slave landed with a cry of pain on top of Nathaniel. Immediately behind, Moses came tumbling down the steps after him. He had taken a gun-stock blow to the head. Tears streaking her cheeks, Lyndel covered all three men with her arms and shouted at the slave hunters, "Leave them alone! They have done nothing wrong!"

The man who had struck Nathaniel with his rifle laughed from the second landing. "Why, yes they have, ma'am. Them slaves is plantation property, no different than the horses and cows and cotton fields. They ran, and that runnin' is against the law. And your beau, well, he tried to prevent me from takin' 'em and that's what the legal folk call obstruction of justice."

He walked down the stairs, his boots thudding on the wood, his men behind him. Hauling Charlie and Moses upright he shackled their hands and their feet while another held his torch and gun. On the second floor Lyndel's mother was hugging and kissing the three girls and telling them everything was going to be all right. Moses looked straight into Lyndel's eyes, and at the pain in his eyes, she felt things falling down and breaking apart.

"Back home, we'd burn your house to the ground for harborin' and abettin' fugitives," the leader of the slave hunters said. "But ye're godless Yankees and you don't know no better."

Levi and the ministers had stayed rooted at the table during the forced entry into the home. Now Abraham Yoder stepped forward.

"We need no lectures from you on godliness, you who would desecrate a man's home and frighten his children and treat the guests sleeping under his roof worse than brute beasts."

The slave hunter grinned. "Why, they ain't nothin' but brute beasts, mister. That's God's truth."

Now Levi shook off his fear and shock and stood beside Pastor Yoder. "I will tell you what God's truth is—there are neither slaves nor freemen but all are one in Christ Jesus. And I will tell you something else that is God's truth—no slaveholder has a place in heaven."

The slave hunters' faces darkened and Lyndel saw their fingers move in and out of the trigger guards of their weapons. She saw the leader's face twitch between annoyance and anger and rage. Finally he jerked at the door and told his men, "Get our property out of here and into the wagon." The men dragged Charlie and Moses through the doorway in chains. Charlie glanced at Lyndel with a look she knew she could never erase. Nathaniel, finally coming to himself, stood to his feet.

The leader gripped his rifle more tightly. "Am I gonna have more trouble from you?"

"No, you're not," Sheriff Jackson finally spoke up, "because you're not going to be here. You've got what's yours. Now get out and get back to Virginia."

"These people broke the law, sheriff. Not Virginia law. *Federal* law."

"Get going and get across the state line before the folk in Elizabethtown wake up. A lot of them might take exception to slave hunters roaming about in their midst. They have more guns than you do and they won't treat you as gently as these Amish folk have."

"Is that a fact?" The leader nodded to himself. "I guess it's gettin' close to the time Virginia joins in with Mississippi and Texas and Alabama and has its own country. Yes, I reckon it's long past time." He bent his head. "Thank you kindly for your hospitality. Come and visit the Hargrove Plantation sometime and we'll see if we can't do you one better."

He left, and Lyndel followed Nathaniel and Levi and the pastors out onto the porch. The wagon of slave hunters was already moving down the lane to the main road. Moses and Charlie sat in the middle, flames from the torches lighting their faces. Moses had an expression like stone. Charlie was broken, his cheeks wet, holding a hand to his side. In a few minutes the wagon was no more than half a dozen torches floating in the darkness.

"We failed them," said Nathaniel in a quiet voice. "We had them under our protection and we let the slave hunters drag them away."

Sheriff Jackson stepped out onto the porch. "It was the law, Mr. King."

"God's law or man's law?"

"Washington's law. The Supreme Court's law."

"Then perhaps it is time we change the law."

"Oh? And how do you plan on doing that, young man?"

But Nathaniel was staring at the pastors. "You are the leaders of the church. Men chosen by God. Yet you did nothing. Nothing."

Samuel Eby bristled. "We are people of peace, not confrontation."

"You could not even attempt to block their path? To hold the bedroom door shut?"

"That is not our way. You yourself overstepped your bounds and your calling as an Amish man."

"Did I?" Nathaniel looked around him and his eyes rested on Lyndel. "Did I, Miss Keim?" He stared at Levi. "Did I, Levi Keim?" Then his eyes fell on Abraham Yoder. "Did I overstep my bounds, Pastor Yoder?"

No one responded. Nathaniel walked slowly down the porch steps to the ground and made his way to his carriage. He climbed painfully into the driver's seat in a way that made Lyndel want to rush out and help him but she knew he wouldn't want that. He glanced over at them as he flicked the reins in his hands. "We are not much like Jesus in the end, are we? He cleared the temple. He made a whip. We are not able to even clear the temple of Lancaster County of these men-stealers. Because of our weakness, men like Moses and Charlie pay with their freedom and their blood."

His carriage began to roll out of the yard. Lyndel realized that now was the time to tell him what she thought of the words he had said at the table and the stand he had made at the staircase. Tomorrow would not do and a week from now would be too late. Perhaps it wouldn't matter to him, but it mattered to her. Surprising herself as well as the others she lifted the hem of her dress and flew down the steps and across the yard to the carriage. Nathaniel saw her running and reined back.

"Lyndel," he said, "what are you doing?"

She rested her hand on the side of the driver's seat. "I just wanted you to know I heard what you said at the meeting. Everything you said was right. Yes, it was right. And what you tried to do at the staircase was also right."

His face was like granite from his anger at the Amish leaders and the slave hunters. Yet as he listened to her a small smile broke through. "How do you know what I said at the meeting?"

"I was sitting on the staircase."

His smile grew. "Were you? With your father's permission?"

She smiled back. "My mother's anyway."

He looked away. "Well, what I said didn't seem to make much of a difference."

"It did to me."

He glanced back at her. "*Ja*?" Then he stared ahead. "I always come to the Keim house to call on Levi. How about if I come tomorrow to call on you instead?"

She was startled and didn't know what to say.

"Or is that too much too quickly?" he asked.

Lyndel made up her mind in an instant and put a hand on his arm. "For the first time in our lives—yes, come and call on me."

"Well. It was not a very good evening. But this was the best part of it." He flicked the reins. "Do you know what I feel like doing, Lyndel Keim?"

The wagon was moving forward at a walking pace and she kept up with it, her hand still on his arm. "What's that?"

"Giving chase to the slave hunters. Running them off the road. Scaring them into the woods. Rescuing Moses and Charlie and driving like a crazy man for the Canadian border in New York." Suddenly, despite the grimness that hadn't left his face since the arrival of the slave hunters from Virginia, he gave a sharp laugh. "I reckon I don't sound very Amish, do I?"

"It sounds like a good plan," she responded. "But you'd need help."

"Yes. I would. But except for you and Levi and Abraham Yoder, and perhaps your father, I'm not likely to get it in time, am I?" He glanced away from the lane and at her. "What will happen to Moses and Charlie, Lyndel?"

She shook her head.

"Here's the road. We're picking up speed now—take care. I hope to see you tomorrow, Lyndel Keim."

"I'll look forward to that, Nathaniel King."

His buggy turned onto the wide roadway and moved off toward his family's farm. She stood for a while under the stars and as she watched him go, she obeyed a desire to pray for him. *Lord Jesus, have mercy on Nathaniel King…and on us. Have mercy on our country.*

That night sleep was slow to come. Two of her younger sisters were in bed with her, constantly tossing and turning in their anxiety. The other sister slept with their mother. When Lyndel did find a moment's rest, her dreams were torn by flame and gunfire and leering slave hunters and rope. Moses and Charlie were running but they never got away—men on horses always rode them down. She kept telling the men from the plantation to set them at liberty: "America is the land of the free!" But the leader of the slave hunters was there to tell her over and over again, "America is a slave nation, Miss Lyndel. It has been from the beginning and it always will be."

The next morning as she and Levi entered the house after milking the cows, they sat down to a subdued breakfast. Her father read from the Bible and prayed and her sisters helped their mother wash up but few words were spoken.

After eating, Lyndel made her way silently back to the barn and led the herd out to pasture. She lingered to watch a number of the cows head toward the creek that ran through the trees a hundred yards away. The sun had been behind a cloud bank, as if reflecting the Keim family's melancholy mood, but now began to slowly slip free of the gray. Sunlight brought the green of the April grass alive. She closed her eyes a moment and turned her face upward to the sun. How long the winter had been and how unpleasant the evening and night. The warmth felt good inside her and out.

Lord, be with us. There is so much about my world I don't understand anymore.

Cows bawling made her open her eyes quickly and look toward the trees. Had one of the new calves become stuck in the mud of the creek bank? The bawling grew louder and the cows began trotting out between the tree trunks and branches. Lyndel walked swiftly toward them. They passed by her as she stepped in among the trees, under the spread of green leaves yellowed by the morning light. She saw the creek, brown with soil and silt, but none of the herd was there. Glancing to her left and right, she walked farther into the cluster of birches and aspens. Still nothing. So she headed into the sugar maples about a hundred feet away looking for a calf or milk cow in distress or the sign of a predator like a wild dog or coyote. But there was no sound and nothing at all was moving.

Heading closer to the creek she paused to squint up and down the bank in the flood of fresh sunlight that made the dark water gleam. Picking up a small flat stone she flung it sideways. It skipped three times and sank in the middle of the creek. *You'll be sitting there at the bottom a long time,* she thought and turned to start back to the farm.

But then as she glanced off the right, she gasped. She looked closer, then turned away, nausea rising. *It can't be!*

But it was. It was the body of Charlie hanging from one of the sugar maples.

Forcing herself closer, hoping against hope, she wrapped her arms around his legs, instinctively trying to push him upward and take the weight of his body off his neck, but she could only do it for a few seconds at a time. His face was no longer Charlie's, yet she knew it was the man she had cared for. The word *RUNAWAY* was printed clumsily on a sign around his neck.

Softly she spoke. "Charlie..."

She called his name again and again, but he receded from her sight as if he were at the end of a long hallway with walls painted a bright white. Finally she sank to her knees in the long grass, sobbing, her cheeks burning.

Then at once she felt a storm of strength emerge within her and she got up and began to run.

Crossing the pasture as fast as she could she saw her father and brother standing in front of the barn. Shouting out their names, she kept racing for the gate. They looked up and began running to meet her. Her father was through the gate and caught his daughter as she fell into his arms.

"What is it? What is it?" he demanded, his face full of fear.

"Papa...Papa...Charlie is hanging...he is hanging..." Lyndel could hardly catch her breath and pointed to the maple trees. Her father placed her in her brother's arms and set out for the sugar maples, his long legs eating up the distance in what seemed like only a few moments. Levi held her to his chest.

"It's all right," he soothed.

"It's not all right," she gasped. "He's not alive, I know he's not alive."

"You can't be sure. Do you want me to walk you down there?"

"I don't ever want to go down to that creek again for the rest of my life."

"Hey!" It was Nathaniel's voice. They turned to look. He was just driving into their farmyard in his buggy. "Anybody home?"

Levi waved with one hand, holding on to Lyndel with the other. "Over here!"

Nathaniel laughed and headed toward them. In one hand Lyndel could see he was holding a bunch of snapdragons of all colors mixed in with several branches of white and gray pussy willows. She watched him walk up to the gate and saw his boyish excitement at coming to pay a call on his friend's sister. How good it was to see his smile, a smile for her and because of her, so that even in her sadness she felt a short, sharp surge of joy as he unlatched the gate, grinning and green-eyed handsome.

But it couldn't last. No, she knew somehow that everything was going to change forever when he found out what had happened to Charlie. She couldn't guess what that change would mean for him… and possibly for her with this new fondness that seemed to be springing up between them…or even if it might bring about its sudden end. So she savored the last few seconds of his burst of playfulness as he walked up to her and Levi across the grass and then she prepared to let her happiness go.

He took off his broad-brimmed black hat with one swipe of his hand and bowed. Then he extended the snapdragons and pussy willows. "Miss Keim, if I may, I have come to pay you a visit long overdue."

She had told herself not to smile but she couldn't help but respond to his enthusiasm and energy with anything less. She took the bouquet from his hand and pressed it to her face. "Thank you, Nathaniel."

"My pleasure."

"Nathaniel—"

He heard the catch in her voice and immediately his smile faded. "What's wrong? I thought you wanted me to come."

"It's not that."

"Then what?"

"Nathaniel, please go across the pasture to the sugar maples. My father is there. He needs your help."

"Of course. Is something wrong?"

"He is—he is bringing Charlie Preston down from a tree."

"What?"

"They…hung him…Nathaniel…"

So the change came to his face and soul just as she knew it would. He stared at her for several moments, looked at Levi for several more, then began to walk quickly and in a straight line for the trees. She sank her head into her brother's shoulder.

"His eyes changed, Levi."

"Of course they've changed. He will feel responsible. He will wish he had done more. That he had chased after them like he wanted to."

"The boy who climbed out of the buggy, the boy who came to see me is gone. He's gone, Levi."

Her brother did not respond.

Five minutes later they watched their father and Nathaniel coming across the field carrying Charlie's body between them. Nathaniel had his back to them holding the shoulders, while their father had the feet. Nathaniel had taken off his shirt and placed it on Charlie, running the dead man's arms through the sleeves and buttoning it, so that the shirt, too large, fell all the way to his knees and covered most of his body in white.

They took him to a room at the back of the house where firewood was stored out of the rain, a room cool and rich with the smell of earth and trees. It had been Lyndel's favorite room to hide in when she was a girl, and because Levi knew this she was always the first one he caught among their friends and neighbors. Now they gently laid Charlie on a long table and folded his arms on his chest over Nathaniel's shirt. There was a minute of silent prayer before they left. Constantly running her fingers over her eyes to clear them Lyndel caught glimpses of her father, her brother, and Nathaniel and realized she wasn't the only one struggling with the pain of this death. Yet she felt something else thrusting itself up through her shock and anguish that surprised her with its strength and heat.

I said I would protect him. We all said we would protect him.

"I betrayed him!" she blurted.

Her father snapped his head around to stare at her. "What do you mean?"

"I promised him. From the very beginning I promised Charlie I wouldn't let anyone hurt him."

"My daughter—"

"You promised too! You stood there at the barn door and said I could trust you. But you told the others. And one of the others told the sheriff."

"Of course you can trust me."

Lyndel could feel the blood in her face as she curled her hands into fists. "You gave him up to the slave drivers without a fight."

Her father's face turned white. "We are a people of peace. It's not our way to resort to guns or violence. I have an oath to fulfill as an Amish bishop."

"What about your oath to me? Does it mean more to you to be a bishop than to be a faithful father?"

"My Lyndel, I love you—"

"You said I could trust you. You said we would protect him. We failed him! And in failing him, we have failed God!"

Her father took Lyndel's hand and looked into her face.

"Listen to me. It will be an Amish funeral. I will discuss this with the leadership. We will lay his body to rest tomorrow. I must let Sheriff Jackson know what has happened here, of course."

"Oh, the good sheriff."

"Lyndel, please—"

"Our people will only argue he was not Amish."

"He took sanctuary with us. He trusted us as he trusted God. He will be buried as one of us. You must remember who you are and what you believe. You must calm yourself."

"I can't. We betrayed Charlie."

"We have a righteous Judge in heaven who will protect Charlie Preston's soul from all harm and calamity. He is safe with Jesus. I ask you again to calm yourself and to remember what you believe. If you cannot trust me today you can certainly trust God."

"It will take some time, Papa, for me to forgive myself, to forgive all of us."

"Yes. Time. Prayer. In Christ you will find what you need." He put his arms around her briefly. "I'm sorry you saw what you saw. I wish it had been otherwise. I'm sorry you feel I failed you." He stepped back and wiped his face with a large white handkerchief.

"Bishop Keim." Nathaniel's face was white and blank as a field of snow. "I apologize. But I need to be on my way and I wish to speak with you before I leave."

"*Ja, What* is it? Do you need to borrow one of my son's shirts?"

"Thank you. I always keep a spare one under my seat in case the one I'm wearing gets dirty. What I wanted to say—do you recall how I asked in December if I could visit the families in Indiana who left to settle with the Amish there and help them out?"

"Of course I remember your request."

"Perhaps now would be a good time for me to pay our people that visit."

Bishop Keim looked at him a long time and then nodded. "You may be right. I will discuss it with the pastors tonight when I call them together about the funeral. If you would be so kind as to ask your parents for their approval and blessing."

"Yes, I will."

Nathaniel began to walk toward his carriage and his horse. Lyndel, feeling completely depleted, watched him go. *Well, that is it, Lord. He has come and gone. But thank you for his walk from the carriage to the pasture gate just the same. I saw his eyes then and his eyes were for me.*

Nathaniel rubbed Good Boy between his ears and spoke to him for a few moments. Then he pulled a white shirt from under the seat of the buggy, tugged it on, and began to climb up. Suddenly he stopped and looked at Lyndel. Despite the weight she knew he carried over Charlie's hanging, a bit of life returned to his eyes for a moment.

"Weren't we supposed to have a visit today?"

"Yes. But the day has changed."

"It has changed but I still would like to have that visit. What about the day after tomorrow?"

"The day after Charlie's funeral?"

He nodded. "I think—Charlie Preston would smile and whisper it was a good thing."

"That would suit me, Nathaniel King."

"God willing, I'll be here." He finished climbing up into the buggy and took hold of Good Boy's traces. "I have something important to ask you."

Lyndel narrowed her eyes. "Important?"

"Get up there, Boy. Yes, very important."

"Are you serious?"

"I am."

"And you are just going to drive off?"

"I am."

The King buggy rattled toward the road. Lyndel's father looked at her. "Is there something between the two of you I have missed?"

"I'm not sure, Papa."

"There is nothing?"

"I didn't say there was nothing. I said I'm not sure."

"Well," said Levi, "I have this for you anyway, whether you're sure or not sure."

He held out a jar that had collected some rainwater.

"What on earth is that for?" she asked him.

"It's for your snapdragons and pussy willows." He placed the glass jar in her hand. "If they last a little bit longer, perhaps God will grant that whatever you and Nathaniel feel or don't feel for each other may last a little bit longer as well."

4

A light rain was falling the next day, April 4th, a Thursday. The showers and clouds suited the Amish community's mood, thought Lyndel. The Keim house was full of church families dressed in solid black. Charlie's body was washed and dressed and laid out in a special room just off the parlor. He still wore Nathaniel's white shirt, and his pants were a dark pair that belonged to her brother. The collar of the shirt was up in order to hide some of the marks of the rope on his neck. Lyndel was grateful the swelling in his face had gone down so that he looked once again like the young cheerful man who had asked her to read the Bible in the lamplight.

People filed into the room to pay their respects and found a seat. Lyndel sat back in a nearby chair to watch others walk slowly past. Nathaniel and Levi entered the room together. Levi rested his hand on one of Charlie's, stood there a long minute, then moved on. Nathaniel was struggling, the veins on his neck suddenly standing out as he stood over the young man's body. Lyndel saw him slip a small piece of paper under Charlie's hands. Then he whispered something in Charlie's ear. His face set and resolute he walked out of the room without looking at Lyndel.

It was a hard thing, this funeral, such as it was. It should never have been happening. Charlie should have been alive. But he wasn't. It was at least some minor solace that at last night's discussion about the service, not a single man had argued against a funeral service for Charlie Preston, not even Samuel Eby or Solomon Miller.

So Lyndel wasn't surprised that as the service began, it was Solomon who gave the first funeral sermon, followed by Samuel. She also wasn't surprised that the words the two ministers spoke weren't the words they had used in the debate about slavery on Tuesday night. Lyndel felt that much of what they said and the Bible texts they used could have come from Abraham Yoder's lips, or Levi's or even Nathaniel's. Samuel preached for half an hour, Solomon for another three-quarters of an hour. By the time they had finished and her father was praying, she glanced over to see that Nathaniel had reentered the room some time during the preaching. She noticed that the hard lines on his face had relaxed.

When they left the house Charlie's body was placed in the same sort of carved pine coffin that all Amish were buried in. The three pastors held one side of the coffin on their shoulders while Bishop Keim, Levi, and Nathaniel took the other side. They placed it in a carriage in which the six of them sat together as the bishop drove. All the other Amish carriages fell in behind. Normally, Lyndel knew, this would be the extent of the procession to the graveyard. But word about what had happened at the Keim farm on Tuesday and Wednesday had spread through Elizabethtown, and many Pennsylvanians were waiting quietly outside the house as the Amish emerged with Charlie's coffin. Once the last Amish buggy had joined the long line winding its way along the main road, the residents and farmers of Elizabethtown fell in behind. Even Sheriff Jackson was there.

The six men carried the coffin to the opening in the ground and lowered it with thick ropes. Bishop Keim prayed and opened the Amish hymnbook called the *Ausbund.* He read a hymn hundreds of years old about suffering for Christ and enduring the hatred, scorn, and violence of the world.

"If we suffer with him," the bishop finished, looking out over the faces of women, men, and children, "we shall also reign with him. Amen."

Amen, the people responded, even those churchgoers who were not Amish or didn't belong to any church at all. Then the bishop and pastors, along with Levi and Nathaniel, took up shovels and slowly covered Charlie's coffin with earth, filling the grave completely. Lyndel wanted to ask Nathaniel what he had written on the piece of paper he had buried with Charlie and what he had whispered in the dead man's ear, but once the task was completed, Nathaniel got into the buggy with the other five men and they promptly returned to the Keim house.

A large meal had been prepared by the women of the Amish church and for an hour or two, Amish and non-Amish sat side by side, talked, ate, and listened to one another, some sitting at tables in the house, some at tables in the barn. Lyndel was in the parlor with her mother and sisters, while Nathaniel was with her brother and father and the pastors in the kitchen. Talk of children and weather and crops mingled with discussions about President Lincoln, the secession of the Southern states, and what might happen next. Only a few tables away Joshua Yoder, Abraham Yoder's son, held a newspaper clipping in his hand while he spoke rapidly to the men sitting beside him about the enshrinement of slavery in the Confederate Constitution.

"Listen to what they've voted on and agreed to since early March," he said. "This is from Article Four, Section Three, and Clause Three: *The Confederate States may acquire new territory...In all such territory the institution of negro slavery, as it now exists in the Confederate States, shall be recognized and protected by Congress and by the Territorial government; and the inhabitants of the several Confederate States and Territories shall have the right to take to such Territory any slaves lawfully held by them in any of the States or Territories of the Confederate States.* You see? They will pound their podiums and say they're fighting for freedom and states' rights and a fully independent nation, and so they are— freedom to take away other men's freedom, the right to enslave human beings made in the image of God and to fight for a slave nation fully independent of any sense of right or wrong when it comes to the lives and souls of African men and women and children. Why, they even invoke the favor and guidance of Almighty God to help them establish justice, tranquility, and liberty—for themselves, of course, not for anyone else, certainly not for anyone like the man they lynched out in the Keim pasture yesterday."

Lyndel closed her eyes and rubbed her forehead with her thumb and fingers as Joshua went on. She hated the violence of the word *lynched* but she couldn't argue that Joshua wasn't right in using it—Charlie had been lynched, not just hung, and he had been murdered, he had not simply lain down and died.

She stood up and told her mother she wanted to take a quick walk outside. Putting a cape over her shoulders she went through the doorway into the farmyard. The rain-washed air and the scent of green growing things overcame the painful images in her mind and the dark feelings in her heart for a few minutes.

Lord, what will become of our nation, the nation you gave us to reside in? Shall we truly split into two countries living side by side? What can prevent us from becoming ill-tempered and feuding neighbors with no love between us?

Avoiding the route to the pasture, she skirted the barn and the people seated inside and opened a gate to one of the hay fields. The hay was short and she wandered across the large field, not choosing any particular direction, sometimes glancing up into the soft rainfall, other times keeping her eyes on the ground just ahead of the toes of her boots. She found the creek and a grove of birch, but this was far from the place where Charlie had been, so she didn't turn away, but walked on, watching the brown water that now moved swiftly between the banks, swollen with fresh rain. A long time she stood and prayed and thought, not hearing the person approaching behind her through the wet hay. When a hand gently touched her arm she leaped ahead and almost stumbled into the water, except the hand suddenly gripped her tightly and held her back.

"I'm so sorry—it wasn't my intention to startle you."

Nathaniel looked so awkward and embarrassed, his eyes and mouth drooping, his face reddening, that Lyndel found she could only glare at him for a few moments.

"You scared me half to death," she said, her eyes and lips narrow.

"I wanted…to surprise you."

"Well, Nathaniel King, you certainly succeeded at that."

He released his grip on her arm and stood back. "You were having time alone and with God, it seems. I should go. Once again, I'm sorry. I will be by tomorrow evening if you still wish it."

Lyndel regained her composure, turned her glare into a small smile, and said, "You may come for supper."

When he nodded and smiled, then turned to go, Lyndel said, "You don't need to go. Stay, please…for a while. I've had quite enough time alone praying prayers and thinking thoughts. Some human company would be welcome."

"Are you sure? It was not my intention to intrude—"

"You're not intruding. Stop being a gentleman, please, Nathaniel, and go back to being my brother's best friend—and my new friend."

A small smile went over his face. "All right. *Gut.* How are you, despite everything—despite today being the day of the funeral?"

She paused, then said, "On the one hand, Charlie is with the Jesus whose words he loved to hear me read. On the other hand, I can't help but feel he left us too soon. And then there is Moses Gunnison—I can't stop thinking about him and wondering how he's faring on that Virginia plantation."

"I know."

"And you, Nathaniel, how is it with you today?"

He shrugged and put his hands in his pockets. His eyes were dark under the broad brim of his hat, raindrops falling from its edge. "Would you mind walking with me? We can follow the creek for a while, perhaps for miles."

"Miles?" She smiled at him, the rain beading on her face. "Do you have a lot to say?"

"Depends."

They began to make their way side by side, she with her hands folded under her apron, he with his still in his pockets. For a long minute nothing was said and there was just the sound of their boots in the mud and wet grass of the field. She glanced up at him.

"Are you waiting for me?" she asked.

He shook his head, suddenly gray and somber as the weather. "I'm not sure how to begin. I wonder what you will think of me."

"Well, once you start we can find out. Is this the big important thing you wanted to tell me?"

"*Ja, ja,* I guess it is." He puffed his cheeks with a breath and then blew it out rapidly.

"If it's that difficult to get out perhaps you can tell me something else in the meantime."

"Tell you what?"

"You whispered in Charlie's ear. You put a slip of paper in his coffin."

He glanced at her. "So closely you were watching?"

"Indeed I was."

"I told him…that where the Spirit of the Lord is there is liberty—from the Bible—and on the paper I wrote some of the words from a song the slaves sing while they work."

"And what were the words?"

Nathaniel cleared his throat. "Some of these mornings, bright and fair, I thank God I'm free at last. Going to meet King Jesus in the air, I thank God I'm free at last. Free at last, free at last, I thank God I'm free at last."

Lyndel gazed at him, her mouth partly open. "You astonish me, Nathaniel King. Where on earth did you learn that? It's beautiful."

"I…I just thought…I could picture Charlie singing it while he was in the fields—"

"What a—different sort of man you are. I never guessed it." She smiled. "But it is a good different, Nathaniel King."

He shrugged. "I suppose the leadership think of me as something of a wild young colt, what with my talk of clearing temples and making whips."

"Well, it's in the Bible, Nathaniel, so they can't say too much, except perhaps that clearing the temple was the task Jesus was called to perform as the Son of God, not you."

"Your father told me over the meal that I was free to leave for Indiana, so they can't be too badly disposed toward me."

"Put your fears aside. I'm sure the pastors have a high opinion of you. My father does too. I hope telling you this doesn't swell your head." Her eyes smiled along with her lips. "It must be very exciting for you. When do you plan to leave?"

"My father asked me to stay on until the seeding of the barley, oats, and wheat is completed, so I'll be here at least another three weeks, perhaps as long as a month."

"Oh, will that have you champing at the bit?"

"Four months ago, three months ago, even a few days ago, yes. Now I'm content to leave when my timing is God's timing. You know, I thought it would be a good idea to see how another Amish community lived out its faith, one that was far away from Lancaster County, and to find out if I feel the same way about my beliefs in Indiana as I do in Pennsylvania. In addition, I thought I might…meet someone…"

He paused and Lyndel felt a sharp pang run through her. The sensation was annoying and she frowned. What did it matter to her if Nathaniel King found an Amish woman to marry in Indiana? Up until a day or two ago the only thing the two of them had had in common was her brother Levi. Nathaniel caught her frown and wished he could retract his words.

"I'm sorry," he said and watched her blue eyes darken to black in response.

"What on earth do you have to be sorry about?" she snapped.

"I didn't mean you to think I've never noticed you."

She stopped walking. "Really, Nathaniel, what *are* you talking about? Notice me in what way? Haven't I always simply been your friend's sister?"

"That's true, but—"

"So why should I care if you run off to find yourself a bride west of the Ohio River?"

Her vehemence startled herself as well as Nathaniel. Confused at the strength of the reaction storming up inside her at his words, she stood and watched while he started and stopped a sentence three or four times, the words always dying on his lips. Abruptly she turned around and began striding back the way they had come.

"This whole thing is ridiculous!" she called back over her shoulder. "Talking to each other at all was a mistake! Please don't come calling tomorrow evening! You stay Levi's dearest friend and I'll stay his sister and that's the best we can hope for!"

"It's just that I never knew how to tell my best friend's sister how beautiful she was!" Nathaniel blurted as she strode away. "How do you do that with someone you've always teased and called 'Tomatoes'?"

Lyndel stopped and turned around, her mouth open. "What?"

Nathaniel's face was flushed again. "How do you…how do you tell someone who was always the red-haired nuisance that she is a woman now—and a remarkably beautiful woman at that?"

Lyndel felt the blood come into her own face.

"I can't even tell you when it started—this change in how I thought of you—but on Tuesday, when I saw Lyndel Keim take charge of the situation surrounding Charlie and Moses, when I saw the risks she took—" Nathaniel shrugged and smiled in a weak, lopsided way. "Was there ever anything on God's green earth more beautiful than you with your eyes ablaze? And not just your eyes—your whole face and body were on fire. How do you talk to someone nicknamed 'Tomatoes' about things like that?"

Lyndel felt like ice, then flame, then ice again. Her mind had stopped. Nothing came to her so she continued to stare at him and dared not speak. He bent down, picked some hay, and rolled it around in his fingers.

"So I thought the hanging, the funeral, the pain, that it would cool everything down and put all my feelings in their proper place." He kept looking at the stalks of hay in his fingers. "But it's just getting worse. So maybe now I'm running to Indiana to get away from this…sudden beauty…who is my closest friend's sister. At the same time, I want to call on her. What do you think I should do, Lyndel Keim? What would you do if you were in my shoes?"

Lyndel found that she was finally able to focus her thoughts. This involved stepping toward him and placing her hand on his arm. It also involved smiling at him with all the richness and depth that was inside her and, at that moment, burning through her blood.

"Well, if she's truly that beautiful," she told him in a quiet voice, "then I would throw all caution to the wind and I would call. Yes,

Nathaniel King, if I were in your shoes, that's what I would do. And this time, considering the strength of your feelings, you might contemplate bringing roses instead of snapdragons, lovely as snapdragons are. The only flower I can think of that goes with the sorts of things you are saying to a woman are roses, whether that woman is Amish or not."

5

"Bishop Keim! Bishop Keim! They have shelled Fort Sumter and the commander of the fort has surrendered!"

Lyndel was up in her room letting her sister Becky comb out her long red hair when Joshua Yoder drove up to their barn shouting and calling her father's name. She and Becky ran to the window and looked down as their father came quickly from behind the house where he had been piling firewood.

"What is this hollering about, Mr. Yoder?" he demanded. "Calm yourself."

It seemed to Lyndel that Joshua practically stood to attention before her father. "The South bombarded the fort in Charleston Harbor, sir. It surrendered last Saturday on the 13th. President Lincoln called for 75,000 troops to put down the rebellion, and when Virginia got word of it their government took a vote and they seceded from the Union yesterday."

"I knew about the surrender, young man—may God help us— everyone knew about it by Monday. But I have not heard about the call to arms or Virginia's secession."

"We've been too busy with spring planting and our own affairs but all Elizabethtown is buzzing. I have papers here from Boston and Phil-adelphia and, look, the *Daily Dispatch* from Richmond for Wednesday the 17th. They say more states will be joining the Confederacy."

Lyndel watched her father take the papers from Joshua's hands. A coldness came into her arms and chest. She had hoped the fort's surrender would be the end of it, that people would realize things had gotten out of hand and wiser men would put a stop to further violence. But now the president was calling up militia. Why would he do that unless he expected a battle? She closed her eyes and leaned her head against the windowpane.

"What's the matter, Lyndy?" asked Becky. "Do you feel sick?"

"Yes, I do a little."

"Do you want me to get Mama?"

Lyndel pulled her head away from the glass. "Thank you, Becky, but this is not something mother's medicines can fix."

"Can Nathaniel help?" Becky smiled a quick little smile. "I know he's coming again tonight."

"Oh, Becky, it doesn't take a great talent to figure that out. He has dropped by almost every evening for the past two weeks."

"And not to see Levi either."

"No? He and Levi went out in the wagon two nights ago."

"Once. You have been out in the buggy four times with Nathaniel."

Lyndel reached down and messed her sister's hair. "Who's counting?"

"*I'm* counting."

"So who taught you to count? Stop going to school."

The first time Nathaniel had come to call, the day after the funeral and their walk in the hayfield, he had indeed brought her the roses she'd asked for, holding them behind his back. She had protested she had just been teasing him and hadn't really wanted expensive flowers—the Amish community would look down on such an extravagant gift. Then he had brought them out from hiding and she saw they were young wild roses, very pink, very small, half of the bouquet still buds.

"They are not so much, I guess," he'd told her.

But Lyndel had been as ecstatic as a ten-year-old girl with a sweetheart, even rushing the flowers to her mother who was working in the kitchen. "Mama, look, Nathaniel has brought me wild roses."

Her mother had smiled broadly. "Where does a young man find roses so early in April?"

Nathaniel was in the doorway, feeling oddly out of place for the first time at the Keim house. "Mrs. Keim, ma'am, there is an ash heap behind our barn and I have often seen them growing there spring after spring. I just had no good reason to pick any until today."

"So my daughter is a good reason?"

He laughed. "It suddenly occurred to me over the past couple of days that, yes, she is a very good reason. I'm just sorry it took me so many years to finally figure it out."

Lyndel and Nathaniel had not talked much about what was happening in America, preferring to discuss their feelings for one another, feelings that seemed to have just dropped down out of heaven, and childhood memories of playing together with Levi and other Amish boys and girls. But the political events had continued to intrude on them all the same. Her father fretted that war might come, a war that would ravage the land and kill thousands, perhaps tens of thousands. Often he asked Lyndel to excuse Nathaniel so he could join Levi and himself at the kitchen table and talk about what the Amish must do and also to pray. She would wait in her room, choosing not to hide on the landing and listen in. Her father always sent Becky to knock on her door when they were done. Then she would come down and Nathaniel would be standing on the porch, smiling when she stepped outside and joined him.

"What do you find to talk about night after night?" she asked.

"It is the same thing. Good reasons or not, slavery or not, the breakup of the nation or not, the Amish do not bear arms."

"Don't you agree?"

"Sure, I agree. It is not *gut* to see people die, is it? Remember when Old Man Zedekiah fell off the roof of his barn? Or Matthew Yoder drowned and we saw them pull his body out of the river? Who in their right mind wants war and death?"

"But?" For she already knew him well enough to know he was holding something back.

He hesitated. Then blurted, "There is the way Charlie was killed and the reason he was killed. How long does that go on?"

"So long as God lets it go on."

"*Ja*? Or does he want us to do something about it? Does God come in a mist and plant our corn for us? Harvest our wheat while we watch? Hitch our horses to our wagons and plows and carriages? So why do we think he will stop evil without our hands and feet and hearts?"

The day Joshua Yoder roared into the yard with his newspapers like a nineteenth-century Paul Revere, as Papa grumbled later, Nathaniel also arrived in a hurry and asked, in a tight voice, if Lyndel could go for a drive with him. They hadn't even turned onto the main road, a soft blue and red sky spread in the west before them, when he said to her in an agitated voice, "My brother Corinth has run off to Harrisburg to join the army."

This, of course, explained Nathaniel's mood to Lyndel in an instant—or, at least, most of it. "What? Isn't this the second time?"

"Right. He tried to do it last year when South Carolina and Mississippi seceded."

"Are you going to go and look for him?"

"Papa and my other brother, Simon, they left on the train this morning. Papa hopes to find him before the community finds out. But I think that's a futile wish. He went with another boy from Elizabethtown and that boy's parents have been telling everyone who will listen that it's not their son's fault, that Corinth was the bad egg. I'm sure your father will find out before the morning milking."

"How old is Corinth?"

"Sixteen."

"But looks nineteen."

"Yes, so who knows if he even is in Harrisburg anymore? They're forming militias everywhere. He could be in Pittsburgh or Philadelphia, someplace he thinks it will be harder for us to locate him. I wish I knew his reasons for doing this."

"Maybe they are the same as your reasons."

"Me?" Nathaniel glanced over at her. "I don't want to join the army."

Lyndel raised her eyebrows and made what Nathaniel was already calling her *pixie face*. "Perhaps not. But you want to end slavery."

Nathaniel snorted. "I doubt Corinth's ambitions are so lofty. My sense of it is he wants to wear a uniform and have girls toss flowers at him as he marches down the street with his regiment. Then he wants to lick the South single-handed and become a hero. After that, he will return to Elizabethtown with fame and fortune."

"Well, he is a handsome boy—all the girls think so. And he is always respectful and has a big heart. I can well imagine the girls of Pennsylvania would toss flowers his way. But surely they won't sign him up."

"Of course they'll sign him up. The president wants every able body he can get. Tall and strong and quick as he is, they'll slap him in a uniform and ship him off for training overnight."

"Will you be going to help your father and brother?"

"On Saturday, *ja*. But Simon has to return first. We won't leave Mama without a man around the house."

"Other families would lend her a hand."

"Of course. But we don't want anyone to know." He shook his head. "So what does it matter? Your father will know by morning milking, I reckon."

The sunset had deepened its colors and added purple. Nathaniel pulled the buggy over to the side of the road.

"Look at that. Enough talk about armies and soldiers and rumors of war. Do you see that bit of cloud on our left?"

"No."

"That one. It's the same blazing color as your hair."

She laughed. "Oh, it is not, Nathaniel. You exaggerate. Besides, what do you know about my hair? It is always up and the *kapp* covers most of it."

"I see plenty. Besides, your *kapp* has blown off on more than one occasion."

She looked at him in astonishment. "What? You have been keeping track?"

"Last fall. At the October bonfire. Off it went in a stiff breeze that I thanked God for. And some of your pins came loose too, remember?"

"I remember. I'm just surprised you do."

"I guess my wheels were starting to turn by then. Strands of your hair were moving in the wind just like fire. The same color as the maple leaves. Yes, that may have been when all this started. Who knows? Hey, a star there."

"And do you wish on stars?"

"Sometimes." He leaned back, still gazing at the evening sky. "Do you mind if I put my arm around your shoulders?"

"I don't mind. But our friends and neighbors passing by might mind. Are we courting?"

Nathaniel looked at her in surprise. "Courting? Why, things have happened so quickly, who has had the time to think about courting? Is that what you want?"

She patted his knee with her hand. "It's not necessarily what I want. But you asked to put your arm around me. Our church will permit that if we are courting. Not before."

Nathaniel let out a lungful of air. "Rules, rules."

"And with my father being the bishop, that makes it even more important that we abide by the *Ordnung*."

"Well, to tell you the truth, it's been so interesting getting to know Tomatoes that I hadn't really given courting much thought."

"Nor have I. And we certainly don't have to be in a rush about it. Unless of course you absolutely *must* have that arm around my shoulders."

"So—would you like it there?"

She smiled. "Sure. Why not? But you will have to talk to my father first. Then, if the leadership approves, we are an official couple on our way to the altar."

"Oh, boy. That's a lot to think about."

"It is. So I suggest we don't think about it. Not yet. As you say, things have happened very quickly. We have some time, don't we? Or are you racing off to that woman on the other side of the Ohio tomorrow morning?"

They both laughed. He turned in his seat to get a better look at her. She saw his hand lift to touch her face and she moved aside, shaking her head gently. He rolled his eyes.

"Why did I have to fall for the bishop's daughter?"

"You can change your mind. Indiana waits."

"Indiana. I scarcely think about Indiana anymore. But I think a lot about Lyndel Keim. I don't know if I'll ever go west now."

"If you do, we could write letters. Wouldn't that be fun? And you wouldn't have to stay away for a long time, would you? Just a month or two?"

The sunset colored her face and made her skin glow—red hair gleamed a coppery gold, eyes were a brilliant blue as if, Nathaniel thought to himself, they were a couple of stars from a spring constellation. The impulse to take her into his arms was so strong he looked away and flicked the traces. The buggy moved out into the road and he turned it around and headed back toward the Keim farm.

Lyndel made her pixie face. "Did I say something wrong?"

"You look too good."

"I look too good?"

"Either I go to Indiana so you don't drive me crazy every day or I go to your father and say I would like to court you."

"But we both agreed it was too soon to think about courting and marriage."

"We did. So I must go to Indiana instead."

He saw the sly grin she flashed as she said, "Come, Nathaniel, I can't be that irresistible. Think back to March. You scarcely looked at me twice."

"March? March seems like ten years ago." He glanced at her as they drove. "It won't work for me to stay, Lyndel. Not unless you change your looks completely."

"And would that help you?"

"It would."

"And it is something you want? For me to change my looks completely?"

"No."

"Then where are we?"

"On the road to your house. And a nighttime of dreaming about your face and your hair and your eyes."

Softly she said in response, "I dream about you too, green-eyed

Amish boy." Then she leaned her head against his shoulder and reached out to take his hand tightly in hers.

"Hey," he said.

"You don't mind, do you?" she responded.

"Of course I don't mind. But you said things like this were not permitted. Especially for the bishop's daughter."

"Tonight the bishop's daughter doesn't care."

And she did dream. But most of it wasn't the dreams of the night, but the dreams that came to her by day: of marrying him, holding him, kissing him, running her hands over his back and through his beautiful brown hair. Yet she found she couldn't say the romantic things to him that he said to her and this troubled her. Yes, his words against slavery had excited her and she'd told him so. His attempt to bar the slave hunters from reaching Moses and Charlie had made her proud of him and she'd run across the yard to his carriage to tell him how she felt.

But when it came to letting him know she thought he was handsome, that his green eyes in the sunlight made her long to take him in her arms, that she loved the way he walked, so tall and straight and strong, she couldn't bring the words out of her mouth. What was wrong with her? A dozen girls from the community would gladly trade places with her. Yet she couldn't even respond that he was wonderful, brave, and sweet, after he told her a hundred times how stunning her blue eyes were, or how her red hair flamed, or how beautiful the strength was he saw in her hands and shoulders. Her silence made no sense to her and she couldn't understand what stopped her tongue.

Still, as April became May and May turned into velvet June, with its bright flowers and trees thick with leaves and hay higher than a tall man's head, it seemed to her that she and Nathaniel were getting closer and closer to the point where they both felt it might be time for him to sit down with her father and declare his intention to court her with the aim of asking for her hand in marriage. She was certain this would free her up inside so that she would finally be able to say all the things she wanted about his beauty and manliness and strong spirit. But just as finding Moses and Charlie in the barn that day had changed everything, as had his words of affection to her in the hay field one rainy afternoon, something new burst into their lives once again and stood everything on its head.

Corinth had returned to Elizabethtown in the company of his father and brother the Saturday after he had run off to Harrisburg to enlist. For months, as the North and the South had proceeded steadily on divergent paths with little armed conflict, the young man had been content to remain at his family farm and help with the crops. But when a huge battle occurred at a place called Manassas Junction in Virginia in July, and the North was defeated, the King family woke to find that Corinth had disappeared from their midst yet again. This time a search of Harrisburg's military depots turned up nothing. It wasn't until a letter arrived from Indiana that the Kings learned Corinth had made his way to an Amish community there and was refusing to return home. The man who wrote the letter, kin to the Yoders, explained that Corinth had made it clear he would only talk with his older brother Nathaniel. So Lyndel went out to milk her cows at four o'clock one August morning to find a perfect red rose from someone's garden lying across the top of her milking bucket.

She felt wonderful and sad at the same time. Although there was no note attached, there wasn't a doubt in her mind that the rose was from Nathaniel. It had to do with his affection for her, of course, but she felt it was also about beginnings and endings and this stirred up the mix of emotions within her. Not knowing what else to do, she upended her milking bucket, sat on it, cried for a few minutes, then tucked the rose in her *kapp* while she went about her chores. She decided that once she had finished milking she would go to her room and carefully press the rose between the pages of her Bible at Psalm 91.

A loud creaking of wheels made her raise her head from her work.

"Hello, the Keim farm!" a man called. "Is anyone about?"

Lyndel stood up and went to the barn door. She recognized the voice. The visitor was Nathaniel's father, Adam King.

"Mr. King." She greeted him with a smile. "*Guten Morgen.*"

He nodded from the seat of his buggy. "*Guten Morgen.* I have come to bring you news. You and your father."

"What news is that?"

"Nathaniel has left on the train. He boarded late last night."

Lyndel bit her lip. "He has gone to Indiana to bring back Corinth?"

Mr. King stared at her. His brown eyes were soft. "He left for Indiana, yes. But not to bring back Corinth. He went to enlist."

Lyndel felt ice move through her body. "What?"

"There is a telegram from Pittsburgh they brought to the house an hour ago." Mr. King extended a slip of paper. "He talks to you."

She reached up and took the telegram from his hand.

Father, I have not gone to fetch Corinth. I have gone to join him. I will enlist in the Union Army and request to be enrolled in the same regiment. Lyndel, I did not know how to tell you. I still don't. I take up arms because I see Charlie Preston's eyes when your father and I cut him down from the tree. No matter what else has gone on since that day his eyes and face are with me. I must put my body between the slave driver and the slave. I realize I may never see you again. But my God knows how much I love you. Goodbye.

6

Lyndel's shock at reading Nathaniel's message soon turned to anger at his unwillingness to face her in person…to at least say goodbye. What if it were true that they would never see each other again? How could he leave like this? Had he been merely teasing when he spoke of courtship?

But as the days turned to weeks, so too the anger turned to forgiveness, worry, and prayers for Nathaniel's safety. The latter, of course, was her main concern. No one had heard a word from him. Where was he now? Was he fighting…or perhaps helping the wounded somehow so he didn't have to bear arms?

Finally the day arrived, three months after his departure, when Lyndel received her first letter from him. No one could remember her being that excited about anything. And even though the letter was not very forthcoming as to his duties, it at least assured her that he was safe…for now.

She realized too that the longer he stayed with the Union Army and the longer he refrained from returning to the Amish in a repentant spirit, the more likely it was that he would be banned from the church.

Her prayers continued to range from protection to repentance to his quick return home. But as the months passed and occasional letters continued to arrive, Lyndel faced the truth that Nathaniel must be far from repentant for his actions.

Her concern was made all the more real by the sad glances her father gave her when she mentioned Nathaniel at the table. And then finally, in the spring of 1862, she found herself walking to the Sunday service in their barn dreading what was about to happen. But no matter what was said today, she had made a decision. She would first talk to Levi and then she would begin to make her plans.

She sat down beside her mother and immediately bent her head and moved her lips, silently praying for Nathaniel and Corinth. They had both been in the army almost a year. How she missed Nathaniel. It had become intolerable. *Please, Lord, bring us together again. Somehow. Either he comes to me or I go to him.* She opened her eyes and lifted her head as the singing of hymns began. And then when the singing was finished, she sat and waited anxiously as her father rose and moved to the front of the gathered people and began his sermon.

"So now it is April again," he said. "Do you remember how it was last year, with our Lord greening the earth, when news came of the assault on Fort Sumter? Do you remember how men chose to fight rather than to pray? To kill rather than to forgive? To make war rather than find the pathway to peace?"

Lyndel's father paused. She could see the shine of tears at the edges of his eyes and reached over to grip her mother's hand.

"How very hard this is for him," whispered her mother. "Remember that."

"I know, Mother. I hold nothing against him."

"Are you sure?"

"I harbor no ill feelings, I promise you."

People all around them, seated in the Keim barn on rough benches, waited while the bishop closed his eyes to pray. Then he spread his hands. Light from cracks in the barn walls glistened on his damp cheeks.

"It is never too late to return to Christ's fold. Though we may err, there is always forgiveness with our God and with his people. The gate is never shut to the broken and contrite of heart." He turned to look behind him briefly. "It was here that Moses Gunnison and Charlie Preston took shelter." Then he gazed over everyone's heads as if he could see the pasture and creek and sugar maples through the open barn doors. "It was among the maples by the stream that men took Charlie

Preston's life from him. The rope hangs from the tree yet. I have never removed it." His eyes fell on the people with a sudden fierceness. "But they could not take his life from God. The Lord holds Charlie's soul close to his heart. No man can take Charlie from the God of heaven and earth."

Amen, murmured dozens of men and women, including Lyndel and her mother.

"We do not pray for God's creatures to be enslaved. We pray for them to be free to follow the Lord's will for their lives. But God has called us to be Amish. And the Amish do not free men by killing other men. The Amish will not add more grief to the homes of Northern families or Southern families. We heal. We bless. We comfort. The Amish of America believe God cares for and loves all Americans, regardless of their color or creed or the sins they commit. Always with the Lord Jesus Christ there is mercy, there is hope, there is peace for the turmoil of the human heart and the tumult of nations."

Briefly he picked up a newspaper and let it fall down upon the clean straw.

"News comes of a terrible battle near Shiloh in Tennessee. Tens of thousands dead and wounded. Mothers in tears. Fathers' spirits broken. Some of you ask me why I bother to read the papers when the burden they put on a man is so pernicious. My brothers in Christ, my sisters in Christ, I read them so I know how to pray for our country—not North or South but for our whole country. And to weep with those who weep, as our Lord commanded."

He nodded at the pastors, who sat near him at a front bench, and they stood up and gathered on both sides of him—Abraham Yoder, Samuel Eby, and Solomon Miller. They knelt as one and folded their hands before them in prayer.

"Corinth King left us to bear arms but he had not yet been baptized, not yet taken his vows." Her father's eyes rested on Lyndel. "Nathaniel King, on the other hand, was baptized two years ago. He is one of us. He is Amish." Her father moved his head to seek out Nathaniel's parents. "Last year we waited months for confirmation that he had joined a regiment in Indiana. He himself confirmed he had enlisted by writing to me and confessing it was so.

"Many of you know that he and I wrote back and forth all winter as I endeavored to get him to change his mind, to repent, to return to us a man of prayer and of peace. But he has insisted he feels called to make a whip as Jesus made a whip and is clearing the temple of our nation. When I told him it was not his place to take on the role of our Lord he replied that we had to imitate Christ in all things. I responded that just as Nathaniel could not take on the sins of the world on the Cross so he could not take on the sins of the nation and bear a whip to cleanse the temple that is America. But he has proceeded on his own way. He has forgotten the commandment, 'Thou shalt not kill.'"

Lyndel saw that her father's tears were flowing freely now. She heard others begin to cry and a tightness came to her throat. She had sworn there would be no tears on her part but she found she couldn't stop them and so she bowed her head, raising a small white handkerchief to her face.

"So now the papers from Philadelphia and New York tell us of his Indiana regiment and how Nathaniel performed bravely under fire at Lewinsville in Virginia last fall and how he has been promoted to corporal. I have failed to persuade him to return to the ways we as a people have been called upon by the Lord to follow. So, in grief and with our eyes toward the righteous Judge who weighs the hearts and the motives of all men, I and the leadership…" he paused as if he hoped that somehow it had all been a bad dream and that by wishing it so, he might open his eyes and find a repentant Nathaniel King kneeling in front of him, "must with great regret declare Nathaniel King excommunicated, *exkommuniziert,* from our church. He may not be spoken with. Letters may no longer be written to him or letters received from him. It must be as if he were not alive, so that one day, repentant, he may return to us as one who is alive—a young man joined again to his Amish people and joined to the Lord and Savior of our souls. Amen."

Amen, the people responded but Lyndel did not open her mouth.

There were baptisms that day—Sunday, April 13th, 1862—and

Communion and then a huge meal but, as she had done the day of Charlie Preston's funeral, Lyndel wandered off alone to the hay fields near her farm, fields where the grass was short and green and wet from spring rains. And, as Nathaniel had followed her into those fields the year before, she was followed again, this time by her brother Levi, who caught up with her and stood just behind her, calling her name and waiting for her to turn.

When he saw her white face and swollen eyes he removed his broad-brimmed hat. "I'm sorry, Lyndel. This is not much of a day."

She didn't greet her brother but merely asked, "What does your newspaper friend from Elizabethtown tell you?"

"He was in Virginia only a few days ago. The 19th Indiana is camped on a creek called Cedar Run at Catlett's Station. The men are relaxed and in good spirits."

"Did he see Nathaniel?"

"No."

"Where is Catlett's Station?"

"Not far from Manassas Junction."

"Isn't Manassas where the great battle was fought last summer?"

"*Ja*."

"Is there going to be another fight there?"

Levi shrugged. "Who can say? For now the Rebels have fled, leaving a trail of knapsacks and food and dead horses. Nathaniel's regiment is less than a mile from the Hargrove Plantation."

Lyndel's eyes became a dark blue. "Are they going to march on the plantation?"

"They have no reason to do so."

"Thank you, brother. Are you still with me as far as our plans go?"

He nodded. "I am. But…it does not feel right slipping away without a word to mother and father."

She smiled in a halfhearted way. "I know. Every time I pray, the Lord touches on that very thing. I will tell them, brother. Just before we leave. It would be wrong to act as if we were abandoning them."

"I would like to be there when you speak with them."

"Of course."

He played with the brim of his hat. "It can't be until after spring planting."

She gave a short laugh. "Every April it is the same. Nothing can happen until after spring planting. Perhaps the war will end at spring planting."

"I pray to God it would."

"So are you thinking of June?"

"I am. The seventh. A Saturday."

"Nathaniel's regiment will no longer be encamped near Manassas, will it?"

"I think it's unlikely. They move them around like knights and rooks on a chessboard. But my friend will find the regiment. The Philadelphia paper has assigned him to the Virginia theater of operations permanently."

Lyndel put her arm through her brother's. "See me home, would you? One day I should like to meet this newspaperman of yours and thank him. Now that I can't send Nathaniel mail or receive his letters, your friend's information will be more important than ever."

"Once we're in Virginia I will introduce you."

"Has he gone ahead and tried to make the arrangements I—we—requested?"

"He has. He has spoken with a Mrs. McKean, who is a matron at the Armory Square Hospital in Washington. She seems inclined to take you on as a nurse."

"Without ever meeting me? Why?"

"Oh, I suppose I have talked you up to my friend. And being a writer, he has embellished everything I have said."

"Levi! How will I live up to whatever nonsense you have told her? She probably thinks I am ten feet tall!"

"To tell you the truth, my friend mentioned Mrs. McKean was impressed by the fact you were a farm girl. I guess she expects that means you are strong and hardworking. And that is so. I believe you will have no trouble being hired as a nurse."

"If God wills, then may it come to be."

Lyndel had scarcely entered her bedroom and washed her face, pouring fresh rainwater from a pitcher into a basin on the washstand, than her little sister Becky tapped on the door and called to her.

"What is it?" asked Lyndel. "I'm cleaning up."

"Papa wants to see you in the kitchen."

"Do you know what it's about?"

"Well, I see he has a letter on the table by his cup of coffee."

Lyndel quickly dried her face and went down the staircase with Becky. When they reached the kitchen, their father smiled, caught Becky's eye, and nodded his head in the direction of the door to the porch.

"Your sisters need someone to hold the other end of the big skipping rope."

"All right, Papa."

When she had gone out the door he looked at Lyndel. "Sit with me, please. Would you like something to drink?"

"Not right now, Papa, thank you." She sat down next to him and saw that his eyes were dark and swollen just as hers had been.

"You understand how difficult a day this has been for me as well as you?"

"Yes, Papa."

"It is hard on the entire community. Please understand that."

"I do understand it."

His longer fingers tapped against a white envelope on the tabletop. It was stained with dirt and splotches of ink.

"This came yesterday. I did not tell you. I wondered if there should be any mail passed on to you. I knew the *Meidung* would be coming into force. But as the day has worn on, as I have prayed and listened and worshipped, it has become clear to me this is your letter and you are meant to have it. There can be no others after this."

Lyndel sat up. "Do you mean to let me have that letter, Papa?"

"I do. And it is right that you must be permitted to respond. Then there must be no further correspondence until he has laid down his weapons and repented."

"I may write him back once more?"

"*Ja.*"

Impulsively, she got up from her chair and threw her arms around her father, the chair clattering backward onto the floor, her father surprised by the strength of her hug and the two kisses on his cheek and beard.

"Oh, thank you, thank you!" she cried.

"Hey, hey, my girl, it is only a letter."

"Papa, you know it's not *only* a letter."

"So you love him?"

Clutching the envelope she wiped at her eyes with the back of her hand. "I don't say that I love him. But I care about him so much. He is so sweet. And he has declared his love for me."

"Has he?"

"*Ja, ja.*"

"Well, perhaps the day will come when he weds you in the way a good Amish man takes a good Amish wife to himself." His eyes strayed to a window that overlooked the pasture. "It started with Charlie Preston. And in a way I cannot blame him—I too cut Charlie from the tree—no, I cannot blame him. He must lay down his whip, he must lay down the musket and bayonet, but God knows he saw great evil and wanted to right it. His intent is pure even if his path is violent and dark."

She sat back down and took one of his hands in hers. "Papa, may I ask you something?"

"*Ja?*"

"You said in your sermon the Amish are people who bless. Who heal."

"I did say it."

"Would it be wrong to nurse a wounded soldier back to health?"

"What is this?"

"You read in the papers how Clara Barton and other women helped tend the wounded in Washington after the battle last summer."

"After Manassas? Yes, I read that. They did good work."

"Holy work?"

"Holy work?" Her father ran a hand over his dark beard. "Inasmuch as you did it to the least of these you did it unto me. Yes, I would have to say—holy work, the work of love."

"If I…if I were to do such work…someday…would I find favor… in your eyes?"

He stared at her. "Is this what you are thinking? Will you also leave us for this terrible war?"

"Not for the war, Papa, for the healing, to minister to the sick—"

"Still. You are involved in the war. Clara Barton is not Amish. You are. Your calling is different."

"If we are both called upon by God to heal, it is not so different."

Her father shook his head and waved his hand, standing up from his chair. "The church would not approve. I would be called on to order the shunning of my own daughter. Would you take me to such a place?"

Heat came to Lyndel's face. "Why may I not heal others in the name of God?"

"There are always sick here. You can nurse the sick of the church or Elizabethtown. You do not need a war."

"But the war is where I'm needed most. Here a few are ill with fever or stomach cramps. There young men are torn to pieces. Balls of lead are in their arms and chests. Their blood is pouring out onto the ground. They cry out for their mothers while the doctors saw off their legs. Tens of thousands, you said. There are not enough nurses to help. I could make a difference, Papa."

"You would be part of the war. The Amish are never part of a war, never—not in any way are they part of a war."

"Not even in a good way?"

He shook his head again, slowly and forcefully. "There is no good way."

"Not even if it is Christ I nurse? Not even if it is Christ whose skin is burnt black from the explosion? Not even if it is Christ who is crying out as the life flies from his mangled body? 'And the King shall answer and say unto them, Verily I say unto you, Inasmuch as ye have done it unto one of the least of these my brethren, ye have done it unto me.'"

Her father did not move, listening, thinking. Then he turned away.

"If this is what you will do, please say goodbye to your mother and me first. Will you do that?" He stopped at the door, partly opening it so that the laughter of his three younger daughters filled the kitchen. He looked back at Lyndel. "Do you find it in yourself to at least give us that?"

She wiped at her eyes with her fingers. "Of course, Papa."

He gazed at her, nodding. There was a very faint, faraway smile. "I am grateful to the Lord for you." Then he went out and closed the door gently behind him.

Lyndel made it to her room, threw herself full length on her bed, and wept. It took more than ten minutes before she was able to prop herself on an elbow, her eyes red, tears still running across her face, and open the envelope with Nathaniel's letter inside.

Dear Lyndel,

I hope this letter finds you well, you and your family and the entire community. All I can tell you is we are marching back and forth in Virginia. The bread is not soft Amish bread and the cooking is not like what I'm used to at my place or yours. Corinth and I are the only Pennsylvanians mixed in with the boys from the 19th regiment and we tell everyone we are from Elkhart County, Indiana, which is true enough as that is where our Amish settlement is located. A few others are from that county, but most hail from different parts of the state. Along with the Hoosiers—that is what the Indiana boys like to call themselves— our brigade is composed of troops from

Wisconsin—the 2nd, 6th, and 7th volunteer regiments (I hope it is all right to say so in my letter and to give out the numbers). We get along well enough but it is no Amish church meeting as you can imagine. Our brigade commander, General Gibbon, is tough as a plowshare and not liked too much, but the officer who is in charge of the 19th Indiana, Long Sol Meredith, well, we all respect him and will pretty much follow him anywhere.

But that's enough soldier talk. Since I last wrote I have been going through Isaiah in the Old Testament and Ephesians in the New. I also reread all your letters and the boys rib me about this but I don't care. I love the way you write and what you have to say and I love the scent you leave behind on the paper—it's that soap your mother makes with lilacs, cinnamon, and roses. I keep your letters in my Bible in my knapsack and sometimes I stick that Bible in the blanket I roll up for a pillow—so there are your letters and Paul's letters and Peter's all jumbled together and holding up my head.

I must go—a corporal's duties. Will write you again when I can. It takes forever for the mail to catch up with us but I hope the next mail call will have a card or note from you. Lyndel,

you mean so much to me. May God keep you
safe.

Are we courting yet?

Love, Nathaniel

Lyndel smiled as she read and then quickly got up from the bed and went to her desk. She laid out a fresh sheet of paper, lit the lamp at her elbow, and dipped the tip of a goose quill in her bottle of ink. Then she began to smoothly spread her flowing script across the page, dipping the quill after every third or fourth word.

My dearest Nathaniel,

I have just read your latest note to me and I have to write to tell you they will not let me send you any more letters after this one. It is, of course, on account of your enlisting and taking up arms against the South and slavery. They have given you a year to return home and you have not done so. But do not be dismayed, my darling, they still love you, only they want you to come back to being a true Amish man again. I confess that sometimes I'm confused about the whole matter but I know this—what happened to Charlie was wrong, and slavery must be stopped one way or another. I also know I can no longer sit here while this war drags on. Wounded men need care and if other women can nurse the soldiers so can I. Was not Christ a healer?

And it's not only that. I simply can't let
another year go by without seeing you. This
past winter was difficult enough but at least
we had our letters to one another to sustain
us. Now that those are being taken away,
another winter, even another summer, would
be impossible. So here is my news to cheer
you—I am going to come to you, I am going to
find you, even if I have to go through all the
Union and Confederate armies to do it. Levi
is escorting me and he has a newspaper friend
following the war, who will also assist us. I
intend to nurse the wounded and sick and my
objective is to be assigned to the surgeons in
your regiment. I'm not sure how I will get
permission to do this but I believe God is with
me in this enterprise and that He will make
a way—I have every reason to believe I will be
successful if I only begin the journey and take
one step at a time.

So place this note under your pillow and dream
for the day it will be true and that I will
stand before you and let you take me into your
arms—oh, yes, I will, even if my father and
the whole Amish church and President Lincoln
himself are watching.

My most earnest desire is to see you again. God

bless you and keep you from harm. Our reunion
will take place very soon.

With all my heart, I am,

your Lyndel

7

Lyndel and her brother didn't leave in June as they had planned but early on a July morning. Levi spent the extra weeks working with his father in the fields, Lyndel with her mother and sisters around the house and the barn.

When the day finally arrived, their mother stood like stone on the porch as the buggy pulled out of the drive and onto the road in the darkness of the pre-dawn morning. Waves of guilt surged over Lyndel as Dancer trotted toward the depot. Levi gripped her hand as their father drove.

"I do so worry," Lyndel whispered to her brother. "I hope they can manage without us."

"Remember, I'll be back for harvest," he said softly. "They won't be alone for long. I'll escort you to Washington and see that you are properly settled. And if I can be of any help to the effort, short of taking up arms, I will do what I can. By September I will have returned."

"I feel I am doing the right thing," she groaned quietly. "But now that we are actually leaving I wonder…"

"We can ask Papa to turn around."

Lyndel considered this for a moment and then said, "The papers are full of the fighting around Mechanicsville and Frayser's Farm and Malvern Hill. The casualties are pouring into the hospitals. This isn't simply about finding Nathaniel's regiment and asking to serve with their surgeons. It's about keeping as many of the boys and men alive as possible. Even you can help with that."

Levi nodded. "I intend to…if I can."

"Here we are." Their father brought the buggy to a halt. "Let me help you with your bag."

"It's light enough, Papa," said Lyndel as she stepped down. "Don't trouble yourself."

"It's no trouble." Taking his daughter's bag, he walked ahead of them to the station platform, where they stood quietly waiting for the call to board the train.

Finally, their father spoke. "As your father, I must say what I must say and then I must trust you to our God. Above all things, I want you to remember who you are and what you believe. Perhaps nothing will come of it since Levi is only escorting you, Lyndel, and you are simply going to be nursing the wounded. But some will say that makes both of you contributors to the war effort. Who knows what will come to pass? I'm sure I can give you three months before others insist on the *Meidung*."

"I'll be back before that," Levi said.

"Still. They may ask you to repent upon your return."

"I won't have so much as lifted a rifle," Levi protested.

"Nevertheless. In your way you have supported the war by helping your sister."

"Helping her to heal the sick just as our Lord did."

"Nevertheless."

"Perhaps I will be home very soon as well, Papa," Lyndel spoke up.

He looked at her. "Do you truly think so?"

"They're always talking about fighting one big decisive battle, aren't they? Perhaps that will happen this summer. Then the South will surrender."

"There have already been many battles, daughter, and the South has won most of them. Why would they surrender? No, the fighting has decided nothing. It has only succeeded in placing more young men in the ground."

"I hope to keep some of them away from the grave, Father, if I can."

His dark eyes remained on her a long time. Finally he said, "I know. Let me pray for both of you before it's time to leave."

He removed his wide-brimmed straw hat, put it by his feet, and placed a hand on each of their shoulders, praying in High German. Levi took off his hat as well. Lyndel felt herself calm as her father spoke with God. Then he put his hat back on his head and stepped back, his hands behind his back. The locomotive had taken on water and coal and was building up a head of steam.

A short man with a cigar walked by and spoke in a dull voice, "All aboard!"

"Well, then," their father murmured. "You must board…and I must get back to your mother."

Lyndel put her arms around his neck. "I'll miss you, Papa. God bless you."

He patted her gently on the back. "And Christ be with you, daughter."

Levi shook his father's hand. "I will not be long."

"I pray not. May his will be done on earth as it is in heaven."

He went and stood by Dancer and the carriage and was still there when the train pulled out of the station. Lyndel and her brother faced each other at window seats and both lifted their hands to him. Their father nodded. Then he and Elizabethtown were gone and the sun rose, coloring the land by laying down layer after layer of light as the train moved through.

Lyndel closed her eyes and pressed the fingers of one hand against her forehead. "This is so difficult."

"*Ja*," Levi responded, almost in a whisper.

"Even though I believe it's God's will it's still difficult."

"*Ja.*"

Even so early in the day tall white clouds had begun to pile up in the east and form thunderheads over the green land. Farms came and went. It seemed to Lyndel to be only moments before they were approaching Harrisburg. She hadn't visited the city in years. The sudden sight of hundreds of soldiers in blue uniforms lined up beside the tracks startled her—she had only seen two or three in Elizabethtown over the past year. Several large black cannons chained to flatcars made her dig her fingers into the fabric of her seat. The train slowed as it approached the station, passing more soldiers and horses and artillery. Suddenly it stopped before the platform was even in sight.

"Why are we stopping here?" she asked.

Levi shrugged. "Who knows? Harrisburg is a busy place now. There's an army camp and many trains running through from east and west."

"Can't you look out and see?"

"Of course."

Levi stood up and tried to open the window. It was jammed. He worked at it and banged it with the heel of his hand before he was able to get it to respond and he could thrust his head out. All he could see was rolling stock and soldiers. A sergeant with a pipe in his mouth glanced up at him.

"They're filling up the cars with troops just ahead of you, lad," the sergeant said with a distinctive accent. "It will be a few more minutes."

"Couldn't we just climb down and walk to the depot?" asked Levi. "We need to change trains."

"Ah, no, they'll not let you do that. Too dangerous to be wandering about on these tracks. Trains are coming and going by the minute and the engineers aren't always extra careful. Where are you headed?"

"Washington."

"What's there?"

"My sister is going to nurse."

The sergeant spotted Lyndel and raised his hat. "Wonderful. Grand." Then he looked back at Levi. "And you—are you going there to enlist?"

The train suddenly shook itself and lurched forward.

"Thank you!" Levi called to the sergeant and sat back down as the locomotive inched its way ahead. He shook his head at his sister. "I'm glad I didn't have to answer that question."

"You can always say you are going to nurse as well."

"I don't think that's the answer a soldier is looking for."

"I'm causing everyone a lot of trouble. Mama, Papa, my sisters, you. I'm sorry for that."

"I'll be all right." Levi stared out at a column of soldiers marching along a street. "What has Nathaniel told you about Lewinsville?"

"What do you mean?"

"You never told me how he became a corporal. Did he shoot someone?"

Lyndel stared at him. "My goodness, no. Is that what you think?"

"He had to do something."

"He saved some of his men from Jeb Stuart's cavalry. They would have been captured. He kept them hidden until Stuart's troopers rode off."

"Is that all?"

"I suppose he kept everyone calm and helped keep his company organized. So his captain thinks he's a natural leader."

"Has he ever fired a shot?"

"No. A few of his boys fired their muskets at Lewinsville. But none of them have ever been in a battle and Lewinsville was no battle. For which I thank God. I would like all of this to be over before Nathaniel has to aim his weapon at anyone. Or have them aim their weapons at him. Didn't he talk to you about this in his letters?"

A small smile came over Levi's face. "Not much. Most of all he was asking about you."

"But he and I were writing each other."

"He was afraid one of the other men from church would ask to court you."

Lyndel half-laughed. "As if I would say yes. Does Nathaniel think I'm as fickle as an English girl?"

"It's been over a year that he's been gone. And he tells me you've never told him you loved him."

Lyndel struggled to reply. "It's not...that I don't care for him...I just need to see him again before I...speak those words."

"Why?"

Lyndel felt the blood in her face and throat. "I need to find out... what I feel when I see him."

Levi frowned, the lines wrinkling his young, handsome face. "You mean you don't know what you feel?"

Her blue eyes had become gray. "As he says, it's been more than a year. I can't…use those words until I see him face-to-face. That's all. Please don't ask me about this again, Levi."

"All right."

"You find that strange?"

"I find women strange." He looked out the window at a long string of cavalry mounts. "I'm glad it's enough for me to shoe horses."

"What about Mary Yoder?"

Levi continued to stare out the window. "I will let you know when she asks to be shod."

They didn't miss their train for Baltimore, but they had scarcely pulled out of the station before they came to a stop for two hours. When they did start up again the train traveled slowly for another hour. Lyndel tried to rest, her head pillowed on Levi's jacket, which he had rolled up against the window for her.

"*Danke*," she murmured, closing her eyes.

He didn't wake her at Baltimore, where the train only stopped for half an hour before continuing on. By the time they began to slow for the Washington station a sudden thunderclap made her sit up, blue eyes wide and glittering. Lyndel stared out the window as if the train had taken them to the moon. "Where are we?"

"Washington."

It was now late afternoon and the sun was setting in a thick bank of red and black clouds that shimmered with lightning. Still perplexed, Lyndel gazed at faces lit by gas lamps, faces that seemed to have emerged from her dreams. Her skin was pale.

"Are you all right?" Levi asked.

"I just…can't seem to orient myself…I was sleeping so deeply and thought we were marching with the army…searching for Nathaniel and Corinth." She paused to look at Levi. "Wasn't that friend of yours supposed to meet us?"

Levi pointed. "He's right there on the platform. Hiram Wright."

"Why, he has red hair just like me."

"Not just like you. His is shorter. And the color of sweet potatoes."

"Whereas mine is like tomatoes?"

Levi grinned. "That's for you to say, Ginger. Nathaniel would tell you it was a glorious crimson flame."

The train had lurched to a stop, and the two travelers stood and gathered their things and made their way through the now crowded aisle to the exit.

As they made their way to where Hiram Wright stood waiting, the young man doffed his derby and took Lyndel's suitcase from her hand. "Your reputation precedes you, Miss Keim."

"Thank you, Mr. Wright. What reputation is that?"

"Your brother said I would find you fascinating."

"He said that?" She shot a quick glance at Levi, her eyes narrow. "How can you find someone fascinating you've only seen for less than one minute?"

"Hair. Face. Posture. The way you carry yourself. You must remember I'm a journalist. I'm used to sizing people up quickly. Now, please follow me and we'll make our way out of here." He turned and led them through a crowd of people and soldiers.

"I trust you won't have to rewrite your first impression a week from now," Lyndel said.

"Not unless it's to use more superlatives, Miss Keim." He grinned, turning in her direction, the freckles that covered his face moving with his mouth and lips. "Levi tells me you have a beau with General Gibbon's brigade."

Lyndel hesitated at Hiram's use of the word *beau* but decided not to make an issue of it. "He is in Colonel Meredith's regiment."

"Right. The 19th Indiana. The rest of the brigade is from Wisconsin. I saw them on parade once. A distinctive bunch. Tall black Hardee hats, you know, like short top hats, but slanted in toward the top. Some with the brim pinned up on one side. Black ostrich plumes. Long jackets. Very different in looks from the other Union brigades."

"What is your opinion of their—spirit?"

Hiram glanced at Lyndel as they walked. "They were fine at Lewinsville."

"But Lewinsville wasn't a battle."

THE FACE OF HEAVEN ⁓ 77

"No, it was not." He pointed to his carriage. It was drawn by two horses. "They are a good bunch of men. A little rowdy. On July 4th they held horse races and foot races while the other regiments lazed about—it seems the Indianans have an overabundance of energy. They're spoiling for a fight, Miss Keim, that's the only way I can put it. One day they'll get it."

"Do you know their whereabouts, Mr. Wright?"

"Virginia. Out and about in the vicinity of Manassas Junction. But Stonewall Jackson isn't there anymore. So there's no fight to be had. However I'm of the firm belief that Stonewall will be back. He's not a man to back away from a contest."

"You consider war a contest?"

"I do not, Miss Keim. But some of the commanders in both armies do. And Stonewall Jackson is one of them."

Lightning flashed over their heads, followed by a long, low rumble. "Perhaps it will be all over this summer."

Hiram's youthful face turned yellow in the sudden flare of a gas lamp. "I know that's the common opinion. I do not share it."

"What *is* your opinion, Mr. Wright?"

"It will take years for the Union to win this war, Miss Keim. And they could very well lose it with the generals we have."

The horizon filled with light and then went black. The thunder was moving farther to the south and east. Hiram's words brought a tightness to Lyndel's stomach.

"I hope you're not correct, Mr. Wright," she said.

He placed her case in his carriage. "It happens on occasion. Though the occasions are infrequent." He climbed into the driver's seat. "There is room up here for the three of us. Welcome to Washington, both of you. We'll drop by the hospital first, Miss Keim. The matron, Mrs. McKean, asked me to bring you by when you arrived."

"And that is the one called Armory…Armory…?"

"Armory Square. Just over on the mall in front of the Capitol dome." Hiram flicked the reins. "Away we go, Sally. Away we go, Kate. You'll be boarding with a prominent Washington family. Levi will be bunking with me in Georgetown. I hope these arrangements are acceptable to you."

"Thank you very much for all your work on our behalf, Mr. Wright. Though I'd be just as happy taking a blanket and pillow with me into someone's barn."

Hiram laughed as he steered through the traffic of carriages and pedestrians. "That would be rich. Ladies don't sleep in barns out here, Miss Keim. And the truth is, there aren't that many barns anyway. You'll have to settle for a four-poster bed with a canopy."

Levi sat between Hiram and his sister. She leaned forward to get a better look at Hiram to see if he was teasing her. "Mr. Wright, I'm just a plain girl who is used to plain Amish ways. I certainly do not require a four-poster with a canopy."

"Plain you are not, Miss Keim, not with hair and eyes and face such as God has given you. The bed you will have to take up with your hosts. Perhaps they have a spare stable where you can spread your quilt."

Armory Square Hospital consisted of rows of long, low white buildings like barracks neatly laid out, with a picket fence in front. Hiram pulled up in front of one with an arch and a sign over its door. He helped Lyndel step down onto a small wooden platform and avoid the mud and puddles of the street. Then he escorted her inside, with Levi following.

Mrs. McKean had seen the carriage drive up and was waiting. Tall and broad, in a white dress and apron with her hair pinned to perfection and tucked rigidly under a cap, she extended a large hand to Lyndel. "Welcome, Miss Keim. I understand you have come all the way from Pennsylvania to volunteer?"

"Yes, ma'am."

She looked Lyndel up and down. "You are perhaps too pretty to nurse wounded soldiers. But you have a firm grip despite all that. Hiram said you were a farm girl."

"I am, ma'am."

"Please call me Miss Sharon. This will be infinitely harder than milking cows or churning butter."

"I have nursed wounded men, ma'am—Miss Sharon."

"Have you? Where?"

Lyndel struggled under the onslaught. "Two…runaways…hid in our barn last spring."

Miss Sharon raised her thick eyebrows. "Did they? And was your nursing successful?"

"I believe so, yes."

"You believe so? What became of them?"

"One was recaptured. The slave hunters—hanged the other."

Miss Sharon paused. Lyndel fought to keep her face strong but she could feel her lower lip trembling as she thought of Charlie Preston swinging from the sugar maple. Miss Sharon flicked her eyes over Lyndel's navy blue dress and black apron and *kapp*.

"Your attire is—different. But suitable, I suppose. I prefer white aprons and caps however."

"So we dress in Lancaster County, Miss Sharon. I just came from the train. I haven't had time to change."

"Nor will you. I have five nurses down with typhoid fever. I apologize for throwing you in at the deep end of the pond but I need you right now and I need you to stay through the night." She looked at Hiram. "Thank you for bringing Miss Keim here, Mr. Wright. I will see she gets to her lodgings in the morning. George will drive her."

Hiram held his derby hat in his hands. "It's no trouble for me, Miss Sharon. Or her brother here, Levi Keim."

Miss Sharon briefly inclined her head. "Mr. Keim. I'm told you will be going to the front in Mr. Wright's company to enlist with the ambulance service."

Levi had removed his broad-brimmed straw hat. The news surprised him and he twisted the hat about in his hands. "I had thought I might be of some use here."

"No doubt you would be, Mr. Keim. But we lack strong, healthy men at the front to carry the wounded safely from the field, sometimes under fire. A strapping boy like you would be of enormous benefit to the Union as an ambulance attendant."

Levi glanced at Lyndel. "Well…"

Miss Sharon caught his look. "Your sister will be quite safe here, young man. Believe me, my girls are treated with honor and respect in this hospital and in the community. No fear of that."

Levi nodded quickly. "Yes, ma'am. Of course."

"Now you two had best be off. Miss Keim has much work to do and not much time to learn it before our next casualties come in from Virginia. Thank you—you may come by for her at eight o'clock if you insist."

She shooed Hiram and Levi toward the door like cattle. Levi craned his neck to look back at Lyndel. "My sister's been traveling all day, ma'am."

"She's young and strong. She'll be fine."

"I'll telegraph Mother and Father and tell them we've arrived safely," he called to his sister.

She smiled. "Thank you."

Miss Sharon shut the door behind Levi and Hiram. Then she picked up a lamp.

"Follow me, Miss Keim. You may leave your travel bag here by the desk for the present."

Lyndel walked behind Miss Sharon down the hall into a ward with beds neatly lining both sides. The lightning from the east ignited the room for a moment and clearly showed what the quiet moans and gasps had already told her—bearded heads sunk on pillows, bodies without arms, legs without feet, faces without eyes. She smelled blood and clenched her hands into fists. The thunder banged and almost made her jump. The storm had moved closer to Washington again.

Once the lightning was gone, the ward was dark but for two or three lamps. There was only one nurse and she was bending over a bed at the far end. Miss Sharon continued to stare at the soldiers, holding the light in her hand at eye level. For the longest time she said nothing and Lyndel waited, praying.

Lord, this is why I have come. What did you feel like inside when you saw all the suffering and death? Help me to make a difference at least something like the way you made a difference.

"They need to be shaved and have their hair combed, Miss Keim,"

Miss Sharon suddenly spoke up. "Their wounds and sores need to be cleaned again and dried. Fresh bandages must be applied. If they are hungry, feed them. If they are thirsty, give them something to drink. Should they ask for hot coffee there is a pot on the kitchen stove. If they are restless, comfort them. If they are sleeping, let them sleep." She turned to face Lyndel and her eyes glistened in the light she held. "I have found such simple things save lives. Just such simple things. If we could do that for all of them within an hour of their wounding we'd save so many more.

"But nurses like you and me are not permitted on the battlefield. It takes days to bring them to Washington. Think how many more would live if we were there with them, Miss Keim."

Lightning stabbed at the windows again. The thunder roared almost immediately. The storm was right on top of them. Suddenly rain began to crash against the roof and the panes of the windows.

This was only one of many buildings full of casualties. And Lyndel was aware that Armory Square was only one of many hospitals in Washington. The South had their hospitals too. All of them with room after room of shattered men.

She shivered as she continued to stare at the soldiers in their beds. Miss Sharon watched her carefully. Then she spoke quietly, "You will be all right, my dear. You will get used to it."

Lyndel didn't take her eyes from the men as rain whipped the building and thunder made the walls shake.

"I have come to the war," she whispered.

Miss Sharon stared at her and finally nodded, the lamplight gleaming on her face and hands. "Yes. You have come to the war."

8

August 28, 1862

Dear Lyndel,

We are camped in a field of clover thick with grasshoppers—why, one has just hopped onto this page I'm writing on. Somewhere out there is the town of New Baltimore. Everyone is dead asleep. We marched all the way from Sulphur Springs yesterday.

Corinth and I are in the same company now as I was transferred to his because they needed another noncommissioned officer. He foraged a couple of chickens and a knapsack full of green corn and we roasted it all and ate it before turning in about 11:30. Corinth is getting pretty good at this soldier game though I still can't teach him to call me corporal. Not that I care but the captain does. In any case, the men love him. Not just for his foraging skills. He has a good word for everyone and a slap on the back for each of his comrades in arms. And you were right about the girls. Every time we march through a town he seems to get the most flowers and the most smiles. Once a gal even kissed him. He's quite the boy.

I decided to get up early and write you this note. My pocket watch says it is 3:30. I expect we will be marching the entire day and I won't get another chance. I know you told me months ago they would not permit you to receive my letters on account of my being shunned but who else can I talk to about the things that swirl about in my head? And I have a wallet full of three-cent stamps—what am I supposed to do with them if I can't write my mother or father or you? I intend to send letters to Lyndel Keim until I run out of those stamps, which may not be long because I keep selling them to other soldiers who can't get their hands on any. Where my mail winds up is in the Lord's hands. Perhaps the postmaster in Elizabethtown will slip one in your pocket regardless of the rules and maybe you will read it anyway.

I was reading Psalm 91 just before I fell asleep last night. Here is what I think God is saying to—

"What are you doing, Nathaniel?" a voice suddenly whispered.

Nathaniel glanced over at his brother. "Catching up on my mail," he whispered back.

Corinth was propped up on one elbow. "It's not even four in the morning."

"I know."

"And it's pitch dark."

"My eyes are used to it. I can see fine. It's not a long letter."

"Who can you write to? We're shunned."

"I hope they'll get my note anyway."

"You're writing Lyndel, aren't you?"

"So what if I am?"

Corinth flopped back onto his makeshift pillow. "You have it so bad. A horse must have kicked you in the head. It's been more than a year since you've seen her. How can you even remember what she looks like?"

"Her hair is red and her eyes are blue."

"Naomi Miller has black hair and green eyes but I hardly think of her anymore. It's so long ago."

"Naomi Miller never held your hand."

"Is that all? Lyndel Keim only held your hand?"

"And put her head on my shoulder."

The ring of the bugle cut through the silent dark.

"That's it," said Nathaniel. "Up early to march circles around Stonewall Jackson."

"Or maybe he's marching circles around us."

Nathaniel grinned. "Maybe."

"Corporal!"

Nathaniel jumped up. "Right here, Sergeant."

"Shake the platoon out. We'll get an hour's march out of the morning before we have breakfast."

"Yes, Sergeant." Nathaniel grabbed his Springfield musket, his unfinished letter to Lyndel, and his Hardee hat. "I'll make sure the boys are up. Then I'll come back for my bedroll."

Corinth rolled up his own bedroll as he listened to his brother calling out names in the dark: "Hey, Nip. Hey, Stewart. Crum. Harter. Rise and shine. Time to find Stonewall and trim his beard."

Corinth strapped up his knapsack, ran a hand once or twice over his head of tight blond curls, and clamped his Hardee hat on. He stopped a moment and smiled in the dark.

"Naomi Miller," he said out loud. "Huh."

The brigade went a mile and stopped for breakfast. Corinth got a fire going for the platoon and Nip, a boy not much older than him from Indiana's Delaware County, scrounged some flour and baking soda from someone and made flapjacks.

"If only we had honey and butter," one of the men said, squatting by the fire and eating one of Nip's flapjacks with his fingers.

Nathaniel nodded. "Or maple syrup."

"I don't believe I've ever had maple syrup, Corporal."

"Why, Ham, tomorrow morning I'll get eggs, honey, and maple syrup and we'll have ourselves a feast," smiled Corinth.

"Where you gonna find all that?" Ham was licking his fingers. "You're mighty sure of yourself."

"I have a nose for forage. If it's in Virginia, I'll find it."

"Likely Stonewall has it in his kit."

"Then I'll borrow the fixings from him and invite him to a sit-down meal."

Ham laughed. "I believe you mean it."

Corinth put his hands on his hips. "An hour's truce is all I need. We could end the war with a good meal. The Rebs'd realize there's no sense in going on fighting when we all could be sitting down and eating instead."

The platoon laughed. The sergeant began pouring mugs of what he called his rough coffee, smiling under his large black mustache. "Well, that's something to look forward to, Private King. I hope you can deliver on your promises."

"Oh, that's strong brew, Sergeant!" One man shot to his feet, his face twisted and turning red. "Hot as a stove and sharp as a bayonet. What did you put in it?"

"Same as always, Private Jones. Generous measures of rock, sand, and Pennsylvania coal. And some of that good black grease the wagoners slap on their wheels."

"Don't joke. I believe what you're saying when it hits my stomach."

"Who's joking? What else does the army give me to make coffee with? When they get us out marching again you'll be glad you had a cup. It'll keep you ramrod straight. You can't never fall down when you've had a shot of Tippecanoe County coffee."

A man got up and stowed his cup in his pack. "You're saying not even a mess of minie balls could knock me over, Sergeant Hanson?"

"That's what I'm saying, Corporal Nicolson."

"You reckon I'll ever get a chance to find out?"

"Well, Corporal, if we keep marching long enough I expect we'll wind up in Stonewall Jackson's kitchen before the year's out. He might take offense and then you'll have your hat full."

It was a long day of marching and Nathaniel noticed they were soon on the Warrenton Turnpike. After a while the brigade was ordered off the turnpike and stood waiting in the heat with their columns pointed toward Manassas Junction. Men gulped from their canteens and put wet cloths under their tall black hats. The breakfast had worn off and he knew the troops were famished. Still there was no movement forward and no order to forage for food. Finally General Gibbon had an ox killed and the meat given out to the regiments and their companies. Nip and Corinth started roasting the platoon's beef before the fire was little more than a few smoking sticks.

"You're in an awful hurry," grunted Ham, squatting far away so that he didn't feel the heat.

"I know enough about the army," Corinth replied, laying out the slabs of beef on rocks, "to know we'll no sooner start eating than the captain will tell us to start marching."

"Sergeant Hanson!" the second lieutenant yelled, reining in his brown mare.

The sergeant had been poking a large chunk of beef toward the flames that had suddenly burst upward from the wood. He jumped to his feet and saluted, leaving the beef to sizzle. "Yes, sir."

"Have the men fall in. We're getting back on the Warrenton Turnpike."

"Any idea where we're headed, Lieutenant Davidson?"

The officer shrugged. "I hear we have Stonewall surrounded. Who knows?"

"What about the ox meat, Lieutenant?"

"Eat it. Quickly." He galloped off.

"I knew it," groaned Corinth.

"Take your knives," said Nathaniel. "Cut off a portion and swallow it whole if you have to. It will be hours before we get a chance to eat again."

Nip made a face. "It's not cooked."

"Wave it over the flames once or twice. That'll have to do."

Ham crammed a huge piece in his mouth. "Rare, smoked, roasted," he said around his chewing. "I'll take it anyway it comes."

"Fall in! Fall in!" thundered Sergeant Hanson, a strip of undercooked beef in one hand. "We've got a lot more marching to do before your mother kisses you goodnight."

"Where are we headed?" asked Corporal Nicolson, wrapping raw beef in a piece of paper and stuffing it in his pants pocket, the blood quickly seeping through the paper.

"I told you before. Stonewall's kitchen table. Are you ready for the sweet potatoes and greens he's got spread for you?"

The marching continued for hours. Nathaniel found that thinking about Lyndel, or what he remembered of the face and smile that passed for Lyndel, made the walking go by more quickly. It was something he had been doing for more than a year. Not just entertaining a few thoughts now and then that flitted in and out of his head. He strove to recall all the minutes of all the hours they'd spent together, the buggy rides, the meals at her mother's dinner table, every word she had spoken, every movement of her face and hands, no matter how slight. He found he became so immersed in his memories that the miles peeled away under his boots.

When the 19th Indiana entered a strip of forest and cannons rumbled like a thunderstorm a little ways off, his green eyes suddenly focused as he quickly glanced around him.

"You just come back to us from Lancaster County?" smiled Corinth as they marched.

"What was that I heard?" asked Nathaniel.

"Artillery. Or a storm brewing up. Take your pick."

"Which direction is it coming from?"

A sudden shriek made the brothers and the troops in their regiment stop marching and look up. Treetops exploded and rained down bark and branches. More shells struck the trees and spat wood splinters and the soldiers ducked and cringed. The air filled with whistling and howling as artillery fire kept crashing in. One cannonball hit and bounced and plowed a long rut along the side of the road, coming to a stop just by Corinth's left boot. He and Nathaniel looked at the ball and then at each other. Corinth's grin broke through the fear tightening his young face.

"Pretty big marble to play with, brother," he said.

Lieutenant Davidson came racing along the turnpike on his mount. "Get off the road, men! Move into the trees on the Douglas Brawner farm here! Stay in your platoons and companies and keep your heads down! General Gibbon has Battery B up after them!"

Nathaniel and Corporal Nicolson and Sergeant Hanson yelled at the men to get into the trees north of the road. They crouched there as shells continued to fall. Then the fire slackened as Rebel gunners engaged the Union gunners. Suddenly the firing swelled again as more Rebel cannon sounded as if they were firing at the Union guns from a different direction. This went on for ten minutes or more before Davidson came galloping along the turnpike once again.

"General Gibbon has sent the 2nd Wisconsin up the slope to the farmhouse!" he shouted. "They'll put a stop to Johnny Reb's artillery! Just stand at the ready!"

Corinth said softly, "Listen. I can hear the skirmishers."

The *crack-crack-crack* of musket fire came to them through the trees.

"Just like a few Fourth of July whizbangs going off," responded Nathaniel, also speaking as if it were important he keep his voice low.

Suddenly the musket fire broke open into one loud roar. A few moments later there was another explosion of massed firing. Half a minute later another thunderous crash of gunfire.

"That's volley fire," hissed Sergeant Hanson who was nearby. "The 2nd Wisconsin has run into something more than a few cannoneers with popguns."

The volley firing continued without letup. Nathaniel found his mind was split into three parts: one part focused on the fighting going on up the hill, another worried about a blister that had developed on his left heel, the third part lingering on thoughts of Lyndel, who was smiling at him and offering him a bowl of corn on the cob. He ignored the thoughts about the blister and went back and forth between Lyndel and the musket fire.

"Steady, men, steady!" It was Lieutenant Davidson yet again. "Our regiment is ordered forward to support the 2nd Wisconsin on its left! Colonel Meredith wants every man to do his duty by the Union and in honor of the great state of Indiana!" He drew his sword and pointed up the hill through the forest. "Form line of battle! Advance!"

"Corporal Nicolson! Corporal King!" shouted Sergeant Hanson. "Shake out the platoon into line of battle! Shoulder to shoulder with our company and our regiment!"

"Line of battle!" yelled Nicolson and Nathaniel at the same time. "Let's go, boys! Advance with the regiment!"

They went about three hundred yards through the trees, Corinth on Nathaniel's right, Nip on his left. The smell of burnt powder became stronger and stronger. Once the regiment broke into the open the grass sloped up to a house and several farm buildings and clouds of white and gray smoke, where the 2nd Wisconsin was holding their ground and firing into another bank of smoke lit yellow by the flashes from Rebel muskets.

"Double quick! Let's go!" came Lieutenant Davidson's voice. "Up the hill to the left of the brave Wisconsin boys! Go, go!"

Nathaniel moved out ahead. "Up to the fence on the crest, platoon! Heads down! Move, move!"

Corinth raced out ahead, taking the lead. The regiment half-ran up the field after him and clambered over the gray fence, re-formed, and began to advance toward the Brawner farmhouse. Corinth was still at the front. Nathaniel felt an odd sensation that made him look twice at a fence and some haystacks less than a hundred yards ahead. One moment it was just the haystacks and the long fence. Then it was a crowd of men in gray uniforms raising hundreds of muskets, the barrels pointed at the 19th Indiana.

"My boys!" Nathaniel cried out. "Corinth!"

But the volley fire came before hardly anyone saw what was happening. Nathaniel heard the zip-zip of the balls tearing past and saw his men fall, some with short, startled cries of pain and surprise, others dropping in silence. The Rebels had their ramrods out and were quickly reloading, one eye on what the Indiana regiment was going to do.

"Platoons, steady! Company, steady!" they heard Lieutenant Davidson's shout. "Aim low! Aim low or your shots will go over their heads!"

Nathaniel lifted his musket without thinking and aimed at the men staring at him across the grass.

But they are Americans too, came a quick thought.

"Fire!" yelled Davidson.

On Nathaniel's right and on his left the Springfields cracked and spewed smoke and sparks. The noise deafened him and closed up his ears. Men in gray dropped like sacks. A few of the faces looked surprised. Then the Rebel muskets were pointing at him again. The gray line burst with smoke and flame and the zinging sound of near misses made Nathaniel's ears pop open once more.

"Indiana will respond!" Davidson thundered. "Reload!"

Nathaniel was still not thinking, only reacting. Nothing seemed real or normal to him, though far back in his mind an image of Lyndel still flitted, and that image seemed more actual to him than the muskets and the firing and the rip of the balls over his head.

He placed the hammer on his Springfield at half-cock. Dug a paper cartridge from a leather cartridge holder on his hip and bit off the twisted end. Poured black powder down the barrel of his musket. Tore the ball free of the paper wrapping and pushed it point up into the muzzle. Took the metal ramrod from its slot under the barrel and shoved the bullet all the way down until he felt it was seated firmly on the powder charge. Slid the ramrod back into place. Cocked back the hammer all the way on his weapon. Plucked a percussion cap from a box in a pouch on his other hip. Jabbed the cap onto the nipple underneath the musket's hammer. Imagined the hammer striking the cap and making it burst, shooting a small streak of flame into the barrel and the powder. Imagined the explosion and the ball being thrust forward at high speed at the men facing him—some young, some old, some bearded, some clean-shaven.

Then he pulled the trigger and the cap spat, the barrel boomed, the musket stock kicked back sharply into his shoulder, and smoke blocked his sight. When he could see clearly a moment later a tall youth in a farmer's broad-brimmed hat, directly in front of him 60 or 70 yards away, clapped a hand to his head, dropped his musket, and fell backward without a cry. The gray men raised their barrels at him again and he saw the black holes of the muzzles while he half-cocked his own, pulled another cartridge from his holder, bit off the end, and shook in the powder.

"What secesh regiment is that?" he heard Ham shout.

"See their colors?" Sergeant Hanson was ramming a bullet into his musket. "Them's not just any old johnnycakes we're fighting. That's the Stonewall Brigade itself. You see those flags, Corporal Nicolson?"

"I see them, Sergeant."

"I guess we found our way to Stonewall's kitchen sooner than I thought."

"I'm still on my feet, Sergeant."

"You can thank God and Tippecanoe County coffee for that."

Gunfire drowned the men out. Nathaniel glanced at his brother while he was reloading. "You all right?"

Corinth's face was going gray from powder residue. He bit off the end of a cartridge and spat out the paper. "Hot work. Just like harvest and Daddy in a mood. Only I'm praying now too. Don't pray much at harvest time."

Corinth knelt and fired. Then reloaded again. A Confederate soldier seemed to scream directly at him and waved a flag, taunting. Corinth stood up, aimed, and shot the flag staff in two. The Confederate's mouth opened wide. Then he dropped to his knees and gathered the flag up in his hands, quickly tying it to the longest of the broken pieces of the staff. Scrambling back to his feet, he howled and shook the flag at Corinth a second time. The young man shot the flag off the top of the pole. The soldier dove out of sight.

"Private King!"

"Yes, Sergeant Hanson!"

"I admire your marksmanship. But I need Stonewall's men out of the fight. Not their flags and banners."

"Yes, Sergeant." Corinth glanced over at his brother. "I prefer shooting the flags to shooting the men."

"I know."

"I wish to God we and the Southern boys could settle this some other way."

The balls of lead continued to zing past their heads. Nathaniel looked up and down the line at the other men. Several were sprawled in the grass, clutching wounds but still trying to reload their muskets and fire back at the Stonewall Brigade.

"You men who are wounded, get back down the hill to the field stations!" he called to them. "Go on—you'll fight another day—get your wounds tended to so's we don't lose you!" He saw a figure that was not moving. "Is that Stewart?" But no one replied as muskets were lifted and flames stabbed through the billows of smoke.

"They're charging!" Ham was pointing through the haze that reeked of rotten eggs. "They're coming at us!"

"Steady!" Nathaniel heard himself shouting. "Reload! Aim low! Turn them back! Fire at will and turn them back!"

The Stonewall Brigade was scrambling over the fence they had been hiding behind at the beginning of the battle, all of them yelling and screeching and starting to run at the 19th Indiana over the short stretch of grass. But Nathaniel's platoon never fell back and neither did the rest of the company or regiment. They held firm and fired and Nathaniel experienced a strange mix of emotions that included relief no one in his platoon had turned tail, pride that the regiment was going toe-to-toe with the Stonewall Brigade, fear that something could still go wrong and the army would retreat, as well as a cold sickness that men and boys were falling and dying and he could do nothing to stop the killing—he was part of it now.

The Stonewall Brigade drew back to the shelter of the fence under heavy fire from the 19th but Nathaniel could see the Rebel officers and sergeants and corporals calling to their men and whipping them up to make another charge. Once more the gray men swarmed over the fence, once more Nathaniel shouted himself hoarse, once more the accuracy and intensity of the Indiana fire made the Rebel troops stop and turn and melt back.

"Think if this was our farm," said Corinth. He was on his knees and digging his extra rounds of ammunition out of his pack while the balls threw dirt into the air all around him. "Daddy'd be fit to be tied. Bullet holes in the new siding on the house. The barn looking like a colander. Horses and cows hollering and running off into the countryside never to be seen again."

"It could still happen, brother."

Corinth shook his head. "The war will never come to Pennsylvania."

It was ten minutes after seven and the sun was dropping in the sky, when Davidson rode past and told them the whole brigade was engaged. Gibbon had sent the 6th and 7th Wisconsin in on the right and the 76th New York and 56th Pennsylvania had filled in a gap in the battle line. No Union regiment was yielding an inch.

"Stonewall's a good Presbyterian," Davidson said before he moved off, "but he must be wondering whose side God is on tonight."

The sky turned from blue to copper to red. The firing never stopped, guns flickering through the smoke and sunset like lightning flashes in a thundercloud. Men's muskets were fouled with burnt powder—some soldiers were jamming the ramrods into their barrels and then banging the rods against Brawner's barn or house or a tree or rock to seat the bullet. Others just picked up Springfields left in the grass by the wounded or dead and used them if their barrels were clear.

"I'm getting low on ammo, brother," Corinth said, the sunlight red on his young face.

Nathaniel grunted. "Get it off the wounded. Get it off the men who have fallen. How much more do you need?"

"A heap. I don't plan on going anywhere soon."

"There's a pile of packs right behind you. Dig through them and see what you come up with. What happened to your extra rounds?"

Corinth smiled in the sunset. "I gave 'em all to Stonewall. Fast as I could."

Nathaniel gave a sharp laugh. "I'm sure he's thanking God you're here today to lend him a hand."

Rebel cannon began blasting at the Indiana regiment but Company B and Company G turned their musket barrels on the artillerymen and silenced the guns. As Stonewall poured more troops into the fight, Colonel Meredith pulled the regiment back to the shelter of the rail fence they had climbed over when they first arrived at the Brawner farmhouse. Seeing an opportunity, the Rebels leaped their own fence a third time with fixed bayonets and charged the Indiana line, screaming, Nathaniel thought, like a spring twister.

Now Captain Langston pounded up on his black gelding Nighthawk and began to bellow lines from a song called "Hail, Columbia." Nathaniel recognized the tune, though it was never sung among the Amish for it was a patriotic song of warfare and bloodshed. It was America's anthem and he listened while the men in his company picked up the melody and shouted out some of the lines.

Hail, Columbia! happy land!
Hail, ye heroes! heaven-born band!
Who fought and bled in Freedom's cause,
Who fought and bled in Freedom's cause,
And when the storm of war was gone
Enjoyed the peace your valor won.

Firm, united, let us be,
Rallying 'round our Liberty,

As a band of brothers joined,
Peace and safety we shall find.

The anthem Langston had begun in his cavernous baritone broke out into a mix of cries and yells and roars that drowned the howl of the Rebel charge. The company rose and aimed and threw fire again and again into the gray men and brought down their colors. The entire regiment blazed like a bonfire and the attack fell to pieces, Rebel troops running back to the rail fence and waving their flags in an act of defiance. The sky darkened but yellow and orange sparks still burst from men's guns. No one would stop. Even when Long Sol Meredith went down, his horse hit by a bullet and crushing him in its fall, the Indianans simply loaded more quickly and fought with increased ferocity as his aides hauled the colonel to safety.

Then it was black. The Stonewall Brigade's fence line flashed with white light and their muskets boomed. The Indiana fence line erupted in response. Again and again the two lines lit up, refusing to break off the fierce brawl with one another. Three times Lieutenant Davidson came quietly down the line, dismounted, telling his company to retire.

"You're the bravest of the brave," he said to them. "But the regiment has to withdraw. Stonewall keeps feeding fresh units into the battle line. Our scouts tell us his whole army is only a mile away. Twenty thousand men. Come morning they'll roll over us like the sea. We need to draw back."

But no one in his company would listen. Not a soldier in the entire 19th Indiana regiment would listen to his captain or lieutenant. Certainly not Corinth. Nathaniel watched him kneel and fire, kneel and fire, lit up by the flash of his Springfield each time he pulled the trigger, his hat gone and his hair caked black with powder. Nathaniel realized that, after all his platoon had been through, he felt no inclination to yield the Brawner farm they'd fought to hold either. But Gibbon insisted and finally it was up to the corporals and sergeants to get their soldiers to head back to the edge of the forest three hundred yards behind them. A few grumbled and argued but men like Nicolson and King and Hanson persisted until platoon by platoon, company by company, regiment by regiment, the whole brigade was crouched at the tree line ready for whatever Stonewall's veterans would throw at them. Minutes went by as they waited for the Rebel yell. But nothing happened. Crickets began to fill the night with their sounds and wounded men could be heard crying and begging for water.

"Someone…Yank…I don't care if it's a Yank…have mercy…just a sip from your canteen…I won't take much…just a drop…Yank…"

"Billy? Tommy? Help me out here. Both my legs are shot through. Help me out here. I think I've stopped the bleeding."

"Water. My Lord God, please bring someone to me with water. Help me. Help me. Water, please, my God, water."

Nathaniel sank down in the grass and dropped his head into his hands. His Hardee hat fell off and lay by his knee. He tried to pray and to bring Lyndel's beauty to mind. But he could not see her.

Vater unser, der Du bist im Himmel…Our Father which art in heaven, hallowed be thy name. Thy kingdom come. Thy will be done, in earth as it is in heaven. Give us this day our daily bread. And forgive us our debts, as we forgive our debtors.

Nathaniel prayed rapidly in High German, as if he were at an Amish church meeting. It was all he could think of. The prayer Christ had taught was the only words that came to mind. A hand gripped his shoulder.

"Corporal. Are you hit?"

Nathaniel got to his feet. Sergeant Hanson was holding two lanterns in his hand. "I'm all right, Sergeant."

"I need volunteers to help collect the wounded. We can't get to the ones around Brawner's house, of course—the Rebs have that spot now. But there were plenty that crawled away, I'm thinking."

Nathaniel picked up his hat and put it back on his head, then took one of the lanterns. "I'll do it. Some of the others will help."

"Good man. Corporal Nicolson has a crew out looking to the right of our position here."

"I'll search the field in front of us." He lifted the lantern and looked about him. "Nip? Corinth?"

"I'll help." Ham stepped into the small circle of Nathaniel's lantern light.

"Where are Nip and Corinth?"

"No idea, Corporal. They may have already taken some of the wounded down through the trees to the ambulances."

Ahead of them, exactly where the regiment had made its stand by the farm buildings, they could see lights moving from place to place as Stonewall's men searched for dead and wounded.

"It looks like fireflies," said Ham.

Nathaniel started toward a voice that was moaning for water and trying to speak out the words from a hymn he knew the English liked to sing.

"Do you have much water in your canteen, Ham?" he asked.

"The secesh put a shot through it early on. But the boys gave me four or five of theirs."

"Anything in them?"

"They only took a swig or two to rinse the grit out of their mouths. The canteens are pretty full."

Though like the wanderer, the sun gone down,
Darkness be over me, my rest a stone,
Yet in my dreams I'd be
Nearer, my God, to thee
Nearer, my God, to thee, nearer to thee.

Nathaniel lowered the lantern to look at the singing man's face. "Nip!"

He and Ham immediately dropped to their knees to help him. Nip was cradling a man's head in his lap.

"Water?" Nip asked like a child. "May I have some water?"

"Where are you hit?" Ham unslung one of the canteens. "Sure, I have water for you. Go ahead and drink all you want."

"Not for me." Nip ran his hand over the hair of the head in his lap. "For him. To clean the wound. Wash away the blood."

Nathaniel held the lantern closer. "Who's this?" Then he saw the tight blonde curls stiff with powder and drew in his breath sharply as the light fell on Corinth's cold and empty face.

Nathaniel knelt down at his brother's side and took his hand. The other men were silent. Nip placed a hand on Nathaniel's shoulder and squeezed it gently.

Sergeant Hanson broke the silence, "Orders to move out, men. Now!"

Nathaniel bent down and kissed his brother's cheek. "I will join you soon, my brother."

9

"There." Lyndel straightened up from placing the bandage on the young soldier's arm. "Good as new. You're one of my success stories, Ben."

The soldier sat on the edge of the hospital bed in his nightshirt and smiled quietly under a head of thick black hair she had washed and dried and combed a few minutes before.

"I expect you've made more of a difference than all the doctors and medicines and vittles," he said. "That's what I've written my mother and Aunt Sarah."

Lyndel smoothed back the hair from his forehead. "You remind me of my brother. I haven't seen him for weeks. He's with an ambulance unit in Virginia."

"I guess you're some proud of him. The boys think a lot of the ambulance crews. Some are brave enough to haul wounded off the field even while the fighting's going on."

"That's what happened with you, am I right?"

"Yes, Miss Lyndel."

Lyndel gathered up her washbasin and comb and soap. "I'll miss you once you're gone. The doctor says Sunday's the day."

"Father is coming down from Boston to collect me. Will you be working Sunday?" His eyes followed every movement she made.

"I believe I'll be here in the afternoon and evening."

"I want Father to meet you."

She brushed strands of her red hair back out of her eyes and smiled.

"Of course, Ben. If I'm not in this building, ask one of the other nurses. They'll let you know where I'm hiding."

The door to the ward flew open. Hiram Wright came rushing along the aisle between the beds as patients lifted their heads. Miss Sharon was right behind him, her face flushed. Lyndel and Ben stared at the grim look in his eyes and at the length of his stride.

"Gently, Mr. Wright," Lyndel said softly, going to him and laying a friendly hand on his arm. "The men in this ward need quiet. Not a strong dose of your energy."

"But I have news, Miss Keim," Hiram blurted. "Urgent news. May we step up to the front room?"

Lyndel nodded and followed him and Miss Sharon as they strode from the ward. In a few moments Hiram was able to begin.

"There's been a battle. Another terrible battle at Manassas Junction. And we've lost it. Washington's in a furor." He took both her hands in his. "Nathaniel's regiment was engaged."

She clenched her hands around his. "When?"

"It all started Thursday at a farm near Gainesville. But the important battle was Saturday the 30th, yesterday."

"What do you…what do you know about Nathaniel?"

"Nothing. But the fighting the 19th Indiana was involved in was heavy. It was Stonewall Jackson's troops they were up against. His own brigade. I know Indiana made a stand. But General Pope bungled and his flank was turned. The army had to flee. The 19th and their brigade covered the retreat. The casualties are frightful. They need you."

Lyndel's mind swirled in tight dark circles. "Who needs me?"

"I've spoken with Clara Barton. I know you worked with her here two or three times."

"Yes—"

"Her team is heading to Fairfax Station today with three carloads of medical supplies to treat as many of the wounded as possible. The idea is to save those who would die on the long trip here. Miss Sharon has agreed to Miss Barton's request."

"You and I have talked about it before, Miss Keim," Miss Sharon said. "Hundreds of lives would be spared if nurses could bandage and

give food and drink to the wounded as they're brought off the battlefield."

"Miss Barton is willing for me to join her?"

"Yes," Miss Sharon said. "You and your friend Morganne David.
But you must get down to the station immediately. Within the half-
hour."

Lyndel pulled away from Hiram. "I can be ready in less time than
that. I don't need to go back to the house. But Morganne is sleeping in
our room there. She worked all night."

"I'll fetch her. Then come back for you."

"How is it that Miss Barton can get us so close to the front lines?"

"The surgeon general has given her a pass." Hiram turned to go but
paused to glance back at Lyndel. "You understand nurses have never
been permitted this close to the battlefield before?"

"I understand that, yes."

"There will be some risk involved. Rebel troops could attack."

Lyndel lifted her chin and her eyes turned a deep indigo blue. "I'm
going."

He nodded. "All right. I'll be back with Morganne shortly."

As always, Miss Sharon's face was chipped from stone. "Do well.
Leave nothing undone. The army will watch how you and the others
care for the wounded. Bring credit on our calling."

"I will endeavor to make you proud of me."

"Never mind pride. Work hard. Save lives. If the Rebels should capture you, ask to treat their wounded."

"I'll do just that, of course," Lyndel smoothed down her white
apron. "I need to gather up my things."

Miss Sharon caught her by the arm as she stepped past. "Miss Keim,
I would prefer that you return to us."

Morganne had rings under her blue eyes and was trying to pin her
blond hair up when Hiram brought Sally and Kate to a stop in front of
the hospital. Lyndel climbed up beside her and Hiram shook the traces
and clicked his tongue. The horses moved out into the muddy street
again. Rain was starting to fall so Hiram had the roof of the carriage up.

"I'm sorry, Davey," Lyndel said to her friend, using her pet name.

"No, I'm fine," Morganne mumbled around the long pins in her mouth. "I had four hours' sleep. Who needs more than four hours' sleep? Especially when there's a war on."

Lyndel leaned forward to look at Hiram. "Do you know where Nathaniel's regiment is?"

Hiram shook his head, his eyes on the carriages and wagons and horses all around him. "As I mentioned, his brigade was the rear guard for the army. Pope has the troops double-timing it to the fortifications at Fort Buffalo in Upton's Hill. Not far from here. Though they can't stay for long."

"Why not?"

"All the reports I've seen at the office have Southern units pressing into Maryland. The army has to go after them. There will be another battle. And we'd better win this one, or Washington will be wide open to the Rebels."

Lyndel found she was squeezing her hands together so tightly her knuckles were white. "Do you…do you think the 19th will be at Upton's Hill too?"

"If not today then tomorrow."

"Would the army still be there when I return from Fairfax?"

Hiram glanced at her. "Miss Barton will stay in Virginia until every wounded man is brought off by rail. It will be days."

"Are you—perhaps you'll be traveling with us?"

"I'm afraid not, Miss Keim. The army has not granted me a pass to report on their latest debacle."

The thought Lyndel dared not think slipped into her mind without permission: *If Nathaniel is among the wounded or the dead it will not matter if you get to Upton's Hill.*

Clara Barton was waiting for them at the station, hands on her hips, bonnet on her head to keep off the rain and a red bow at her throat. "Miss Keim. Miss David. You're just in time. Otherwise you would have had to join me by horse-drawn ambulance."

Hiram tipped his derby. "We came as fast as we could, Miss Barton.

The city is in a bit of a to-do, what with the defeat and Lee invading Maryland."

She nodded. "Defeat does not bring out the best in anyone. Or fear of defeat." She looked at Lyndel and Morganne. "I asked you two to join me because I've seen how hard you work at Armory Square. You will have to work twice as hard in Virginia. No Sabbath rest for us. Still interested?"

Lyndel and Morganne said yes at the same time. Miss Barton finally smiled.

"My two Pennsylvania girls. Well, get on board. You'll have to find a place among the bandages and medicines and jars of New England preserves. These ladies are Mrs. Morrell and Miss Haskell. They will be helping as well. I expect another to join us later. My goodness, Miss David, what is that contraption?"

Morganne was taking her luggage from Hiram, who was handing it down from the carriage.

"This? This is my Martin guitar. Mr. C.F. Martin has his shop in my hometown of Nazareth."

Miss Barton pinched her lips. "You won't have time for that."

Morganne's blue eyes flickered with fire. "I have time at Armory Square despite how busy it gets. The soldiers say it soothes them. Miss Barton, I have heard you singing to the patients."

After a momentary pause, Miss Barton said, "Well, *first* they get bandages and poultices. Then they get food and water. When all of the wounded have that, then you may serenade them."

Morganne inclined her head, her eyes a rock blue. "Thank you. Now I'd like to get it in out of the rain. Excuse me." She climbed into the boxcar and found a seat on a crate.

Hiram helped Miss Barton and Lyndel up into the car. "You two ladies take care of each other as well as the wounded."

"That's in God's hands," said Miss Barton. "We can only do what is right in his eyes and leave the rest up to him."

"Make sure you come back with a good story I can put in the paper."

"No doubt I will. Carry on, Mr. Clements."

The young engineer had poked his head out of a window in the steam locomotive. Now he gave her a quick salute and his head disappeared. A whistle blew three times and the engine began to move, its string of cars behind. Hiram waved, the rain streaming off his derby.

"You'll ruin your hat," called Lyndel.

"I'll go to Upton's Hill, Miss Keim," he called back. "I'll see who I can find."

"Oh, thank you, thank you."

Miss Barton glanced at Lyndel as she pulled the door to the freight car shut. "Do you have a brother in the army? Or a beau?"

Lyndel found a seat on several hard, lumpy sacks. "A friend, Miss Barton. From my home in Elizabethtown." To avoid Miss Barton's eyes she removed her black *kapp,* shook the water off, then placed it back on her head.

Miss Barton made herself comfortable on top of a barrel that swayed with the movement of the train. "What unit is he with?"

"His regiment is the 19th Indiana."

"But you're from Pennsylvania."

"So is he. But he was living in Elkhart County, Indiana, for a short time and that's where he chose to enlist."

"May I ask his name?"

"Nathaniel King."

Miss Barton nodded. "If I run into him I will know to tell you."

Lyndel met her gaze. "Thank you."

There wasn't much talk. Morganne was still simmering and kept her eyes on the walls of the car. Miss Barton chatted with her two friends a while but the talk soon petered out. Lyndel prayed through a list she kept in her head: her family, especially her brother with the ambulance service; Nathaniel and Corinth and their family; the Amish of Elizabethtown; the Amish of Elkhart County. The news that Nathaniel had been in a battle focused her attention on prayers for him and Corinth. The more she prayed the better she felt, though she realized she would never feel settled until she knew whether he and his brother were all right. If they weren't all right she would pray about that and deal with it when she had to.

I am not going to give in to fear and worry. I know what that's like and it never helps. It only makes a person more distraught, worn out, and miserable.

The train finally stopped at Fairfax. Miss Barton and Miss Haskell pulled back the sliding door of the freight car with the engineer's help. The sky was overcast and rain was spattering over the tracks and the station. Lyndel stepped down expecting to see soldiers lined up in neat rows inside the depot. Instead, when she walked around to the front of the hissing locomotive, she saw hundreds of men laid out on a grassy slope with nothing under them but hay from bales that had been broken open. Their uniforms were wet and caked with blood, their faces and arms and hands dripped with rain, and she heard many of them groaning and crying out for water. The bodies seemed to her to cover acres. She put her hand to her mouth.

Oh, my Lord. What are we going to do?

Miss Barton clapped her hands together.

"The trains will be taking these men to Washington hospitals. But no man, absolutely no man, goes on any train before one of us has tended to him. Water, food if he can keep it down, wounds dressed, arms in slings if necessary, poultices or compresses kept wet—all these things are critical. When you've finished working on one soldier please indicate that to the men here, who will then place that man on a stretcher and put him in a car. Any questions?"

None of the women spoke up. Like Lyndel they continued to stare at the hundreds of bodies and the ambulances that were driving in with even more wounded.

Clara tied a gingham apron over her dress. "Then let us begin. Perhaps we could all start in different locations. Excuse me." She turned to an officer who was standing and watching them. "We're nurses from the capital. There are medical supplies and food in three of the freight cars. Can you ask some of your men to unload them for us? The bandages are especially important."

The officer looked at her more closely. "Are you Clara Barton?"

"I am, sir."

"It's an honor, ma'am. You're helping our boys. We'll do all we can."

Lyndel and Morganne went together to the soldiers far on the right and began to work side by side, Lyndel with one man, Morganne with another. They took bandages and other material to make poultices and slings, as well as several canteens to offer mouthfuls of water. Lyndel's first soldier had a large bullet hole through both of his cheeks. His teeth had been damaged and his tongue was swollen and he couldn't chew. Slowly she tipped the canteen against his lips and let him take as many short swallows as he wanted. Then she cleaned the dirt and grit and caked blood out of the wounds and out of his mouth.

She went to Miss Barton who was bent over a soldier hundreds of feet away. "Can I make soup for a soldier who can't chew solid food?"

"Of course. Go right ahead."

"There is hardly anything to cook with."

She looked up at Lyndel. "Empty a can of red beans and feed someone else with them. Then use the can for a pot. That's all we can do."

Clara worked at getting a small fire going in the drizzle, something not easily done, so that when Lyndel came up with her can of homemade soup there was a place to warm it.

"Thank you, Miss Barton," she said, crouching beside her.

"We can all make good use of this fire. Let's make sure it doesn't go out."

"Will there be enough blankets for those who have to remain outside tonight?"

Clara shook her head. "No. I have only what I have. And the army has nothing."

"I could make coffee. Very good coffee for the men that will help them stay warm. If we have beans. And sugar."

"We have beans and sugar. But nothing to grind the beans with."

Lyndel smiled. "You have done a great deal with very little, Miss Barton. I think God can multiply my loaves and fishes too. There are other ways to grind beans. Once I feed my soldier his soup he'll be ready for Washington. Then I'll take a few minutes to make some coffee for the wounded."

Miss Barton stood up. "Wonderful. We will need it too in order to stay awake."

"I'll keep it going so long as we remain here."

"We remain here until every soldier is bandaged and fed and on the train. It will be days."

Lyndel looked up at her while she continued to heat the can of soup. "If we have enough beans there will always be the coffee."

"I'm glad you're here, Lyndel. Now I must get back to my boys."

Lyndel got to her feet. "I also. The soup is more than ready."

But Clara didn't walk away. "Your black apron works better than the white ones."

"I think so too."

"You told me at Armory Square one night that you were Amish. I spoke with a senator from Pennsylvania about it. He said you were not a people given to battle. That you would not fight in a war such as this."

"That's true."

"Yet here you are close to a battlefield, a place very few women would dare to go."

Lyndel laughed. "My father is also not sure I should be nursing wounded soldiers. You sound like him." Then the laughter left her face. "This is the road to Jericho, Miss Barton. These men have been beaten and robbed and left to die. Jesus tells me to care for them as they are my neighbors. So I clean and bind up their wounds. Then I put them on the train that takes them to the inn where they will get rest and, I pray to God, a restoration of their health. This is what I do as an Amish woman. Of course it is the war that hurts these men. But it is God who would heal them."

"You have a lively mind, Lyndel. I'll use that illustration the next time I'm called upon to speak at a church." She paused to wipe rainwater out of her eyes. "Now we must both get back on the road to Jericho. I fear your soup is turning cold."

The women worked through the day and into the night. Every time she cleaned, bandaged, and fed a man, Lyndel prayed over him, sometimes in English, sometimes in German. Many times they grasped her hand tightly in thanks. After she had prayed she called stretcher bearers to carry the soldier to a waiting train. Once a train was full it left for Washington. Soon another would take its place.

When night fell, they had a pair of lanterns to work with and a handful of candles in the damp and the drizzle. Blankets were wrapped around the men they felt needed it the most—they didn't have nearly enough to go around. But they carefully covered the others with fresh hay from the bales stacked under the eaves of the station house. There were plenty of woolen socks and they placed these on the feet of every soldier.

At one point, stumbling over her feet, Lyndel crawled onto one of the bales and slept from three until five. Then a familiar voice woke her and she instantly sat up and strained to listen.

"Hey, you! Hey, yup!"

A team of horses pulled up to the station, an ambulance rattling and bouncing behind it. Lyndel jumped down and ran through the darkness to where lanterns swung from the front and back of the ambulance wagon. The driver peered at her through the mist and she said softly, "Levi, it's me."

He sprang down from the driver's seat and caught her up in his arms, lifting her feet off the ground.

"How I've missed you," he said, almost too loudly.

"Shh, shh, the wounded are sleeping." She smiled. "I've missed you too. It's so good to see your face."

"What on earth are you doing at Fairfax Station?"

"I'm helping nurse the soldiers from the Manassas battle. The nurse in charge was given a pass to permit her to bring us this far forward."

"But it's much too dangerous. Lee's army is moving into Maryland. Some of his troops will come through here."

Clara Barton walked up to them holding a lantern. "So is this your beau?"

Lyndel laughed quietly. "Oh, no—this is my brother. Levi, I would like to introduce to you the nurse in charge of our work here, Miss Clara Barton."

Levi removed his rain-soaked cavalry Stetson with its wide brim. "Miss Barton. The soldiers speak well of you."

"Do they? I've done little enough to deserve their praise."

Levi looked quickly at Lyndel. "I must cut this short. I have several badly wounded men who need your attention."

"Bring them on, then," Miss Barton said.

Levi disappeared briefly to the back of his wagon and returned carrying the first of the injured and set him in a vacant spot under a tree that Miss Barton indicated. The two nurses bent over him immediately.

"Get water into him, if you can," said Miss Barton to Lyndel, "and then some hot soup or coffee. After that wrap a cold compress to his temple. A train is due within an hour. I must assist your brother in laying out the other wounded. Where is Morganne?"

Lyndel lifted her head in the morning dark and scanned the lines of wounded on the grassy slope. "I know she didn't sleep. She told me she could rest when we were back in Washington. There she is. Under that cluster of trees. Making a sling for someone, it looks like to me."

Clara followed her gaze and nodded. "Very good. I knew I didn't go wrong in asking my Pennsylvanians to join this little entourage." She stood up and smoothed her apron as best she could—it was stiff with blood. "Come, Mr. Keim, let us remove your passengers to a softer bed than your wagon."

Lyndel looked back to the man—no, the boy, for he could barely be more than sixteen—she was attending. He rose slightly to spit out the lukewarm water Lyndel put to his lips but then readily took in the hot coffee she offered him in small mouthfuls. Then she went to a small stream, soaked a cloth in it until it was ice cold, folded it, and wrapped the compress tightly over the injury on the side of his head. She began to pray over him in High German at the same time as a locomotive blew its whistle and creaked to a stop at the station.

The boy looked at Lyndel through still-dazed eyes and asked, "Where am I?"

"Fairfax, but we're about to put you on a train for Washington."

The boy's green eyes now looked past her. "We were fighting in the dark. We never gave an inch to Johnny Reb. Never gave an inch."

"Shh. Shh. I know."

"Something knocked me down. Everything went white."

"You will get better."

"Will I? Will I really…my folks at home…they need me."

"Yes, I'm sure they do. And we shall do our best to see that you return to them. What's your name?"

"Les. Les Goodfellow."

"The perfect name for you!" Lyndel said with a smile.

"Where will they take me?"

"I think you will be taken to Armory Square Hospital."

"May I ask your name, ma'am?"

"My name is Lyndel Keim."

"Would you remember me? Would you pray for me?"

"I've prayed for you already. I will continue to do so. I will pray God's hand upon your young life."

The boy nodded and closed his eyes. "I think I need to rest."

"Miss Keim, you really must move on to the next man," Miss Barton cautioned.

"Of course," Lyndel replied. She patted the boy on his calf and said, "Here come the boys to put you on the train."

Two soldiers approached and lifted the boy onto a stretcher and began to carry him toward the tracks.

The boy opened his eyes and said, "God bless you, Miss Keim."

Lyndel stepped toward the stretcher and halted the soldiers while she bent over and gave the boy a soft kiss on the cheek.

"When I return to Armory Square, I'll ask for you, Les Goodfellow."

The men resumed their walk to the train and Lyndel returned to aid the next soldier with a prayer on her lips—for Les Goodfellow and for Nathaniel King.

10

"My dear Lyndel, I lost the last letter I was writing to you. I must have dropped it in that field of clover when they blew reveille. I have no idea what the grasshoppers or Rebels will make of it. Now it is about two weeks later, the 16th of September, a Tuesday. It is hard, very hard, to tell you we lost Corinth during our first fight back in August. I don't even know what happened. We found him in the field by the farmhouse and I saw no sign that he was breathing. I swear I feel as low and dark as a deep cold well. The army retreated again and I had to leave his body behind. I could only pray over him. I asked God what was the point of his death. Our brigade held but the rest of the army broke so his sacrifice made no difference. The people have cheered us mightily here in Maryland, that is where we are marching now, but it does not matter to me. Corinth is gone and it seems to me that pretty soon the Union will be gone too. So much for our holy crusade to end slavery and preserve a nation of liberty for all."

"Who are you talking to, Corporal?"

Nathaniel glanced to his right as the regiment trudged along a road of dust. It was Ham. "No one," he responded.

"Were you praying?"

"No."

"Speaking with your brother's spirit?"

"I was not."

"Well, you were talking to somebody and I'm the closest one to you and it weren't me."

"Never mind. I was only writing a letter out loud."

There was the *pop-pop* of gunfire in the distance.

"What's that, you reckon?" asked Ham.

"Skirmishers tangling. It won't amount to anything."

"South Mountain started with skirmishers and it amounted to something."

"South Mountain wasn't much of a battle. Just charging a stone fence."

Ham snorted. "Ain't you in the devil's mood? Our fight at South Mountain the other day was no small affair. Those Georgia and Alabama boys wouldn't give us that fence or that slope. We had to keep pushing and pushing to get them to appreciate it was our mountain now. And come morning that's the way it was. We'd given Lee a spanking and he had to change his plans. The South pulled out and the brigade stayed. They should've renamed it North Mountain."

Nathaniel grunted. "The boys had courage."

"General McClellan didn't retreat after South Mountain the way Pope had us skedaddle after the brawl at Brawner's Farm. We had those secesh licked, high and mighty, at Brawner's—we stopped Stonewall cold with six regiments. But Pope made us retreat. Good thing McClellan's in charge of the army now. You ought to thank your God for that."

Nathaniel grunted a second time, conceding another point to Ham. "I do."

"McClellan saw us take on the secesh at South Mountain, you know. He was mightily impressed."

Nathaniel looked over at Ham. "Who told you that?"

"The talk's come down the line. Little Mac was there. Speaking to Hooker, the First Corps commander. We're on the National Road, remember? Then it's up the slope, moving the secesh off the mountain and away from that stone fence of yours. Shoving those gray bellies all the way back to Turner's Gap. They're blasting away at us but we never break."

Nathaniel's mind instantly filled with the smoke of thousands of muskets firing and Rebel troops falling back inch by inch. He could even taste the sulfur of the powder on his tongue.

Ham went on. "So Little Mac asks Hooker, *Whose men are those fighting in the road?* Hooker tells him, *That's General Gibbon's brigade of Western men.* Little Mac says, *They must be made of iron.*"

Nathaniel snorted. "That's a big story."

"I got the Boston paper in my pack. I'll show it to you when we bivouac. They're calling us the 'Iron Brigade' now."

"I don't believe it."

Ham shifted the nine pounds of his musket to his other shoulder. Nathaniel decided it was time to do the same.

"You're a real ornery one these days, ain't you, Corporal?" Ham grumbled. "All those pretty Maryland girls blowing us kisses and waving the flag. You even caught one of them bouquets they threw in Frederick—and the gal who tossed it looked better than a sweet sunrise over Indiana. Everyone else is feeling their oats again except you. We know your brother's death has brought you down to your boot heels. But you'll see. The big battle's about to be fought. Bobby Lee's run and hid in a barn in Sharpsburg and Little Mac is going to flush him out. The Iron Brigade will do its part and the rebellion will be over before Christmas. Corinth helped get us here."

Nathaniel took some water from his canteen. "Will slaveholding be over before Christmas too?"

Ham nodded. "You bet." He spied some chickens at the side of the road. "Your brother was always a great forager. We could use him now." He changed shoulders with his Springfield again. " 'Cept we're not allowed to forage in Maryland. It's a Union state."

Gunfire swelled in the distance once again, dropped, then burst out with a fury before trickling away into occasional pops and bangs.

"South Mountain," said Ham. "This time we send 'em farther back than Turner's Gap."

"Atlanta?" suggested Nathaniel.

"Atlanta. Richmond. Charleston. All them places. Hey, they can go all the way south to that Rio de Janeiro if they want. Just give us our country back."

The afternoon became twilight and still they marched. The brigade moved along the Hagerstown Turnpike with the Potomac glinting and dark to their right. The town of Sharpsburg was just ahead of them. Nathaniel found he was beginning to drag his feet. The night before the 19th had been placed on picket duty and had guarded until reveille. Companies and platoons had taken their turn but no one had gotten enough sleep. He hoped they would have a chance to get a decent rest tonight. He even prayed for it.

Ten minutes later, near nine by Nathaniel's pocket watch, Captain Langston told the company to retire on the east side of the turnpike. Clouds covered them and a light rain dampened their hats and frock coats and muskets. The 19th and the rest of the brigade—the 2nd, 6th, and 7th Wisconsin—made camp all around. Nathaniel's platoon brought out their blankets next to a barn.

"Another farm," grunted Corporal Nicolson. "It's always another farm. The farm boys must be getting sick of us peppering their outbuildings with lead and trampling their crops into the ground."

"A good number of the crops should be harvested by now," Private Jones told him, wrapping his Springfield in a large cloth. "I'd give the corn a couple more weeks though."

"Well, I can't see what this fellow's got growing but I wish him the best with it when we start charging about in the morning."

Sergeant Hanson was pulling a loaf of stale bread from his pack. "We won't be fighting here, Corporal. Lee's army is two miles farther ahead in Sharpsburg, sitting pretty and waiting for us. If there's farms thataway it's their crops you should be worried about. Not this gentleman's—I think Lieutenant Davidson told me the map had it as a Joseph Poffenberger's place."

Nicolson also dug through his pack. "I'm not worried about anyone's farm. If Joseph's neighbor loses his corn instead of him I guess that's Joseph's good fortune and his neighbor's bad luck. There. I knew I had some apples left from that orchard we marched through." He bit into one and glanced at the sergeant's bread. "How's that loaf?"

"Harder than your apple." Hanson gnawed on it unhappily. "If I had the energy to get up a fire in this drizzle I'd fry it in gun grease. I tell you, I miss that young Corinth some. We'd probably be dining on beefsteak and gravy with buttermilk biscuits if the good Lord had left him with us."

Nicolson nodded as he finished one apple and picked up another. "There'd be a fire, that's for sure. Whole platoon'd be a lot drier and warmer."

"Not much of a platoon these days," Ham spoke up, wrapping his blanket around him.

"The captain said there'd be recruits before the next fight," the sergeant told him.

"We got them at Upton's Hill. And lost a slew more at South Mountain."

"Sergeant!"

Sergeant Hanson rose to his feet. It was Lieutenant Davidson. He saluted. "Sir."

Davidson looked down at him from his mount. "There are wagons just catching up to us with recruits. A number have been assigned to your platoon."

"Thank you, sir."

"Some of them specifically requested to be assigned to this regiment, this company, and this platoon."

Hanson lifted his thick eyebrows. "That surprises me, Lieutenant."

"It surprises me too, Sergeant. I hope you can see them safely through this battle."

"I'll do my best, sir. The rest is up to God."

"So it is." Davidson wheeled his horse. "Long Sol is in no shape to command the 19th tomorrow. Can't lick his injuries from Brawner's Farm. Lieutenant Colonel Bachman is taking his place. You can pass that along."

"I will, sir. Bachman is a good man."

"He is a good man. Goodnight, Sergeant. Catch up on your sleep. The drumroll comes early."

"I will, sir. Thank you, sir."

Hanson sat back down, running his fingers over his large mustache and glancing at Ham. "There you are, Private. An answer to your prayers."

Ham snorted. "What? The recruits? By tomorrow night we'll be asking him for another dozen."

Nip came out of the blackness, his blanket draped over his shoulders. "Does anyone want a fire?"

The men looked at his thin body and sunken cheeks in the wet dark.

"Don't trouble yourself, lad," said Hanson. "We're about to turn in."

"How about some mutton or beefsteak?"

"Ah, no. We've just dined on soldier's food. You can do us up proper tomorrow night after the fight."

Nip stared at the sergeant. "Is there going to be another fight?"

"There is."

"With who?"

"General Lee."

"What about Stonewall?"

"He'll be there."

"Will we lick him?"

Hanson nodded. "We will. I promise you we will." He patted the damp grass. "Why don't you lie down now and get some rest?"

"Hanson. First Sergeant Hanson. 19th regiment. The Indiana regiment. Sergeant Robbie Hanson."

A covered wagon lit by a lantern was creaking along the turnpike and a man was calling from the driver's seat. Nathaniel had already pulled his blanket up to his neck and lain down with his head on his pack. He was staring at the wall of the barn and, as his eyes continued to grow accustomed to the night, watching small drops of water gather enough weight to roll down the slats of wood. He heard Private Jones call that the sergeant was just at hand and listened as the wagon rattled to a stop.

"Sergeant Hanson?"

"Aye."

"Indiana regiment?"

"You've found us."

"I have recruits for your platoon here."

"That's good news."

"Private Levi Keim. Private Joshua Yoder. From Elkhart County."

Nathaniel sat up. Unable to see the recruit's faces clearly he got to his feet and stumbled toward the turnpike, where Hanson and Jones stood talking with them and the wagon driver. As he emerged from the darkness he saw that it really was Levi Keim when the young man turned his face toward him.

"Nathaniel!"

They embraced, Nathaniel feeling the stiffness of the new uniform under his hands, a uniform beaded with drops of water.

"You were driving ambulance," Nathaniel said, trying to take in the sight of Levi in a Hardee hat, frock coat, and knapsack. "What happened?"

But Levi did not answer him at first. Instead he extended his hand to Joshua Yoder. "Look who I have brought with me."

Nathaniel and Joshua shook hands.

"Brother Nathaniel," Joshua greeted him.

"I am frankly astonished." Nathaniel looked back and forth from Levi to Joshua. "How is it you both enlisted with an Indiana regiment?"

"Why, we made plans to meet up with each other in Washington," explained Joshua, tall and straight in his Hardee hat with the gold bugle symbol for infantry on its front. "We have been writing for months. Even sending telegrams now and then."

"So you told the recruiters you were from Elkhart County?" asked Nathaniel.

Joshua smiled. "Didn't you? And I have more cause—that really is my family with the Amish community there. I told no lies."

"Nor did I." Levi was smiling. "I simply said I had close relations in Indiana and that was good enough. Just like you did, Brother King."

"But what kind of training have you had?" demanded Nathaniel.

Levi shrugged. "A few days of marching and bayonet practice. I can load and shoot." He winked. "Shoot straight." He unslung his musket and placed the stock firmly on the ground. "I suppose they needed any warm body they could find after Manassas Junction and South Mountain. The fact I'd been with the ambulance service made a difference too."

"But what will the church say about this?" Nathaniel was still trying to grasp what they had done by joining the army. "What have you told your mothers? What have you told your fathers—one is a pastor and the other is a bishop?"

The smiling stopped.

"I did nothing behind my father's back," said Joshua. "Or my mother's. After the losses at Mechanicsville and Malvern Hill I told my father I must enlist. I said I could not let the Union be defeated and allow a country conceived in liberty to be ruled by slaveholders. David and Jonathan fought for Israel, I told him. So I will fight for our New Israel, America."

"Didn't our ancestors come here in freedom?" asked Levi. "How can we stand by and pray and watch that freedom disappear without doing a thing?"

"Prayer is doing something," Nathaniel responded.

"Yes," replied Levi. "And it is prayer that brought me here." He glanced back at the turnpike as if looking for someone. Then he fixed his gaze on Nathaniel and the sergeant while the men in the platoon listened. "What would you have done? Under a flag of truce I was retrieving wounded from Manassas and Chantilly and inside the Maryland border. I saw Rebel troops rounding up African families—men, women, children. Neighbors told me many of these people had never even lived in the South, had never been slaves, they were freemen.

"But it made no difference to Lee's soldiers. They beat them and cursed them and chained them and sent them back to Virginia in wagons. One of the officers was the slave hunter who came to our home that night, Brother King. Yes, it was him, a major now in the Army of Northern Virginia. They called him Georgey Washington. Can you imagine that? So I remembered Charlie Preston and realized there would be many more Charlie Prestons unless we put an end to the Confederate States of America and became one country again. I cabled my father and mother: *I prayed, I searched the Scriptures, now I have taken up arms and put on the uniform of a common soldier of the United States of America."*

Hanson nodded and shook his hand. "The Hoosiers are proud to have you fight alongside them. Especially with solid stock from Elkhart County in your blood." He turned to Joshua and shook his hand as well. "The same goes for you, Private Yoder. Have you two had anything to eat?"

"Hanson. First Sergeant Robbie Hanson. 19th Indiana regiment," a voice called from the turnpike.

The wagon driver smiled. "Here's your second set of recruits." He called out as the wagon came alongside his, "What took you so long, Billy? Take the road into Virginia by mistake, did you?"

The other driver reined in his team. "No need scaring the recruits to death their first night in the field, so's I took my time. Are you the platoon sergeant?" He was looking at Hanson.

"I am," Hanson replied.

"I have here privates Plesko, Campbell, McKeever, and Groom in the wagon. All from Indiana."

"Thank you. They'll be welcome."

It was Nip who spoke up and asked, "Are any of you good at foraging?"

Lyndel returned to Washington from Fairfax Station on Wednesday, the third of September, and went to her house to change clothing before reporting for duty at Armory Square.

To her dismay, she had fallen asleep and the host family had tucked her in. She slept, exhausted, for more than two days.

She awoke to frustration and anger at herself for having lost so much valuable time. Further, now that she had experienced Fairfax, closer to the front, she was no longer content to work in a Washington hospital. No, now she knew she had to get closer to the front and nurse soldiers within minutes or hours of their wounding.

Accordingly, she proceeded to knock on the doors of Indiana congressmen and senators and officials. For more than a week she persisted, but all to no avail. Brandishing letters from two Indiana captains she had cared for after Manassas brought praise from the Indiana statesmen, but no efforts to procure a pass through the lines so she could work with the ambulance service on the battlefield.

"I'm not asking to go everywhere and do everything," she pleaded in office after office. "I just wish to assist the surgeons and ambulance men of the 19th Indiana. I want to keep Indiana boys alive. You mustn't think of me as weak or a coward. I was at Fairfax when we fired the station and fled by rail from Rebel cavalry."

The men all nodded and thanked her, but nothing was done. They pointed out that Clara Barton was already in the field, traveling by wagon in the steps of McClellan's army. They couldn't ask the army to authorize a pass for yet another woman.

"Suppose something happened to you," a congressman argued. "Think of the scandal. Think of the disgrace. Indiana sends a woman to war and then isn't able to protect her from the enemy. Impossible. Your plan is well intentioned but far too risky for yourself, the state of Indiana, and this federal government to undertake. You're greatly needed at the hospitals here. The wounded will reach you soon enough."

Lyndel's' blue eyes had blazed white. "That's the whole reason for my appeal to you, Congressman. They will *not* reach me soon enough! They will die on the way. What if it was your own son lying on the field without so much as a mouthful of water or a bandage or a word of hope?"

On Sunday the 14th there was another battle involving Nathaniel's brigade—the 19th Indiana and the 2nd, 6th, and 7th Wisconsin. They fought so bravely the papers were calling his men the Iron Brigade—if Nathaniel was even alive! Now there was talk of an even greater fight looming like thunderclouds over Sharpsburg and Hagerstown in Maryland. How could she stay in Washington when the soldiers were going to be fighting and dying a hundred miles away? What if Nathaniel was still with his regiment and needed her? Clara Barton had already left with the Army of the Potomac weeks ago. How was it possible God had left her here in Washington when any of a dozen other young women could easily take her place?

Lord, can't you do something? Why put this fire in my heart and then give it no place to burn? Can't you move somebody's soul to grant me passage to the battlefield? How can I help the wounded man on the road to Jericho if no one will even permit me to put a foot on the road to begin with?

Lyndel arrived late at Armory Square. The outside of the hospital was thick with carriages and soldiers and a crowd of civilians. An armed man blocked her way.

Still steaming from the disappointment of her last meeting, Lyndel was curt. "Excuse me, young man. I have to get to work."

"I'm sorry, ma'am. The new shift has already come and gone. How do I know you're a real nurse?"

He was the wrong private in the wrong place at the wrong time. Lyndel locked eyes of fury on him. "What? Do you think I've just come from a costume shop? This is my hospital. Stand aside or I'll treat you like I would a wayward cow on our farm."

The crowd swirling around them laughed. The private, who had thought himself pretty lucky to be assigned duty in Washington rather than meet up with Lee's army in Maryland, was now wondering if he hadn't got the short end of the stick. He made things worse by blurting, "No one gets past me. Especially not an itty-bitty farm girl."

Lyndel felt she was a shot about to be launched from a cannon, the wick burning rapidly down to the powder. Amish or not, she wanted to nab him by the ear and twist it as hard as she could and bring him crying and red-faced to his knees. He saw in her eyes she was about to do something and raised his musket up higher on his chest. That's when Lyndel started to entertain the idea of kicking him as hard as she could in the shin with her boot.

"One war at a time is enough, Private, don't you think?" An officer tipped his blue Stetson to Lyndel. "My apologies. I've seen you nursing here on numerous occasions. Private Hanks is perhaps a little too zealous today. The president is inside, you see."

Lyndel's temperature dropped immediately. "Mr. Lincoln?"

The officer nodded. "It's an impromptu visit. That's why you were not made aware. However, I'm sure your staff would like to have you inside helping them out rather than outside and contemplating making Private Hanks another casualty of our domestic conflict. Please carry on."

"Thank you, Captain." She patted Private Hanks on the arm. "No hard feelings, soldier. God bless you."

As the red-haired beauty swept past him the private's face flushed at her touch. His eyes met his captain's. The captain smiled.

"I wouldn't wash that perfume off my uniform any time soon if I were you, Private Hanks. It'll bring you good luck."

Lyndel rushed to her ward. It was empty but for Morganne David, who was shaving a patient with a straight razor and humming the Southern tune "Dixie." Lyndel scanned the room and asked, "Where's the president?

Morganne didn't look up at her friend but kept humming and shaving off the wounded soldier's beard.

"Davey!" Lyndel almost shouted.

Morganne's pale blue eyes flickered up. "The president's in another building." Her eyes flickered back down again.

"Is Miss Sharon mad I wasn't here?"

"I doubt it. The mob hasn't been in this ward yet. They walked off somewhere else after the president unfolded himself from his carriage."

Lyndel took a deep breath and calmed down. "All right. Good. No one noticed my absence and they probably won't be back."

Morganne applied more shaving cream to the soldier's beard. "What were you doing, Henry? Trying to win the war by growing a bigger beard than Jeb Stuart?"

"What do you know about Jeb Stuart?" mumbled the soldier.

Morganne swiped shaving cream into his mouth. "I saw his picture in the paper. I can read, you know. I'm not some farm girl fresh out of the barn." She looked up at Lyndel with a sharp-edged smile. "Sorry, Lyn."

Lyndel started making a bed that had been left rumpled. "Oh, I don't care. I like the barn."

"Your attention, please, ladies. The president of the United States."

A short and round officer with gold braid all over his shoulders had stepped inside the ward and was holding the door open. Soldiers and civilians spilled into the room followed by the long lanky figure of the president. He was dressed in a black suit and held his black top hat in his hand. He nodded to Lyndel and to Morganne—who had decided to stop whistling "Dixie" for the moment—and began shaking the hands of the patients in the beds. Lyndel didn't know what else to do so she finished the bed and then stood beside it as the crowd made its way down the row. When he reached her the president stopped and smiled.

"I reckon you don't get too many empty beds," he said.

"No, Mr. President. I'm afraid it won't stay empty for long."

He nodded. "Well, I am sure you are doing your best for our boys." He took her hand. "My thanks from a grateful Republic."

As he moved away a thought flared up in her head and made its way to her lips. "Mr. President. Mr. Lincoln. I could do more."

She saw Miss Sharon's face turn into a thunderstorm.

The president stopped and turned back to her. "What do you mean? Do you not have enough supplies at Armory Square?"

"We're fine here, Mr. President. But we lose so many of our boys getting them here. More needs to be done for them right on the battlefield."

"We have our surgeons and our ambulance crews."

"But our surgeons have their hands full performing amputations. And our ambulance crews have their hands full getting the men off the field and setting them down by the field stations. No one has time to give the wounded men water or clean their wounds or put on clean bandages and poultices. Especially if the fighting is going on somewhere nearby." She plucked the letters from the Indiana captains from the pocket under her apron and extended them to the president. "I was at Fairfax Station, sir. Working alongside Clara Barton. I know we were able to save many of the men simply because we were able to treat them a short while after they were wounded. These officers will attest to that in their statements."

A colonel stepped up to her. "Thank you, Miss. The president has a busy schedule. I'm sure he could read your letters another time."

But Lincoln was pulling a pair of glasses from a suit pocket. "That's all right, Bart. I want to hear what these captains have to say."

The room was silent as Lincoln, glasses perched on his nose, read first one letter and then the other. Lyndel realized she was holding her breath and finally exhaled. Lincoln peered up at her from over his glasses.

"It appears you have quite a following in the 19th Indiana."

Lyndel hesitated. Then decided to take the plunge. "Mr. President, it is I who would like to follow them and nurse the boys on the field where they have fallen. You know the beds will be full in a few days.

You know there is going to be another battle with General Lee. I want to save as many as I can." She stood as straight as she could and tilted her chin as she plowed on. "Please, sir, will you write me a pass that will allow me to travel to the front lines and assist the surgeons and ambulance crews as their nurse? You're a Western man, Mr. Lincoln. Why, Illinois is one state farther west than Indiana. Let me travel with the 19th Indiana. Let me ride with the ambulances. As much as I would like to, I can't save the whole Army of the Potomac. But I can at least save our Western men, our soldiers from Indiana and Wisconsin." Her and the president's eyes locked. "You only have one Iron Brigade, Mr. President. They stood up to Stonewall Jackson for you. Please, stand up for them. Let me be their nurse."

No one moved. Lincoln paused, his eyes still on Lyndel. Then he bent his head and whispered something to an aide. The soldier nodded, drew a fountain pen from the leather satchel under his arm, and handed it to Lincoln.

The president smiled at Lyndel. "He assures me it is full of ink. Just as you are full of spirit." The aide held the satchel flat while Lincoln turned over one of the captain's letters, spread it on the satchel, and began to write across the white paper in his small script. "You were there when we fired Fairfax Station to keep it from the Confederacy?"

"Yes, sir."

"Did you spot the enemy's cavalry?"

"They were riding down the hill just as we pulled out of the station with the last of the wounded, Mr. President."

He glanced at her over his glasses, pausing in his writing. "Weren't you afraid?"

"Yes, Mr. President, I was quite afraid."

"I'm glad to hear it."

"But not afraid enough to dissuade me from doing my duty."

Lincoln's eyes remained on her but he said nothing.

She plunged on. "If Clara Barton and I hadn't been able to get the last of the wounded on board, we would have remained behind with them."

"Are you certain of that?"

"Yes, Mr. President. We were those men's nurses. We would not abandon them."

His eyes dropped back to the page. "What is your name?"

"I am Lyndel Keim, Mr. President."

"With a *y*?"

"Yes, sir."

"Do you mean to go it alone?"

"There is one other nurse—if you could arrange for her passage— I trust her with my life."

"And what name does she go by?"

"Morganne David. Two N's, sir," Lyndel said with a grin. "And an *e*."

The president finished writing and handed the paper to her along with the other letter. He returned the pen to his aide and folded his glasses, placing them back inside his suit pocket.

"Take good care of our Western boys, Miss Keim," he said, unsmiling. "The battle that you anticipated will come and very soon. The bottom is out of the tub. We will need our Iron Brigade, every man of them, if we are to stanch the flow. May I wish you Godspeed?"

"Thank you, Mr. President. My prayers are with you and with the whole nation."

"Then those are prayers I reckon will count for something where it matters the most."

He went back to shaking hands with the wounded. When he came up to Morganne and her razor and shaving cream he said something Lyndel couldn't catch, which made Morganne and all the others laugh. As he continued on to the far side of the room she looked at what he had written on the back of the captain's letter.

This note permits the bearer passage to the battle lines for the nursing of the wounded of the 19th Indiana and all the regiments of their brigade. The nurses named in this letter are Miss Lyndel Keim and her companion Miss

Morganne David. They are to work alongside the army surgeons and ambulance crews and render them every assistance. Please help these ladies on their way with all due courtesy and respect.

Yours truly,

A. Lincoln

September 15, 1862

Lincoln nodded as he passed Lyndel on the way out of the ward. She and Morganne looked at each other once they were alone.

"My good word, Lyndel! And I thought I had nerve," Morganne finally blurted. "Miss Sharon is going to cut your head off and roast it whole."

"Never mind about my head. I thank God for the meeting with President Lincoln. Now you have to finish shaving Henry and we have to ask Miss Sharon to get some of the new nurses to take over our work here. We need to catch up to the army."

"How are we going to do that?"

Everything had happened so fast. Lyndel rubbed her fingers against her forehead. "I guess I don't know."

"I would be happy to be of assistance. Provided your pass is legitimate, of course."

Hiram Wright stood in the doorway. He looked at Lyndel and shook his head and laughed. "My, oh, my. Miss Lyndel Keim of Elizabethtown, Pennsylvania—you do beat all. Accosting the president of the United States. Lady, you do beat all. For General Lee's sake, I hope he takes you into account when he draws up his battle plans."

In less than two hours the three were on their way north to Sharpsburg and Hagerstown. Hiram had procured a covered wagon from his newspaper and Lyndel and Morganne had filled it with medical supplies, including sacks of Canada wild ginger and comfrey root Lyndel's mother had dried and mailed to her over the summer. Miss Sharon had not so much as mentioned the manner in which Lyndel had appealed to Lincoln but had given her yards of cotton for bandages and dozens of bottles of laudanum, morphine, and brandy to assuage the pain of the wounded.

"Now, girls," she'd told them, "nurses need to be much closer to the front in this war. The officers and politicians will be watching. Save the young men. Assist the surgeons and ambulance corps. Show them what the women of the Commonwealth of Pennsylvania are made of." In an act that astonished the two young women Miss Sharon had roughly taken their hands and kissed them each on the cheek. "God bless you," she'd said and abruptly turned away.

At first their wagon moved quickly, Sally and Kate seeming to enjoy the open road and fresh clover Hiram let them stop to graze on every couple of hours. Then they caught up to the wagon train that followed the Army of the Potomac—food, ammunition, powder, saddles and tack, medical supplies—and their pace slowed considerably.

Lyndel pointed. "Why are the ambulances so far in the back? They should be right behind the troops."

Hiram pulled back on the traces. "Muskets and cartridges and extra bayonets are at the front."

"It's nonsense."

Hiram grunted. "That's the way the army thinks. Plan on changing their minds too?"

Morganne was sitting between Hiram and Lyndel. Lyndel leaned forward to get a better look at the young reporter. "Did I change somebody else's mind lately?"

"Only the mind of the president of the United States."

"Oh, that. I just had to help him realize what he already knew." She sat back. "It troubled me to see him look so careworn. I did not wish to add to his burdens."

Hiram smiled. "I'm sure you made his day. Blue eyes and red hair and a smile like sunshine."

"Hiram, not everyone sees me the way you do."

"You mean the world has gone blind?" The wagon began to move more quickly as traffic surged forward. Hiram's grin had come and gone and now he looked like stone. "He has plenty to be careworn about. We can't afford to keep losing battles and expect to preserve the Union."

Morganne turned to him. "Didn't we win at South Mountain?"

"Sure, Nathaniel's brigade gave Lee a caning. There's no doubt in my mind the Rebels were headed for Pennsylvania and Lancaster County and had to change their plans after Sunday's fight. Now they're waiting for McClellan at Sharpsburg instead."

Lyndel leaned forward again. "Lancaster's my home. There's nothing for General Lee there."

"Yes, there is, Miss Keim. It's a fast route to Harrisburg. And Harrisburg is a major military center and rail link. Lee would love to get his hands on it and paralyze our movements."

Lyndel sat back and shook her head. "They would bring warfare right to the door of the most peaceful people in America."

"It hasn't happened yet. But if McClellan runs like Pope ran, who knows what might happen next? Lee could put a choke hold on the Union." He glanced at his two passengers. "Talk among the correspondents who cover the war for the big papers in Boston and New York has Britain and France granting recognition to the South by Christmas or New Year's."

Morganne turned pale blue eyes on him. "What exactly does that mean?"

"They would call the Confederate States of America a legitimate nation. Send her ambassadors. Supplies. Maybe even help her win her independence from the United States."

"No." Morganne's eyes turned a much darker hue.

Hiram shrugged. "It's looking that way. A few more victories for the South might be all it would take."

"What about slavery?"

"Well, Miss David, Britain and France wouldn't mind a weaker United States, so they are looking the other way on Southern slaveholding right now. But the truth is, much of the support for Richmond comes from the aristocracy of Europe—they sympathize with the Southern gentry and the plantation owners."

"What about regular people like you or me?"

"The working man? The regular citizens of France and Britain? That's another story. Some of them feel like white slaves themselves so they have something in their hearts for the Africans. And the British and French know what it is to be laborers. The North doesn't have a slave economy, it has a lot of laborers, so European folk feel a strong connection there too—yes, Miss David, they have a real sympathy for the Union cause."

Morganne's pale blue eyes remained on him. "If that is so, why is there a danger of the British or French supporting the South's bid for independence?"

Hiram clicked his tongue at the horses. "If you put the vote to the common man in France and England and Ireland they'd say hurrah for the Union. But it's the aristocracy who run the governments in London and Paris. And they are leaning South."

Morganne continued to stare at Hiram. "That's a mouthful, Mr. Wright. But everyone says one big victory by the North will settle it."

Hiram made a face as if he had swallowed something bitter. "Sorry, Miss David. A Union win over Lee will hold the lion at bay for a while. But there would have to be quite a few more solid victories before you could say the South was backing down. I will tell you that whatever happens this week will make a difference. We lose and the politicians in Europe will meet with representatives from Jeff Davis's Confederate government. We win and we buy ourselves some time."

"Perhaps," Lyndel spoke up, "Mr. Lincoln has a plan."

Hiram nodded. "No doubt he has. It may even be a very good one. But it's out of his hands." He glanced over at her. "It's in the hands of men like Nathaniel."

Morganne gave a short laugh. "You are no patch of moonlight on the waters, are you, Mr. Wright?"

"I'm sorry you find me a disappointment, Miss David."

"On the contrary. Now I see you have more behind your freckles and sweet-potato red hair than a dab of charm. You're more interesting to me now than you were an hour ago."

"I'm glad to hear it."

"Are you?" Morganne faced forward again, settling her hands in her lap. "Let us see what the long journey brings our way."

They traveled through the night, moving slowly, the horses plodding along half-asleep. Morganne rested her head on Hiram's shoulder and closed her eyes while Lyndel lay down in the back. By noon on Tuesday the 16th they were drawing close enough to the front for officers to ask not only for Hiram's correspondent pass but repeatedly for the pass Lyndel carried. Often enough her sheet of paper brought a grunt of surprise.

"Well," said one captain handing it back to Lyndel, "it's a strange thing to have you ladies so close to the cannon fire and musketry but I reckon Father Abraham knows what he's doing."

At sunset Hiram finally pulled off the turnpike and into a field where other wagons had stopped for the night.

"Is that it?" complained Lyndel.

"Yes, ma'am, that's it," replied Hiram. "The horses are beat and I'm beat, and there are so many Federal troops everywhere I would guess we're pretty close to Lee's army. I'd rather not drive past our pickets and wind up at Stonewall's campfire by mistake."

Lyndel called out to an officer who was riding past with several aides. "Excuse me, sir, can you tell me where we are?"

The officer reined in and smiled. "Ladies so close to the front? To what do we owe this honor?"

"I am Lyndel Keim. This is my companion Morganne David. We are nurses. Our driver Mr. Hiram Wright is a war correspondent."

The officer tipped his Stetson to Morganne and Lyndel. "I am Lieutenant Colonel Alois Bachman, ma'am."

"Miss, if you don't mind."

"Miss it is then. May I see your pass?"

Lyndel produced the folded sheet of paper. Bachman strained to read it in the dark and drizzle. "President Lincoln? Nurses for the 19th Indiana and its brigade?" He looked at her in surprise. "But I am the commander of the 19th Indiana."

Lyndel was equally startled. "Where is Colonel Meredith?"

"Battle injuries prevent him from retaining command for this battle." Bachman folded the sheet and handed it back to her. "Don't let the ink run. No one will permit you and your friend to remain here without it."

"Where is the 19th, sir?"

Bachman pointed. "Bivouacked by the turnpike a mile or so ahead. But you are probably as far as you need to go tonight, nurse or no nurse." He nodded at the women and said, "I thank you for caring about our men. Please form up with our ambulance corps in the morning and inform the surgeons of your presence. The wounded will be grateful for your skills once the battle is joined."

"Thank you, Colonel," Lyndel replied. "I wish you and your men well. And a speedy recovery to Colonel Meredith."

"Yes, we all are hoping for the best for the Colonel. I pray whatever sacrifices are made tomorrow will not be made in vain." He tugged on the brim of his hat. "May God protect you and Miss David. I will see you in the field. Two young ladies will be a marvel at a time of bloodshed."

He rode off with his cluster of lieutenants and second lieutenants.

Hiram began to unharness the horses. "There. Now you know you are close to Nathaniel."

"If he's with them."

"Why wouldn't he be with them?"

"You couldn't find him at Upton's Hill."

"Miss Keim, I only had one afternoon there and the whole 19th regiment hadn't even arrived. Courage. Has his name ever shown up on any of the casualty lists in the papers? I feel in my bones Nathaniel is alive. What do you feel in your bones?"

"Aches and pains from being jolted up and down all the way through Maryland." Morganne was grinning. "May I spread my bedroll under the wagon?"

"Best place. At least you'll have a roof." Hiram began to lead the horses into the darkness. "I'm going to water the horses. The Potomac is just over to the right. There's a creek called Antietam around here as well if I can find it."

"Don't be long," called Morganne.

"Ten minutes, Miss David, no more."

Lyndel had her hands on her hips. "Fancy him?"

One side of Morganne's mouth curled upward in a smile. "I have since we left Washington. Didn't care for him much before that."

"What's changed?"

Morganne stretched. "Oh, the scenery."

Lyndel flicked a hand in her direction. "Suit yourself. He's a good friend. I think I'll sleep in the wagon."

"Is there room?"

"More room than there was in Miss Barton's boxcar."

Lyndel made her bed close to a stack of bandages. She lay on her back and listened to the movement of horses and wagons on the road. Someone was calling for a Sergeant Hanson. Then she heard Hiram return and a laugh spring like silver from Morganne's throat. Lyndel smiled in the dark. Well, why not? They were both persons she cared about. Maybe it would work out for them in the long run.

Thinking of Morganne and Hiram as a couple turned her thoughts toward Nathaniel. Hiram had faith that he was alive. Why didn't she? Despite the wagon wheels and horse hooves and voices around her she was able to pick out a cricket as it talked to the night. What if Nathaniel was lying in his bedroll a mile up the turnpike? Was he listening to the wheels creaking past too? Could he hear the crickets? While he lay there, did he still think of her? Was he writing letters and trying to mail them even though he knew her father would never let her have them?

Or is he in the stone-cold ground?

She turned on her side. Morganne tapped on the bottom of the wagon and she tapped back. She drifted in and out of sleep. Suddenly there was the *pop-pop* of muskets far ahead. Then a silence deeper than the silence of a quiet night on the farm in Elizabethtown. A feeling

134 ~ MURRAY PURA

crept over her arms and legs like the feeling she used to get when she was a little girl and frightened of ghosts. A feeling that something large and cold and wicked was approaching the door to her room. That it would wait a few minutes for the right moment. Then it would strain against the wood and hinges until not only the door would bend but the whole house collapse upon her head with a roar.

12

Nathaniel pulled out his pocket watch. It was 3:30. Just like the morning of the battle at Brawner's Farm. He heard another pop. Picket fire had awakened him.

He tugged a small Bible from a pocket in his coat. Stared at the pages until his eyes adjusted to the lack of light and he could make out letters and words. He read Psalm 91 twice. Then lay on his back and thought he could see a few very small stars.

They had feasted on some foraged chickens until it felt to Nathaniel like the end of the war. And he wanted it to be the end of the war. No more battles. No more wounds. No one being left for dead in the grass. He wanted to head home.

And on the way pick up Lyndel. A nurse in Washington—how was it possible? Why had her parents let her leave the Amish community and spend her days among the suffering and the dying? Did she have any idea that her brother was in the army now and not the ambulance corps? Levi had never told her. What would happen to Lyndel if they took her brother back to Washington on a stretcher with his arms blown off?

Lord, it must not happen, it must not happen today. But what can I do to prevent it? Keep Levi at my right hand? Corinth was on my right at Brawner's Farm and I still lost him. What about Joshua? How do I protect him? How will I face his father if he falls today…and Abraham Yoder says I set the example his son followed? How will I escape the blame and judgment if all the boys from Elizabethtown are shot down and only I survive?

What right would I have to live and breathe and return home to help with
the harvest while they're planted in the hard ground of Sharpsburg?

Nathaniel sat up. There was no use thinking this way. It didn't help.
It didn't change anything for the better. He should just pray, dwell on
the thought of Lyndel a few moments as he always did, give the day to
God, then get on his feet and drink some of Sergeant Hanson's coffee
and make sure his musket was clean and dry. Get the men up and get
some hot food into them. March. Fight. Tear down the Rebel flag and
with it the slave markets of Richmond and Atlanta and Charleston. If
he couldn't accomplish those things, he shouldn't be here. If he couldn't
do those things the South's way of life would win over the North's and
a million Charlie Prestons would be born into slavery to be lynched at
a slaveholder's whim.

He took a small newspaper clipping from his Bible. Nip had picked
it up from an abandoned Rebel campsite in Virginia and was going to
use it to light a fire. Nathaniel asked if he could keep it. He propped
himself on one elbow and read it for probably the twentieth time,
squinting in the blackness.

SLAVES! SLAVES! SLAVES!

**Forks of the Road, Natchez. The subscribers have just arrived
in Natchez and are now stopping at Mr. Elam's house, Forks
of the Road, with a choice selection of slaves consisting of
mechanics, field hands, cooks, washers and ironers, and
general household servants. They will be constantly receiving additions to their present supply during the season and
all will be sold at as reasonable rates as can be afforded in
this market. To those purchasers desiring it, the Louisiana
guarantee will be given. Planters and others desirous of pur-
chasing are requested to call and see the slaves before pur-
chasing elsewhere.**

Gunfire crackled all around him. He got to his feet and watched
musket barrels sparkle a few hundred yards away. Nip rolled over and
jumped up, his face white.

"Are we under attack?"

Nathaniel shook his head. "Nervous pickets. The armies are pretty close together."

Nip stared at the flashes as another half-dozen Springfields went off. "I kind of hoped Lee's army might pull out during the night."

"Robert E. Lee? He's not like our good old John Pope."

"I feel kind of hollow in the stomach." Nip half-smiled. "Maybe the Rebs put something in the ham to turn Yankees inside out."

Their eyes met.

"Stick close with me today, Nip," Nathaniel said. "Since I lost Corinth, you're my brother now, like it or not."

Nip offered up a half-smile.

"All right, let's get the fire going!" boomed Hanson. "Who can sleep with all the pickets shooting at hobgoblins? Let's fry some bread while we have the time. I'll brew the coffee that stops minie balls cold." He looked at Nip. "How are ye this morning, soldier?"

"I reckon I could use some of your minie-ball coffee, Sergeant."

"You still know how to set the wood ablaze?"

"I do."

"Have at 'er then." He looked around him. "Corporal Nicolson. Corporal King."

"Sergeant."

"Sergeant."

"Shake the platoon out. Make sure every man has forty rounds in the cartridge box on his hip and another sixty in his pack. If someone's short, get what he needs from an ammunition wagon. Check that the boys have plenty of percussion caps too. Especially the recruits. And listen—" Hanson stepped up to Nicolson and King and lowered his voice. "When the shooting starts I want you to sing out the loading sequence loud and clear. For two or three reloads. I want to be sure the new lads get it straight. They might freeze up once the Rebs open fire. All right?"

Nicolson and King nodded. And then began to move among the sleeping men.

"Harter. McKeever. Groom. Sala. Ham." Nicolson's voice rang out.

"Up and get squared away. You have a busy day ahead of you. We have to help Bobby Lee get packed for his return trip south."

Nathaniel went toward the farm buildings. "Jones. Keim. Yoder. Plesko. Conkle. Rise and shine and check your cartridge box and cap box. We have some stiff work to do and you'll need full boxes to do it. Make sure you have another sixty rounds in your pack."

Nip was feeding sticks into a knot of flames. "Where's Crum?"

"South Mountain," Nathaniel said.

Soon the platoon and a few extras from the company were seated around Nip's small fire, warming their hands, frying bread in butter that had gone bad, choking down Sergeant Hanson's coffee.

"Private Plesko. Will ye have a mug of America's finest?"

The young man with soft eyes looked up from the fire. "Thank you, Sergeant." He extended his tin cup and Hanson poured, the steam rising up.

"Where from, Plesko?" asked Nicolson.

"Indianapolis."

"What about your family name?"

"Slovakia, Corporal. We're from Slovakia in Europe. It's close to Russia."

Ham whistled. "Too far to walk."

"How long have you been in Indianapolis?" pressed Nicolson.

"Ten years. Father felt it was right we help the country that helped us. I enlisted on my eighteenth birthday."

"Good man," grunted Hanson, standing nearby and taking pulls at his coffee with all the muscles in his face straining.

Plesko sipped at the coffee, stopped, looked at it, and smiled. "Father would say it needed a little more grease."

The men laughed.

"So McKeever," said Nicolson, intent on going through all the recruits. "Irish, am I right?"

McKeever nodded. "Not so hard to figure out."

Nicolson went on. "Campbell. You Scottish?"

Campbell tried to bite into his fried bread but it was too hot and he winced and almost dropped it in the dirt. "Not been there for a hundred years but yes, sure, Scottish. American first, Corporal."

"We're all Americans first, right, lads?" thundered Hanson. "Look what the good Lord's put together here. Jones is Welsh. 'Keever's Irish. Plesko is Slovak. Campbell's a Highlander. Keim, Yoder, and King are German, by the sounds of their English. Groom—what's that?"

"England." Groom stared up at him, the coffee in his hand untouched. "Before 1700 we were here. Fought in the Revolution."

"Well done. On the winning side, I'm guessing."

The young man with curly black hair didn't smile. "Grooms are always on the winning side."

"Are they? Then we should make quick work of the Army of Northern Virginia today."

"I should think so." Groom poured his coffee slowly into the ground. "Not fit for Jeff Davis, Sergeant."

Hanson frowned. "That's magic elixir there, Private. It doesn't do to go wasting it."

"I imagine an oak tree will spring up from this spot. An oak tree could handle your concoction. Not having a stomach."

Joshua Yoder lifted his cup and tried to break the feeling Groom had cast over the breakfast fire. "It may not work for him. But it works for the Germans among you, Sergeant. My family background is Westphalian, mind you. Though I suppose there's not much difference."

"Fine brew," agreed Levi. "Is there enough for a second?"

Hanson shook off Groom's insult. "There is. Just enough, lad." He leaned over and emptied the pot into Levi's cup. "You get the bottom too, Private. How's that?"

"It will keep me going all day. I wish I had this on the farm."

"I'll send you the recipe when the war's over."

"Maybe today then," smiled Nip who was happily seated beside Nathaniel.

"That's the spirit," grinned Hanson.

A drumroll broke in upon their chatter. Lieutenant Davidson walked his horse along the turnpike as the drum continued to beat.

"Sergeants. Prepare your men to move out. Get what food you can inside you."

He stopped and looked at Hanson's platoon by the fire. "Isn't that a cozy sight? Were you up all night, Sergeant?"

"Since about four, I'd say, Lieutenant."

"All set for a good morning's work it looks like."

"We are, sir. There's no coffee left or I'd offer you a spot."

Davidson laughed and moved on. "I've heard about your coffee. I think we should serve it up to the Rebs. They'd head back to Virginia and Alabama lickety-bang."

Hanson watched Davidson urge his mount along the road. "Very few appreciate the finer things in a soldier's life."

"Like Grandma's Tippecanoe coffee," said Nicolson getting to his feet.

"Aye. Grandma's Tippecanoe coffee. Had your fill then?"

"I have. Ham's had. Everyone's had—except perhaps Private Groom and a few others."

"They'll regret it when the balls are whistling past their ears," growled Hanson. "The breeze alone will knock them flat."

He glanced over at Campbell and McKeever and Plesko who were still squatting by the fire. "What is it, lads?"

"Will we…will be marching today, Sergeant?" asked Campbell.

"Marching? Aye, there'll be marching, there's always marching." He smoothed down his mustache with his hand. "But there's likely to be some brisk work too. Today you're going to see the elephant. Stick close to your corporals. Stick close to the man on your left and on your right. Do what they do. Go where they go. You're part of a proud regiment and a proud brigade. We look out for one another. You'll be all right." He winked. "And you've had the coffee."

Nathaniel gathered Joshua and Levi around him. "I'd like to offer up a prayer. We are Amish. We fight not because it's something we enjoy. None of us would be regular army, would we? The three of us have volunteered to bear arms because we want to live in a free country and we wish all the people within her borders to have that freedom. No one is to be left out, *ja*? It's not freedom for some men or women over there but no freedom for these men and women over here. It's one grand liberty for each human being. And we pray that all may one day have that same liberty of the spirit in Jesus Christ by their faith, *ja*? Today we load the gun and fix the bayonet so that tomorrow the African woman and child and man sit down at their table without fear, without the whip, without a price on their heads. Through Jesus Christ our Lord."

Nathaniel removed his black Hardee hat, bowed his head, and prayed in German. Levi and Joshua took their black hats from their heads as well. All about them bedrolls were tied to packs, muskets were checked for dirt or rust in the dim light, men went to munitions wagons by the side of the road for extra cartridges and caps. But the three stood within a circle of peace. It seemed to each of them, for those few minutes, that they had returned to Pennsylvania and, when they opened their eyes, they would see the barns and porches and chokecherry trees and smile. When Nathaniel finished and they lifted their heads and lifted their muskets, not one of the men didn't feel some measure of disappointment—instead of barns and haystacks and chokecherry trees and rocking chairs on porches they saw cannon and cavalry and soldiers with long dark guns.

General Gibbon had the Iron Brigade moving out of their bivouac by Joseph Poffenberger's farm. Columns of men in blue were marching into what little light five o'clock in the morning gave them. Rebel artillery began to boom far ahead and shells crashed onto the turnpike among the soldiers advancing toward Sharpsburg. Nathaniel watched Levi's and Joshua's faces whiten as they saw bodies tumbling through the air or fall shattered to the ground. Captain Langston pelted up the turnpike on his mount with Lieutenant Colonel Bachman at his side. Bachman shouted at the 19th Indiana to cross to the west side of the road by David Miller's barn. They had no sooner lined up there than Gibbon ordered them into the woods. The 7th Wisconsin went in with them.

"Take a look at the enemy's standards!" called Langston as his company climbed a fence and went into the trees with the rest of the Indiana regiment. "It's time to reacquaint ourselves with some old friends!"

Nathaniel's mouth was a thin straight line as he examined the Rebel flags a hundred yards ahead. "It's Stonewall."

Balls zipped through the trees, clipping leaves and snapping branches. The 19th Indiana and 7th Wisconsin returned fire. Nicolson and Nathaniel barked out the loading sequence for the recruits in their platoon: "Half-cock your musket! Cartridge! Bite off the twisted end! Powder in the barrel! Round in the muzzle! Ramrod! Seat the round on the powder! Return ramrod! Percussion cap on the nipple! Musket to full cock! Aim low! Fire!" White and gray smoke billowed through the tree trunks.

Battery B raced up to the Miller farmyard and unlimbered its guns. As soldiers pulled the artillery horses back out of harm's way the guns began to fire at the Rebel troops in the woods. Nathaniel couldn't see the cannon but he could hear them and the rough brogue of Lieutenant James Stewart as he shouted out aiming instructions to his cannoneers.

"You hear Old Jock?" he asked Joshua and Levi who were loading and firing off his left shoulder. "Stonewall's boys don't have much of a chance against a force from Indiana and Wisconsin and Scotland."

Bullets ricocheted off rocks and trees. Men in gray fell. Men in black hats fell. But it was Stonewall and the Rebel troops who gave way. Captain Langston hollered that there was a Dunker Church just ahead and he wanted it captured and held. The 19th Indiana and 7th Wisconsin pushed against the gray wall as they had pushed against it at South Mountain. And stone by stone the wall caved in.

A ball burned across the back of Nathaniel's left hand, taking some skin with it and leaving a streak of blood, but he only noticed it when he was lifting his musket to fire. An image of Lyndel sprang into his head and he saw her washing the wound, bandaging it, and patting him on the cheek with a smile: *You're fine, darling. Go ahead. Get back in the fight and finish this war as swiftly as you can.*

"They're running!" Ham shouted. "They're running!"

The platoon paused to watch as Stonewall's men broke from the woods and headed across the turnpike into a cornfield.

"There goes the crop," lamented Nicolson.

The 2nd and 6th Wisconsin were charging through the field, taking on hundreds of Rebel soldiers, so that the corn fell in bushels as if scythed. Union cannons added to the shower of fire. Men were dropping everywhere as if they were the cornstalks themselves and had just been cut. Flashes of flame slit the banks of thick smoke. The two Wisconsin regiments pushed the Rebels toward the church, were shoved backward, then stormed forward once again and cracked the Rebel line. Men in gray and butternut tried to climb the fence that separated the cornfield from the road but were shot as they made the attempt. As more and more corn was sliced by gunfire, and the ground beneath the stalks exposed, more and more men could be seen strewn among the cobs and husks.

Just as it seemed the Wisconsin regiments had put an end to the Rebel resistance Nathaniel was startled to see waves of gray troops explode from the trees behind the white Dunker Church the 19th Indiana was advancing toward. The Rebels roared across the turnpike and crashed into the Wisconsin men, throwing them back through the battered cornfield and into David Miller's barns and farm buildings behind it. The gray troops surged forward, screaming and shooting, knocking down everything in their path.

"They're going to capture our cannon," said Nip, looking at the artillery stationed at the farmyard behind them. "Old Jock's guns. And use them on our Wisconsin men."

Nathaniel heard officers crying out commands up and down the line. At once hundreds of men in black hats emerged from the trees and aimed their muskets at the gray wave engulfing the cornfield and farmyard and turnpike. Lieutenant Davidson ran up to the company, his face spattered with blood and beads of sweat, pulling his horse by the reins.

"Save our brave boys!" shouted Davidson. "Wheel to the left and fire into the Rebel flank!"

The 19th Indiana and 7th Wisconsin burst into a sheet of white flame and smoke. The Rebels hadn't counted on this and were caught by surprise as dozens of their men staggered and collapsed from the volley. It was followed by another rage of fire and another. Lieutenant Colonel Bachman made his way to the front of his Indiana regiment, slashing his sword through the morning air.

"Follow me, boys!" he yelled and charged across the turnpike into the cornfield.

"Fix bayonets, Indiana!" hollered Sergeant Hanson. "Forward! Double quick! That's John Bell Hood's Texas Brigade and Evander Law's Alabama boys. Let's give them the old Hoosier hurrah and end the war by lunch!"

The Indiana men poured across the turnpike after Bachman, shooting and yelling and climbing the fence into the corn patch, pursuing the Rebel troops that were fleeing back the way they had come. Nathaniel saw that Levi and Joshua were still on his left, their faces blue and black with powder, and Nip on his right, skin streaked gray in a mix of powder and sweat. As they trampled the cornstalks still standing he caught glimpses of Campbell and McKeever and Plesko and Groom. McKeever was without his black hat, had blood on his neck, and was caught up in the momentum of the charge as the men tore through the corn and into an open field.

The white church was there, just on the other side of the road, and Nathaniel couldn't help but think, for an instant, of open Bibles, men and women praying and singing hymns, and little children waiting for a story about Jesus. Then he was reloading, firing, and running, reloading, firing, and running as the platoon roared with the rest of the regiment after the Rebel troops. But as he lifted his musket in the middle of the furor he saw a bullet strike Bachman and spin him around and then a second bullet rip through his back. The lieutenant colonel fell.

Now the Texans and Alabamans stopped running. They turned and gathered their numbers and gave a shout as loud as cannon fire. And then attacked the leaderless regiment. Firing and reloading as quickly as they could, the Indiana men were forced back into the cornfield among the bodies of the wounded and dead who lay in mounds of gray and blue. The two armies blazed at each other at point-blank range, corn-stalks and husks and caps sailing up and spinning through the sky.

"Hold them! Hold them!" Davidson was practically screaming. Then Nathaniel saw him drop like a stone. A wounded horse squealed and plunged through the corn, its reins trailing on the ground. The saddle was peppered with bullet holes. He recognized it as Captain Langston's mount.

The 19th yielded ground angrily, firing at each step they took back, but for many their muskets were fouled and unshootable, while for others all they had left were a final half-dozen cartridges. Pinned to the fence between the cornfield and the road they made their stand, defying men Hanson called some of the best in Lee's army.

"Stand like iron!" Hanson thundered. "You looked Stonewall's Virginians square in the eye this morning! Now stare down Hood's Texans!"

The Indianans stood and fought alongside the 7th Wisconsin and 26th New York, Battery B blasting over their heads into the Southern men and the corn. Balls and lead shot whirred through the air. Great heaps of white, black, and gray smoke blinded Nathaniel, who often could only fire at the gun flashes of the Texas and Alabama muskets, never seeing the human faces behind them. The stink of sulfur stung his nose and the taste of it made his tongue burn. Nip fired from one knee, Levi and Joshua stood. Their faces were so black it looked as if they'd been smeared with tar and soot.

Then a shout went up from behind the 19th Indiana. Rebel troops charged from the woods across the road where the 19th had fought Stonewall's forces earlier in the morning. Bullets raked the ranks of the Indiana, Wisconsin, and New York men. With more and more of their friends falling into the stubble they turned to face the new threat from the road, returning fire with the rounds they had left or could scoop from the packs and cartridge boxes of dead and wounded soldiers. Pulling back over the road in front of their enemy they made a new stand at the barn of David Miller. It was the exact spot where they had begun their attack into the woods at the break of day and routed Stonewall's men.

"Steady! Steady!" bellowed Hanson. "Fire rocks and stones if you have to! We're not going any farther back, boys! I'm tired of walkin', I tell ye!"

Hanson identified the new Rebel troops as Virginians from Jubal Early's brigade and the artillery as that of Jeb Stuart, who had battled them at Lewinsville. Stuart used canister shot that spread hundreds of balls in vicious bursts through the Indiana columns. But the 19th Indiana and 7th Wisconsin of the Iron Brigade, along with the 26th New York, stood firm despite the fire being hurled at them. Across the turnpike the rest of the Iron Brigade, the 2nd and 6th Wisconsin, even though they had lost scores of their comrades in David Miller's corn-field, stood by the cannons of Battery B and poured what bullets they had left into the Texans and Alabamans who were trying to overwhelm the Union position and capture the artillery. Old Jock used canister just as Jeb Stuart did, and he double-shotted them, so that Rebel dead fell before the Wisconsin men and the cannons by the score. When General Gibbon finally ordered a withdrawal to Joseph Poffenberg-er's farm, where Wednesday, September 17th, had dawned for the Iron Brigade, what was left of the Confederate troops had no intention of following them.

Nathaniel's platoon took up a defensive position on the east side of the road by the Poffenberger farm with the rest of the brigade. The artillery pointed its snouts menacingly toward Sharpsburg. But no one ever came after them. Men gulped from their canteens and listened to the terrific crash of muskets from across the fields and forests of the battle-field as the fight swept back and forth throughout the rest of the day.

Levi sat with his head in his hands under a tree and could scarcely speak. Joshua knelt on the grass and said he was looking for a lady-bug he had brushed roughly off his uniform, thinking it was a wasp. Nicolson and Nathaniel counted heads as they passed out fresh car-tridges. McKeever was gone. Campbell was gone. Nip was gone. Har-ter was gone.

"Did any of you see them go down?" Nathaniel asked his men. "Are they wounded? Are they dead?"

"Davidson's dead," someone said.

"Yes." Nathaniel's face was dark blue and looked like a death mask. "I saw that."

"Bachman's dead," Ham spoke up. "And Harter took a shell right in the chest."

"Captain Langston's dead," mumbled Joshua.

"What about Nip? McKeever? Campbell?" Nathaniel glanced around him at the weary faces. "Didn't anyone see them?"

"I guess not," muttered Nicolson.

"Saw Nip being loaded into an ambulance," one of the men spoke up. "Don't know what shape he was in."

"Are you certain?" asked Nicolson.

"Yes, sir. It was him."

"Thank God. Thank God. I pray he's all right." Nathaniel sank down on the grass. "You know, I can't hear too well."

"Neither can I," admitted Nicolson.

"Where's Hanson?"

"Meeting with Gibbon. He's company commander now."

"We didn't keep the cornfield."

"No," admitted Nicolson. "But who would want it? The crop is ruined."

"We have wounded lying there."

"I know. But we can't get them now. Not until there's a flag of truce or the Rebels withdraw."

Nathaniel stared at him. Nicolson's skin was as dark as his. "Do you think they'll withdraw?"

Nicolson shrugged. "Who can tell what's going on? Listen to those volleys." He paused a moment as the roar of muskets reached a crescendo hundreds of yards south and east of them. "If we took Stonewall and Hood out of the fight we did our part."

"I still worry about the wounded. We could save them."

"The Rebel surgeons will look after some of the boys. Though I expect they will see to their own first."

"Their own! We are all Americans!" Nathaniel felt like screaming. "This is madness! Today's slaughter is madness!"

"Easy, Corporal," Nicolson said quietly. "The men need to see your strength now."

Nathaniel nodded and looked out across the turnpike. "Yes, yes, you're right."

"If it's any help I saw the ambulance corps pull some of the wounded out of the corn when the fighting was closer to the church. I think they managed to rescue a couple dozen before the battle came back into the cornfield again. I saw a woman working with the wounded."

Nathaniel nodded. "Dark skirt and red bow at the throat? That is how the newspapers describe Clara Barton. A brave woman."

Nicolson frowned a bit as he thought back to the moment and took a drink from his canteen. "No, nothing like that. This woman was wearing a blue dress with a black apron. And she had some kind of black cap on her head. I'll never forget the hair. It was all pinned up but you could spot that woman from a mile away, I swear. Every strand on that pretty head was the color of fire."

13

Nathaniel moved double-quick along the Hagerstown Turnpike in the fading light, one hand gripping his musket, the other on his black hat to keep it in place. Two wagons full of fallen soldiers passed him and turned off the road to a burial pit. He ran past soldiers in groups of two or three and cannon pointed south toward Sharpsburg and Lee's army.

Meadowlarks and robins were singing to the dusk. Gunfire all over the battlefield had ceased. Before leaving Poffenberger's farm Nathaniel had checked his pocket watch and the hands had been just shy of seven. He guessed he would be at the Miller farmyard in a few more minutes. Once the barns and farmhouse came into sight he saw stretcher bearers and ambulance wagons and men carrying bodies through doorways. Then he saw the cornfield and the fence that separated it from the road. He slowed to a walk and clenched his teeth.

During the fighting he had scarcely noticed the bodies of the fallen. They lay three and four deep along the fence and at the side of the turnpike. The corn patch was dark with death, black hat and gray coat tumbled together as if a twister had torn through David Miller's farm. Farther ahead he could see mounds of soldiers sprawled on the grass by the Dunker Church. A sickness came and went in his stomach and his head. Lanterns were lit and moving between the buildings. One floated by the church, disappeared behind it, then reappeared again.

He continued to approach, squinting at the figure by the church. As he came closer he realized it was a woman. He thought it might be

Clara Barton assisting the surgeons here. The light fell on the woman's hair and shoulders. She bent and set the lantern on the grass to tend to a man at the far corner of the church. He watched her raise a canteen to the man's lips. His uniform was gray. A voice carried to him through the twilight.

"There's plenty, don't worry, plenty for your friends. Drink up. Drink up for me, *ja?*"

His throat tightened. His stride lengthened. He stepped off the turnpike and walked toward the church, past the tangle of bodies to a clear stretch of grass. The woman's face was turned to the injured man.

"The bullet didn't hit the bone," she was telling the soldier. "You'll keep your arm, sir."

"God bless ye," said the bearded officer.

Then, as she bent toward the wounded man, the light from the lantern fell on her face. Powder and grime streaked her skin. Loose hair dangled into her eyes and she kept pushing it back with hands stained by dirt and blood. She was over a year older than the last time he had seen her. But her beauty was no less. It was her.

"Ginger," he said.

Her head came up sharply. "What? What did you call me?" She jumped to her feet, picking up the lantern and holding it toward him. The light fell on his face and she stopped as if she'd been struck. "Oh!"

She all but dropped the lantern onto the ground and ran to him.

The impetus of her rush threw them behind the Dunker church and away from the dead and wounded. Nathaniel's face was dark with burnt powder but Lyndel clasped his head in her strong farm-girl hands and kissed it again and again. "Nathaniel, you're alive, thank God, you're alive! How I've prayed for you!" She pressed her lips against his and they held the kiss for a long minute while the night rang with birdcalls and the rasp of crickets. "Stay with me. I need your help here. Miss Barton has a whole crew but I just have Morganne and Hiram to tend the wounded and help Indiana's surgeons. The 19th needs you more at David Miller's farm than it does at Joseph Poffenberger's."

He ran his hand over her cheek and played with the loose strands of her hair.

"Your eyes are so blue," he said.

She laughed and put her fingers to his lips. "You can't see my eyes in the dark."

"Yes, I can. Your skin is so smooth and your hair is so wonderful. I wish it would all come undone."

"Perhaps if we work hard enough on the wounded you will get your wish."

He kissed her on the lips again. "How beautiful God has made you."

"And how handsome my man is. Even under all that war paint." She took a damp cloth from a pocket and wiped at his skin until some of the grime began to come off. "My sweet Nathaniel. A corporal."

"Sergeant now. After today."

His eyes were large and soft. She held him against her again, tucking his head into her shoulder. "So many brave boys. I pray their sacrifice will make a difference. I pray Lee will withdraw. He must withdraw." She removed his black hat and kissed his hair. "But I need you with me. I do, Nathaniel. I couldn't bear for you to walk off into the dark after only a few moments together. Won't you stay close? Won't you help me nurse the men here?"

Nathaniel lifted his head. "Captain Hanson knows where I am. He doesn't want to see me until reveille. Said he'd put me in the brig if he glimpsed so much as the tip of my boot before drumroll." He kissed the top of her head just in front of her *kapp*. "I'll stay with you until four. Then I'll have to skedaddle. There's no telling if Lee and McClellan will mix it up again tomorrow." He kissed her hair again.

"You picked a heck of a spot for a tryst, Yank."

The voice came from the front of the church.

Nathaniel and Lyndel stepped around the corner. Nathaniel smiled and squatted beside the Rebel officer Lyndel had been nursing. "You can't blame me, can you, Captain? This farm would be a place of beauty but for the quarrel we've had here."

"I expect. Don't think many of the dead would begrudge you, son. Could they rise, they'd hope you were first in line at the county-fair kissing booth." He grinned through a beard matted with powder. "If there's a heaven, they're better off than you and me right now. And if there's nothing, they won't know it. Now if there be a hell, that's something else again. I hope the Lord has mercy on all these boys."

"Yes, sir." Nathaniel dug into his coat pocket. "Have you something to eat? Would you care for a couple of buttermilk biscuits?"

The captain propped himself up on his good elbow. "Where on earth did you come by those? You Black Hats have one of your grandmothers following you around in her wagon, woodstove and all?"

"A comrade in arms made them." Nathaniel's voice caught as an image of Nip came to his mind.

"Thank'ee." The officer bit into one of the biscuits Nathaniel offered him. "Soft too. Before your girl showed up I thought I could drink the Chattahoochee dry. Didn't have a thought for food. Now she's poured half a canteen into me I think I could swallow a dozen of these. The butter's off but that's nothing for a soldier. Am I talking too much, ma'am?"

Lyndel was washing both sides of the wound where the ball had passed in and out. "Talk all you want. No one's going to give you chloroform tonight." She brought cloth and dried leaves out of a satchel she'd placed on the grass and made a poultice.

"What's that?"

"Canada wild ginger."

"Why you putting it on me?"

"You fought through all this and now you're going to go and get scared on me, Captain? It draws out the poison, keeps the wound clean, helps the skin bind back together. How's that?"

"Feels good, all right."

Lyndel stood up. "Can you walk a bit? Sergeant King here would be pleased to help you away from this carnage and find you a barn to lean against or a tree to lie under. Please take this canteen with you."

"Why, thank'ee. I expect I would like to take that walk. I'm fair tired of the sight of this spot."

He put an arm over Nathaniel's shoulder and tottered up the road past the cornfield to the Miller farmyard.

"Not a barn or the house or anywhere they're doing the surgery, son," said the officer. "I swear I heard enough screaming today to last me a hundred year."

"How about the old tree over there?"

"That suits."

When Nathaniel headed back he saw Lyndel was walking about the cornfield with her lantern, examining men's faces. The light passed over face after face and then left them to return to the dark. Dozens of black hats and black feathers lay battered in the dirt. He came up quietly beside her and saw the glint of water on her face.

"The captain's settled," he said softly.

She wiped the back of her hand over her cheeks. "Thank you, Nathaniel. I'm sorry. I just would like to have seen more young men survive."

"I know."

"Miss Barton was working here right after the Rebels withdrew and that was early on. The battle had moved east toward Antietam Creek. I came about noon. We were with casualties in the West Woods first, the place your men fought Stonewall Jackson. I watched it from time to time with Hiram's spyglass, you know. When I could bear it."

Nathaniel touched her gently on the arm to stop her from walking any farther. "There's something you should know."

Lyndel looked at him. "What? Please give me no bad news."

He made a small smile. "War brings only bad news, Ginger. The worst of it is that I've lost Corinth to a Rebel bullet. He's gone."

Lyndel gasped.

When she regained control of herself, she asked, "There's more?"

"*Ja*. Your brother and Joshua Yoder enlisted in the 19th Indiana. They're in my platoon."

Lyndel gripped his hand. "Don't say so!"

"They fought today."

"Oh—is Levi—is he all right? Joshua?"

"Neither of them is wounded."

Lyndel pulled her hand free and wandered among the dead and the cornstalks until she reached the fence by the road. She climbed over it still holding the lantern and began to walk beside more bodies. The light touched on hands and eyes, it touched on heads of curly hair, on those who still wore their black hats or Confederate caps. Nathaniel climbed over the fence after her.

"Why did they do it?" she asked as she walked. "Did they tell you?"

"Your brother saw Lee's men abduct Africans in Maryland. They took free men and women and children captive and sent them south to the plantations. Joshua—well, he couldn't abide the thought of the North being conquered. Of living in a slave nation. I believe Levi also mentioned Charlie Preston."

Lyndel was silent a few moments. The light swung in her hand and the light played on rigid faces. He knew she was hoping to see movement or hear a groan.

"Do you think we'll ever meet up with Moses Gunnison again?" she asked suddenly.

"I don't see how."

"Or that leader of the slave hunters?"

"Levi's seen him."

"Where? When?"

"Just a couple of weeks ago. After Manassas and Chantilly. Your brother was collecting Union wounded under a flag of truce. Said the Rebs called the man Georgey Washington. I suppose it was in jest."

"George Washington! Some George Washington!" She suddenly dropped to her knees. "His leg just moved."

Nathaniel squatted by the black hat. "Soldier, can you hear me? I'm Sergeant King with the 19th Indiana."

A struggling voice whispered, "7th Wisconsin."

"Do you know where you're hit?"

"Arm. Right arm."

"I have a canteen here." He put it to the young man's mouth. "Drink your fill. This woman's a nurse. She'll take good care of you. Things are going to get a whole lot better from now on."

"I'm going to clean and bandage your wound, soldier," Lyndel said, taking her satchel from her shoulder. "Then we are going to get you up to the surgeons."

"Am I—am I going to lose my arm?"

"Perhaps not. At least not all of it. And your other arm will be just as good as it is now."

He closed his eyes and turned his head away.

"Private, can I offer you something to eat?" asked Nathaniel.

"No, thank you, Sergeant."

Lyndel finished bandaging the bone that had been fractured by a bullet. "We need stretcher bearers."

Nathaniel peered through the dark. "Can't tell where they are. It doesn't matter. This boy's young and slender as a birch sapling. I've got him."

"Are you sure?" asked Lyndel.

"I'm sure. Just sling his arm so it doesn't get knocked about."

Nathaniel picked him up and carried him to the stables where the 19th Indiana's surgeons were at work. Lanterns hung from the rafters, and the stable doors had been unhinged and were being used as operating tables. Soldiers lay groaning on the straw while Morganne mopped their brows or gave them sips of brandy to prepare them for the amputations. She glanced up at Lyndel in the black and gold light. Her eyes seemed to have no color.

"Just lay him here." Morganne patted her hand on a patch of straw stained with blood. "It will be another hour. Is it a leg or an arm?"

"His right arm," Lyndel told her as Nathaniel lowered the boy gently down beside Morganne.

"So young," said Morganne quietly.

A shriek made Lyndel jump but Morganne scarcely noticed. Hiram leaned into a bearded Union corporal whose leg was being sawed off above the knee. Then he replaced a thick strip of harness leather in the man's mouth.

"Bite, Jack," he said. "Bite for all you're worth. The doctor's almost done."

Hiram's arms past his elbows were red.

"Miss Keim." A surgeon looked up from a second stable door. "Would you give this man more chloroform while I probe for the bullet in his shoulder?"

Lyndel poured the sweet-smelling liquid from a bottle into a clean cloth she found on a shelf next to a rack of farrier tools. She held it over a young soldier's mouth and nose. He writhed and twisted as the surgeon poked deep into a muscle. Both the surgeons were covered with blood and grime and sweat. Once the soldier lay still, Lyndel took another cloth, dipped it in a bucket of water, and quickly and firmly wiped first one doctor's face and then the other's.

"Thank you, Miss Keim," said one of them. "Before you head out into the night again I wanted to tell you how much we appreciate the supplies you brought us—sharp saws, the chloroform and brandy, quinine and morphine and opium pills. Our own army has not brought up the supplies we need for fear the battle may resume tomorrow and the enemy capture the medical wagons."

"I took a page from Clara Barton's book, doctor. She is always bringing supplies to the field stations."

"I'm glad you learned so well. Now some of our assistants are over in the tool shed just behind us. I have no idea how they're fixed for horsehair for suturing or whether it's even been boiled to render it pliable. Do they have enough morphine to rub into the worst of wounds to deaden the pain? Or oiled linen and sticking plaster for bullet holes?"

"I promise I will look in on them before I head back to the battleground."

"Miss David!" called the other doctor loudly. "I need you here. Bring a sponge and basin and take care of this blood from the amputation. Then administer some turpentine or tannic acid to stanch the flow."

Morganne set the bottle of brandy to one side. "I'm coming."

"Fetch some laudanum as well, will you? And I will need you to apply a tourniquet."

"Yes, sir."

"Hiram," the doctor went on, "you may lift the corporal down now and lay him on some fresh straw at the back. Then I'll thank you to bring up that lad with the neck wound there."

"Nathaniel!" Hiram looked at his friend and half-smiled. "I've not had a chance to say it's good to see you. Can you help me lift this man down and the other up?"

"Of course." Nathaniel scrambled to Hiram's side and together they took the corporal from the stable door that was propped up on sawhorses. Morganne was still applying turpentine to the amputation as they set him in the straw. Then they picked up a soldier with blood running through the bandage on his neck.

"Thought you'd be looking for the nearest telegraph station to file a story," Nathaniel said to Hiram as they placed the soldier carefully on the door.

"In the morning." Hiram grunted. "First light I'll ride out so the pickets can see who I am. Unless the fighting resumes."

Nathaniel stared at him. "Do you think it will start up again?"

"Depends what McClellan does. He's fought Lee to a standstill. I don't think Lee will push for any more. It depends whether or not Little Mac wants to try to put an end to the Army of Northern Virginia. We still have more than twenty-thousand in reserve while Lee has none."

"But Little Mac is no risk-taker, Hiram."

"No, he's not."

The other doctor spoke up around a scalpel clamped in his teeth. "We've never had casualties like this, not at Manassas, not at Gainesville or South Mountain. I honestly don't know who McClellan can summon up to fight."

"The reserve would be enough, doctor. But I don't know if Mac'll do it. If he doesn't, Mr. Lincoln will want to know why. So will the Congress."

"There's been enough slaughter for one battle. More than enough."

Hiram put his hands on his hips and watched the doctor work morphine into a large gash in a soldier's side. "That may be, sir. But if Lee's army lives to fight another day you'll see this again and again and again. The war could go on for years."

Lyndel went outside the stables and headed for the tool shed. Suddenly she felt faint and sagged against a tree. She tried to remember what she was setting out to do. Then an arm went around her shoulder and back and held her up.

"Are you all right?" asked Nathaniel.

"I thought I was." She leaned into him. "I've worked at Armory

Square for months. I tended the wounded with Clara Barton at Second Manassas. I don't know what's wrong with me."

"Some of the wounds are pretty bad."

"It's…it's more than that. Do you ever think back to our families in Pennsylvania? How much they disapprove of our being here? Sometimes the weight of their censure is just too much along with all the blood and killing." She looked up at his powder and blood dark face. "Nathaniel. I feel alone and far away from myself."

"No," he responded, kissing the top of her *kapp*. "You're not alone."

14

October 3, 1862

Antietam Creek

Dear Mama and Papa,

I'm hopeful you received the letter I sent on the 20th of September telling you the Elizabethtown boys are all right. Levi does not have a scratch on him, you may thank God. Joshua Yoder is also fine and was not wounded in the battle. In addition, Nathaniel is well just as I wrote you. You know, I'm sure, that Corinth King is with God now.

A friend, Mr. Hiram Wright, who is a war correspondent for a Philadelphia paper, told me he sent a telegram to you on my behalf on the 19th. Did they bring that to your door?

I don't wonder you're angry that your Amish children are here, the cost of war is so terrible.

Every day we lose more of the very men that we rescued from the battlefield on the 17th and 18th of September. Yet some are saved and will return home to their families and I'm grateful to our Lord Jesus I can be part of that.

Solomon Meredith is in command of the 19th Indiana regiment once again since Lt. Col. Bachman, a very nice man, was killed. One of the first things Colonel Meredith ordered done was the burial of our slain with wooden headboards placed at their gravesites. The 19th Indiana was called upon to bury the Confederate dead also. It took several days and the heat made it a harder job than it already was. Much as you hate this conflict—don't we all?—you would be glad to hear what one of Nathaniel's men said, a Private Plesko: "I would bury them no matter who they were, not just because they're Americans but because they are human beings and they too are made in the image of God."

We feel the Emancipation Proclamation of September 22nd has made at least some of the sacrifice worthwhile. The president would never have issued it except that General Lee withdrew from the field here the day after the battle and retreated to Virginia. Mr. Wright is adamant the decree will prevent Britain and France from recognizing the South as a sovereign nation. Even though it won't take effect until January 1st, as you know, and only pertains to those states in rebellion against the Union (not the four slaveholding states that did not secede), Mr. Wright believes it will incalculably harm the Southern cause by making slavery a critical reason for the conflict. Perhaps some of the states that left the Union will return by January 1st because of the Proclamation, as Mr. Lincoln hopes—who but God knows? Yet slavery is the reason your Amish boys have taken up arms, much to your grief and displeasure, and I'm glad the president has taken up arms against it as well and by so doing declared their intentions honorable and righteous.

I have mentioned President Lincoln several times in this note. He is here now. The Amish Brigade, as I call it because Nathaniel, Levi, and Joshua are in it (though the newspapers call it the Iron Brigade) was formed up for hours yesterday in the hot sun. However, Mr. Lincoln and General McClellan did not appear. That was an aggravating experience for the troops. Everyone says we shall see the president today but so far nothing has occurred in that respect. I have a great deal to do when it comes to the wounded in any case—

"Lyndel!"

"I'm in our tent writing a letter, Davey!" called Lyndel.

"The boys are forming up in the field. President Lincoln really is here this time. Hurry!"

The men stood in straight rows, regiment by regiment, backs straight but uniforms faded and tattered. Lyndel realized there were nowhere near the numbers there should have been. The president looked rugged in his untrimmed beard and black suit, his face sunburned, but his step steady and sure on the green grass. The reek of dead horses left where they had been killed during the battle two weeks before saturated the warm air. The president didn't appear to notice. With General McClellan beside him he gazed long and hard at the ragged but proud appearance of the Iron Brigade and Lyndel saw the pain pass over his face.

The flags of the four regiments, many of them full of bullet holes, some shot to pieces, dipped in salute to the president of the United States. Lincoln, tall black hat in his hands, bowed low in response. Lyndel saw Nathaniel formed up with his platoon, Captain Hanson and Lieutenant Nicolson on one side of him, Ham a corporal now, on the other. It seemed to her that Lincoln searched out the platoon in the formation and rested his eyes on Nathaniel, Levi, and Joshua, as if someone had pointed out these were three Amish boys who had taken up arms to preserve the Union.

Perhaps I have imagined it, she thought.

Lyndel was gathered off to the side with the 19th Indiana's quartermaster and surgeons and chaplains. The president slowly made his way toward them. Briefly he shook a few hands. Then he spotted Lyndel and Morganne and inclined his head.

"The nurses of the Indiana regiment."

"Mr. President," they both replied at the same time, bowing their heads and each making an attempt at a curtsy.

"This was a terrible ordeal for you," he said.

"It was an honor to help these soldiers, sir," Lyndel said. "They bore the brunt of the battle. To have saved some from the bullets and shellfire is a privilege."

Lincoln nodded. "I see that by the look in your faces. You do not find the field conditions too rough? You have been encamped here more than two weeks."

"They are not rough, Mr. President," Morganne spoke up. "The troops afford us every amenity they possibly can. They treat us as if we were their own sisters with all grace and respect."

A smile came to Lincoln's face. "Do they? I'm sure you've done your best by them to deserve it." He nodded as he walked away. "Perhaps I may not have to meet you under such circumstances again if the fortunes of war favor us."

"We shall pray to that end, sir," Lyndel said as the president moved slowly on.

That evening Nathaniel came as he usually did to the primitive hospital that had been set up not far from Miller's farm where Lyndel and Morganne also had their tent. Since he was bivouacked with his men near the Potomac he didn't have far to walk. Lyndel and Nathaniel made their way along the Hagerstown Turnpike but didn't hold hands.

"Sometimes I feel guilty," Nathaniel said. "I can have my evenings with my sweetheart while other men cannot."

"I understand," she replied. "Would you rather we did away with these walks altogether?"

"Oh," he said with a laugh. "I don't feel *that* guilty, Miss Keim. I guess if they could, my men would do the same as I'm doing right now, so I'm not ready to let go of you just yet."

"I'm glad. According to Hiram we may have little enough time left together as it is."

Nathaniel made a face. "What's his latest theory?"

"Pouting makes you less handsome," she teased.

"Does he have us on the march by the end of the week?"

"It's Friday now. That would be short notice indeed. He believes your brigade will receive substantial reinforcements in a few days and that you'll be back in Virginia by early November."

"Under McClellan?"

She picked up a long stick and pretended for a few moments that she was moving cattle, swishing it about in the air. "Well, for all the affection the men hold for the general, it's not generally shared by those in the capital, according to Hiram. Congress feels he should have gone after Lee the day following the battle and torn the Army of Northern Virginia to pieces. It might have ended the war then."

"It certainly would have killed more men."

Lyndel's look darkened with the sunset. "I know. It's so easy to talk when you're seated in a warm room far from the shellfire. But Hiram's sources tell him that if McClellan continues to find excuses not to pursue Lee's army it will be his undoing. Hooker or Burnside may be given orders to take his place."

"Hooker or Burnside?"

"I don't mean to upset you. Let's talk about something else. What did your men think of Mr. Lincoln's visit today?"

"It was better than the one yesterday when he didn't show up," Nathaniel said. "They're not much for standing out in the hot sun like blades of grass. But they allow as Lincoln is one of us since he wears a tall black hat."

Lyndel laughed and Nathaniel took pleasure in seeing her eyes shine. So often her eyes were tinged with the pain of those who tend the dead and the dying.

"Mail came today," Nathaniel mentioned as they continued to stroll, horses and soldiers moving by on either side of them. "Did you hear anything from your mother or father?"

"I wrote them and sent it off. But I don't know why I bother, Nathaniel. They're not talking to me."

"You think they've shunned you and your brother?"

"Levi has taken up arms. He has fought in a battle and killed other men. Most certainly he is shunned."

"But you—"

"I'm a nurse who contributes to the war, you know that. I help nurture men back to health and some of them return to their units to fight."

"I suppose your being with me has something to do with their silence."

Lyndel swung her stick back and forth. "You've been shunned for almost a year and I'm speaking with you and…consorting with you. Most certainly that's another good reason for Bishop Keim to enforce the *Meidung.*"

"Still, they might have sent you a letter to explain their thinking rather than leave you in the dark."

Lyndel made a final swipe and tossed her stick to the side of the road. "*Ja.*"

Nathaniel coughed. "Here come the other lovebirds. It looks like they might have walked clear to the Pennsylvania border and back."

Lyndel squinted. "How can you tell who that is? It just looks like two black specks to me. You must have the eyes of a falcon."

"Hiram has a particular swagger."

It was indeed Hiram and Morganne. Once the two couples came within greeting distance of one another, Morganne began to talk rapidly, her face a mixture of pleasure and annoyance. "Hiram has been relating to me the most astonishing things."

Nathaniel smiled. "If he didn't, you would soon realize Hiram Wright wasn't the man courting you."

Morganne's blue eyes narrowed. "No one is being courted, Nathaniel King. However I am being dazzled and bewildered. Mr. Wright here claims General McClellan is against emancipation of the slaves. That he said he would turn runaway slaves around and send them back to their rightful owners."

Hiram shrugged. "Anyone who covers Washington politics knows that. The general believes slavery's a constitutional right. Our constitution, not just Jeff Davis's. Lincoln felt the same way until this past summer."

Morganne folded her arms over her chest. "You see?"

"Go read his speeches in the papers. Plain as day, the president said if he could preserve the Union without ending slavery he would do it and had no intention of interfering with it."

Lyndel saw that Nathaniel's face looked very sharp-edged. "Why did he change his mind then?"

"Our losses in Virginia," replied Hiram. "He realizes it's going to be hard to defeat the rebellion. So freeing the slaves in the Confederate states is a blow against the South's culture and its cotton industry. It also alienates France and Britain from the Confederacy. Lincoln is a good man, Nathaniel, but he's a politician and a war president and his priority is to win the war and save the Union. I honestly don't know how much he cares for the plight of the slave apart from that."

"Only God knows the heart of a man, Hiram. I doubt President Lincoln knows himself what he really believes about all the matters at hand. But if what you say is true, I will pray he changes his mind one more time."

Hiram shook his head. "So he can be like your Amish platoon? A lot of the Northern boys don't think much of the African race, Nathaniel."

"I've heard the talk," Nathaniel replied. "That too can change just as the president can change."

Hiram had a look of disgust on his face. "With prayers and hymn singing?"

Nathaniel's face was cold. "Yes."

"I wish," Lyndel quickly interrupted, "this had all been dealt with in 1776."

Hiram, aware he had offended Nathaniel, awkwardly put his hands in his pockets and looked away from his friend to Lyndel. "It was. Thomas Jefferson put the clause in the Declaration of Independence. Or perhaps Benjamin Franklin and Thomas Paine worked hard to make sure it was there. It doesn't matter. A lot of American patriots wanted a clean start for our country when it came to slavery. But South Carolina and Georgia wouldn't join the Union against Great Britain unless slavery in the colonies was retained. So the Declaration was mangled for their sakes. The Continental Congress never even knew about the antislavery cause, they never debated it, they never put it to the vote."

"So then we're fighting a second revolution to correct the errors of the first," Nathaniel said. "Whether Abraham Lincoln is aware of it yet or not, the day will come when he'll know the truth of this in his heart and soul. You talk about McClellan saying he would return all runaway slaves to their rightful owner? Good. Their rightful owner is

God. That's what me and my Amish platoon are fighting for, Hiram. But you're mistaken if you think we're the only ones."

He moved ahead along the turnpike and Lyndel rushed to keep up with his long strides.

"I hope you're not angry with me," she said.

"Why should I be angry with you? Hiram fills his head with too many words and arguments. He's smart about some things but not so smart about others. And he always leaves God out of it. As if anything worthwhile is going to happen without prayer and faith." He suddenly stopped walking and looked at Lyndel. "I'm sorry. Fifteen minutes ago the only thing that was in my head was wanting to ask if you would be coming with the brigade when we march."

Lyndel put her hand on his arm. "When the surgeons pack up I pack up too. We may not leave on the very same day, Nathaniel, but the doctors and ambulance corps will not be far behind the army. And neither will I."

"I love you, Lyndel Keim. You know that?"

"*Ja*, I know it."

He put his arms around her. "Hiram told me we would be on our way to Virginia before the end of the month. But I'd like more time here with you. Perhaps he's wrong about the marching just as he's wrong about how many of us are fighting for a nation free of slavery and slaveholders."

But Hiram wasn't wrong about the brigade's marching orders. They moved out of their bivouac on October 20th and left the cornfield and the Dunker Church and Dave Miller's farm behind them, slogging through torrents of rain and days of heat, until they crossed into Virginia on the 30th of October, a new regiment of recruits marching with them, the 24th Michigan. Not long after, Lyndel, Morganne, Hiram, and the ambulance corps followed the brigade along the same muddy roads, Lyndel parting company with her friends for a night and taking a wagon into Washington to gather fresh supplies.

Her old residence was quiet but the butler knew her well and let her in. He said the Palmer family had retired but that her room was always left clean and ready should she come in from the battlefront and require it. Smiling her thanks, Lyndel walked softly up the curving staircase to the second floor carrying a candle he offered her. Opening the door to her room she was startled to see a lamp lit on a table and make out a figure seated in a chair.

"Who are you, sir?" she demanded.

The man turned up the lamp so that she could clearly see his face.

"Have you and I changed so much in one year," he said, "that you no longer know your own father?"

15

They held each other tightly. Lyndel felt tears come quickly, as did her father. His hug almost made her bones crack, but to her it was a welcome sensation.

Over and over again he spoke in Pennsylvania Dutch of how much he loved her and how Lyndel's mother pined for her and her brother Levi.

"Papa." Lyndel smiled as her eyes continued to fill. "It's so good to see you. But it's such a long journey for you."

Bishop Keim stepped back and used his handkerchief to wipe at his face. "I've been in Washington a week. I knew the army was on the march and I hoped I might catch you here. I pestered them at the Armory Square Hospital until they told me where your lodgings were. Your hosts have been good enough to give me a room. I was standing at my window when I saw you come up the drive in the wagon." He stopped to smile again, then added, "I quickly came up here to surprise you."

"You certainly did that, Papa."

"I knew I wouldn't be able to see Levi but I thank God he has brought us together."

"*Ja. Gelobt sei Gott.*"

He nodded and put the handkerchief away in a pocket. "Your mother and I have been praying about this trip for weeks. You might have carried on with the army and gone into Virginia but God has arranged for you to be here." He paused. "I have come to bring you home."

Lyndel stared at him. "What did you say?"

"If I could bring Levi with us I would, but he has enlisted. You have not. You have done your best to alleviate others' suffering. It is enough now. You are only making the war worse. It is time to return to Pennsylvania."

Lyndel felt a sharp cut inside. "I'm not making the war worse, Papa."

"Of course you are. You patch them up. They return to their regiments, *ja*? Fight again. Kill again."

"Many of them go home to their families."

He lowered his voice. "Let us speak softly. Our hosts are asleep. Your mother and I have discussed this. Asked of the Lord. It is prayer that brought me here."

"Papa. It is prayer that brought me here as well."

"Please pack your things. There is a train to Harrisburg in a few hours."

"I hope you are not serious about this."

"*Ja*, I am serious. Why would I travel all this way and leave your mother, who is already alone enough?"

"But—I am of age now—and doing what I feel the Lord wishes me to do—the surgeons and the other nurses count on me—there will be more fighting—more wounded."

He folded his hands in front of him. "*Ja*. And more fighting and more fighting. The conflict will drag on for years. Why did any of us expect it to be over in a few months? These are Americans battling Americans. Neither side will easily surrender. Never."

Lyndel felt the skin on her face tighten. "All the more reason to have experienced nurses to help with the casualties. Many more lives may be saved."

His eyes darkened. "Do you enjoy it so much, daughter?"

Heat filled her head in an instant. "No one loves to see men die—no general, no soldier, not President Lincoln or Jefferson Davis. The slaughter at Antietam Creek was terrible. If the next battle is the last battle, I thank God. But until it is over I must heal men. Not sit back from a safe distance and watch them bleed and cry out for water while their wounds suck their life from them."

"Healing. This is not what Jesus did. Show me where he placed his hands on injured soldiers so that they could return to the battlefield."

"Did he not heal the Roman centurion's servant? When did he tell the officer to stop being a soldier?"

"So and you will lecture me about David and Jonathan and Gideon next. I am not here for a debate. You do not understand. If you do not return with me it is finished."

"What is finished?"

"You and I are finished. Your brother and I are finished." The lamp flared and his eyes flared with the leap of the flame. "Already the people blame not only Nathaniel King and Corinth, now gone from us forever, for setting the example that caused others to stumble. They point the finger at you. They point the finger at Levi. I am the bishop of the church and they accuse my children of dragging others into sin." He turned his back on her and began to pace the bedroom. "Even Abraham Yoder confesses he harbors bitterness in his heart. He feels young Joshua would still be on the farm but for his letters back and forth with Levi."

"Oh, Papa, that's not fair. Joshua was caught up in the affair between the South and the North from the beginning. Always scanning the papers. Debating with others. He even read the Confederate constitution."

"It doesn't matter what he did beforehand. It was all a young man's talk. But Levi convinced him to take up the bayonet."

"No—"

"Abraham showed me the letters from Levi that Joshua left behind in his room."

Her father paused to look out the window at the street. "So I ask you to return with me. Confess your sin. Repent. Then there will be no shunning or excommunication. You can write your brother and young Joshua, write Nathaniel, one final time and implore them to turn from violence and the gun to a life of peace and prayer. The church will look favorably on your act of contrition."

Lyndel clenched her fists. "But I am not contrite. I have not sinned."

He stared at her. "Of course you have sinned. The Amish beat their swords into plowshares centuries ago. You are Amish. You took those vows of peace when you were baptized. Now you have broken them."

"I have never lifted a weapon, Father."

"You have aided hundreds who do. Men you have nursed have returned to the fields of war to kill other men."

"I have not broken Amish laws. I have not broken God's laws. He commands me to love my neighbor as myself. That is what I do on the battlefield. So do others. We do not kill, Father. It's life we wish to restore to the young men. Suppose it was Levi lying wounded in the mud? Would you rather people stood by and did nothing for him? That they let him die because they didn't wish to soil their hands in warfare?"

"There are others who can do this work, daughter. It is not for us. We are called to be Amish. That is our ministry to America and to the world. It is for us to *live out* the Sermon on the Mount, not discuss it as they do at Harvard and Yale. We must exemplify forgiveness and mercy. In our bodies we must live like Jesus Christ, who gave his life for others."

"I *am* giving my life for others. So is Levi. So is Joshua. So is Nathaniel. So did Corinth."

"Always you will use slavery as an excuse."

"An excuse?" Lyndel's eyes widened. "I saw Charlie Preston, Father. Before I ran to you for help I tried to lift his body and take the pressure of the rope off his neck. I thought he might still be alive." Tears cut across her face. "I saw the wounds on his back. Do you think I didn't notice how they had whipped him to the bone? Do you think covering him with Nathaniel's shirt meant I would forget what I had seen?"

"I am sorry, my child—"

"How many men like Charlie have been murdered since this nation began? How many have been scourged like Jesus and worked to death? Do you feel ashamed at their blood? Do you cry out for their broken bodies like you do for the broken bodies at Antietam Creek and Manassas Junction?"

Her father extended his hands and came toward her. "Lyndy."

She stepped away from him. "I do not want anyone's blood shed. But it may be that blood for blood is what it will take to make this nation whole again. I do not wish it, but I cannot say what is required. I only know I'm called to be Amish and a follower of Jesus and because of that, I'm obliged to be on the battleground binding up wounds. Just as Levi and Nathaniel feel obliged to bear arms to put an end to wickedness. Yes, Father, in the same manner in which Jesus shall come a second time to right wrongs and establish justice on the earth, mounted on a charger, sweeping away evil with the sword."

Bishop Keim dropped his arms to his side. "How you have changed." He went to the doorway. "I'm going to get my case. I did not travel with very much and I am ready to leave. If you wish to join me, we can walk to the station together."

"You know I can't, Father. I am…where I believe God wants me to be."

"You understand it will be impossible to receive any more letters from you, although we have thanked the Lord for them?"

"*Ja.*"

"That there will be no more parcels from your mother with the wild ginger?"

"I'm sorry to hear that. The plants help us to cure the wounded."

He lifted his hands. "From the moment my train leaves Washington you are cut off from us. You and your brother and the others. There is nothing I can do. And you have made it clear there is nothing more I can say."

"The priest went on his way. And the Levite. But the Samaritan stopped and had compassion."

Her father's face filled with blood. "Do not quote the Scriptures to me."

She stood in the hall as he picked up his case from his room, along with a heavy coat he threw over his shoulders, and began to walk down the staircase.

"I love you, Papa," she said quietly.

It looked as if he was going to carry on without stopping but at the foot of the stairs he hesitated and glanced up. "I love you as well, my daughter. May Christ be with you."

The front door opened and shut. She went to her window and looked out. His tall slender figure moved along the street, one hand gripping his case, a wind stirring dark autumn leaves, a fine mist softening the night and blurring the glass of the windowpane. He vanished in the shadows but she remained at the window a long time, finally leaning her head against it, unwilling to sit down or take to her bed. She prayed, she slept for a few minutes, she woke, she prayed again, her head still resting on the windowpane. Then she heard the train's whistle crying over the city and the war and taking her father back to a world of crops and harvest and draft horses and hymns. She went to the chair he had been sitting in when she entered the room and remained there throughout the night.

Lyndel didn't see Nathaniel again for more than a month. A quick visit to Armory Square gave evidence of the great need for nurses to tend the wounded brought in from Antietam Creek, so she went to work. One day became two and three and then thirty. She slept four or five hours a night and returned to the hospital each morning well before dawn.

Letters arrived from Nathaniel imploring her to return to the regiment and she sent back hastily written messages expressing her love and promising she would rejoin the ambulance corps and surgeons' wagons as soon as she could. She didn't tell him she had no intention of making her way back to the Army of the Potomac until there was a reason for her to be with the troops other than to hold Nathaniel in her arms. It was crucial that she work. The visit with her father had filled her with a darkness that could only be kept at bay by saving as many wounded as possible.

There was a bright moment when she discovered Nip in one of her wards. He had been shunted from field hospital to field hospital and had never been strong enough to pen a note or get word to his platoon. An infection had almost ended his life but further removal of shell fragments and constant cleansing of his wound, followed by quiet recovery at Armory Square, had him ready to return to his regiment by late November.

"You tell the boys how much I miss them," she instructed Nip the morning he headed out.

"Anyone special?" he teased.

"I'm sure you're bright enough to figure that out. If you have the courage you can give him one of these." And then she kissed him on the forehead.

He smiled his small smile. "I might summon up the courage, Miss Keim. But I'm not sure that Nathaniel won't belt me, even if I say the kiss is from you."

"Not Nathaniel. Remember, at heart, he's an Amish boy, even after all this."

"Even so, I've pulled out of this last scrape by the skin of my teeth. I don't want to push my luck or God's favor."

Morganne sent a telegram the second week of December warning her that the army seemed to be preparing for an assault. Lyndel repacked her case and took a train as far forward as she could and then talked her way onto an ambulance drawn by four black horses. She arrived just as the army crossed the Rappahannock River on pontoon bridges and began to occupy Fredericksburg.

Stunned, she watched as Union troops ransacked the town, smashing windows, stealing clothing and furniture, and setting buildings on fire. The town hadn't surrendered, she was told, and this was its punishment. She made her way, with a military escort, to Nathaniel's platoon, an anger gathering inside her as she stepped through streets full of broken glass, bayoneted couches, and scorched rugs. The Iron Brigade was not committing any of the depredations—in fact Nathaniel and other sergeants and officers were trying to quell the looters, but all Lyndel could think of was what her father would say about armies and wars and the sin the troops were committing.

"How can we tell the world we're fighting for a better America when we're treating fellow Americans like this?" she blurted out in her anger.

"Can't you see I am trying to stop it?" he said in defense. "I don't like it any better than you do!"

She stormed away with her military escort and eventually found where Morganne and Hiram and the medical units were located. They were a half-mile from Fredericksburg on the other side of the

Rappahannock at a place called Stafford Heights. She agonized all night that Nathaniel could be killed in the morning's attack and they had parted in the middle of an argument.

Led by General Burnside now, not McClellan, Union forces crossed a canal on three narrow bridges the next day once the fog had burned off and attacked a high ridge known as Marye's Heights. After the first assault was thrown back by entrenched Rebel forces Lyndel was too busy with casualties that came to them to fret over Nathaniel and the rough words she had hurled at him.

Smoke billowed over Fredericksburg as if the fog had settled back down over houses and churches again. Gunfire rolled and roared from the ridge, where the slopes were increasingly covered in the blue uniforms of the wounded. After the fourth assault was repulsed Morganne told her they were asking for nurses in Fredericksburg and just below Marye's Heights.

"Clara is already in the town," she said. "Hiram is over by Marye's Heights and sent me a note. He said the wounded are in desperate straits."

"Then we should go," Lyndel replied. "Our surgeons here can get plenty of help from others."

"We'll have to cross the Rappahannock into Fredericksburg and then cross the canal to the battleground."

Lyndel's eyes became steel-gray. "If Lee wants to shoot us he can shoot us."

Slipping across the Rappahannock on the pontoon bridges the Union army had placed, they hurried through town. Wounded were being carried by stretcher bearers into houses and buildings. After a short prayer the two began to approach one of the slender bridges over the canal. Hundreds of decks of playing cards were scattered on the ground in front of them.

"What's this?" Lyndel was looking down at a queen of hearts.

"The devil's instruments," said Morganne. "No soldier would wish to risk facing his Maker with those in his pocket."

They began to cross even as shells crashed into the water and balls sent up splashes all around them. Before their very eyes, soldiers in front of and behind them were killed and toppled into the canal.

Shocked and angry, Lyndel's eyes lit as if by a white phosphorus match. She stopped in the middle of the bridge and stared defiantly up at the gray troops she could see crouched behind a stone wall on the heights.

"What are you doing?" demanded Morganne. "Keep moving!"

"Let us see what sort of men war has turned these Southerners into!" Lyndel snapped. "Let us find out if they will stoop to firing on unarmed women!"

She and Morganne stood still for a full minute while the battle shattered the sky above them. Gradually the splashes from bullets became less and less until they ceased.

"Are the Confederates firing on us?" asked Morganne, looking upward anxiously.

Lyndel shielded her eyes with her hand and peered through a haze of black powder smoke and sunlight. "No. I thank God."

They finished crossing the canal. Hiram rushed up to them from a spot where a number of war correspondents were hugging the ground.

"What are you two doing here? Have you lost your minds? Burnside will be sending up a fifth assault any minute."

A bullet plucked his derby from his head and the three of them crouched low.

"You told us the wounded needed help," Morganne reminded him.

"Yes, yes, but to come here when the air is thick with lead—"

Lyndel seized Hiram's hand. "Tell me what's happening with Nathaniel and his men."

"They haven't been engaged. Except for the 24th Michigan, who put up a stiff fight, the Iron Brigade hasn't been used at all."

"I thank God. But why have they been spared?"

"Ask Burnside. And while you're at it, ask him why he didn't send troops upstream and downstream and come at the Rebels from the sides and back as well as the front. All he's doing is slaughtering our young men."

"Where are the wounded being assembled?"

Hiram pointed, his hatless red hair blowing about in a sudden breeze. "See the field hospital over there by the water? Then the stretcher bearers get them across the canal into Fredericksburg or all the way across the Rappahannock back to Stafford Heights."

"Do you think you'll see Nathaniel and Levi?"

"I don't know."

"If you do, please tell Nathaniel how much I love him. And tell them both—and Joshua—that I'm praying for them."

Hiram nodded. "All right."

"Lyndel." Morganne's pale blue eyes were locked onto her friend. "They need us."

"Then let's go to them."

Morganne kissed Hiram quickly on the cheek. "I'll be fine."

"I'm going back across the canal to send a telegram. Then I'll join you and try to help out." Hiram held her hand a moment. "I don't believe a Rebel sniper would target you intentionally. But there are ricochets. And cannon fire is just as indiscriminate. You shouldn't be here."

She smiled and touched her lips gently to his. "Yes. I should."

The two nurses crouched and ran to where surgeons were working on the most severe injuries. They began to clean and dress the wounds of those who were to be carried back across the canal into Fredericksburg.

Soon their hands and faces were streaked with blood. At one point, as Morganne rose to get water from the canal, a bullet passed through the hem of her dress, tugging so sharply she thought she had been snagged by a thorn. An hour later, as another attack was being launched against Marye's Heights and the stone wall, a ball laid open Lyndel's cheek and knocked her to the ground. Blood trickled down her face and smeared her neck.

"You must get back into Fredericksburg," a surgeon commanded when she came for bandages. "We can't care for you. There are too many who have been shot."

"I'm not here for your help," she replied. "Only to get supplies for the wounded."

"You can't work like that."

"Yes, I can. The blood will clot soon enough."

"Miss Keim. I could order you."

She stared at the doctor. "You could, sir. But I can't hear you very well. The musket fire is deafening."

The assaults ended with the quick coming of the December night. Morganne found Union coats full of bullet holes that had been thrown to one side and the two women wore them as they nursed in the cold dark until three or four in the morning. There were no more attacks the next day, December 14th, but the cries of the wounded that had pained Lyndel all night continued into the morning. Splashing icy water on her face she went back to cleaning and binding wounds and examining tourniquets she had fastened earlier.

Early in the afternoon she and Morganne watched in silence while a Rebel sergeant crisscrossed the ground in front of the stone wall, canteens dangling from his body, eventually giving hundreds of injured Union soldiers water. No Northern soldier targeted him. Both armies faced each other, guns leveled, a few hundred yards separating them, as his gray form moved from one blue-uniformed soldier to another. It went on for hours as he handed out blankets and coats as well. Then Burnside asked for a truce so that he could bring the wounded down from Marye's Heights. Lee granted the truce and the nurses joined the stretcher bearers as they climbed the slopes to reach the thousands of Union casualties. The two nurses treated as many as they could before the men were carried off the ridge.

Lyndel briefly came near a Rebel sergeant who was standing by the wall watching her. She knew who he must be from all the canteens still slung from his body. Approaching him she extended her hand. Surprised, he took it and held it a few seconds and then removed his hat.

"May I have the pleasure of your name, sir?" she asked.

"Kirkland, ma'am. Richard Kirkland. From Flat Rock in South Carolina. Kershaw County."

"Sergeant Kirkland, I am Miss Lyndel Keim from Elizabethtown, Lancaster County, in Pennsylvania. God bless you for what you have done today. The water you brought to the wounded saved scores of lives."

He looked away. "I had to do it."

"But they are your enemy."

His eyes returned to her. "We're in a fight all right. But I don't think of them as such."

"Nor do I think of you as such. Thank you again, Richard Kirkland. I will remember you. I will pray for you. You are a man close to God's heart."

He smiled. "I am grateful for your words, Miss."

Lyndel returned to bandaging the wounded and stanching blood flow with tourniquets. Soon Hiram was working alongside Morganne, his good Philadelphia suit and shirt stained with blood and dirt. Lyndel asked about the 19th Indiana. They were stationed on the army's left flank, he told her. No, he hadn't seen Nathaniel or Levi but the regiment had never seen action. If Burnside decided to renew the assaults that would probably change.

They worked into the night. Lyndel found the constant activity prevented the winter cold from getting into her bones. A sudden display of the aurora borealis sent white whirls and silver streaks across the sky. She often paused to look up at them as they twisted and turned and shone onto the battlefield.

"I'd say it's likely most of those Southern boys have never seen them," Hiram told her and Morganne. "Even this is pretty far south for a display. They'll probably think it's a sign from heaven to honor their victory."

Lyndel wiped loose hair from her eyes as she stared at the loops and spirals of white against black. "We call them Northern Lights in Pennsylvania. They could just as easily be taken as a sign by the Union not to despair, that in the end Northern forces will overcome." She glanced at Hiram. "Do you think this fight is over?"

"I do. We may be in for another string of defeats just like it was before Antietam."

"What makes you say that?"

"Burnside will be sent packing for the high number of casualties here. I expect Hooker is next in line and I have no more confidence in him than I do in Burnside."

"I thought we might have turned the corner at Antietam Creek."

Hiram bent to wipe his hands on the grass. "With victories at Perryville, Kentucky, and out west in Corinth, Mississippi, I thought so too. But I'm afraid this is looking like the familiar pattern reasserting itself."

Morganne had her hands on her hips. "You might be wrong, Hiram."

"Wrong?" He straightened. "Well, in the vagaries and vicissitudes of war and life things sometimes come full circle. One day it might be us dug in on the heights and entrenched behind the stone wall. Then we'll see if Robert E. Lee fares any better than we did today."

The next morning Union troops began withdrawing across the canal and the Rappahannock. In the marching and the turmoil Lyndel glimpsed the black hats of the Iron Brigade but couldn't spot Nathaniel or her brother. She and Morganne remained at Marye's Heights and Fredericksburg for several more weeks, caring for the wounded men before they were sent on to hospitals in Washington and elsewhere. Hiram disappeared to file his story for his paper and then returned.

The days were cold and harsh. Two letters came from Nathaniel that she devoured, sitting in the kitchen of an abandoned house in Fredericksburg. When she picked up a pencil in her gloved hands to write a short reply she found she couldn't focus on the characters of the alphabet; they kept blurring or shifting positions.

Getting up to make herself a cup of tea and set things to rights she felt dizzy, and she steadied herself on the back of the chair. She took a careful step, and then as she made ready for another, the dizziness enveloped her completely and she collapsed, knocking over the heavy wooden chair that had been her support.

Morganne, washing up in the next room, came running and found Lyndel unconscious on the floor. She flew down the street for one of the surgeons, who quickly saw Lyndel had developed pneumonia in one of her lungs and that it was likely to spread to her second lung in her weakened condition.

"She's worn herself thin," the physician scolded. "You both have. Not enough sleep. Few proper meals."

"The wounded always come first for us, Doctor," replied Morganne. "You can't budge us on that."

"Miss Keim will need to go somewhere clean and quiet in order to recuperate, and soon, or we will lose her."

"Hiram Wright can get her to Washington by wagon and rail. We have a residence there. The Palmer family will take her in."

"Are you certain of that? She will require care if she is to recover."

Morganne's eyes were dark. "I'm sure the Palmers will take her in. Just as I am sure she will get the care she needs."

The doctor folded up his stethoscope. "Whatever arrangements you can make, do them now. If she is to survive, Miss Keim must be transported to Washington immediately."

17

Nathaniel pulled open the wooden door of the small log cabin the men in the brigade had built for their winter camp in Virginia. Levi had removed a section of the roof for the daylight hours and sun poured into the normally dark enclosure. He looked up at Nathaniel from a Bible he was reading as he sat on an overturned cracker box. Joshua was on the edge of his cot with a newspaper spread over his knees.

"Any mail?" Joshua asked without glancing up from the paper.

"Not for us," Nathaniel replied. "At least, not from home. Miss David sends me a note saying Lyndel rallies some days but does poorly on others."

Levi's face was in a shadow. "We ought to pray together for her."

"*Ja.*"

Joshua, with his eyes still on the newspaper said, "When Fighting Joe Hooker took over command of the army from Burnside he said he'd take care of his men. And he has. The whole brigade is loaded down with parcels from home he's ordered through the lines at the pace of a lightning bolt. Ham got a bunch of summer preserves from Indiana just yesterday and not one jar was broken."

Levi answered, "Hooker didn't reckon on the intractability of the Pennsylvania Amish. When they sent those goodbye letters in October they meant them. Lyndel told me they even stopped sending packages of medicine and bandages."

Nathaniel sat on his bed. "That's true. She still mails them letters but who knows if anyone reads them? Before she took ill she sent them a note saying everyone was alive, that none of us had been injured at Fredericksburg."

"If they read the casualty lists in the paper they'll know that," said Joshua.

"So would your father read such lists?" asked Nathaniel.

"No."

Nathaniel nodded. "Most won't. Perhaps Bishop Keim makes a habit of it so he knows how to pray. Well, boys, the fact is, we can't stay gloomy all winter because others get food parcels and we don't. I went to the sutler and purchased a few items." He dug into the deep pockets of his frock coat and pulled out four red apples. "One for each of us. At least they're hard as rock." He tossed them to his friends and reached into another pocket and pulled out a glass jar of peaches. "Use your spoons to scoop up a few mouthfuls. No need to save it. Eat the peaches up now before one of us gets dysentery like Jones or Groom and can't enjoy them."

He handed Joshua the jar first. Joshua swooped under his cot and pulled out his mess kit. Then he unscrewed the lid and spooned about a fourth of it onto his tin plate before passing the jar on to Levi. Nathaniel got what was left. He tipped the jar back to let the peach slices and juice slide into his mouth.

"My, my, that was good," Joshua said as he bit into his apple. "Thank you, Brother King. I don't suppose the sutler sold them at a bargain price?"

"He always says he has a family to support and that their house has twice been shelled by Rebel artillery."

Joshua snorted. "Some boy likely put a stone through his window with a slingshot. But his wares are worth it. Amish that have been orphaned need to find good food wherever they can get it. My treat next time."

Levi finished his apple. "I don't wish to disrupt the festive occasion, but have you heard any more news about the…execution? Have they changed their minds?"

The cabin grew silent. Nathaniel shook his head.

"And Nip?"

Nathaniel blew air out of his mouth. "He has to be part of the firing squad. There are fifteen of them from the regiment."

"Did you speak with him?"

"No. Captain Hanson had taken him aside."

"Execution. Such a hard sentence for a young man who was afraid." Levi looked up at the scrap of blue sky and then at his companions. "Can we have that time of prayer now?"

They slowly nodded. All three knelt by their beds. Levi began to pray out loud in German. He began by asking mercy for the soul of the boy of seventeen who was going to be shot. Then he moved on to those who were ill in the brigade's winter camp, especially those from their platoon and company. After that he asked that his sister's life be spared. Joshua followed him, then finally Nathaniel. There was no time for the *amen*. A muffled and grim drumroll interrupted their thoughts and worship.

Joshua's face was white. "The boy and I—*Wir sind im gleichen Alter*. We are the same age."

The February afternoon remained bright and cool with pale clouds to the east. The 19th Indiana formed companies and stood rigidly at attention. The soldier was brought forward to stand in front of an embankment. Solomon Meredith, who commanded the Iron Brigade now after Gibbon's promotion and appointment to another unit, sat on his horse staring straight ahead while the charges were read. Mounted next to him was the 19th's new colonel, Samuel Williams. A captain barked an order and the firing squad marched forward.

The platoon spotted Nip right away, the shortest man in the group. There had been much rejoicing in the company when he had reappeared in their midst just before the Battle of Fredericksburg. Ham had promptly dubbed him Lazarus. Now Nathaniel felt the muscles of his stomach tighten for both Nip and the deserter. If only Meredith or Williams would rescind the decision and spare the two young men the agony of the moment. But the blindfold was tied over the deserter's eyes and the fifteen muskets were raised as the commands were snapped out. The youth stood alone, swaying a bit in the cold breeze off the nearby Potomac, as if he were a thin sapling. Then the guns cracked and he fell.

When the regiment was dismissed Nathaniel watched as Joshua made for Nip and put an arm around his shoulder. Nip did not shrug it off. *God have mercy,* he prayed, thinking of Nip and the boy whose body was sprawled on the hard earth next to a wooden coffin, *Christ have mercy, Christus erbarme dich.* He began to walk back to his winter cabin on a makeshift street lined with scores of similar cabins.

I did not reckon on firing squads, Lord, when I prayed about bearing arms to put an end to slavery.

"Sergeant King." It was Captain Hanson.

"Sir."

"What word do you have on our regimental nurses?"

Nathaniel was at attention. "Miss David is at Armory Square Hospital until the army commences its spring offensives. Miss Keim is still recovering at a private residence."

"Stand easy. We're not on the parade ground here." Hanson handed Nathaniel a slip of paper. "Here's something that's better than money. Or a jar of summer peaches."

Nathaniel glanced at the note. It was a three-day pass to Washington. His eyes returned to Hanson in surprise. "What is this about?"

Hanson smoothed the sides of his mustache. "What does it look like it's about? We want you to get our girl back on her feet before the regiment moves out in April. Surely you can make a difference to her if anyone can. It's Tuesday. I have no desire to see you back here until Saturday. Is that understood?"

"I believe it is."

"Once you return you can think about the sermon you'll be preaching to the Hoosiers on Sunday."

"Sermon?"

"You know the trouble we've been having with our chaplains. We never seem to have one around when we need a good stiff morning of preaching. You're from a religious family. You'll fit the bill. Miss David has even agreed to come down and play a hymn for the boys on her guitar."

"I have no idea what to preach about. I've never done a sermon."

Hanson fixed him with a sharp gaze. "The regiment is much like the rest of the brigade and the Army of the Potomac when it comes to the Emancipation Proclamation—they didn't sign up to fight for the darkies; they say they signed up to fight for their country. I'd like you to work on softening their opinion of the Africans. While you're at it, bring the Father, Son, and Holy Ghost into it. You've told me several times why you enlisted and exactly what the slave hunters did in your farming community in Pennsylvania. Now tell the lads. Then bless 'em."

Hanson clapped a hand to Nathaniel's shoulder. "There's a steamer at the landing taking on sick for hospitals in Washington. Two men from your platoon are already on it, Jones and Groom. It'll be heading up the Potomac in an hour. Get whatever gear you think you need and be on it. Mind you get that woman up and about again. Two months will go by like a racehorse and we'll be on the march and looking for a fight with Stonewall and Lee."

It was not a long trip. Nathaniel chatted with Jones and Groom and afterward stood by the bow of the steamboat and let the edge of the February air fall sharp on his face.

At the dock he made his way off the vessel and struck out for the Palmer house, where Lyndel and Morganne boarded. He was welcomed warmly, a cup of coffee was pushed into his hand, and then he was led to the sick room, where Lyndel slept. A nurse from Armory Square who had been caring for her got up from her chair and left him alone. He stood over the bed and lightly touched her hand but she didn't stir.

I didn't think you would be so pale. Or so quiet. I thought I might finally get to see your scarlet hair in all its glory but they've tucked it up under a white cap. Where is your prayer covering? And what is this scar on your cheek?

The fire was almost out in the hearth. Nathaniel peeled off his coat and pack and hung them from the back of the chair the nurse had been sitting in. Bending down he added several small logs to the dying flames and blew on them until the wood ignited. He returned to the bed, kissed Lyndel on a forehead that felt colder than the winter air, glanced at the edge of a mustard plaster he could see at the collar of her flannel nightgown, then turned and sat down in the chair. Pulling a thick black Bible from his pack he flipped through its pages, found the passage he wanted, and read a few verses in English followed by several in German. After several minutes of his voice Lyndel's eyes opened. They were a blue, he thought, as brilliant as the February sky.

"What is that you have been reading?" she asked.

"Psalm 119. It's very long."

"May I have a drink of water?"

There was a tall glass and a pitcher on a table behind him. He got up, poured her a glass, and took it to the bed. Placing one arm under her shoulders and head he lifted her so that she could drink properly. When she'd had enough he carefully placed her head back on the pillow. Her eyes followed him.

"What day is it?"

He smiled down at her. "A Tuesday. February 10th."

"What year?"

"It's 1863."

"They told me it was still 1862."

"A little over a month ago they might have said that."

She frowned and her face took on a bit of color. "No. They told me that yesterday."

"Well, today it's 1863."

Lyndel stared at the ceiling. "Am I not better yet?"

"Not quite."

"I was told the pneumonia hadn't spread to the other lung."

"That's my understanding also."

He took her hand. She looked at him and tugged it away.

"You're being quite free."

Startled, he didn't know how to reply. "I apologize."

"I like your voice, however. Perhaps you could read a while longer. How about the Gospel of Matthew?"

He sat back in the chair, found Matthew, and began to read out loud again. Once he reached the Sermon on the Mount she stopped him. "What is your opinion of turning the other cheek? Is it something that is practicable?"

"Christ practiced it."

"Sometimes. Not so much when he cleansed the temple. Or when you come to Matthew chapter 23 and he calls the religious leaders sons of hell and a brood of vipers."

"Still he didn't harm anyone or kill anyone."

"No. He was not a man of violence." She stared at him, the blue in her eyes brightening. "Is turning the other cheek something that can be practiced in war?"

Nathaniel closed the Bible on his thumb. "It would be difficult on the large scale but possible between one man and another."

"Explain yourself."

"I mean it would be hard to practice on a battlefield but easier between one soldier and another."

Her eyes roamed back to the ceiling. "Yet I've seen it done on the battleground. A sergeant of the Confederacy took his life in his hands to walk out plainly among the Union wounded and offer them water. No guns were fired at him. Nor did he consider the wounded soldiers his enemy."

"*Ja.* I've heard about that."

"Then there are the pickets from both sides who exchange food and pleasantries. Some have even crossed the river and sat by each other's campfires."

He nodded. "They can get in trouble from their commanding officers but a good number do it just the same."

"I see by your clothing you are a soldier."

"I am, ma'am."

"Addressing me as Miss will do. And where are you stationed at the present?"

"Belle Plain. Just over the border in Virginia. On the banks of the Potomac River."

"Some church folk think you can't follow Christ and fight in this war. How would you respond to such an assertion?"

"For two years I have tried to do it, Miss."

"Have you succeeded?"

"I don't know."

"But God knows. Though you would hardly call all the fury and killing of battle turning the other cheek, Sergeant."

"No. Yet I have not hated. I have not rejoiced in the flow of another man's blood." He leaned back in the chair. "Sometimes in the fight I do feel, even there, I'm trying to turn the other cheek. It's hard to put into words. I'm sure a religious person who was against war would say my thoughts on the matter made no sense. Especially while I was squeezing the trigger."

Her eyes were upon him again. "How strangely you talk. I could let you ramble on all day but I'm growing tired again." Her eyes closed. "How odd that I could be so intimate with a total stranger."

She was suddenly as deeply asleep as she had been when he first entered the room. As the heat from the fire continued to fill the small space he settled back and closed his own eyes and also slept. There was the sound of their breathing and the sound of the flames and that was all.

18

I have seen Him in the watchfires of a hundred circling camps,
They have builded Him an altar in the evening dews and damps;
I can read His righteous sentence by the dim and flaring lamps;
His day is marching on.

I have read a fiery gospel writ in burnished rows of steel:
"As ye deal with my contemners, so with you my grace shall deal;
Let the Hero, born of woman, crush the serpent with his heel,
Since God is marching on."

Glory, glory, hallelujah!
Glory, glory, hallelujah!
Glory, glory, hallelujah!
Since God is marching on.

Morganne David stood in a navy-blue dress and bonnet in the cold February light and strummed her Martin guitar. Colonel Williams and a number of officers stood on either side of her. It astonished Nathaniel that she sang in such a clear strong voice, totally unlike her speaking voice, and that she didn't lose the tune or miss any words or fail to rouse the 19th Indiana to bawling out the song at the top of their lungs. The troops hurled the words to the blue heavens with even more power than they did on the march with songs like "John Brown's Body" and "Battle Cry of Freedom." The band, at a nod from Morganne, came in on the last verse and chorus, and the din from the band and the men's throats and lungs caused the officer's horses to toss their heads and skitter sideways. The quiet following the singing was like the sudden quiet after a massive explosion or the end of a battle.

It was now time for Nathaniel to speak. He felt as if he were going into a sharp fight with his platoon, only this time he was on his own and his men weren't behind him. The Amish boys had promised to pray for him, of course, and so had several others in the company, but when he first walked up from the ranks and faced the regiment his mind and body felt cold and he didn't know how to begin. Captain Hanson was nearby. As Nathaniel continued to hesitate Hanson hissed: "Tell them who you are."

"Good morning, men," said Nathaniel finally. "It's a fine Lord's Day and I am Sergeant Nathaniel King."

"*Louder!*" came Hanson's hiss a second time.

Startled, Nathaniel shouted in his battle command voice: "I ENLISTED IN ELKHART COUNTY!"

The troops, who had been standing at ease, jumped. Then they began to cheer and applaud, a huge roar rolling over the encampment that caused the other regiments of the Iron Brigade to look up from their own Sunday worship services or chores and wonder what had got into the Indiana boys this time.

"I guess I was raised in Pennsylvania but adopted by Indiana in time to fight for our country!"

More cheering and hurrahs.

"I've been with you since Lewinsville and Brawner's Farm and South Mountain! South Mountain is where they gave us and the Wisconsin boys, the Badgers, the name Iron Brigade!"

The men roared again and many of the Wisconsin troops, listening in on all the commotion, roared with them.

"At Fredericksburg the Michigan troops won their black hats by their courage and now the Wolverines are part of the brigade too!"

A shout went up from the 24th Michigan camp.

"Easy, lad," whispered Hanson. "It's a church service. Not the Battle of Antietam."

Dozens of soldiers from the Wisconsin and Michigan regiments were converging on the Indiana parade ground. Nathaniel scarcely noticed them. Suddenly the words he wanted now began to come to him quickly and easily.

"I won't keep you long, men. You can look forward to this evening, when General Meredith has promised a brigade bonfire where Miss Morganne David will lead us in singing our great old songs and General Hooker has offered us some roast ox."

More clapping and cheering.

"But I have a message I would like to bring to you. Something I believe God has laid out clearly in his Word to inspire us. In the first book of the Bible—Genesis—we're told that man is made in the image of God. *All* men. None are excluded. Then in Acts chapter 17 and verses 25 and 26 this same idea is carried forward, where it is written that God *giveth to all life, and breath, and all things; and hath made of one blood all nations of men for to dwell on all the face of the earth.* All the human race is one, regardless of the color of our skin, and that is the way God has made it and wants it."

Silence descended over the crowd of troops standing on the frozen field.

Nathaniel heard it and understood it but plunged on. "Some of you are wondering about the Emancipation Proclamation. If you were a slave, would you want to carry on being a slave or be free? Some of you are wondering about slaves enlisting and fighting the ones who enslaved them. If an African soldier was fighting with his regiment and stopped a Rebel attack on your position and saved your life, would that be a good thing or a bad thing?"

Interspersed among the quiet troops Nathaniel heard murmuring.

"If I were a slave and had a chance to be free, to live in my own house and raise my own family without the threat of being whipped or chained or sold off like cattle, I would do it, wouldn't you? If I had a chance to fight for my freedom, if I had an opportunity to bear arms to keep myself from being enslaved again, I would pick up my musket and fight for my life and my family. Wouldn't you?"

Again the murmurs, but now Nathaniel felt the silence had changed

THE FACE OF HEAVEN ⌐ 195

from one of resistance to one charged with force and emotion, ready to erupt.

"I'm fighting for a free country—aren't you? I'm fighting for freedom for everyone in our country—aren't you? I'm not just bearing arms to keep Indiana and Wisconsin and Michigan at liberty. I'm bearing arms so that the whole country can be at liberty and everyone in South Carolina and Mississippi and Alabama can be at liberty. I'm fighting so that our nation can be one again and free again under God. Under *God*!"

Now the men exploded. Black hats were thrown in the air and hands raised and the brigade roared like a burst of summer thunder. Voices shouted *Amen* and *Preach it, son*, and at the back of the excited troops Nathaniel saw General Meredith seated on his horse, the only two things not moving among the arms and hats and cries of the troops. Meredith's eyes were on him dark and strong.

As the soldiers quieted again—though their quiet was now one of restless energy, of leaves rustling and moving about in the air before a storm—Nathaniel decided to speak the final words that had come to him and finish the message. "All men, yes, and all people, men and women, are made in the image of God. All the men of all the nations of the earth are of one blood. And one man's blood was shed for all people so that all could be saved and draw close to God.

"Before the war began, some slave hunters came to our farm, men. They caught two fellows who had been slaves on their plantation, men who only wished to live free and die free. The hunters scourged one to the bone and *lynched* him. The other they took back to slavery. Even though both men were made in the image of God—and both men were of one blood with all the nations of the earth—and both men had been in Christ's heart and mind when he died for the sins of the world on the Cross.

"I don't know about you but I'm here to fight for the African who is American as well as the German who is American and the Irishman who is American. Let us make the nation God has gifted us with hallowed ground for everyone, North and South, man and woman. Let us be done with chaining a man's body and soul. Don't we remember?

Have we forgotten? 'We hold these truths to be self-evident, that all men are created equal, that they are endowed by their Creator with certain unalienable Rights, that among these are Life, Liberty and the pursuit of Happiness.'"

As the troops shouted and cried out yet again, Morganne gave a quick nod of her head to the bandleader and started in on the last verse of "The Battle Hymn of the Republic":

In the beauty of the lilies Christ was born across the sea,
With a glory in His bosom that transfigures you and me:
As He died to make men holy, let us die to make men free,
While God is marching on.

Glory, glory, hallelujah!
Glory, glory, hallelujah!
Glory, glory, hallelujah!
While God is marching on.

Before the 19th Indiana and various soldiers from the rest of the brigade had finished hollering the chorus three times, Captain Hanson leaned toward Nathaniel's ear. "I don't know if I was just part of an abolitionist rally or a convention to save the Union or a Holy Ghost campfire meeting. But it certainly wasn't an Episcopalian church service like Robert E. Lee is attending in another part of Virginia." He shook Nathaniel's hand. "Well done, Sergeant. God bless ye."

Colonel Williams came up and Hanson and Nathaniel snapped to attention and saluted. He returned the salute and extended his hand to Nathaniel.

"As fine a sermon in a time of war as I've ever heard, Sergeant, with just the right amount of gusto for the men. I truly wish Father Abraham had been present today."

"Thank you, sir," replied Nathaniel, taking the hand.

"Now if you'll step this way, General Meredith's compliments and he would like a word with you."

Nathaniel hesitated. "General Meredith?"

"He's just over here, Sergeant."

Long Sol Meredith remained in his saddle on his battle horse. Nathaniel came to attention and saluted. Meredith returned the salute and eyed him carefully.

"Elkhart County?" Meredith asked.

"Yes, sir. By way of Lancaster County, Pennsylvania."

"Are you of Amish stock, by any chance, Sergeant?"

"Yes, General, I am."

Meredith smiled and laughed quietly. "What will America make of us? I'm a Quaker and you're Amish. Neither of us is supposed to fight."

"That's true, sir. But I couldn't stand by and watch our country turned into a slave nation ruled from Richmond."

"No. Neither could I. Though the Rebels would argue they didn't want to conquer the North. Just be left to themselves in the South."

"Clashes over the acquisition of new territory in the West would have been bound to occur regardless, sir."

"Yes. And one day the Confederacy might have felt it was necessary to move on Washington and be done with it. That would not be to my liking or yours, Sergeant. No slave nation."

"No, sir."

Meredith reached down and patted his horse's neck. "I do not agree with all your sentiments regarding the African race, Sergeant, and I doubt most of the men here do either. But no one can argue with your spirit or your patriotism. Or your Christian faith. I understand you only have one lieutenant in your company?"

Nathaniel nodded. "Lieutenant Nicolson, sir."

"Now you have two. Congratulations. I trust we will see you at the bonfire tonight, Lieutenant?"

Nathaniel saluted as Long Sol Meredith moved his horse away. "I'll be there, sir. Thank you, sir."

Nicolson came over smiling and slapped him on the back. "Another man for the officers' mess."

"I was pretty comfortable in the noncommissioned officers' mess."

"Grass was growing under your feet. Time to move on."

Hanson grunted. "Congratulations, Lieutenant. First time in the United States Army a soldier's been promoted for giving a sermon."

"I do find it a bit bewildering, Captain."

"Now I have to make one of my corporals a sergeant. Ham or Nip. Any thoughts on that, Lieutenant King?"

"No, sir."

"Well, give it some thought."

"Yes, sir."

General Hooker found a number of ailing oxen for his Iron Brigade that night and after Nathaniel had sat down with his platoon and enjoyed the roasted meat he stood off by himself to watch the flames stretch skyward, sparks making stars in the darkness.

Several things were bothering him. The first was his sermon—what had gotten into him? His own father wouldn't have recognized the young man preaching a message that sounded like it came from the mouth of a fiery patriot or a Radical Republican. Or the man with the tune the soldiers loved to march to, John Brown, the abolitionist who had led a raid on Harper's Ferry to get the guns stored in a Federal arsenal.

Truth be told, he didn't sound Amish anymore. He didn't look Amish anymore in his tall black hat and uniform. Next he would be growing a mustache like Captain Hanson and scandalizing his community in Lancaster even more. Amish men never grew mustaches because that is what soldiers did and they were against soldiers.

But the biggest problem, the matter he prayed about the most, was Lyndel's health. He had gotten past the point where he feared she might not live. He thanked God for her recovery. Yet she did not know him. What if the amnesia persisted and she never recognized him again? It might be that they had no future together—none—and he didn't know what to do with that knowledge or even which words to use in his prayers about it.

A hand was laid gently on his shoulder. It was Morganne David.

"There seems to be a great deal on your mind, Lieutenant King."

"Hello, Miss David. I was just…thinking over the Sunday service.

Your music was perfect. My message, I think, was somewhat—overdone."

"If it were peacetime, perhaps. But in a time of civil war? No, you said things that needed to be said and you said them in a way that the soldiers can hear. Didn't I see a number of them coming up tonight and shaking your hand?"

Nathaniel put his hands in his pockets. "Many of them said I had taken them forward a few more steps. That I had given them something to think about, *to chew over thoroughly,* as one corporal from Michigan put it. I wonder what Hiram would have thought?"

She laughed. "Hiram? He would have gone against the grain of your sermon, of course. Let's see—he would have pointed out that thousands of Africans are serving in the Confederate Army, that both slaves and freemen fought against you at Antietam, and that they want nothing to do with an end to slavery in the South or Mr. Lincoln's Emancipation Proclamation."

Nathaniel turned to look at her in the waves of light from the huge fire. "You can't be telling the truth."

"I am. Hiram showed me articles from Southern papers as well as recruitment information. Nathan Bedford Forrest has a good many Africans among his troops. One freeman wrote to a newspaper to say that just as his people had fought for Louisiana at the Battle of New Orleans in 1815 they would fight for their home state in whatever other battles came their way."

"It makes no sense. Why wouldn't they want to be free?"

"Some of the freemen have slaves themselves. And some of the slaves are on good plantations and are taken care of very well—they think they would be worse off and unemployed as freemen in the North. Many are under no illusions about Northern hospitality either. They feel they're not wanted up here, not only because of their race but because they'll take jobs from white laborers."

Nathaniel looked back at the yellow and red flames. "You'd think they'd want freedom regardless of the difficulties that came with it."

"But many people aren't like that. And it's not just slaves who think that way. Plenty of other people are afraid to make changes because what they know may not be good, but it's good enough compared to how risky a new sort of life might be." She patted him lightly on the back. "Nathaniel, I care for Hiram very much, but he is a discourager. He thinks that's the only path afforded him if he wishes to be realistic about life. I, however, like to think of myself as both realistic and an encourager. You said the right things this morning and you pointed us in the right direction. You can be sure many more slaves will seek their freedom rather than stay entrapped on their cotton fields. We see droves of them passing through Washington every week. Hiram told me that this summer Africans will be fighting the Rebels and they will be doing so as Union troops within their own African regiments."

"Well, that's something. It will improve the soldiers' attitudes toward the African race."

"No doubt it will. But we're still talking about many years before North or South accept them as equals."

"How many years?"

"A hundred, Nathaniel. Likely more. Three or four generations. From grandparents to parents to children and then to the children's children."

"I thought you were the encourager."

"I *am* the encourager. Hiram would say two hundred years. Or never."

"And I reckoned I had things on my mind before." Nathaniel rubbed the back of his neck. "Where is Hiram anyway? I haven't seen him at Belle Plain for weeks."

"His paper sent him west. He's campaigning with General Grant."

"Grant? I heard he's a drunkard."

"That's not Hiram's opinion. He thinks Grant is the best fighting general we have, one of the few the South are actually leery of."

"Does he? So you said yourself he always goes against the grain of opinion. Often enough he's right."

"Often enough indeed."

"Did you...see Lyndel before you left?"

"I did. I had to pick up some items from my room. She asked after you."

Nathaniel stared at Morganne. "Asked after me? She doesn't even know me anymore."

"Of course she knows you. She just knows you—and likes you, by the way—as another person."

"Oh, that's all. So what am I supposed to do? Court her all over again as another person?"

"No. As yourself. She doesn't know who you are anyway so you might as well be yourself." She smiled. "Except that now you are an officer and a gentleman."

Nathaniel's eyes were black and troubled. The firelight, instead of illuminating his eyes, actually moved the shadows back and forth and obscured them. "Do you think she'll ever recover her memory, Morganne?"

Morganne's face went in and out of the light. "The doctors don't know. I pray for her every day but I don't know."

"Miss David!"

A cluster of women were calling to her. Nathaniel saw they were the wives of officers who had come down that afternoon. They would stay with their husbands in well-built log cabins until campaigning began again.

"Miss David! The men are impatient for their campfire sing-along!"

"I'm coming!" she called back.

She looked at Nathaniel and squeezed his arm. "Cheer up. From what the nurses tell me, no one gets her so animated as you."

"How would they know? They always leave me alone with her."

"They listen at the door, Nathaniel." She began to walk toward the officers' wives. After a few steps she paused and turned. "Get leave to go to her again as swiftly as possible. She may not know you but it's your love for her she's responding to. If you can book passage on a steamer tomorrow morning, do it."

19

Lyndel drifted in and out of consciousness. She heard bits and pieces of conversation, glimpsed a white-lace curtain hanging over a window, took cool water into her mouth, listened to the strings of a guitar being strummed softly. She was certain she saw Mrs. Palmer's face and Morganne's and Miss Sharon's, as stern as the prow of a naval frigate. A quiet voice, a man's voice, read the Bible over and over. Sometimes he seemed to be close to her ear, other times on the far side of the room. Each time he read there was the snap of logs burning.

> *He that dwelleth in the secret place of the most High*
> *Shall abide under the shadow of the Almighty.*
> *I will say of the Lord, He is my refuge and my fortress:*
> *My God; in him will I trust.*

"Why am I not at Fredericksburg?"

Lyndel sat straight up in bed and stared at the red flames in the fireplace and at Nathaniel, who was sitting in a chair in his frock coat and a scarf, his black hat on the floor by his feet. A thick black Bible was open in his lap. He closed it and set it down by his hat. Then walked to the bed and kissed her on the cheek.

"Good morning, beauty," he said.

She took his hand. "What am I doing here? What are you doing here?"

Nathaniel was startled, stopping his movements for a moment. "Why…do you know who I am?"

"For heaven's sakes, don't play games. Of course I know who you are, Nathaniel King. Did you think I had mistaken you for the man in the moon?"

Nathaniel grinned. Then he laughed and kissed her hands. "This is wonderful, wonderful! You know who I am! Glory to God in the highest!"

Lyndel's eyebrows slashed down. "What is the matter with you? You're carrying on as if this is some sort of backwoods revival meeting. Stop playing the fool. Put an end to this glory-hallelujahing right now and tell me why I'm here."

Nathaniel struggled to calm himself for her benefit. He sat on the edge of the bed, his face still brilliant with joy and astonishment. "You've been fighting pneumonia, my love. For a while, it had even affected your memory. But you're looking very well today. If a little pale for an Amish farm girl." He laughed again and shook his head despite her fierce eyes. "I can't believe it. I thank God you're back."

"I should be at Fredericksburg. The cold ground will be giving many of the wounded the same illness you say I have."

"Shh. Fredericksburg is over. The wounded are in Washington and Philadelphia hospitals."

"I remember…that the army retreated…the heights were never taken…the grass was thick with bodies…"

Nathaniel gently placed her head against his chest. Strands of scarlet fell over the thin scar on her cheek. The white cotton cap still covered her head.

"It's a new year. You've chatted with Miss Sharon about the prospects for 1863."

She gripped his hand more tightly. "I can't recall that conversation."

"It was about hope. She said you gave something of a sermon."

"You're joking."

"About three days ago."

She lifted her head and looked at him. "How long have I been in this room?"

"A couple of months. You're still in the Palmer house."

"How many times have you been at my side?"

"I don't know. Eight or nine or ten."

"Did you desert the army to nurse me?"

"Captain Hanson permits me to come this way to check on our regimental nurse. We are in winter quarters at Belle Plain in Virginia. It's a short steamer trip down the Potomac to you. And nothing much else is going on except doing hard drill and eating bad food."

"Levi…and the others?"

"They're fine. They send their best wishes and their prayers. You get stronger every week. This isn't the first time you've been sitting up and speaking with someone."

She put her head back on his chest. "My mind does not feel strong. I can't remember a single conversation or a single aspect of the battle."

"In time perhaps it will all come back."

She clenched his uniform in her free hand. "I do not want everything to come back."

March 25, 1863

Washington, DC

Dear Mama and Papa,

I have no idea if you are reading my notes to you but I am going to keep sending them anyway. I wrote you after the Battle of Fredericksburg in December to tell you Levi and the other Amish boys are all right. Now I'm writing you to tell you that I am all right. I wouldn't mention it except I'm never sure what sort of news or rumors may come your way and I wouldn't wish you to be left confused and fretting.

I did have a bout with pneumonia but I thank
God it didn't spread to my second lung. If you
read this, you will be glad to know I am now
much improved. Nathaniel got leave to visit me
from his winter camp a number of times. They
say he doted on me day and night while I lay
on my sickbed but I had no idea he was there.
I hope to be back nursing by the first of April
if the recovery God has granted me continues at
its present pace. After a week of rain the sky
is blue and the sun quite warm so Nathaniel
is due to take me on my first outing in nearly
three months. Ich lobe Gott. I miss you both
and of course I miss Sarah and the girls.

your loving daughter,

Lyndel

"You look a little tired."

"I suppose my legs don't have the energy I require at this stage of
my recovery. Could we sit on that bench there?"

Nathaniel frowned. "You'll take a breeze off the Potomac on that
one."

"I need a breeze. I'm overheating in all the clothes you made me
bundle up in." Her blue eyes flashed in the sunlight and she put a
gloved hand to his face. "It's all right, dear. I'm not going to fall to pieces
on you. Bear in mind God did not fashion me out of porcelain."

"You've been very ill—"

"But the danger has passed. The doctor says so. Even Miss Sharon
agrees that I'm almost myself again."

"I've seen soldiers with a sickness who appear to get well and I've watched them rush about with an astonishing burst of strength. Then they've suddenly dropped dead."

Lyndel laughed as she settled herself on the bench. "Thank you for your encouraging words, my dear. They certainly refresh my flagging spirits."

"Well—"

"Just hold me and I will be all right. I promise."

Lyndel took one of his hands in both of hers and leaned against his shoulder with its bright gold second lieutenant's epaulet. She wore a black bonnet along with a dark navy coat and cape and a vivid red scarf Nathaniel had purchased for her. At first she had balked at putting the scarf around her throat because it wasn't plain. But then she considered that her church and family had cut her off and Nathaniel was trying to show the love to her they could not and would not. So she had wound it about her neck and made Nathaniel's eyes gleam. He bent and kissed her quickly on the lips while they were still in the hall of the Palmer house and no one else was nearby. She put a hand on the back of his head and kept him close, prolonging the kiss.

"I've missed you," she had told him.

Now, seated on the bench by the Potomac, she felt completely loved and completely safe. God and Nathaniel would guard her from all harm and any further illness. The fear she had first experienced of never regaining the full use of her mind or memory was gone as each day brought more experiences back to her. Nathaniel's love and affection was so passionate and so abundant it seemed to her she was constantly wrapped in some sort of spiritual Amish quilt that would keep her warm regardless of the winds and rough weather of life. The cannons and armies were far in the distance and she hadn't tended a wounded soldier for months, so it seemed the conflict didn't exist. It was as if Richmond and Washington were at peace and all warfare had ended.

Steamers puffed their dark smoke into the sunshine and sailboats glistened as they spread their canvas. She watched soldiers load and unload supplies at the docks. Men rowed back and forth from ship to shore, their oars making small white splashes in the blue water. Gulls swung in loops over the harbor and cried the rough cry Lyndel loved.

The scent of tar from the pilings made her close her eyes and breathe in as deeply as she could.

I am alive and in love. Thank God, oh, thank God.

Several families of African-Americans walked off a steamer with various bags and bundles, squinting in the spring light. For the longest time the children stayed close to their mothers. Then one of the girls, her long hair tightly braided, saw something on the wharf and raced after it. Soon all seven of them were chasing what Lyndel couldn't see. A mother and father laughed, and laughed fully, as they watched the boys and girls run.

"Freedom, Nathaniel," she said softly. "This is what you're fighting for. It's why we've left our church and our home. But not our God."

Nathaniel's smile was weak. "They make a pretty picture. But will they find their freedom here? Or more of what they left behind in Virginia and South Carolina?"

"Davey told me about your conversation. And your sermon. We can't change everyone's minds, Nathaniel. We say and do what we think is right. Some people join us. Others ignore us or despise us. I nurse. You soldier. We both pray. That's all we can do to change our little corner of the world. But God is with us."

"Your father and mine wouldn't agree with you."

"We are Amish. Regardless of what they say at the Amish community in Elizabethtown. And what matters is we both believe in Jesus Christ."

"Lyndel, our people will not call me Amish again until I lay down my musket and bayonet and come back to them on my knees saying I was wrong." He turned his head to look at her. "I can never do that. I believe I'm right to fight against slavery. How can I ever honestly repent of what I am doing?"

"You're not going to repent. They may cut us off, but God will never do that to us. There are plenty of Christians who are fighting on both sides. We think they're wrong and they think we're wrong. But God loves all of us despite our errors and sins. You don't have to be Amish to be a Christian. And our people's way of understanding what it means to be Amish isn't the only way." She smiled at him with as much strength as he'd seen since her illness. "We can start our own Amish church on the other side of Elizabethtown. We can call ourselves the King Amish."

"Are you serious?"

"Yes. I'm serious. Others have done it. You know yourself there are many different Amish churches."

"We will have our own farm?"

"Our own farm. And you will be the region's farrier. People will come from miles around for your services."

Nathaniel watched a warship spread all its sails and head south on the Potomac. For some reason all its cannon had been run out. He kept his eye on it for a few minutes. Neither he nor Lyndel spoke. Then he leaned his head back and gazed at three white clouds moving slowly.

"Our parents won't come to have me shoe their horses," he finally said.

She gripped his hand tightly. "No. But there will be others who will be like parents to us. You'll see."

"You say that so easily."

"I say it quickly because it's not easy to say. But I've turned over these matters a great deal since I began to think straight after my illness. We can't spend our lives waiting for our parents to choose us over their religion. We can only carry on and welcome them with open arms if they should ever decide to cross the threshold of our home."

"Our home." He smiled at her. "You make it sound like we're already married."

She laughed. "Oh, I know, I'm just talking—who knows when the war will be over, but we need to look ahead and think about where we will live since we can't go back to the Amish community in Elizabethtown again—"

"I wish we wouldn't wait."

"Wouldn't wait for what?"

"To be married. It's quiet now before the summer campaigns begin—I'm an officer, you could join me at Belle Plain, see more of your brother as well, we would have a month together, truly together, perhaps more if the spring rains are heavy—"

Lyndel sat up and faced him, her eyes a deep sea blue. "Nathaniel King, what are you saying? Are you proposing to me?"

Nathaniel struggled for his words. "*Ja*, I guess, *ja*—I don't see the point in waiting for three or four years when the war might be over or might yet be dragging on—why can't I hold you in my arms now, take care of you as you grow stronger? You could work at the field hospital in Belle Plain…every day there are soldiers who are ill and some of the sickness is serious and it's often hours before they can be transported to Washington by steamboat—"

Lyndel put her white-gloved hand to his mouth. "Shh. I don't need to hear your courtroom argument. Just ask me what you want to ask me."

"Well, I…" Nathaniel stopped talking, looked at her and suddenly took her face in both his hands. "I love you. I so wish you would agree to be my wife forever."

Lyndel threw her arms around his neck. "Oh, *ja*! Of course, I will." She kissed him with such a surge of energy that she knocked his head back against the wood of the bench. Then she laughed and drew him forward and kissed him again, oblivious to soldiers and citizens walking past and glancing their way. "I pray to God there will be buckets and buckets of rain and that the army will not move out of their winter camp for another six months."

20

The wedding took place on Sunday, March 29th, just a few days after Nathaniel proposed. The day began with a heavy rain that eventually dropped off to a mist that fell like silk on Lyndel's hands. She closed her eyes and turned her face up to it.

It is like a gentle baptism. Thank you, my God, thank you, my Friend.

By the time she was standing on a knoll among spring trees at Belle Plain, looking over the chaplain's head at the silver Potomac, the silky mist had melted to soft blue skies and round white clouds. A breeze turned the young green leaves first one way and then the other and moved like Nathaniel's hand down her face. Looking at her, he smiled, sunburned and handsome in a new black hat with a tall ostrich plume and a new blue coat and pants the quartermaster had ordered him to don. One of the great surprises during the flurry of the days leading up to the ceremony was the fact the new uniform fit and was neither too tight nor too large.

"A miracle," grunted Captain Hanson as he brushed off Nathaniel's uniform before the service and polished his sword. "You'll have me believing the Almighty is taking a personal interest in your affairs, Lieutenant."

It wouldn't do to have Nathaniel dressed for a cathedral while his best man, Levi, looked as if he had just fought a third battle at Manassas, so the quartermaster was besieged by platoon and company to come up with something equally miraculous for the young soldier. He growled he had done enough and disappeared into his stack of stores until a group of officers' wives swooped down and refused to leave until something could be done. A new set of blues surfaced for Levi that needed a bit of work with a needle and thread, as well as a black hat that was missing its feather. A black plume was found, not from an ostrich but an eagle. Levi didn't mind the change.

Lyndel had caused the greatest problem because she objected to being married in white. The Amish tradition put brides in plain dresses that they could work in and be buried in. Yet Lyndel's dresses from Lancaster County were beginning to look as tattered as Nathaniel's old uniform, and Morganne, her maid of honor, insisted that if the groom had to wear a new set of clothes so did the bride. Lyndel argued for a dress that looked at home milking the cows, but the women of the regiment overruled her by providing her with a simple gown of white silk purchased in Boston and brought to the door of the small cabin she shared with Morganne on Saturday evening.

It was obvious to Lyndel, looking at the harried but triumphant faces of the five women standing in her doorway, that they had gone to a great deal of effort to get to Boston and return in time, having only one of her old Elizabethtown dresses to work with for measurements. She took the gown from their hands and thanked them, still uncertain, but showing them only her smile and, as Morganne put it a few minutes later, her grace.

"Did you hear how they coaxed the tailor to sew my dress in less than a day?" she asked her friend afterward.

"I did."

Lyndel had held the gown at arm's length. "I feel guilty about this."

"Why?"

"I didn't earn it."

"Do you have difficulty accepting gifts, my dear?"

"No…I…may have trouble with extravagant gifts…but it's also that this dress is so far from being Amish…"

Morganne lit the lamp that sat on a cracker box. "You told me you and Nathaniel were going to become a new sort of Amish."

"We are. Still…I can't reconcile this with the beliefs I hold in my heart." The lamplight made the dress shimmer as it ran through her hands. "Oh," she said, taken by the beauty and sparkle of the silk. She allowed herself to imagine for a moment how it might feel on her and how it might look to Nathaniel.

"What will he think of me if I wear this?" she asked out loud.

Morganne smiled. "That's easy. He'll think how blessed he is to be marrying a woman of such rare beauty. You'll turn his head for the rest of your life."

So she wore the dress. The officers' wives were happy, Morganne was happy, and as Nathaniel gazed at her while the chaplain spoke, the sun sliding out from a cloud and lighting the silk and the Potomac, it was clear to Lyndel that her man was amazed and delighted. As she spoke the vows that made him her husband and her his wife she finally relaxed into the gown and let it be one of the many gifts of a day laden with wonder.

"You're perfect," he whispered as the chaplain told them to kiss and their lips came together.

"My hair is still up," she teased.

He kissed her once, smiled, then kissed her a second time. "Not for long."

As they had planned, Morganne lifted the black *kapp* from Lyndel's head and replaced it with a white one.

"Somehow you manage to look Amish even with the silk dress and in these military surroundings," Nathaniel said.

"No matter what Elizabethtown would think about me today, I'm still Amish to the core."

Miss Sharon had come down by steamer for the ceremony and so had the Palmers. The company and platoon were formed up twenty or thirty feet away, uniforms patched and freshly washed, muskets polished to a sparkling brilliance, and even the 19th Indiana's commander, Sam Williams, stopped by to hear the vows. Congratulating them following the service, and after the company had raised a loud hurrah, he presented Nathaniel with a four day pass co-signed by Long Sol Meredith.

"Disappear to New York," he said. "That's an order."

Dear Mama and Papa,

I am writing a quick note from New York City to tell you that Nathaniel and I have married. Of course this will be a shock to you—if you are even reading this—but we didn't want to wait until this long war ended or until you were prepared to forgive us for taking part in it. The ceremony was done with the Bible and a chaplain and my kapp is now white instead of black as any married Amish girl would have it. We have been granted a brief honeymoon in this great city and are thoroughly enjoying ourselves. I even got Nathaniel to sleep in until seven one morning. Most of the time we walk by the docks and take in the sea air and watch the sailing vessels and steamers come in and out of the harbor. So I wanted you to hear about the marriage from me and not someone else. I love you both. God bless.

Your daughter,

Lyndel

When they landed back at the Belle Plain wharf on Friday, Lyndel expected to return to the cabin she and Morganne had used for a few days before the wedding. It had been built by two privates who had both succumbed to old wounds from Antietam at the field hospital and whose bodies were now buried in the regimental cemetery. Morganne, she knew, had gone back to Armory Square in Washington and her room at the Palmer home so the cabin would be vacant.

Cramped but cozy.

The 19th Indiana had a surprise in store. Levi spotted them as Nathaniel and Lyndel made their way toward the cabin and came rushing up, hugging his sister and pumping Nathaniel's hand.

"Welcome back," he greeted them. "We held quite the barn raising while you were gone."

"Barn raising?" Lyndel stared at her brother as if he'd sprouted extra legs and a second head. "What on earth are you talking about?"

"Do you see that log building?"

She looked where Levi was pointing. "The one with the stone chimney and porch?"

"Yes, that's it. What do you think of it?"

"Almost too lovely for an army camp. Does that belong to General Meredith or Colonel Williams?"

"No, no." He grinned. "It's yours, sister."

"Mine?"

"The 19th threw it together while you were on your honeymoon. I've never seen anything like it, even back home at Elizabethtown. Men scurrying about like ants, stripped to the waist, felling trees, fitting logs, smearing caulking. I don't know how many carpenters we had going at the same time. We all helped of course. Ham built the table along with Joshua and Nip. I did the fireplace with Captain Hanson and Lieutenant Nicolson. Groom and Jones made it back from Armory Square the day after you left and put together four chairs. That young Plesko worked on the floor."

"Stop, stop!" Lyndel's face had filled with blood. "This is too much! Nathaniel and I have done nothing to deserve this!"

Levi stopped smiling. "Of course you have, Ginger. You're an army nurse. You came close to giving your life at Fredericksburg for the wounded. Let alone what you did for the 19th and the rest of the brigade at Antietam Creek. For a few weeks you and your husband deserve a home. The men have given you that. Please don't spurn the gifts God gives you through others' efforts."

Lyndel put her hands to her eyes. "I can't…I don't know what to say, Levi—"

"The words will come to you, I have no doubt of it." Levi looked at Nathaniel, "What do you think, Brother King?"

Nathaniel shook his head. "It's altogether surprising. I am blessed because of the woman I married."

"No. It's not just that. The men remember the sermon. They remember *you*." He clapped a hand on Nathaniel's shoulder. "We even got help from the Wisconsin and Michigan boys because of that."

"Truly?"

"Yes, truly."

Nathaniel gazed at the log house and at the smoke rising from the chimney. "It seems to me someone has already moved in."

"Just a fire to keep you warm at night. Sam Williams is tending it."

"You can't be serious, Levi. Colonel Williams is reduced to fetching kindling for our hearth?"

Levi put an arm around his sister. "I don't believe he would put it that way. The colonel wanted to be the first to welcome you both into your new home. He saw you come off the steamboat. And he has a battle flag he wants you to take care of for him."

"Why is he giving it to me?"

"I expect he will ask you to make the presentation. It's the regiment's flag from Antietam, brother. President Lincoln is coming."

It was only a matter of days before the president galloped onto the parade ground on as beautiful a bay as Lyndel had ever seen. The ground had begun to dry out and dust sprang from the hooves of Lincoln's mount and General Hooker's gray. A cluster of officers rode behind them, as well as a group of lancers with pennants streaming.

Lincoln raced down the line of columns of the First Corps troops, the regimental flags dipping as he went by, head uncovered, hair and beard being tugged backward in the wind he created. He reined in beside Hooker and the assortment of majors and colonels and generals and sat erect as the soldiers began to march past him. His black top hat reappeared and he brought it from his head every time a different regiment went by.

The 19th Indiana's turn came and Lyndel watched them stop briefly in front of the president, lower new flags with their bold colors not yet faded by storm or sun or combat, and mark time while Nathaniel detached himself from his company and approached Lincoln. He saluted and lifted two flags, neatly folded, up to the president. Nathaniel and Lincoln exchanged a few words and the president leaned down from his horse, extending his hand, which Nathaniel shook. Then Nathaniel saluted and returned to his company. With a roar from Samuel Williams, the regiment continued marching.

Lincoln kept the flags on his saddle, one large hand resting on the tattered banners of cloth, as the entire First Corps of the Army of the Potomac moved past his eyes. Lyndel knew one of the flags was the regimental standard and the other the stars and stripes from Nathaniel's company. Both were shot full of holes. An aide brought his horse over and tried to take the flags and hold them for the president but Lincoln shook his head. One gnarled hand seemed to clamp down even more tightly on the two banners after that. With the other he continued to lift his black hat.

After the review Lyndel continued to stand with the knot of surgeons and ambulance drivers she had attached herself to. Mrs. Lincoln was in a carriage pulled by four bays and her carriage followed the president as he dismounted and spoke with various soldiers and officers, his ten-year-old, son, Tad, accompanying him, dressed in a blue uniform with a small sword and riding a pony. She saw father and son speak with Lieutenant Stewart of Battery B and examine Stewart's horse, Tartar, which had lost its tail at Second Manassas. The president wandered off to speak with others but Tad stayed with Stewart—Old Jock—and the horse. With apparent intent, Lincoln drifted toward the doctors and ambulance corps and began shaking the physicians' and drivers' hands. Lyndel noticed that the flags were tucked up under his left arm.

"Miss Keim, isn't it?" Lincoln was smiling down at her. The carriage had reined in behind him and he nodded his head toward his wife. "May I introduce Mrs. Lincoln?"

Lyndel inclined her head. "It's an honor, ma'am."

Mrs. Lincoln smiled. "Thank you."

"How has the long Virginia winter been for you, Miss Keim?" asked the president. "I expect you have been nursing here at Belle Plain?"

"Yes, Mr. President. But I've just been married and am Mrs. King now."

"Mrs. King! Why, congratulations. Who is the lucky fellow?"

"An officer with the 19th Indiana, sir. Nathaniel King. He is the one who presented you with those standards."

"That was your husband? You make a fine pair."

"Thank you, Mr. President." Lyndel had a sudden thought and tried to fight it back. "I...I wish you had been in attendance when he spoke to the regiment about the importance of your Emancipation Proclamation. Both of us heartily applaud it and your support for the African troops. I know you have taken much criticism from various quarters, sir—some who say you have gone too far and others who declare you haven't gone far enough. But we are behind you. I know my husband made every effort to persuade the troops to side with your point of view."

The president listened, his face growing more and more somber, the tired lines reemerging across his face. He took her gently by the elbow and led her away from the group. "Excuse us a moment, gentlemen." When they couldn't be overheard he removed his top hat and stood awkwardly before her, as if she were the person of note and he a petitioner who had come to ask for a great favor.

"I have always been against slavery," he began. "But I haven't known how to rid the Republic of it and keep the Republic intact at the same time. I am not a John Brown. It was my belief a gradual emancipation might be best. Or the paying out of sums to the plantation owners to recompense them for setting their slaves at liberty—this is what Wilberforce and his supporters convinced the British to do, something he didn't live to see. But their slavery was thousands of miles away in the West Indies, not an hour's drive out of London or Liverpool, while ours is precisely that, yonder a few miles on the far side of the Rappahannock. I've come to realize slavery cannot be eradicated, nor the Rebellion suppressed, without a surgery, an amputation, such as your doctors must perform on the battlefield. The Emancipation Proclamation is one of my saws. Our armies are another. I amputate not to kill the nation or even the South but to heal it. I cut away the wounded limb of slavery to heal the enslaved American too."

Lyndel watched the changing expressions on his face and the play of light and dark in his eyes. She hesitated a moment when he had finished and spoke up again. "Thank you, Mr. President. Some say you don't care for the African man or woman or child. Nathaniel and I do not believe that's so."

Lincoln kept his eyes on her. "I confess I don't always know what to make of the African race, Mrs. King. Yet every month that goes by, my intolerance for their enslavement intensifies and my admiration for their spirit, in chains but unbowed, grows like a tall field of summer corn. I don't doubt but they will alter my perspective yet further, and soften the disposition of many toward them, once they bear arms against their enslavers and show a passion for freedom and independence as strong as any man's. It's true I don't progress to where God may want me fast enough for the abolitionists or the Radical Republicans or the freemen. But like the tortoise, I expect to make it across the line the Lord has fixed for me, and I expect to win."

Lyndel reached out and took his hand. "The Iron Brigade and the 19th Indiana will do all it can for you in that respect, Mr. President."

"I know it. And it grieves me to think many of the young men who marched before me today will not live out the summer. Great sacrifices still have to be made to save our nation." Lincoln took the bullet-shattered flags from under his left arm and examined them, opening the stars and stripes with the company's letter embroidered in its middle. He looked back at Lyndel. "I won't leave your husband and his men to make their sacrifice alone. I have my part to play. I have my cross to bear. Believe me when I tell you I intend to bear it for the sake of all our people, South and North, white and black."

"I know that, sir."

"May God have mercy on you and your husband, Mrs. King. And may you save as many of our boys as the good Lord will allow."

He turned to go, folding the standards again before tucking them under his arm, and pausing to place his black hat back on his head.

"Our prayers remain with you, Mr. President," Lyndel said.

He smiled and turned back briefly to face her. "I thank you. It may be that this July or August the door of war will creak back on its hinges enough to give us a glimpse of sky and an early sun rising from the crops. I don't expect an end. But I should like that crack of light from the old open door and the sight of a round sun rising free and easy from the land." He began to walk briskly over the flattened grass of the parade ground. "For the present, the nation's future aside, I see I must rescue Lieutenant Stewart from Tadpole or risk losing a fine artillery officer to my son's unyielding advance of burnished steel."

From that day, the month of April flew like pigeons through Lyndel's hands. Nathaniel was up before the dawn each morning to drill the men of his company and platoon and didn't return until supper. Lyndel was always back from the field hospital well before that and had a meal prepared using the pots and pans the women had placed by the fireplace. Most evenings they were able to spend together and this brought into her soul a peace and contentment she hadn't known since leaving Elizabethtown the year before. She couldn't forget it was spring planting for the Amish of Pennsylvania but she saw that God was putting seed into the ground of her heart and mind with each moment Nathaniel and she had alone.

"Do you not miss the people of the church?" he asked as he held her in the spring dark of their home, no lanterns lit, only the flicker of the soldiers' fires making its way through the bedroom window to move across the walls and their faces. "Do you not miss watching the hay come up in your family's fields?"

"It came up too slowly to watch. I'd rather be here with you."

"You could be there with me also."

"No. I couldn't. You would still have enlisted and left me, married or not." She pulled away to look at him in the play of light. "Am I not right?"

He didn't answer for a moment. "It would have been difficult to leave a young wife so beautiful as you," he finally said.

"Still. You would have done it."

"To save the country. To free the slave. Yes."

She came back to his arms and his chest. "So and I would have become a nurse and followed your regiment just as I have done. Why begin all over again? We're together. Let's remain where we are and stay together."

Often enough the officers and their wives were invited for evening get-togethers. And often enough the men from the platoon and company came for a bonfire and to enjoy popping corn, which Lyndel purchased by the sackful for them. Private Groom now drank Captain Hanson's rough coffee as part of his regular diet, allowing that it fashioned a cast-iron stomach that was proof not only against Confederate minie balls but all forms of dysentery, bad food, rank water, and biting insects. Nip and Levi used the fireplace to concoct different stews and soups with forage from their many expeditions to the Rebel side of the Potomac—forays that Hanson, Nicolson, and Nathaniel pretended to know nothing about. Ham enlisted the help of Jones and Plesko in working on an elaborate house of cards they added additions to every time they visited the King home.

For Levi and Joshua it was a garden. They confessed that farming was in their blood—they couldn't pretend they didn't enjoy seeding and growing and harvesting, so they planted vegetables in a plot they worked at the side of the house that faced south and west. Using manure and shovels and cultivating as rich a soil as they could manage, they purchased seeds from the sutler and planted radishes and lettuce and peas, hammering poles into the ground for beans as well.

"I know the radishes and lettuce will come up quickly," Lyndel laughed, "but who will be here to tend the peas and beans in July?"

Levi was on his hands and knees in the dirt and putting the beans to bed. "You follow the regiment as our nurse, that's true. But I'm hoping a few of the officers' wives will stay on at Belle Plain after the army has moved out. I intend to ask a few of them to take care of the harvest."

"Levi, all of the women will go back to their homes once their husbands have left."

"A few may linger. Like a late spring rain. It's not so bad here, Ginger. You never know."

The hundreds of cards Ham, Plesko, and Jones used came from decks thrown away by men who had sworn off gambling and found faith in God. Ham declared he was grateful the soldiers and God had met one another and left sin and card-playing behind them. In celebration, with pockets full of kings and queens and aces, he decided they should expand their house of cards into a cathedral and they began to fill Lyndel's twelve-foot harvest table from one end to the other.

"Mind you have that done by the fall," Lyndel would tell them. "I'll need that table for my pumpkins and squash and corn."

"Mrs. King," Ham would reply, "by harvest we'll be too busy chasing Stonewall and Lee south to Atlanta to be tending to our card house. You may do with our engineering marvel whatever you wish at that time."

"A door gets slammed or a draft darts in and I have to rebuild one of your rooftops or walls," she pretended to complain.

Ham laughed. "Mrs. King, we all think you enjoy playing about with these cards as much as we do. So we slam the doors and leave the windows open on purpose to give you the opportunity you crave."

"Nonsense, Corporal. Wherever on earth did you get that idea?"

Yet, in truth, when Nathaniel was out and Lyndel hadn't yet reported to the field hospital, she sat at the long table and added another wing or repaired a collapsed corridor of jacks and deuces, finding a certain quiet and a deep satisfaction in balancing card edge against card edge and establishing something that remained erect simply by an act of air and paper and faith. She didn't say so to the men, not even to Nathaniel, but she called the vast structure the New Jerusalem.

One evening near the end of April, well aware that the Army of the Potomac would soon be ordered out against the Army of Northern Virginia, Lyndel and Nathaniel worked side by side to refashion a broken roof. At first their attempts were not successful as card after card fell to the tabletop, often bringing others with it. Eventually, however, they found a rhythm and speedily fixed the roof and added a new wall. They were about to erect a tower, when a knock thudded against their heavy wooden door. Lyndel looked at her husband.

"Perhaps this is it," she said.

"We'll see." He turned in his chair to face the door and barked, "Yes? Who's there?"

"Sorry to disturb you, sir." It was Ham. "But Private Plesko was on picket duty and was approached near the wharf by a sergeant wishing to speak with you."

"It's quite late, Corporal. Can't the sergeant wait for the morning?"

"He says he'll be gone by morning, sir."

"Gone? Gone where?"

"West, sir, to campaign with Generals Grant and Banks in Mississippi. He only has a few hours and insists on meeting with you and your wife."

"Me and my wife?" Nathaniel got to his feet. "My wife? Whatever for?"

"Calm yourself, dear," Lyndel said softly.

"I don't know, sir."

Nathaniel started for the door. "What is the sergeant's name? What unit is he with?"

Nathaniel threw open the door before Ham could respond. A mixture of firelight, moonlight, and wood smoke tumbled into the house. Beside Corporal Ham in his black hat was a tall man in blue uniform with the stripes and diamond of a first sergeant on his sleeves. Nathaniel stared.

"Sergeant…" he began but didn't finish.

Lyndel pushed back her chair and stood up. "Who is it, Nathaniel?" Then saw the man's face.

"Sergeant Moses Gunnison, First Louisiana Native Guard, assigned to the Department of the Gulf under General Nathan P. Banks," said the visitor cheerfully. "I was hoping I'd find the two of you at home this evening. And I hoped you would allow the intrusion."

21

They talked for hours, seated at the small table where Lyndel and Nathaniel ate their meals, the short candle at the center fluttering in the air from an open window.

McClellan's battles with Lee the year before had disrupted life on the Hargrove Plantation where Moses worked as a slave. A skirmish that swept through the farm fields and barns provided enough confusion for him to make his escape through Maryland and Pennsylvania and New York, this time getting across the border into Ontario. The war prevented pursuit but Confederate agents were present in Ontario planning raids into Northern territory and he had to elude several bands before finding a community of ex-slaves who had settled there. Most of them had crossed the border by means of the Underground Railroad before the war started.

"I prospered there," Moses told them, sipping at what Nathaniel called his Cannonball Coffee. "I had many skills that brought me good money from the Canadian farmers. Some of whom were Amish. After the Emancipation Proclamation came into effect Frederick Douglass sent recruiters into Canada to enlist ex-slaves. They were having trouble getting a great many to sign up in the Northern states."

"Why was that?" asked Nathaniel.

Moses bit into one of Lyndel's oatmeal biscuits. "Same as with the whites—everyone was roaring for a fight in '61, when they thought the war would be quick and easy and over by New Year's. But freedom is never easy—not to get it, not to keep it, not even to live it. What with all the hard fighting and dying in '62, and here we're heading into our third summer of warfare, none of my people are much interested in trading what they finally have now for a fight in which they could lose everything—their very lives. We Africans are doing well in New York and Ohio and everywhere else—liberty, employment, a working economy, our own roofs over our heads. Up in Canada, we're living high on the hog too. Why, all black men can vote in Ontario, can you imagine? I confess I felt no great urgency to enlist in the army to do battle with Jeff Davis and the Confederacy."

Lyndel pushed the plate of oatmeal biscuits and a tub of butter at Moses. "I know the South has threatened to hang Africans who put on the uniform of the Union army."

"That gives some men pause. There are others who are worried about coming up against blacks in combat, those fools fighting in gray for the slaveholders so they can hold on to the miserable scrap of a life they've got. Myself, I'd run a bayonet through them as easily as I would a slave driver. They're traitors in my book the same way Stonewall Jackson and Robert E. Lee are traitors to Washington and the Constitution. No, none of that made me hold back. It was the freedom and the peace I was enjoying."

He leaned back in his seat with the fresh coffee Nathaniel had poured him. "Charlie changed my inclination. Come at me in my dreams like one of them fiery seraphim with a sword. Showed me the marks of the rope burn on his neck. Practically walked me through the South, plantation after plantation, all the slavery and whippings and degradation. Asked if I was going to let this carry on another two hundred years while I got rich and fat north of the 49th. My heart was going like a steam engine when I woke up. So I came down to Boston and they put me in the 54th Massachusetts, a black regiment, which was the unit I trained with. More recruits started coming in so they made up a sister regiment, the 55th, and had a mind to transfer me over to give the new troops some feeling of stability."

But a general found out Moses had originally come from New Orleans and been sold at an auction for more than 15,000 dollars before being carried off to Virginia in his twenties. African units were being formed in Louisiana and were certain to see action long before their eastern counterparts. There was a strong need for New Orleans men to serve as noncommissioned officers. So Moses was on his way west to the Mississippi.

"That's the long and short of it." His pocket watch chimed. He pulled it out of a pocket and opened its silver lid. "I've got a bit more time. Big Frank said they'd be unloaded and ready to head back to Washington by two."

"Moses." Lyndel put her hand over his. "We gave Charlie a proper funeral. He's buried in the Amish cemetery at Elizabethtown."

Moses nodded. "I'm glad to hear it." He fixed his eyes on her. "What puzzles me is finding the two of you here. I read about the lieutenant's promotion in the newspaper. You I've read about several times as Miss Lyndel Keim the nurse. The other day I caught mention of your wedding in Belle Plain. So I got leave to ship up here for a few hours before they send me west to serve under Generals Grant and Banks." He stared at them. "I never forgot your names. And I'm pleased to see you married. But you're Amish, aren't you? It was my understanding you don't take up arms or resort to any form of violence."

Lyndel folded her hands on the tabletop. "No, we don't. But I felt from God I must nurse the wounded. Nathaniel felt he must resist slavery. There are two other Amish men in his platoon, including my brother."

"What do your people think of this?"

She looked at her hands. "Well, they're not pleased with us. They won't talk to us anymore, won't send letters or packages of food or warm socks or even healing herbs for the battlefield casualties. We are cut off."

Moses shifted in his chair to gaze at Nathaniel. "How is it for you, Lieutenant?"

Nathaniel half-laughed. "No better. We're orphans now."

"You know that *Thou shalt not kill* is a poor translation from the old Hebrew tongue of the Bible. The commandment actually means *Thou shalt not murder.* God made allowance for Israel's people to fight in wars for national survival and to defend themselves from personal assault."

"*Ja, ja,* so the chaplains have explained to me. Still, when I came out of winter camp last year I felt ashamed to march with a gun on my shoulder. It's now 1863 and I still feel guilty. Perhaps more so, for I have slain other men."

"Who would have slain you."

"I realize that."

"And have slain my people by the thousands."

"*Ja.* I'm not turning back now. My hand is to the plow. If the Lord wishes to condemn me, he must do as he sees fit. I wish we could have resolved this with prayer and goodwill. But that didn't happen. But suppose we had marched without guns, fallen to our knees, and recited the Lord's Prayer while the Rebels lifted their muskets to shoot? They are a religious people. I've read about how Lee and Stonewall and other officers are concerned to have less profanity and drinking and gambling among their troops. In particular Stonewall and Lee are anxious to get Bibles and gospel literature to their men. Would they shoot while we knelt by the ten thousand to pray?"

"Perhaps not. But neither would they give up their slaves, since they have convinced themselves the Bible permits them to hold men in bondage."

Nathaniel furrowed his brow. "A lazy reading of the Scriptures takes them to such a place. A calmer reading with prayer and due attention to detail shows that the Spirit of the Lord moves us toward liberty of soul and mind—and body. A liberty that allows us to serve God and serve our neighbors freely."

"I had heard you were something of a preacher. Big Frank told me the steamboat crews call you the Reverend King. With very little jest, I assure you." He pushed his chair back and stood up. "I had best get down to the steamer."

Nathaniel extended his hand. "We're glad to have seen you again, Moses Gunnison. You're a good man and will always be welcome at our home."

Moses took the offered hand and said, "Just as you have had to become comfortable with guns, so too have I had to accept a white man's hand of friendship. I have never had a white man as a friend before."

"Then you have one now," Nathaniel said.

Moses looked down at their still joined hands, then glanced over to Lyndel's hands. "You have no wedding bands."

Lyndel grasped Nathaniel's hand and kissed it. "We didn't have the money for it, Moses. Nor is it an Amish custom."

"A man needs his symbols."

"It is not our custom."

Moses stood a moment, thinking and looking at the candlelight flickering in the room. He opened a breast pocket and tugged out two plain gold rings. "My mother and father. Born in America. Died in slavery. The master whipped me to find these but I never let on where they were. Mama and Papa had them since I was a boy, I don't know how. Only wore them at night in our shack. Hid them under the floorboards in a little pouch that was always covered with dirt." He tossed them gently in his hand. "My good luck charms."

"Those are very special, then," said Lyndel. "Did you have them with you when you sheltered in our barn?"

"I did. Hidden on my body. Nehemiah Hargrove didn't think to search me for them."

"Was that his name—the leader of the slave hunters?"

"That's right. Youngest son of the master. He's with the Rebel army now."

"My brother has seen him. He says the soldiers call him Georgey Washington."

Moses snorted. "On account the Hargroves claim they have blood ties to President Washington. Washington set his slaves free when he died, I told them once. Bullwhipped me for that. Was Nehemiah who lynched Charlie. You see him again, God grant you lay him low in the dust forever."

The sharp lines that had appeared on his face with the mention of Nehemiah Hargrove vanished when he put the rings in Nathaniel's hand. "My gift. We orphans ought to help one another out."

"Oh, no, no," protested Nathaniel, immediately giving the gold bands back. "We can't accept such a gift, your parents' rings."

"Prayers are enough for us," Lyndel spoke up. "Truly, Moses."

Moses thrust his hands in his pockets. "I'm not much of a praying man. I believe you'll get farther with the rings. Every time you look at them you need to remember each other. And me. And the ones enslaved." He wouldn't take the bands back from Nathaniel. "It's you who are the praying types. So pray for my people. Don't just fight for them with your muskets and bandages. Fight for them with God and his holy angels. Those are blood rings. They tie you to one another. They tie you to me and my people."

He opened the door and stepped out. The light of a half-moon shone on his face and uniform. He saluted. "Godspeed, Lieutenant King. I hope to see you again when this war is over."

Nathaniel returned the salute. "God bless you, Sergeant."

Moses smiled at Lyndel. "Mrs. King, you do look resplendent. Marriage suits you. I trust you will fare well."

"Thank you, Mr. Gunnison. And I you."

They watched him make his way between the cabins to the Potomac. Lyndel took the smaller ring from Nathaniel and found it fit on her ring finger a little tightly but she left it there. Nathaniel's was too large and loose so he moved it to the next finger. The moon found the gold and made it gleam.

"How strange," Lyndel said, gazing at the rings on their hands, "It was nothing I wished for."

"Nor did we wish for a log house," Nathaniel responded. "But our friends gave us one regardless."

"Stay with me a moment, love." She sat on the step. "I shouldn't ask. Reveille always comes too early."

He lowered himself beside her and she leaned her head with its white *kapp* against his shoulder. His arm went around her.

"How wonderful that Moses is alive," Lyndel said. "I would always wonder what had happened to him."

"Yes."

"And wonderful that he found us."

"We seem to be in all the papers."

"I feel that if he's on his way to the Mississippi to campaign, then it can't be long for you."

"We hear the same things you hear from the officers' wives. Maybe on May 1st or 2nd. Or later."

"I thank God wherever you go our ambulance wagons will be right behind you."

"Let's not talk about it," he said, kissing her red hair. "These hard things come soon enough and talk doesn't lessen the sting."

"The wives complain that Belle Plain is muddy when it rains and the air intolerable with mosquitoes. Then they complain it gets so dusty when it's so dry a person can't breathe. I don't share their ill feelings toward this place. I was married here, had my first home with you here, entertained our first visitors as husband and wife here. To me, Belle Plain is a blessing, a bit of heaven on earth."

"Our time has been so short, I'm sorry—"

"Don't be sorry. Our month here together has been full of wonder. I feel stronger in my body and in my spirit than I have since Fredericksburg. No other woman in the world could feel so treasured and complete and fulfilled as I do."

"I wish I wasn't marching."

"Oh, I long for the day you're a farrier with a shop under a great spreading oak tree. But not before the slavery of men like Moses Gunnison is ended. Didn't you sense God had something to say to us through him tonight?"

"*Ja*, I did. But who knows how long it will take to turn things around, how many more battles? There have been so many defeats and reverses."

She squeezed his hand. "I pray something special happens this summer. Something truly astonishing."

"What would that take the form of?"

"A complete shift in fortunes."

"We thought they had shifted with Antietam Creek."

"I ask for something more then."

He kissed her eyes. "What an interesting person you are. You remain irresistible."

"Just because of my hair?"

"Just because of your mind and your spirit. I'd love to stay put another month and tell you more about it."

She laughed. "Oh, wouldn't that be something? Let's see if we can pray in more April showers and stave off the spring campaign until June or July."

But Lyndel's long honeymoon had ended. A few days later, at noon on April 28th, she stood with the other wives on the knoll on which she had been married, the leaves thick over their heads, and watched the Iron Brigade move off with the rest of the First Corps, the men singing about hanging Jeff Davis from a sour apple tree. They were heading for Fredericksburg again, where Lee's army had spent the winter. All the women but Lyndel had handkerchiefs to their eyes. She returned to her house, the thunder of thousands of men's voices still distinct in the distance, and swept the floor and front step clean.

After that she picked radishes and lettuce, made a salad for two, sat at the table and ate her portion, then opened a window and let a spring breeze take the house of cards down one wall at a time. She turned to Psalm 91 in her Bible, read it, and got up to pack her bag, the words running like a creek of new water between the banks of her fears: *Surely he shall deliver thee from the snare of the fowler, and from the noisome pestilence. He shall cover thee with his feathers, and under his wings shalt thou trust: his truth shall be thy shield and buckler.*

Four hours after her husband had marched deeper into Virginia she sat with Morganne David and three physicians in a wagon that bounced and rolled in his footsteps, dust hanging like gauze in the afternoon light.

No matter what happens, I will maintain hope. No matter how many more defeats, I will maintain hope, Lord, and believe you wish our nation to be free and slavery to come to an end as much as I do, as much as Nathaniel does, and that all the sacrifice will prove to have been worthwhile by the time this mighty storm of war has passed.

22

Lyndel was having a dream. She knew it was a dream, but it was an important dream and even while she slept she told herself she wanted to remember it. Yet as soon as Morganne shook her shoulder gently and said it was time to get up, she opened her eyes, glimpsed briefly the images of the dream, then saw them instantly vanish, never to come back. She sat up in the dark of the covered wagon and looked out at a large mansion with a sagging door and slates missing from its roof. Starlight seemed to be caught in the treetops.

"Where are we?" asked Lyndel.

"That must have been a deep sleep," responded Morganne. "We're at the Fitzhugh House. We pulled in here a few hours ago. The First Corps is scattered all around us. There's going to be an assault by the Iron Brigade across the Rappahannock to clear the way for the rest of the corps. Rebel troops are dug in on the opposite bank. Come on, Lyndy. We need to get our field hospital set up for the casualties."

Lyndel climbed out of the wagon, found a basin and towel on the tailgate, splashed the water onto her face, began to gather up supplies, and followed Morganne in the dark. They came to a large open-walled tent with long tables for surgery. Some soldiers were resting on the ground but others were standing in groups and talking in low voices while a number explored the grounds of the Fitzhugh House.

"Where is the brigade, Davey?" Lyndel asked.

"Already assembled on the riverbank. They're just waiting for the boats. Stay here."

"I didn't see Nathaniel last night."

"As soon as the Rebels spot them they'll come under fire. It's only two hundred yards from one side of the river to the other. You need to stay put and help us get set up." She gave Lyndel a quick hug. "You've got me believing now. While you were napping I was praying for you and your husband. It's my hope that casualties will be light."

Lyndel went back and forth from the wagon to the tent carrying medical supplies—bundles of cotton for bandages, slings, and tourniquets. At one point she gathered a number of surgical saws with various blades, all scrubbed clean after Fredericksburg. She bundled them in canvas and gave them to one of the doctors at the tent.

"Ah, good, I was wondering where those were. We're going to need them in a few minutes."

As soon as he said this Lyndel imagined Nathaniel unconscious on the table getting his left arm sawed off. The blood drained from her face and she put her hand against one of the tent poles. No one noticed. In a moment she felt strong enough to return to the wagon and collect bottles of chloroform. But the fear fastened itself into her head and heart like sharp teeth.

It had been four months since she had treated combat casualties. The patients she had nursed at Belle Plain had mostly been sick from flu or dysentery. Memories of wounded and dead, bent and twisted among the cornstalks at Antietam or sprawled on the slopes at Fredericksburg and begging for water, tumbled into her head. Her heart began to pound in her chest and she had difficulty catching her breath. She leaned against a wagon wheel while everything around her churned.

Once the attack begins, once I'm dealing with the wounded soldiers and I'm busy, I'll be all right.

But after the field hospital was completely ready, there were still no sounds of battle. The two nurses sat on stools near each other, exchanged a few words, and waited. Lyndel's heart sped up and slowed down as her anxieties mounted and subsided and mounted again.

"Are you all right?" Morganne asked, her eyes large in the early morning blackness.

Lyndel had her hands clasped rigidly in her lap. "I…I guess not. It's been so long since I've treated combat wounds, and I wasn't married before and now Nathaniel is my husband and I worry about the saws and the amputations—"

Morganne grabbed her by the hand. "Shh. Shh. Once you start working you'll be all right. And Nathaniel will be all right too." She glanced up at one of the doctors. "What's going on? What's the delay?"

"The boats. The boats they need to cross the river haven't come." He sat by them for a few minutes. "The idea was to take out the Confederate positions on the opposite bank. Then the engineers would build a pontoon bridge for the rest of the First Corps to cross. Hooker has one part of the army coming in on Fredericksburg from behind. What we're doing here is meant to confuse Lee so that he's not sure where the main attack is coming from. Eventually we're supposed to join the other part of the army and come at Fredericksburg from the front."

"From the front?" Lyndel jerked straight up on her stool. "Attack Fredericksburg from the front? It will be another slaughter."

"Lee will be attacked from two directions at once. That will be very different from Burnside's approach last December." The doctor suddenly noticed the lack of color in Lyndel's face. "Are you ill, Mrs. King?"

"I just need...I just need to be doing something..."

"I understand. It can't be much longer. We'll have sunrise in half an hour. The men can't cross the water in broad daylight. They'd be cut to pieces."

The sky lightened minute by minute. Suddenly mule teams appeared pulling wagons with the boats. They moved past the Fitzhugh House and through the thin scattering of brush to the river. The doctor shook his head as the wagons rattled past.

"Too late," he muttered, "far too late. I don't know what the army is going to do now. They can't use the boats at this hour."

The sudden pop of musket fire from the Rappahannock made the three of them jump.

"They're crazy to attack!" the doctor shouted.

He shot to his feet and rushed to his table. Ambulance crews ran toward the sound of the firing with their stretchers. Lyndel and

Morganne stood and looked toward the thick fog that was rising from the river and slowly breaking up. The gunfire increased until it became a steady roar. Then it faded as the stretcher bearers staggered back with the wounded. Those with shattered bones were immediately placed onto one of the three tables while others were lowered onto the grass. Lyndel began cutting away uniforms and washing wounds and applying tourniquets. She quickly noticed that none of the casualties were from the Iron Brigade but that all of them were engineers.

"What's going on?" she asked an older man with a brown beard whose foot she was bandaging.

"They got us to try setting up the pontoon bridge," he told her, wincing as she tightened the cloth. "Of course the secesh were on the other side and opened up. We were fish in a barrel."

"Who was doing all the firing that was so close to us?"

"The 6th Wisconsin and 24th Michigan. Trying to get the secesh off our backs. The 14th Brooklyn got mixed up in the melee too. But it was no good. We got chopped up pretty bad. Can't get that bridge across while Johnny Reb has his guns on us."

Lyndel had scarcely moved on to another soldier when the crash of musket fire shattered the morning quiet again and silenced the songbirds. It went on and on. The gun smoke began drifting through the trees and into the field hospital. The scent of rotten eggs made Lyndel cringe under her navy blue dress. When she ran to get a bucket of water from a nearby stream a physician called Little Falls Run she saw boats being rowed across the Rappahannock to the Rebel side. Black-powder smoke covered both banks as the Confederate troops fired on the boats and the Federal troops near her fired back. The colors of the 24th Michigan and the 6th Wisconsin were in the boats.

Black hats began showing up at the hospital, either walking in or prone on a stretcher. The first one she recognized was Private Plesko, who came slowly up to her, Springfield in one hand, a bloody rag in the other he kept putting to his left cheek. Lyndel sat him down in the grass.

"Let me look at that," she said. "What happened?"

"We're shooting at the Rebels from our side of the river to keep them from shooting at our Wisconsin and Michigan boys. But some-times those Rebels are shooting at us instead of the boats. And they have thick undergrowth to hide in on their side while we're right out in the open but for a little stone wall." He smiled, a large hole in his cheek widening as he did so. "A ball came in one side of my mouth. It must have been spent or it would have kept on going out the other side. It tasted worse than Captain Hanson's coffee so I spat it up. Got it here in my pocket for a souvenir. Do you want to see it?"

Lyndel almost laughed. "I've seen plenty of bullets, Private, but thank you anyway. I'm going to clean the wound and I need you to rinse out your mouth. Here's a canteen."

"The water will leak out the hole."

"Put your hand over it."

"Then what?"

"Then you wait until the serious injuries are seen to and a doctor will suture your wound."

"How long?"

"I don't know, Private. An hour? Maybe longer."

Plesko stared at her, his normally soft blue eyes suddenly vivid and bright. "No, no, Mrs. King. Some of the platoon snuck over in the first wave and your husband was one of them. I intend to be in on the sec-ond wave. I can't be sitting here while they're over there. Just clean it out and stuff in some gauze and wrap a bandage over it. Please."

Lyndel wiped at the blood on his face. "I will do nothing of the sort. You can't run around all day with another hole in your head. It needs to be sutured."

"You suture it."

"I can't."

"Mrs. King. The Lord knows I admire and respect you. All the men in the regiment do. But it's either a ball of gauze or an Amish suturing or I'm gone as soon as your back is turned. Mrs. King, they need me."

A thought darted into her mind: *He could lose his life out there, face wound or no face wound. On the other hand, he might save a life out there too.*

"Very well, Private. Sit still while I get some morphine. That will deaden the pain at the edges of the hole. I expect I have seen enough suturing to do it in my sleep. Let me see to the horsehair. You know there will be a scar once the sutures come out."

"Most wounds we get back home mean nothing. This scar will mean something, Mrs. King."

"I see." On an impulse she leaned over and kissed him on the wounded cheek. "I'll do the best I can, soldier."

His face had darkened with blood at her kiss. "Thank you, ma'am."

She was surprised at how steady her hand was. The young man didn't murmur. He stared straight ahead, only closing his eyes now and then if the pain was sharp. In twenty minutes he was on his way, running through the bushes to the steep riverbank, calling back his thanks as he disappeared. The gunfire had lessened considerably once the first wave landed on the far bank and charged the Rebel forces. So Lyndel had no trouble hearing what she knew was a Hoosier yell and went to Little Falls Run to fetch more water and look at the Rappahannock. Indiana colors were in the boats shooting across the current and Plesko was in the first one, bayonet fixed, jumping out into water that went to his chest before the boat had even touched the other shore, clambering up the bank, and disappearing toward the sound of musket shots and loud yelling.

It's almost like a sport to you men. But, God have mercy on you all, it is no sport.

Morganne, face streaked with grime, also came for water and put her arms on Lyndel's shoulder. "You look much better than you did three hours ago, sister."

"Thank you, Davey. I confess I haven't even thought about all those things that troubled me in the dark."

"Did I see you suturing that young private?"

"One of the physicians gave me permission. He glanced at it afterward and said I had done a creditable job."

They both laughed.

"That old grump," smiled Morganne. "You could have raised the dead and he would have said the same thing—*creditable, Mrs. King, creditable.*"

The Rebels were routed, the pontoon bridge constructed, and the Union troops crossed the river without further hazard. The two nurses tended the wounds of a couple of corporals from the 6th Louisiana, Hayden and Rhodus, who talked up a storm as their bayonet cuts were being dressed—their farms, their families, their churches, and their horses all came into the conversation with the two Pennsylvania nurses. Then the ambulances and medical wagons followed the soldiers in blue to a new bivouac.

For days the wagons rolled behind the First Corps and the Iron Brigade but there was never another fight. What happened with General Hooker's plan came to them in bits and pieces as April ended and the first week of May began. Hooker took up a defensive position west of Fredericksburg at Chancellorsville and watched Stonewall Jackson march his troops right past the front of his line and did nothing, thinking Stonewall was retreating.

Stonewall then slammed into Hooker's right flank and demolished the Eleventh Corps, which was dug in there. In the hours and days of vicious fighting that followed, Hooker, never recovering from Stonewall's assault, allowed himself to be beaten back north toward Washington. The Union leader never called upon the second part of his army, led by General Sedgwick, to attack Lee from the rear, he never called upon the First Corps, he never called upon the Iron Brigade—except when the battle was lost and he was adrift in a concussion from the debris of a Rebel artillery round and the brigade was called upon to be the rear guard for the Army of the Potomac.

It was the same task they had undertaken when the army retreated from the second battle at Manassas the summer before. The rain falling and turning the roads to mud and pools of water, the First Corps and the Iron Brigade returned to the Fitzhugh House on May 7th and made camp. Union forces had been defeated once again and the 19th Indiana and her sister regiments had fought their way across the Rappahannock in April to make absolutely no difference in the outcome of the contest between North and South.

Lyndel's wagon splashed along behind the troops, whose backs bent under the rain and their packs and their loss. She knew Nathaniel was alive because she had seen him only hours before, leading his men on foot, his new sword dangling from his hip, covered in mud, the holster for his new revolver soaked black with water. His head was up and she saw his lips moving as he spoke to his platoon. But she knew his heart would be lower than the ruts the wagon wheels made in the muck.

Oh, Lord, will our fortunes ever turn, will they ever turn—or is it your will that America remain a household split in two?

Back at Fitzhugh House Lyndel worked with the casualties day and night and saw no sign of her husband. But the Monday morning after they returned she was trying to pour herself a coffee, her hands shaking from fatigue, when he took the pot from her, filled her cup, and pressed it into her hands, holding it there.

"I love you," he said.

She clutched the cup and leaned her head into his chest, closing her eyes. "I love you too. Where have you been? I've missed you."

"I was sent out to do reconnaissance the day after we arrived here. They've given me a horse."

"A horse. How wonderful. Where is he?"

"She. A mare. Can you walk with me a few minutes?"

"I can."

Holding her hand, he led her to a tall pine behind the Fitzhugh mansion. A shining black horse was tethered there and it nickered at their approach. Lyndel's eyes took on light and color as she put a hand to the mare's neck and stroked her. The mare swung her head and tried to chew playfully at Lyndel's black apron and Lyndel laughed like a young girl.

"Oh, we're already good friends. What's her name?"

"Libby."

"Why such a name?"

"For Elizabeth. Elizabethtown."

"She's a beauty."

"Perhaps I should have named her Lyndel then."

"No, you would need a sorrel for that. Something with red in its coat."

He tilted her chin and kissed her long and with strength. Finally pulling away she glanced around them and, seeing that no one else was nearby, brought her lips back to his. After several minutes she rested her head on his chest again.

"Where have you and Libby been?" she asked.

He evaded the question with a question of his own. "Did you hear that Stonewall Jackson is dead?"

She immediately lifted her head and drew back to see his face better. "No. We've only heard that he was wounded by his own pickets last week after the attack on Hooker's flank."

"Pneumonia set in after they amputated his arm. He died yesterday. May 10th. The Southern papers say he always wanted to die on a Sunday, the Lord's Day."

Lyndel folded her hands in front of her as she stood. "What do your men say?"

Nathaniel looked away and rubbed Libby between her ears. "I know there's no love lost between certain parties on either side. Some in the South see us as tyrants and some in the North see them as traitors. No doubt many in the Union are thanking God that Stonewall is dead. A few might even wish him in hell. But my boys don't think that way. We've been up against Stonewall several times. At Brawner's Farm he said we fought against him with *obstinate determination*, which is a mouthful of praise from Jackson. There is no hatred in my company for him. We wish he hadn't died. He was an American."

Lyndel nodded. "I feel the same way. All the deaths in all the battles sadden me and his death saddens me too."

"Let's walk down to the river for a minute."

They stood on the bank holding hands and gazing at the sun leaping back and forth across the current. It was impossible not to look at the opposite side where the Iron Brigade had stormed the Rebel defenses two weeks before. Nathaniel kissed the top of her head by her white *kapp*.

"I love the smell of your hair. All around you is blood and mud and dying and you always manage to smell like a bouquet of lilacs."

"I discipline myself to wash my hair every morning. Though sometimes I confess I wonder if it's worth the effort."

"It's worth the effort to me. Even if I'm not there every morning to enjoy it. I miss brushing your hair out for you."

"Well, if we stay here long enough perhaps we can get back to our old married-couple routines like that." She smiled. "I miss hearing you say you love running your hands through the flames."

But he didn't smile, though his eyes came from the river to rest firmly on hers. "There will be some time. I don't know how much. Weeks, I think—you see the men have shoveled out walkways and ditches and put up tents with awnings made from woolen blankets and pine boughs. I believe it will be the same as last year—Lee licked us at Manassas Junction, the brigade covered the army's retreat, and Lee came after us into Maryland and we had a fight. Now he's licked us at Chancellorsville, the brigade's covered the army's retreat a second time, and it's only a matter of time before Lee comes north. He has Harrisburg on his mind again, I'm sure of it. And Washington. If there's one flaw in Lee's makeup it's pride. He means to complete what he wasn't able to complete in '62—the invasion of Pennsylvania, the capture of Harrisburg, the entrapment of Washington, and the destruction of the Army of the Potomac."

"Is this what you've found out by your reconnoitering on horseback?"

"Partly from that. Also from prisoners. From other sources. Stonewall's death will set Lee back a few weeks. But then he'll gather the Army of Northern Virginia together and strike as hard as he can. He's not afraid of us."

"Should he be?"

"Of generals like Hooker and Burnside and McClellan? No. But when the Iron Brigade gets a chance to fight he should reckon on the backbone Stonewall saw in us. The men are in a sour mood because we're frustrated, Lyndy. At Fredericksburg only the 24th Michigan got to put up a fight. At Chancellorsville the 6th Wisconsin and 24th

Michigan led the brawl on the other side of the river there and that was it. We didn't do anything else. The great battles are being decided without us.

"The Lord knows I hate the killing, but the Lord also knows I want the fighting if the fighting can end this war more quickly. At Brawner's Farm we fought Stonewall and Lee to a standstill. We did it again at South Mountain. We did it a third time at Antietam Creek. Let Lee come after us, Lyndy, and may God give us a chance to stand squarely in his path this time like David."

Lyndel watched the green fire tear through her husband's eyes. He seemed to burn the air that moved around him as he spoke. She felt a pricking of fear in her stomach.

"You talk as if the 19th Indiana and the Iron Brigade are ready to change the course of the war and take on Lee's army single-handed," she said.

A softer color came into his eyes and he touched her cheek, playing with a loose strand of her hair and twisting it around his fingers. "We have some time. God has given us a second honeymoon. Let's make the most of it."

Now he smiled again and strong warmth filled her as she saw his love for her.

"*A virtuous woman who can find?*" he recited. "*For her price is far above rubies.*"

He removed her *kapp* and began to pull the pins from her hair until it fell in a scarlet shower upon her shoulders and down her back. She didn't stop him. Nor did she look about her to see if anyone was watching as he ran his hands through her hair and placed his lips against hers.

"*Let him kiss me with the kisses of his mouth,*" she murmured, "*for thy love is better than wine.* Oh, Nathaniel, I wish we had our log cabin back."

"Perhaps," he said as he moved his lips over her long shining hair, "the army will consider letting out the Fitzhugh mansion to us for thirty days. I think I can just swing it on a second lieutenant's pay."

23

The army didn't let the Fitzhugh House out to Lyndel and Nathaniel but it didn't bother them when they met there for privacy. Nathaniel repaired a table and chairs that had been abandoned and set them up in a back parlor. Sometimes the two of them ate there, sometimes they just sat together and talked. It could never be like the log house, for Nathaniel refused to room with his wife while his men slept in the field.

At night Nathaniel lay on the ground next to Lyndel's brother Levi while his wife slept in a wagon next to Morganne. Yet to Lyndel the evenings in the Fitzhugh House by the Rappahannock had a charm and wonder all their own, and no experience surpassed sitting in the parlor with the door shut and one candle between her and her husband—his rugged face and green eyes glowed like gold.

By day she nursed the sick and wounded of the 19th Indiana, the Iron Brigade, and the First Corps while Nathaniel drilled his men. For five days in late May, the 19th Indiana and three other regiments were sent out to rescue the 8th Illinois Cavalry but they only marched in a circle for one hundred miles and came back, finding nothing they'd been told they would find.

Sometimes Nathaniel left for days on reconnaissance missions as the Union did its best to keep an eye on the movements of Lee and the Army of Northern Virginia. She was aware that the cavalry were normally used for this sort of work and wasn't sure what Nathaniel's role was, except it didn't take people long to see that he was an exceptional rider. He wouldn't talk about where he went but now and then there was the whiff of burnt powder on his uniform when she hugged him, and twice she watched him reloading his revolver at the parlor table with lead balls.

At the end of May the commander of the Iron Brigade, Long Sol Meredith, designated the Fitzhugh House as a sleeping residence for the only two women traveling with the army, Lyndel and Morganne. Nathaniel and Levi and the others in the platoon cleaned up two of the bedrooms on the second floor after repairing the staircase, and a pair of beds was put together with the help of some of the carpenters in the company. The women washed and hung curtains they found in an old trunk, and extra blankets donated by various soldiers were laundered and used as bedding.

"We live like queens," Morganne said one night as she stretched herself out upon her bed. "It's soon going to feel like the Palmers' home in Washington if we pick up a few more pieces of furniture."

"Hiram would have a story in this," Lyndel replied, finishing the stitches on a pillowcase. "When do you hope to see him again?"

"I have no idea. His last letter was two weeks ago. He's more enamored of General Grant than he is of me."

"Oh, I doubt that, Davey."

"I don't know if I'm that interested in Mr. Hiram Wright anymore anyway."

But the next day, June 4th, Hiram did show up in an unexpected way, when newspapers came into camp with the story of an assault by Union troops on Port Hudson on the Mississippi. He had written the account for the Philadelphia paper that employed him. What made this battle different from all others before it was that the soldiers who charged the Rebel fort were African-Americans. Lyndel read several accounts in the Boston and New York newspapers but liked Hiram's writing the best and clipped it for the diary she had begun to keep. Her spirit was a swirl of joy and pain as she pasted the columns of type in her small book.

So this day, Wednesday, May 27, 1863, must go down in American history as a day of greatness. No matter that the Rebel fort at Port Hudson wasn't taken—it's under siege now just like Vicksburg and will drop to its knees before the Federal forces at the appointed time. No matter that many a brave man fell on the field this day never to rise until the last judgment when God calls the righteous home—their courage will inspire many another to take up arms against despotism and cruel slavery. The 1st and 3rd Louisiana must be remembered as a force that proved in the most heroic manner the manhood of their race. You may call them blacks or Negroes or Africans or colored, it matters not. God knows them by their heart and he knows them by their soul. He sees no color. Only men.

I spoke with a number of the soldiers before the battle. All of them were eager to take the fight to the enemy and, by so doing, display that they wished to see President Lincoln's Emancipation Proclamation in force from the Mississippi to the Potomac. Alas, not one of the men I interviewed survived the clash of arms. In particular I mourn Captain Andre Cailloux who fell in battle about one o'clock in the afternoon as he urged his troops forward. I also grieve the loss of a soldier who was always at his side and who led the 1st Louisiana on their final attack, proudly gripping the staff that flew the Stars and Stripes as he ran into the mouths of the guns. This man was Sergeant First Class Moses Gunnison.

When they met after the news had swept through the Iron Brigade and the First Corps, Nathaniel and Lyndel did not speak. They gripped each other's hands, the rings on their fingers strong and golden in the sunlight. Several times Nathaniel tried to say something to her but failed at each attempt. Finally he blurted out, "Charlie and Moses." Then he brought her into the embrace of his arms.

"I'm riding out on Libby in a few minutes. We will be gone for a few days."

"I will pray."

"You wonder what it is I do on these excursions—"

"You don't have to explain yourself."

"I'm not sure why I was chosen. There are only a handful of us. The others are all cavalry officers. We ride hard and fast and get in as close as we can to Lee's army. Often we elude the pickets and are on the edges of the camps. We look for unit standards, estimate brigade size, watch for movement north or west. There was a time when we thought Lee might march on the Mississippi to try to lift the siege at Vicksburg. But he has no intention of leaving Virginia except to come after us."

"Is he coming now?"

"There are reliable reports that have just started arriving from our agents and Virginians loyal to the Union that the Army of Northern Virginia began to march yesterday, on the 3rd. They say Lee is going up through the Shenandoah Valley to make it more difficult for us to track him. I and the other officers have to find out if the reports are true."

He grew quiet. Lyndel raised her head. "You have something else to tell me. What is it?"

"None of it has been corroborated."

"Yet it worries you."

"Some say Lee is headed for Pennsylvania as well as Baltimore and Washington. He may go through Lancaster County to get at Harrisburg and Philadelphia."

"Our home."

"Lee is a gentleman. He will not allow his soldiers to lay waste to villages and farms."

"But war is no gentleman."

Nathaniel didn't respond.

"Can he do it?" she asked. "Does he have the men?"

Nathaniel's eyes were the green of a deep forest. "We are pretty sure he has over seventy thousand troops."

"Oh, Nathaniel—"

"I must go." He kissed her on the forehead. "I hope to be back by Monday."

He walked to where Libby was tethered, stepped up into the saddle, and rode off through the throng of soldiers and wagons and tents. Levi and Joshua saw him go and approached Lyndel, who watched as her husband disappeared among the trees.

"Ginger," Levi asked, "what's going on?"

"Nathaniel's just doing what he always does."

"Which is what?"

"I'm sure he's told you."

"No," replied Joshua, "he doesn't tell us anything about his rides."

"Why are you asking me? If he wanted the platoon or company to know he'd have said something."

Levi folded his arms over his chest. "He went out of here like a man with the weight of the world on his shoulders. Grow him a beard and dress him in black and gain him another half foot in height and he'd win the Abe Lincoln look-alike contest sure."

"Rumor in camp has him scouting for Hooker," Joshua prodded. "You think that's so?"

"I can't say."

"It's Lee, isn't it?" Her brother was staring at her, hoping to catch a flicker in her face that would tell him the truth. "He's on the move. We don't see any Rebel pickets posted on the riverfront today."

Lyndel dropped her eyes to avoid his. "Even if General Lee were on the march, Nathaniel wouldn't talk about it. He would be afraid of causing a panic."

"A panic? That would be a cause for celebration in this camp! Ever since South Mountain and Antietam, the brigade's been shoved to one side or left in reserve. We want to fight, Lyndy. All we do is sit around here eating salt pork and potatoes and hardtack. Why, those of us who were new recruits to the 19th Indiana last year never even fought at Brawner's or South Mountain. So we want to look Lee straight in the face like we did at Antietam Creek. We want to knock the Army of Northern Virginia so far south they'll have to change their name."

"Strange words to come from the mouth of an Amish boy and a bishop's son."

She looked up as she said these words. His eyes burned black.

"When I say I will plow a straight furrow I plow a straight furrow." Levi bit out his words. "When it's time for haying I cut the whole field. When it's harvest I work all day and all night if necessary to bring the crop into the barn. So our father taught me. When I say I will fight slavery I mean to fight it until the fight is finished. When I say I will die to keep this nation free if necessary I will die to enable men and women to live in liberty within our borders. All men. All God's children."

He stalked away and Joshua followed.

Long Sol had asked Morganne to lead the men in a sing that night. It was meant to get their minds off gambling, profanity, and whiskey as well as the illicit trade with the Rebels on the far bank of the Rappahannock. It was also an opportunity to celebrate with the 24th Michigan, who had finally got their hands on their black hats a week before, after waiting more than half a year. At the same time the 19th Indiana had received both a new Stars and Stripes and a new regimental flag.

Morganne had wanted Lyndel to join her but Lyndel, feeling out of sorts after quarreling with her brother, chose to remain at the Fitzhugh House. Standing at her bedroom window she could see the flames of the bonfire and Morganne standing slender and dark in front of the wall of light with her guitar. The men's voices, some two thousand of them, easily made their way into the mansion. They had just finished singing "The Girl I Left Behind Me" and now were shouting for Morganne to play a song Lyndel knew had become popular in both the North and the South. Her friend's voice, clear as starlight, reached her before the soldiers joined in like a storm.

"All quiet along the Potomac," they say,
"Except now and then a stray picket
Is shot, as he walks on his beat to and fro,
By a rifleman hid in the thicket.
'Tis nothing—a private or two now and then
Will not count in the news of the battle;
Not an officer lost—only one of the men,
Moaning out, all alone, the death-rattle."

All quiet along the Potomac tonight,
Where the soldiers lie peacefully dreaming;
Their tents in the rays of the clear autumn moon,

Or the light of the watchfire, are gleaming…

There's only the sound of the lone sentry's tread,
As he tramps from the rock to the fountain,
And thinks of the two in the low trundle-bed
Far away in the cot on the mountain.
His musket falls slack; his face, dark and grim,
Grows gentle with memories tender,
As he mutters a prayer for the children asleep,
For their mother; may Heaven defend her!…

He passes the fountain, the blasted pine tree,
The footstep is lagging and weary;
Yet onward he goes, through the broad belt of light,
Toward the shade of the forest so dreary.
Hark! was it the night wind that rustled the leaves?
Was it moonlight so wondrously flashing?
It looked like a rifle—"Ha! Mary, good-bye!"
And the life-blood is ebbing and plashing.

All quiet along the Potomac tonight;
No sound save the rush of the river;
While soft falls the dew on the face of the dead—
The picket's off duty forever.

By the end, the men's usually thunderous voices had softened. Lyndel didn't like "All Quiet Along the Potomac Tonight," for it sang of death. Whenever she heard the words they renewed her fear that Nathaniel would come riding in from his reconnaissance one night and be shot by mistake by a Union picket just as Stonewall Jackson had been shot by his own men. She was grateful that Morganne immediately launched into a more cheerful tune, "When Johnny Comes Marching Home Again." For an instant she was certain she saw Levi get to his feet, clapping his hands to the beat of the song. Soon hundreds joined Levi and blocked him, if it was him, from her sight.

Lyndel knelt by her bed. It was her place to go her brother and ask forgiveness. She had snapped at him the way their father would have snapped at him. No, she didn't want him to enjoy the fighting or look forward to the battles. But without soldiers like him, the war couldn't be won and slavery nailed into its coffin.

And he was more than the ordinary soldier who fought and slept and wanted to go home. He had been reading the Bible to the men in his platoon daily and answering the questions about God and life after death they put to him. Men from other platoons and companies had begun to join in. Even Rebel prisoners that had not been sent north yet. Their father wouldn't be proud to see his son in a uniform but he would be proud to see what he was doing with a Bible in his hands.

"He is a good teacher, ma'am," said one of the prisoners to her. "A powerful good teacher. He'd be welcome back home once this spat is over."

Lyndel was applying a new bandage to the wound on his shoulder. "Really? And what does God think of our 'spat,' as you call it, Corporal Erwin?"

"Not being privy to the Lord's thoughts, I can't say. There are good Christian folk praying for victory on both sides of the Mason–Dixon line. A lot of them are going to be disappointed. But no one is disappointed with a good message from God's Book. No one loses there, North or South."

Another Reb prisoner asked, "I hear the man with the Bible is your brother—is that so?"

Lyndel was bathing a bullet hole in his foot. "That's true, Sergeant Thornton."

"Is he a chaplain?"

"No. Infantry. Like you."

"I would say he has a calling to preach the gospel. I know because I've had such a call myself."

"You're in a strange place for a Baptist church."

He grinned. "How'd you guess I was Baptist?"

"Your hair grows a certain way." She smiled up at him. "Just a shot in the dark, Sergeant."

"If the Lord spares me, I'll have my church and my pulpit and my flock one day. It will be a glorious undertaking. The one thing that transcends all this folly and carnage is the Spirit of the Lord. That's why I can see that what's in my heart is in your brother's heart also."

"If it's folly, why are you fighting?"

"I expect because the South is my home—and y'all have invaded it. But I reckon you're doing what you think is right too. The Lord'll sort it all out. I hope your brother makes it through and honors the call God has blessed him with."

She dried his foot with a clean towel. "Thank you, Sergeant Thornton."

Lyndel's knees began to ache. She tried to pray but the Bible verse kept coming into her head about cleaning the debris from her own eye before she could see clearly enough to clear the debris from her brother's. When she tried to ignore it another verse popped into her head: *Therefore if thou bring thy gift to the altar, and there rememberest that thy brother hath ought against thee; leave there thy gift before the altar, and go thy way; first be reconciled to thy brother, and then come and offer thy gift.*

Yet Lyndel felt a stubbornness rise up in her chest. She ought to go to Levi now, walk down the staircase he had helped repair, make her way to the bonfire, find him, and apologize. But she couldn't do it. Neither could she pray. So she sat on the edge of her bed, looked at the firelight on the window glass, and felt miserable.

She had lain down and drifted off, when Morganne shook her shoulder. "Get up! The army is ordered forward and the men are breaking camp!"

Lyndel sat up, confused. "What? What time is it?"

"Just after midnight."

"But Nathaniel isn't here."

"The tents are already being folded up. Hurry. I need your help with the medical supplies."

They worked through the night and finally got some rest about four in the morning. But they were awakened again at six when the order was countermanded and all the tents put back up again. The two nurses wearily removed the medical supplies from the wagons and placed them in the hospital tent the ambulance crews had staked in place once more. It took most of the day before the camp was back to its normal routine.

On the 6th of June the brigade was sent to Franklin's Crossing in full gear to support a Federal action on the other side of the Rappahannock. Lyndel and Morganne remained at the Fitzhugh camp. In two days the brigade returned. "The only thing that happened," snarled an officer Lyndel treated for severe sunburn on the back of his neck, "was we roasted in line of battle for two days in the hot sun."

Time and time again she saw the troops fall in and be left sitting on the grass for hours before being told there would be no marching and that they were dismissed. Something was giving the army commanders the jitters and Lyndel knew it could only be Lee and his army. But no one at Union headquarters seemed to have the slightest notion where Lee was or what he was up to.

Then Nathaniel rode into camp late on June 10th with a cavalry escort, which brought soldiers running from all directions. There had been rumors of a battle about thirty miles away the day before. He was two days late and Lyndel thanked God he was safe. She dropped the cotton she was cutting into bandages and left the hospital tent to greet him. Once she saw the growth of beard on his face, the darkness in his eyes, and the saber cut across the left arm of his uniform she knew he had been in the fight.

The cavalry dismounted and began to talk to the Iron Brigade soldiers who crowded around them. Lyndel caught the names Culpepper Court House and Jeb Stuart before Nathaniel spotted her and, drawing Libby after him by the reins, led his wife away to where Little Falls Run emptied into the Rappahannock. Once he saw they were alone he embraced her with a ferocity that lifted both of her feet out of the dirt, and kissed her with a strength that left her struggling to get her breath.

"Did you pray for me?" he demanded.

Still trying to get air as his arms pinned her to him she said, "Yes… of course…I always pray for you—"

"Because that's the closest I have come yet. The Reb was taking a swipe at my neck and I threw up my left arm to ward off the blow. With my other hand I put the sword to him. I didn't even think twice. It was me or him. I'm sorry. But what a battle. There must have been twenty thousand of us. It was Jeb Stuart. We caught him by surprise. Brandy Station. It was at Brandy Station just by Culpepper Court House. All cavalry but for a small mob of infantry we had with us."

"I need to look at that wound."

"It hurts like the blazes but I didn't have time to get it looked at. As soon as Libby and I had rested up I needed to get back here. The escort was assigned to make sure I arrived safely. Why isn't the hospital tent packed up? Why isn't the camp on the move?"

Lyndel had plucked a pair of scissors from her pocket and was snipping away the lower left sleeve of his uniform. "Stand still, Lieutenant. I'm glad you missed me so much but I need to get at this."

His bare arm was a furious red and pus lined both sides of the long cut. She bit her lip. "We need to get you to the field hospital and get this lanced."

"But Lee is far ahead, Lyndel. I sent word days ago. Why hasn't Hooker given you the order to march?"

"No one has given us an order to do anything except to stand up and sit down and march to the river and march back again."

"Has Hooker lost his mind? They could be at Washington in days. I need to see Colonel Williams or Long Sol—"

"You need to get this wound properly cleaned, Lieutenant King, before you ride madly off north, south, east, or west."

"You're not taking me seriously."

A rider came pounding into camp on horseback. Lyndel glanced up from Nathaniel's arm, realized it was Hiram—a scrawnier, bonier version, but Hiram Wright nevertheless—and thought, *It's as if we're in a stage play and Hiram is arriving right on cue with a dramatic announcement to back up Nathaniel's concern.*

After all her talk of feeling distant from Hiram and unsure of how she felt about him anymore, Morganne, who was filling two buckets with water just upstream from them, saw who the rider was as he swung down off his horse, screeched in a way she never screeched, and ran to him, the buckets going one way and the water the other.

"My beauty!" Hiram held her and kissed her on the face and neck. "The most astonishing woman! The most intelligent woman! The most adorable woman!"

"Stop talking!" Morganne almost shouted and, heedless of the hundreds of soldiers watching and cheering, gripped both sides of his face in her hands and kissed him on the mouth.

In a moment, one arm around Morganne, Hiram spotted Nathaniel and came toward him, his face flushed with the ride and Morganne's kisses. "Nathaniel. I haven't even congratulated you and Miss Keim on your marriage. Well done, old friend, very well done."

"Thank you, Hiram," Nathaniel replied. "I only just got into camp myself."

Hiram saw his wound. "That's not from a bayonet."

"No."

"Were you at Brandy Station?"

"I was."

"That was a cavalry encounter. What were you doing there?"

"I've been riding with cavalry officers, Hiram. We're keeping an eye on Lee's army."

"Then you know he's gone; that he's making his way north with a bone in his teeth."

"I do know it."

"Then why is this camp still in its undershirts with clotheslines hanging from every oak tree?"

"Hooker's been told. I've sent back report after report. They can see for themselves by taking a long glance over the river with a good scope."

"I'm just back from Mississippi by rail because my paper said something big was up. I was loath to leave. I wanted to be there when Grant takes Vicksburg. Oh yes—he will take it, the siege will break the defenders' resistance, and Vicksburg's capture will be a crippling blow to the Confederacy, absolutely crippling. A big story. But my paper was right—what's happening here is even bigger. What's today? Wednesday? At least one corps of Lee's army will have crossed the Potomac by

Sunday or Monday. Richard Ewell is far out and ahead and will be well on his way to Pennsylvania before we've even reached Washington. We're losing and it's not even begun."

As if the generals had been listening in on the conversation by Little Falls Run, the very next day the Iron Brigade was told to get ready and on Friday it marched. The clotheslines were gone and the tents and the pine boughs and the wagons, this time for good. The Fitzhugh House was left to its ghosts once again and the beds and tables and chairs stood empty within its walls. The pace set for the march was so rapid that men began to collapse in the fierce June heat. Lyndel and Morganne jumped from their wagon to give them water and get them in the shade.

"There is no need to push the soldiers like this," Lyndel complained.

Hiram looked down at her from the driver's seat of the wagon. "This is the best chance Robert E. Lee has ever had. If he plays his cards right over the next couple of weeks he will win the war."

24

"They're not actually going to do it?" Lyndel wanted to look away but couldn't.

"Apparently they are." Hiram's face was pale white stone.

Morganne held Hiram's hand so tightly the blood left his fingers. "Couldn't there be a reprieve? Something from the First Corps commander, General Reynolds? Something from the president?"

Before she had finished her last sentence an order was given and the muskets fired. The young man sitting on the pine coffin with the blindfold over his eyes toppled backward into the dirt. To Lyndel's horror his arms and legs began to move and she could hear his voice.

"They fired too low," Hiram muttered. "Most of the bullets missed and just kicked up dust."

Several soldiers were ordered forward to reload and shoot a second time. They were only three feet from the wounded man when they fired. His arms and legs sank to the ground.

Hiram placed a hand on the wagon brake. "He ran last summer at Rappahannock Station. He ran at Fredericksburg in December. He ran last month when the brigade crossed the Rappahannock by the Fitzhugh House. That's why they shot him." He glanced about him. "We'll be marching again presently."

Lyndel watched them put the body in the coffin. "I thought we had truly stopped for lunch. Now I see the only reason we paused in our mad race north was to kill this young man."

"Well. They waited until everyone had eaten before they carried out the execution."

Lyndel didn't see Nathaniel, but he saw her seated on the driver's seat with Hiram and Morganne. He was sorry she had witnessed the shooting. For a moment he thought about making his way over to her but then the command came to fall in and he was ordering Levi and Ham to get the men on their feet. He walked over to Nip as the platoon tugged their packs over their shoulders.

"How is it with you, Nip?" he asked, picking his black hat off the grass and handing it to him.

Nip avoided his gaze. "Okay, I guess. I didn't have to shoot this one."

"No. Canteen full?"

"Yes, sir."

"I've been over this track more times than I can count over the past month. Water will be scarce for a while."

"Yes, sir." Then he smiled in his small way. "Think someone can rustle up some Rebel chicken on this march? I'm awful tired of potatoes and crackers."

Nathaniel laughed. "I guess we might ask Levi. Truth is, no one is as good at foraging as Corinth was. But we've been fighting over this ground since '61. Even my brother might be hard pressed to find a bird worth eating in north Virginia this summer."

The columns began to move. Nathaniel stayed beside Nip, holding Libby by the reins as he walked. Nip glanced at the horse.

"Why don't you ride, Lieutenant?"

"I like to stretch my legs."

"But you never ride while we're marching."

"Sometimes I do."

"Sure. When you have to see Sam Williams or Long Sol or General Reynolds. The rest of the time you hoof it like an enlisted man."

"Captain Hanson and First Lieutenant Nicolson are always mounted. That's enough. Besides—" Nathaniel grinned at Nip. "If I was going to ride I'd rather be perched up on that wagon with my little red-haired wife."

Talk lessened as the heat cut into their bodies and the dust rose up to their knees or higher. Canteens were emptied and refilled at mud holes where rainwater had collected. Levi took a swig of his warm mud water and spat it out.

"That's good water, Sergeant," Nicolson teased as he dismounted to walk his horse. "When you get really parched you'll wish you could get it back."

"I'm already parched and I hope I find good stream water before I have to swish half the farmland of Virginia around my mouth again."

"Let it settle," Nathaniel advised. "Shake the canteen as little as possible while you march and let the muck sink to the bottom. Then sip it. Better than nothing, Sergeant. There won't be anything in the way of good water on this route for a couple of days."

"No? I guess I'll have to try to liberate some Rebel wells along with the chicken coops tonight."

Nathaniel wiped dust off his face. "Good luck and God bless, Sergeant. There's not a farm for miles in this neck of the woods. The ruts and mud holes are your only friends."

Levi snorted. "My mouth gets dry debating you, Brother King. We'll see what midnight brings."

But midnight brought Levi and the platoon only darkness and exhaustion. He grabbed Nip and made a half-hearted foray into the woods and meadows but they returned without anything to show for their efforts except canteens full of water from a hayfield.

"It tastes better than the mud," he whispered to Nathaniel.

"Only in your imagination," Nathaniel replied.

"Did you see Lyndel tonight?"

"She's too far back. I have no idea where her wagon is. Posting her a letter would find her more quickly than my stomping around in the dark."

"Bet you tried for a while anyway, didn't you, Lieutenant?"

"A while, Sergeant. But after almost getting shot by the third picket I decided to lie down on this Virginia ground and get a farm boy's rest."

The next day the heat whipped their backs as mud holes and wheel ruts continued to offer the only opportunities to wet their mouths. The food was crackers and potatoes and hardtack. When they got meat dished up it was salt pork that made their thirst worse.

Levi swore he would find Rebel chicken and well water that night but Bealeton Station on the Orange and Alexandria railway tracks stymied him.

Sunday morning they were up before daylight and marched in coolness for a few hours before the sun hammered the road and dust filled the air. At nine that night they stopped to build fires and make coffee, Captain Hanson's brew having never been blacker or rougher, then marched another five miles on the coffee until sunrise brought them to a breakfast stop, where everyone was too exhausted to eat and just collapsed. Three hours later Nathaniel and Nicolson and Hanson were shaking shoulders and the First Corps was on the move once again to Manassas Junction, a mile away.

"What happened here?" asked Groom.

"We covered the army's retreat as usual," said Ham.

"Is that all?"

"No. That's not all. This is the same place, right by the rail line here, that we camped the morning after Brawner's Farm. And yonder—" Ham pointed. "Yonder is Brawner's Farm. We fought Stonewall's best there and never gave an inch until our good old General Pope made us withdraw and give them a mile. I'd walk you over there but we don't have the time and I'm too tired. Besides, that's where Corinth King died."

"I'm sorry," Groom responded.

Another five miles and General Reynolds stopped the corps so they could brew more pots of coffee. This time they used Bull Run Creek water. It had the look of Confederate uniforms, thought Nathaniel, and no wonder, since the South had won so many victories here. The coffee bought them another three hours on the road until they reached Centreville and cold water that the men gulped down, their mouths thick with dust and silt. They set up camp for the rest of the day, Monday the 15th, and before the sun had set Nathaniel was on Libby and looking for his wife.

It took almost half an hour but he spotted her red hair and white *kapp* in a cluster of ambulances and horses and galloped to her, jumping out of his saddle and swinging her in a circle.

"I thought," she laughed, "you'd be too hot and tired to come looking for me."

"I am. Libby found you."

"How are your men holding up?"

"Very well. But let's just say I thank our God this place has decent water."

Lyndel kissed him and then stroked Libby's flank. "The poor dear must have needed fresh water as badly as the boys."

"She did."

"How is my brother?"

"Levi's fine. When I left him he was washing his face and hair."

"Ah. My clean and tidy brother."

Nathaniel ran his thumb gently over her eyebrows. "Tell me. Is everything all right between the two of you?"

"Why shouldn't it be?"

"Nicolson offered Levi his horse so he could ride with me to find you and Levi said no. That's not what he would have done a month ago."

Lyndel looked down. "It's something I have to fix."

"I can't stay long. Will you ride back with me?"

"Oh, no, I can't—"

"The men have blisters. You would be helping us out if you took care of a few."

"They'll set up a station here for the regiment and the brigade—"

"Lyndy." He kissed her blue eyes. "I need an excuse to have my wife around. And I want her around. Another day and we'll be off again and marching as rapidly as we can. As far as your brother goes, bear in mind an engagement could come at any time. Washington is just to the east of us and Lee's forces are only a matter of miles to the west. We're racing to head him off. Eventually we're going to collide."

"All right." She made her pixie face without being aware of it. "I'm not dressed for riding, though. I'll need to sit sidesaddle."

"Sidesaddle with my arm around you."

"How is the cut on your arm?"

"Right as rain."

"Let me get a few bandages and instruments."

The sky was crimson as they rode into the 19th Indiana's camp. The first person she saw was her brother, standing and talking with, of all people, the commander of the First Corps, General Reynolds, surrounded by his retinue of officers.

As she dismounted the general moved along to see how other units were faring. Levi was smiling as he watched him go. He turned and was surprised by Lyndel's presence and lost some of his good humor, but not all of it.

"I didn't know he was born in Lancaster," he said to Nathaniel. "Isn't that something? And he didn't know he had Pennsylvanians in his Indiana regiment thanks to the good Amish of Elkhart County."

Lyndel stood before him. "You don't have to pretend I'm not here."

"I see you."

"Can we go someplace and talk?"

"Here's fine."

"All right." She didn't approach him. "I take after Father more than Mother, you know that. I have some of his good points and some of his bad. My temper is my own—and my discomfort with this war and the position it's put us in. I don't know if I'll ever be able to make peace with our parents. But I would like to make peace with you. You are my brother. I love you. I'm proud you have the courage to make such a sacrifice and bear arms, a sacrifice that includes losing your relationship with our father and mother and relatives, possibly for all time.

"I don't like the war. I don't like the grieving it brings to families in Louisiana and Mississippi and Massachusetts. But I'm grateful that it put Moses Gunnison in uniform and gave him a chance to finally fight for his freedom. I'm grateful that my brother isn't afraid to fight for that same liberty for others who will never know his name. I don't want you to love war or worship the army and I don't think that's what you want to do. You're eager to get your hands on the plow and complete the task. I misunderstood and lashed out at you as Father might, but the words were my own. Perhaps you don't wish to be reconciled. If not, I'll see to those in your company who have particularly difficult blisters and be on my way. But I'll continue to pray for you, my brother. And…I am sorry."

She waited a moment but Levi didn't respond. Turning away she removed the bandages and medical instruments from the saddlebags on Nathaniel's mare and walked toward Ham and Jones and Plesko, who were sitting on a patch of grass about a hundred feet away.

"Nurse."

Lyndel stopped and looked at Levi. "What is it?"

Levi dropped down and pulled his boots off. "No one in the Army of the Potomac has blisters like I do. I could use your help here. If you don't mind."

Lyndel came slowly to her brother. "I don't mind."

She squatted by him to examine his toes. "You do have some pretty big ones, it's true. I'm going to lance them and wipe them with alcohol and wrap them. You're going to have to stay off your feet for as long as you can."

"The way we've been marching that may only be another fifteen minutes."

"Even so, that will help."

Her head drew close to his as she brought a large needle to bear. He smiled at her. "Go easy on me, Ginger. I have a healthy dose of Papa and Mama's stubbornness too. I could have come to you at any time to make things right between us. I'm sorry I didn't. I love you."

Tears slipped down her cheeks. "Oh, this is no good. Now I can't see properly. Why do you have to be such a gentleman? It's one of Nathaniel's greatest faults too."

"Come here, sister."

Levi held her in his arms. Nathaniel smiled and then laughed.

"Is this funny?" asked Levi.

"What's funny is our company."

Levi glanced over his shoulder. All the men in the company had their boots and socks off and their bare feet were sticking out in front of them, ready for Lyndel's examination and ministrations. Levi couldn't stop from laughing either.

"What is it?" demanded Lyndel, pulling free. "Can't a sister have a good cry in her brother's arms anymore?"

"It seems there's nothing like a redheaded nurse," replied Levi. "You'll keep the Army of the Potomac on the march single-handed."

The troops stayed where they were through the night and the next day. But word soon came that Lee's Second Corps, commanded by Richard Ewell, had crossed the Potomac at Williamsport on Monday the 15th and were heading north into Pennsylvania.

Monday was the day the Iron Brigade and other units had arrived in Centreville. Once the Union soldiers received the news, they filled their canteens and got as much rest as they could, aware their fast march would begin again in the morning. Wednesday the 17th was like fire, and men dropped by the roadside as they were pushed north under the fierce sun. Morganne and Lyndel lifted the heads of the fallen soldiers and put canteens to their lips.

Day after day, through heat or rainstorm, the regiments were hurried toward Maryland and Pennsylvania. On June 25th they crossed the Potomac at Edwards Ferry at the same time as the rest of Lee's army was crossing at Sharpsburg and the Antietam battlefield. They passed through towns and villages where crowds cheered and young women tossed bouquets of flowers and schoolchildren gazed in awe at the men in tall black hats. On the 27th the Iron Brigade reached South Mountain and made camp. This time Ham showed Groom where the brigade had fought and received its name.

The stone wall they had charged was still there. War and weather hadn't broken it down. But the wooden boards that marked the Union dead were barely readable and the graves overgrown with tall grass. Ham walked Groom over the slope the 19th Indiana had run up, with balls kicking up mud or snapping past their heads.

"We put a knot in General Lee's plans that day," Ham said. "We kept him from Pennsylvania."

"But this time he *is* in Pennsylvania, Corporal."

"And Pennsylvania's as far as he gets. You'll be part of stopping him. It could be a fight as memorable as South Mountain, Private."

He caught Groom's look of dismay at the soldiers' graves that had nearly been blotted out.

"Never mind," Ham said. He turned toward the weathered boards. "We remember you. Your comrades in arms always remember you."

On the 28th they marched through another ecstatic flag-waving crowd in Frederick and camped there overnight. The news came to them that Hooker had resigned due to a dispute with the General-in-Chief in Washington and that George Meade now commanded the Army of the Potomac. The 29th took the Union troops through heavy rain to Emmitsburg.

On the last day of June, the 19th Indiana became the first infantry in the Army of the Potomac to cross the state line into Pennsylvania. There the long march ended—the Iron Brigade bivouacked at Marsh Creek while the 19th were sent ahead to picket the road north. Most of the Indiana troops encamped at the village of Green Mount but four companies were sent farther ahead to keep watch for Rebel forces. One of them was Nathaniel's.

"The farmers say the secesh are all around us," Ham muttered as he checked his Springfield for the fourth time to make sure it was loaded. "Lee's got his whole army up here and ours is still back in Maryland."

"Don't be getting cold feet, Corporal," chided Captain Hanson as he walked his horse past. "The Iron Brigade's enough to keep Lee at bay for a few hours."

"With a bit of work, sir."

"Yes, indeed. That's why you wear the black hat."

The falling sun silhouetted the landscape to the north and west in deep purples and golds.

"What you reckon that hill is, Lieutenant?" Jones asked Nathaniel.

"Don't know," Nathaniel replied.

"Round Top." It was Sam Williams, commander of the 19th, behind them. "You can't quite see it from here, but west of it is Little Round Top. There are several ridges and promontories beyond that."

Nathaniel and the men near him came to attention. "Good evening, Colonel."

"Stand easy, boys. I had a look over the map of the area with Generals Meredith and Reynolds a little while ago. Though I doubt Lee will choose to engage us here. My guess is we'll march farther north before there's a clash. After all, his troops have bypassed Washington and Baltimore. Seems like it's Harrisburg and Philadelphia he's after."

"Yes, sir," responded Nathaniel. "But you never know what Lee's thinking."

"Right you are, Lieutenant. We'll see what the morning brings. My hunch is we'll have breakfast in the town of Gettysburg just ahead here and then move straight on for Harrisburg as quick as we can. Either that or swing east for Lancaster and Philadelphia." He looked at Nathaniel. "I understand Lancaster County is your first home, Lieutenant King, just as it is for General Reynolds."

"Yes, sir, it is."

"I expect you'd rather not see it laid waste. A fight for you and the sooner the better, eh?"

"Harrisburg would suit me, Colonel. Or right here, for that matter. Anywhere but home."

"I understand. I'd feel exactly the same way. I was born in Virginia but I farmed in Selma, Indiana, and I'd sure hate to see the war spread west and scorch the land."

"Halloo the pickets! Don't shoot! We're unarmed—but we have plenty of wings!"

There was sniggering and laughter and somebody cried, "Whoops! I dropped one!"

Sam Williams snapped his head around. "Who in thunder is that?"

"They're wearing black hats, Colonel," his aide said.

"That's my—that's Sergeant Keim, sir," Nathaniel spoke up.

Williams frowned and slapped his gloves against his leg. "It looks like they've been foraging. And we're in a state loyal to the Union."

"Not so. Not so, whoever you are. The young ladies of Green Mount gave all this to us. Have some, will you? Our platoon can't possibly eat it all—pies, chicken, turkey, fresh biscuits, bread, butter. Why, I have five canteens full of cold milk—" Levi stopped when he saw the gold epaulets on Williams' shoulders. He almost dropped the five sacks of food he was carrying as he attempted to come to attention and salute. Plesko and Nip and Groom did let theirs fall. Behind them two more men were approaching the picket line and singing a hymn in German.

Nathaniel was afraid to look at Williams. But then the colonel's voice came easy and not without a stroke of humor. "Looks like Pennsylvania's fallen in love with the Hoosiers, Sergeant. I don't want to rob you, but my aide and I could do with a cherry pie if you have one handy. And I'll gladly exchange my canteen of spring water for one of fresh milk."

"Yes, sir. Happy to help you out, sir."

Levi fumbled with his sacks but Plesko stepped forward with a pie and canteen.

"This cherry pie was given to us by a girl as pretty as the sunset over your shoulder, Colonel. Eat heartily and thank God."

Williams laughed. "Why, I intend to. I think Tom here and I better dig in before we get back to headquarters and make our report. Otherwise General Reynolds will sniff it out and demand a lion's share. Johnny is a great one for the pies and biscuits."

"Yes, sir. And please keep your canteen. This one's on the house." Plesko smiled quietly as he handed the canteen of milk to Williams. "The Union forever."

"Hurrah."

Williams and his aide sat on the ground and dove into the pie while Levi handed out cooked chickens and turkey legs. Nip and Joshua held armfuls of bread and oranges. Nathaniel helped himself to a loaf and asked who had the butter and jam. It was meant as a joke but Groom quickly brought out both.

"This looks like the Fourth of July," said Ham, one eye on the road as he bit into a drumstick.

Nip wiped off a milk mustache. "It will be in a few days."

"I'm used to seeing fireworks."

Nip smiled as he worked on a cookie. "This is better than fireworks."

Williams pulled out his pocket watch. A round moon, almost full, had risen over the fields and lit the watch's face like a lamp. "We'd better get cracking, Tom. Reynolds will be wondering why we took so long to inspect the picket line."

The two climbed onto their horses. Williams saluted Nathaniel's platoon. "You soldiers are the farthest advance of the Army of the Potomac. March or fight, good luck and God bless tomorrow."

They returned the salute. "Thank you, sir."

After Williams and his aide had ridden off in the moonlight, the platoon continued to eat and drink. It took a while before they had had enough. Even then no one wanted to sleep. The moon had stroked the land in white.

"Almost like a field of snow," murmured Jones.

"It is," agreed Nathaniel. "Who's that coming toward us way up the road?"

"Captain Hanson and Lieutenant Nicolson, sir. They were reconnoitering a mile or two on foot. The captain wanted to get an idea how far it was to that next town."

"I thought they'd ridden into Green Mount."

"No, sir."

"I hope we have something left for them."

"Still plenty to go around, sir."

The platoon continued to gaze at the moonlit fields.

"Beautiful farmland," Levi said.

"What's that hill over there?" asked Joshua. "It sure sticks out."

"Round Top," Ham told him.

"It's morning now," Nathaniel said, returning his watch to his pocket. "Good morning, men."

"Good morning, sir."

25

Nathaniel opened his eyes. His watch said 3:30. A light drizzle had wet his uniform and hands and face. Nip was asleep beside him. He sat up. Groom was standing a few yards away with his bayonet fixed, watching the road in the last shimmer of light as the moon set in a bank of clouds to the west. Nathaniel craned his neck and spotted Levi walking softly through the grass with his musket a hundred feet beyond Groom.

Nathaniel lay back and pulled the small Bible from the pocket of his frock coat. Lyndel had borrowed it a few days before and underlined several verses in Psalm 91, which he now turned to.

A thousand shall fall at thy side, and ten thousand at thy right hand; but it shall not come nigh thee…For he shall give his angels charge over thee, to keep thee in all thy ways…Thou shalt tread upon the lion and the adder: the young lion and the dragon shalt thou trample under thy feet.

Nathaniel read the verses twice and prayed a moment: *So, Lord, a thousand men may read this today in both armies but they cannot all survive. How do we know when these verses are simply an encouragement to keep our faith strong and when they are directly and personally meant for us?*

He stood up. Groom saluted and he returned the salute.

"I'm heading down toward Green Mount, Private," he said quietly. "I'm going to check on the rest of our company."

"Yes, sir."

Nathaniel rubbed Libby's neck, untethered the mare, and drew her behind him as he walked along the road, letting her stop now and then to crop grass in the ditch. When he returned from his tour of the company's picket line most of the men were getting up and Hanson had appeared to brew his Tippecanoe coffee. The flames of the small fire were painting Levi's face orange as he stirred something in a pot and balanced a frying pan on his knee.

"What's that you're making?" Nathaniel asked as he came up, Libby brushing her head vigorously against his back.

"*A pretty little lass with eyes as green as grass*," Levi sang. "I have the ingredients I need to make proper Pennsylvania pancakes, *Pfannkuchen,* and the green-eyed Green Mount girl gave me a pound of butter and a jar of maple syrup too. What better way to welcome the boys to the Commonwealth of William Penn than to serve up hot *Pfannkuchen?*"

Nathaniel smiled. "Does the young lady have a name?"

"A name and an address. And Green Mount is not so far from Lancaster County, is it?"

"Not so far."

In less than an hour the platoon was squatting on the grass eating pancakes dripping in maple syrup and butter from their mess kits and taking fast swallows of Hanson's coffee. The sun made its way up over the long green fields, breaking apart the clouds and stripping the gray sky down to a raw blue.

"It goes well together," said Hanson. "The coffee and the syrup."

"Sure," responded Nicolson. "One is sweet and the other sour."

"You can thank my coffee you're still alive today, Lieutenant." Hanson walked up behind Groom and clapped him on the shoulder. "Here's more living proof. There was a time this young man poured my Indiana elixir on the ground."

Groom sipped from his cup. "I repented of that."

"Indeed you did. And that's why your cast-iron stomach is attached to a cast-iron body and the good Lord sees fit to let the sun rise upon thee again today." Hanson brought a handkerchief from his pocket and wiped his mouth. "Now, lads. I wouldn't wish to throw a wet blanket on your party while the rest of the brigade is gagging on sickly coffee and choking near to death on hardtack and salt pork. But we're marching at eight and our orders are to occupy the town of Gettysburg. So let's eat up and clean up and make sure you have the twenty rounds in your cartridge box and the extra sixty in your pack. You can have your second breakfast in town."

After they were squared away Nathaniel took Levi and Joshua off to the side for prayer. They removed their black hats and bowed their heads while Nathaniel prayed in German. When they looked back up after a few minutes it was to see not just each other but the platoon, and not only the platoon but the entire company. Musket stocks were on the ground and black hats had been doffed. Hanson was mounted on his horse and his own head was bare.

"I think the lads would like to have a prayer said over them, Reverend King," he said. "This time in English, if ye don't mind."

Nathaniel took off his black hat a second time. "Yes, sir."

His prayer was Psalm 23. Slowly he spoke the words—*Though I walk through the valley of the shadow of death, I will fear no evil: for thou art with me; thy rod and thy staff they comfort me. Thou preparest a table before me in the presence of mine enemies: thou anointest my head with oil; my cup runneth over.*

After he had pronounced *Amen* Nathaniel looked at the company. "March or fight, remember we're here for our homes and our nation. We want to live in a free country. A free country for all Americans, not just a few. God bless you, boys. God bless the United States of America."

There was a deep silence. Then Hanson threw up his arm. "Hurrah!"

The men grinned and, remembering Nathaniel's first sermon at Belle Plain, threw their hats into the air, hollering, "Hurrah!"

The troops broke apart to await the arrival of the brigade. As they parted Nathaniel caught a glimpse of a blue dress and a white *kapp*. Lyndel stood there in the road. The wagon was behind her with Hiram and Morganne on the driver's seat. Lyndel smiled.

"Hello," she said.

He came to her and her *kapp* fell in the dust. She did not care. She just wanted his arms and his smile and the eyes that saw only her.

"How did you get up here past all the pickets?" he demanded.

"Why, love, remember I have a pass from the president of the United States." She drew an envelope from the pocket under her apron. "And speaking of the president of the United States, this came to me last night. It was included in a pouch of dispatches for General Reynolds."

She put the envelope in his hand. It had already been opened.

"Well, read it," she said.

Nathaniel took out a small sheet of paper.

My dear Mrs. King:

I fear this note will find its way to you long after the announcement is common news. But recalling your family background I wanted to inform you personally that General George Gordon Meade has been appointed commander of the Army of the Potomac and that he is of good Pennsylvania stock. Though some of my advisors think otherwise it is my sense of things that events will conspire to bring the armies of Northern Virginia and the Potomac into battle on Pennsylvania soil. I believe therefore that having a Pennsylvanian in command, another Pennsylvanian as an officer in the Iron Brigade, and a third Pennsylvanian in attendance as a nurse can only bode well for our success against General Lee. My best wishes and my prayers in the fiery trial soon to be visited upon your husband and his men

*and indeed upon yourself and the medical
corps. It is my hope we will meet henceforth in
a stronger Republic because of what transpires
in the Commonwealth in which our glorious
Declaration of Independence was signed.*

Yours most sincerely,

A. Lincoln

"Hiram thinks it's a good omen," Lyndel said when Nathaniel looked up from the note.

"Does he? When I think back on what he wrote about Port Hudson and Moses Gunnison I'm inclined to believe Hiram Wright is becoming a religious man in the best way."

"I think so too."

"So, and where does Hiram think we will do battle?"

"Oh, you know Hiram, always swimming against the tide. Everyone else says Harrisburg or Lancaster or Philadelphia."

"And Hiram?"

She put her hand to his face and her eyes turned a darker blue than Nathaniel had ever seen. "Here. Today." Her lips tightened. "He believes most of Lee's army is in the vicinity."

"And where is our army?"

"Coming. Coming quickly. But perhaps not quickly enough."

"Fall in! Fall in! Form up by platoon and company!" Hanson was riding up and down the road. "Our brigade is marching!"

Nathaniel and Lyndel both saw the dust of the approaching troops.

"I must go," he said.

"I'm marching beside you," she told him.

"Lyndy, you can't."

"Of course I can. If the students at St. Joseph's College in Emmitsburg could march beside you on Monday I can certainly march beside you and your men on Wednesday. Is there any one of them I haven't nursed?"

"Lyndy—"

"This is not open to Amish debate. I have already asked Colonel Williams and he has given his consent. I can march with the regiment until such a…" Here her strong voice faltered a moment. "Until such a time as…the situation warrants a change…"

"I don't scarcely believe it."

Her bold composure returned and her eyes turned a fire blue. "Believe what you like. I'm marching. And we'd better fall in before Hanson leans down from that charger of his and bites us. If you like, I'll hold Libby's reins. Unless you'd rather be mounted."

He stared at her. "I reckon being friends with the president has gone to your head."

"Are you going to ride Libby or not?"

He kissed her forehead. "I guess you've put me afoot."

Once the 2nd Wisconsin and 7th Wisconsin had marched by, the 19th Indiana joined the column ahead of the 24th Michigan and the 6th Wisconsin. Lyndel marched beside her husband and her brother and the men cheered. Hiram and Morganne followed the brigade in the wagon.

The sun was warm on her face. The fields were alive with green, and the sky was as blue as a river. She thanked God for what had been offered to her and hoped she might walk beside Nathaniel and Levi all day. But then she heard cannon booming ahead of them.

"Pick up the pace!" shouted Nicolson from his horse. "General Buford's cavalry has run into a hornet's nest of Rebs just up the road!"

"That's enough now," Nathaniel said to Lyndel.

She lengthened her stride. "No, it is not. I'm a Pennsylvania farm girl. March as fast as you like. I'll keep up with you."

The column moved swiftly. Lyndel did not drop back. The crash of musket fire became as clear as the roar of the cannon. The closer they came to the town of Gettysburg the louder the firing grew. Lyndel realized her time with the regiment was limited. She took her husband's hand.

"I love you," she said and touched her ring to his.

The rings Moses Gunnison gave us, the rings his parents wore in secrecy while they were enslaved on a Virginia plantation, rings they placed on their fingers to show the other slaves the power of a love that could not be stopped by chains or whips.

"Halt! Fall out!" It was Hanson. "Pile your packs at the side of the road! Noncombatants to the rear!"

"Pray for us," said Nathaniel, holding her a final time.

"Of course I'll pray for you." She put her fingers to her eyes.

He smiled. "I'm in love with you, you know."

She laughed as she struggled to keep herself from crying. "Oh, who would ever have guessed?"

"Get the extra cartridges out of your packs!" barked Nathaniel as he broke away from her. "Stuff them in your pockets! We don't know how long we'll be mixed up in this!"

"God bless you, sister." Levi was at Lyndel's side, his pack gone, musket at his side. "May you have a steady hand and a steady heart when the wounded come to you."

She put her arms around his neck and kissed his cheek. "Thank you. Be safe, my good brother. Please watch out for each other. Watch out for…Nathaniel."

"I will. We all will."

Lyndel was startled when the men began to sing, one regiment picking up the tune after another, as they stripped off their packs, checked their muskets, and pushed their black hats firmly down on their heads.

We will welcome to our numbers the loyal, true and brave
Shouting the battle cry of Freedom
And although he may be poor, not a man shall be a slave,
Shouting the battle cry of Freedom.

The Union forever, hurrah! boys, hurrah!
Down with the traitors, up with the stars;
While we rally round the flag, boys, rally once again,
Shouting the battle cry of Freedom.

The 2nd and 7th Wisconsin were already through breaks in a fence that ran along the side of the road. The 19th Indiana came into the field right behind them. The troops were shouting and singing at the top of their lungs as they half-ran over the grass at double-quick. Nathaniel was riding at the head of his company with Hanson and Nicolson, Libby's dark mane flying.

The regiment crossed another road and kept going until they had passed a large brick building that turned out to be Gettysburg's Lutheran Seminary. They stopped and caught their breath and checked their muskets. The gunfire was south of them. They could see another road just ahead.

Suddenly an aide galloped up to Hanson and Nicolson and Nathaniel. "Orders from General Reynolds. Buford's cavalry are being forced back on the road in front of you. Rebel infantry are advancing against them. Attack, you are ordered to attack."

Hanson wheeled his horse. "Fix bayonets! Prepare to assault the enemy! Get into line of battle!"

"Form line of battle!" shouted Ham.

"Get out of column and form line of battle!" Nathaniel yelled. "Fix bayonets!"

The 2nd Wisconsin formed line of battle first and lunged up a nearby ridge, disappearing into the woods at its top, a terrific explosion of volley fire rolling down to the other Iron Brigade regiments. The companies of the 19th Indiana were no sooner in line of battle and ready to charge the ridge when aides raced up with the news that General Reynolds had been shot from his horse.

"He was leading the 2nd Wisconsin!" a young aide shouted, tears slicing through the powder grime on his face. "The bullet cut him out of the saddle, just cut him out of the saddle!"

"How is he, lad?" asked Hanson.

"He's dead! He was dead by the time he hit the ground!"

"Thank you, lad." Hanson turned to his men. "We're needed up on McPherson's Ridge. When Colonel Williams gives the command, move smartly. Remember our general. Knock the Rebels back to Richmond."

The signal came and the Indiana men hurled themselves toward the ridge and up the slope with the 24th Michigan on their left and the 7th Wisconsin on their right. Nathaniel's horse leaped fence after fence and pounded through wheat field after wheat field.

They halted just below the top of the ridge.

"It's General Archer's brigade from Tennessee and Alabama!" yelled Hanson. "They're tearing up the other side of the ridge screaming like thunder! All they can see is the 2nd Wisconsin! They have no idea we're here! Once you spot their heads and chests open fire!"

Moments later gray troops came swarming over the crest of McPherson's Ridge, screeching and shooting at the Wisconsin regiment holding steady at the top. Nathaniel saw their eyes and then banks of musket smoke boiled over them as the Union infantry fired and they were falling or running back down the ridge the way they had come. Colonel Williams thundered up to the 19th Indiana line on his mount, waving his sword and shouting, "After them, boys!" The regiment stormed over the ridge, aiming and firing at Archer's brigade as fast as they could reload.

The Tennesseans caught them while they scrambled over a fence at the top and Nathaniel saw the 19th Indiana's colors go down, go up, and then go down again. Libby vaulted the fence and Nathaniel paused to watch Plesko and Levi and Nip climb over, kneel, fire, and reload as they prepared to rush forward again. Suddenly a corporal had the Stars and Stripes and was running ahead of everyone down the slope. Nathaniel drew his sword and saw the sun burn along its length.

"Into the ravine!" he yelled. "The Rebs don't know what hit them! Get after them before they can regroup!"

"Willoughby Run!" hollered Hanson. "That's the name the good folk around here gave it! McPherson's Ridge and Willoughby Run! Take 'em both!"

The 19th Indiana and 24th Michigan and 7th Wisconsin hurtled down the side of the ridge into Willoughby Run, shooting and howling and ordering the Tennessee and Alabama troops to surrender. Levi was hit and spun around three or four times by the force of a ball before falling on all fours in the shallow stream. Nathaniel jumped off his horse and hauled him to his feet while the fighting filled the ravine.

"Get back up the slope to a hospital!" Nathaniel ordered him.

Blood streaked the side of Levi's head. "I'll be all right in a minute. I'm just a bit dizzy."

"You've got to go back and get looked after."

"They won't have anything set up yet, brother. And to tell you the truth, I don't have the strength to climb back up there anyhow."

Levi suddenly yanked Nathaniel's Colt Navy revolver from its holster and fired. A Rebel officer went down clutching his knee and dropping his own revolver. He groaned and cried out and rolled about in the scrub brush.

"Good you didn't have the holster flap fastened," Levi said. "And good I wasn't back at that field hospital."

Ham was leading the platoon across the narrow run of water and up the bank on the other side, chasing fleeing Rebel troops. "Go on! Get 'em! Get 'em before they get back to Nashville!"

Nathaniel took his Colt Navy from Levi's hand and sat him on a boulder. Then he went to the officer Levi had shot in the knee. Squatting beside him he offered his canteen that the officer drank from with huge swallows. He brought a black handkerchief from his pocket and tied a tourniquet just above the knee that brought the blood flow to a stop.

"How is it?" he asked.

"Worse than getting kicked by a mule. Coulter, Memphis."

"King, Elizabethtown, not so many miles east of here. Can you walk?"

"If I had a crutch."

"There's an Enfield lying here."

"That'll do."

Nathaniel helped him up and put the stock of the Confederate musket under his arm. The officer limped forward, stopped and leaned on the gun, panting. Nathaniel glanced past him. All along Willoughby Run soldiers from Alabama and Tennessee were surrendering by the hundreds. The run was littered with muskets the Southerners had dropped. He saw a Rebel general being led away and heard a captain from another Indiana company say it was General James Archer himself. Soon his Amish platoon was back with several dozen more prisoners.

"You and you!" Hanson pointed to Ham and Joshua. "Take those Confederates back behind McPherson's Ridge and turn them over to the 9th New York Cavalry. The officer with the Enfield crutch—I need you to go with them and get some medical attention." He noticed Levi. "Have an argument with Tennessee, Sergeant?"

"It may have been Alabama, sir."

"Pick up a musket and give King and Yoder a hand. While you're at it drop in on the Lutheran Theological Seminary."

"Do you think I need a sermon, Captain?"

"No doubt you do. There's sin in us all. I was thinking of your body, though, and not your soul. The surgeons are set up there, I've been told. Get your head looked into. I'll need you back here for the next round."

"What next round?"

Hanson took off his hat and wiped his forehead with his sleeve. "We took the first. Our Southern cousins will come at us again to try to take the second. Go. They'll not give us all day before they launch another assault."

Nip brought a rag dipped in creek water and gave it to Levi to wipe the left side of his face. When he was done Levi got slowly to his feet and almost pitched forward into the stream. Nip looked up at Hanson who nodded. He joined Joshua as they escorted the platoon's prisoners and the officer named Coulter with his musket crutch. Nip stayed close to Levi's side.

"Levi," Nathaniel said as they left. "If Lyndy happens to be at the Seminary—"

"I know," replied Levi as he trudged unsteadily up the ridge. "You're madly in love with her."

"That's a mild way of putting it, Sergeant."

Levi glanced back and managed a smile. "I'll try to think of something stronger, Lieutenant."

26

July 1, 1863

Lutheran Theological Seminary

2:00 p.m.

Nathaniel:

I believe the two armies tripped over one
another. Nevertheless this is how Providence
has arranged matters. From what I can see
from the Seminary cupola the Confederates
are not withdrawing from Gettysburg. Indeed
they are adding to their numbers by the hour.
I estimate they have 15,000 in the field at
the present time. Your strength at Willoughby
Run and Edward McPherson's Ridge does not
exceed 2000. Of course other elements of the
First Corps are on the field as well as the
Eleventh Corps but the Rebels are adding to
their force and the Union is not. Before long

they shall outnumber you far more than they do now. Moreover the Confederates appear to be aligning their regiments so as to advance the bulk of them against your position. You may be the Iron Brigade but I do not see how it is possible for you to do anything but break and run in the face of the onslaught the Rebels are preparing for you.

Yet here is the rub: If you break and run pell-mell for the rear, the battle is lost. Meade has not arrived. The Army of the Potomac is not yet in Gettysburg but by the trickle. From conversations with the townspeople I calculate Buford and his cavalry held on for about five hours until the 2nd Wisconsin and the rest of the Iron Brigade came to the rescue. You would need to hold Lee's forces at bay for longer than that in order for the main army to even begin to arrive and take control of the high ground behind us that commands this area—Cemetery Ridge, Cemetery Hill, Culp's Hill, Round Top, and Little Round Top. If the Army of Northern Virginia overwhelms you and gains that high ground instead of us it will be another Fredericksburg. Yet, in all honesty, I do not foresee any other outcome but another Rebel victory. If that is the case I believe the peace movement in Washington will hold sway and Lincoln will be forced to negotiate a peace treaty with the Confederate States of America on Confederate terms.

General Doubleday has replaced the fallen Reynolds. No doubt he and Howard of the Eleventh Corps have surmised all I have related to you and will tell you to make a stand despite the odds against you. I suppose that is the soldier's lot. I have no doubt in my mind but that you and your regiment and the entire brigade will fight bravely and distinguish yourselves. Your enemy already holds you in the highest regard. Perhaps God has a miracle waiting in the wings. I do not know but that your brigade and the scattered units of the First and Eleventh Corps may be that miracle. Regardless of the outcome I pray you may come through this ordeal alive, my friend.

Hiram

Nathaniel handed the letter back to Levi. "Get it to Hanson. He can show it to Williams and Long Sol Meredith."

"I'm sure they are well aware of the pickle we're in."

"Give it to Hanson anyway."

"All right."

Nathaniel watched him walk away. A white bandage was a tight strip around his head. The sun vanished in a cloud and he saw the men of his company in shadows. Rain fell for a few minutes. The cloud moved on and the sun returned more fiercely than before. Plesko and Groom and Jones were laughing about something and clinking their tin cups together. They each drank as quickly as they could, eyes on one another, burst out laughing again, and sprayed Hanson's coffee over their uniforms and the grass. Nathaniel smiled and opened the second note Levi had brought back from the seminary.

> Love,
>
> I stand in the Seminary cupola when there is a pause in the surgery and I look where Hiram points and I use his brass spotting scope. But I can't see the field of gray uniforms he insists is there. I see you. I am certain of it. Who else has so glossy a black? Who else sits so erect in the saddle? Who else still has an intact ostrich feather in his hat? I love you, my dear Nathaniel. Come what may you can rely on that and on the love and power of God. My prayers for you and your men are unceasing. Psalm 91:15.
>
> With all my heart,
>
> your Lyndel

Nathaniel brought his Bible out of a pocket, turned easily to Psalm 91, which he had read so many times, and found the verse. *He shall call upon me, and I will answer him: I will be with him in trouble; I will deliver him, and honour him.* He was reading it a second time when Colonel Williams rode down to Willoughby Run where the 19th was positioned. Several of the company captains and lieutenants were with him, including Hanson and Nicolson.

"Men!" Williams stood up in his stirrups. "Men of Indiana! General Doubleday has expressed his expectation to Long Sol that the Iron Brigade will hold the woods at all hazards! You see the force the Rebels are massing against you minute by minute! The 24th Michigan is arrayed on your right and will face the same fury from the enemy as you! Long

Sol and I and the 24th's commander, Colonel Henry Morrow, have requested repeatedly that our regiments be permitted to leave this slope and Willoughby Run and move back onto the top of McPherson's Ridge! There we would build a fortified position that would require the enemy to make an uphill assault in the face of almost a thousand muskets! But General Doubleday considers the woods below the crest of McPherson's Ridge the critical point in his line! There are no more appeals to be made! The army is counting on us! The nation is counting on us! This is the hardest fight you have ever been asked to make for our state and for our Republic!" The color guard was standing beside him. He reached down and seized the American flag. "Boys! We must hold our colors on this line or lie here under them!"

He galloped away. Nathaniel looked out across Willoughby Run from the slope that rose from the shallow creek. The Rebel formations Hiram could see much more clearly were continuing to form and extended far past the 19th's left flank. They even extended past the flanks of the three regiments from Colonel Biddle's brigade that had been sent to strengthen the left wing of the Army of the Potomac. Thousands upon thousands of men were being mustered against them on the farm fields below. It was as if the Rebels knew the time was ripe to take not only the McPherson high ground by storm but all the rest of the Gettysburg high ground beyond it.

Nathaniel began to walk up and down his company's line holding Libby's reins. Was anyone hungry? Were their canteens full? Did they have plenty of cartridges handy? Plesko? Conkle? Sala? Nip? Everything all right?

Nip was lying on his back looking at clouds. "My uniform is bulging with cartridges. It was hard running through crops and slipping over rail fences with a hundred pounds of lead in each pocket. But now I guess I'm ready for the whole Rebel army."

"There's four of them for every one of us it seems like," said Joshua. "You think you have enough for all that?"

"Enough and to spare for a deer hunt."

"Deer hunt!" Hanson came by on his horse. "I expect all the deer left for Indiana hours ago, Private."

"There may still be a few brave ones, sir."

"Here they come!" Williams hollered. "Fall in!"

Nathaniel saw two lines heading toward them and upward of two thousand troops converging on their left flank. All the Rebels were moving fast. He took out his pocket watch. It was three o'clock. The thought passed through his mind that he had not even been awake twelve hours, yet everything about his world had changed drastically.

"Aim low." It was Nicolson. He had dismounted. "Hit them hard. Don't waste ammo, we don't have any to spare. If your gun fouls, use a tree trunk or a rock to slam your ramrod home. Or pick up another musket. You know what to do."

Clouds gathered again and a shadow ran over the approaching Confederates like the palm of a hand. The sun returned in a rush. Nathaniel held a pistol in one hand and his sword in the other along with Libby's reins and felt annoyed. Why weren't officers issued muskets? What good was a revolver or a sword when the enemy was a hundred yards away?

"Easy, boys, easy." It was Williams. "Remember the stories they told you when you were ten about the Revolution and Bunker Hill. Don't fire until you see the whites of their eyes. Let them get right up to us, right up to the run. Then cut loose. On my command."

The first Rebel line came charging up to the creek bed. Williams gave a shout and hundreds of Springfields blazed yellow fire and white smoke. The Rebel line collapsed as if knocked down by a huge fist. The Indiana men kept up their fire and every Rebel officer or soldier who tried to make it across the creek was shot down. The Rebels pulled back and settled into a killing fight with the Union troops.

A shower came and went and the hot musket barrels on both sides of the run evaporated the raindrops instantly with a hiss. All the men in Nathaniel's Amish platoon were firing as fast as they could tear open cartridges and shove the bullets home. A ball clipped Nathaniel's ear and he could feel the warm blood trickle under the collar of his uniform. Groom was hit and knocked on his back, got up and was hit again, returned to a kneeling position and was slammed onto his back a third time. Nathaniel ran to him. Groom's whole chest was blood.

"Didn't have enough coffee." Groom smiled, blood on his lips. "Shouldn't have spilled any."

"We'll get you to the surgery at the Seminary."

"Lieutenant. I have no intention of leaving the best friends I've ever had right when they need me the most. Grooms don't lose a fight— remember I told you that when I was a recruit at Antietam? Help me get on my belly. I guess I can reload my musket and get a few more shots away."

"Just lie back—"

"No, sir. Each of us has a role to play. All the boys know that if they get past us and the rest of the brigade there's nothing back there to stop them. So we're wasting time. Roll me over. Put my musket in my hands, it's ready to go."

Nathaniel did what he asked and Groom fired the round in his Springfield and slowly and painfully began to reload. After his second shot he fumbled for cartridges in an empty cartridge box. Finally he dug one from his coat pocket but was too weak to tear open the paper with his teeth. Nathaniel took the cartridge and loaded the musket for him, then put it back in his hands.

"Thank you," whispered Groom. "I still got a few shots in me."

"Blaze away. I'll get your gun ready for you. It's better than standing around shouting and waving a sword."

Groom aimed and squeezed the trigger. The recoil made his whole body jerk. Nathaniel reloaded and Groom aimed and fired. This time he couldn't lift the musket up so Nathaniel took it from his hands, reloaded it, and gave it back. Groom fired and fell forward on the musket after the recoil had slammed into his shoulder. Nathaniel could hardly work the Springfield free of the young man's grasp. He saw that Groom was gone.

"God bless you," he said while guns thundered around him and balls threw up dirt and grass. "I'll keep your musket going until the sun sets or I'm stove in."

Nathaniel emptied Groom's pockets of cartridges and stuffed them into his own. Then he reloaded and aimed at a Rebel sergeant trying to creep into the run. There was a roar that was lost in the greater roar and the sergeant fell face first into the creek. Nathaniel reloaded and aimed again.

"It's the 26th North Carolina in front of us!" Hanson was yelling, riding back and forth along the line. "I just got a good look at their flag! Keep pouring it into them! Don't give them a chance to catch their wind and try a charge! And keep an eye on that unit with them! The 11th North Carolina! They're shifting over to our left flank!"

"Biddle's there!" shouted Nicolson. He no sooner said this than his horse was hit by three or four shots from the left. His mount collapsed on top of him and he was pinned underneath.

"Biddle ain't there!" yelled Jones. "There's no one on our left flank but hundreds of screaming Rebels and they're firing right into our backs!"

Nathaniel ran to the exposed flank. He hit Levi and Joshua on their shoulders as he went past at a crouch through the thick haze of gun smoke. "You boys come with me! We'll do what we can to keep the 11th's heads down!"

The three men fell on their stomachs and began firing back at the gray soldiers who were coming up toward the run from the side. Others from the company were sent over by Hanson to help them. The group was able to stem the tide for a while but many of the Carolina troops were shooting over them at the exposed regiment. Men were getting hit by bullets from the front and the back and the side.

"The grass is thick with our dead and wounded," grunted Levi as he aimed and fired. "This isn't working. The regiment needs to get into a new position before there's none of us left."

"Keep shooting and drop back, Indiana!" hollered Colonel Williams suddenly. "Long Sol has set up a second line a hundred yards back up the slope here toward McPherson's Ridge! See him on his horse? Go there! Fire, reload, and drop back!"

The 19th kept up a hot fire at the 26th and 11th North Carolina regiments and slowly edged their way to the new line of defense. Reaching it, men crouched behind trees and poured shot into the Confederate ranks. The creek bank and brush were smothered in scores of gray bodies. The 24th Michigan curled around on its left to present a hundred guns or more to the attack on the flank. Dark smoke obscured the trees and the soldiers and the creek.

Long Sol's horse went down and crushed the general beneath it. He was pulled clear but was badly hurt. The 151st Pennsylvania moved into the gap between Biddle's regiments and the Iron Brigade and fought to control the gray surge but the Carolina troops kept coming. A soldier ran past with the 19th's Stars and Stripes and Nathaniel saw that it was torn apart with bullet holes and its staff shattered. A shot thudded into the tree he was kneeling behind with Nip and a splinter of bark cut open his jaw. Libby, tethered behind them, reared and kicked out with her front legs.

"There's too many of them!" cried Ham. "They're a cloud of locusts! They're going to swarm over us like a biblical plague!"

Hanson pointed with his sword. "Get to the top! Get to the crest of McPherson's Ridge! Do ye see that rail fence to the right of the 7th Wisconsin? Rally there! Go now!"

Nathaniel jumped up, fired, and began to grab men by their arms and propel them up the slope to the top. "The fence at the crest of McPherson's Ridge! Rally on the left flank of the 7th Wisconsin!"

Nicolson was limping up from Willoughby Run, turning every ten or twelve feet to fire with his Colt Navy at the North Carolina soldiers. He saw Jones in the grass with a leg wound and stooped to help him up. Together they made it to the fence where bullets were hitting and sending wood chips flying. Wave after wave of Rebels pursued the Indiana troops, and wave after wave fell apart before the fire of the 19th Indiana, the 7th Wisconsin, and the 24th Michigan. The fire of the 2nd Wisconsin was concentrated against Confederate forces on the right flank of McPherson's Ridge. The 6th Wisconsin clashed with Rebel units on the far side of the Chambersburg Pike, a road that ran between the ridge and the farm fields to the west.

The reek of sulfur, the din of thousands of muskets blasting away life, the rolling smoke, men falling like trees and tumbling down the slopes of the ridge like logs, the screams of horses, the heat that made hands sweat so much that ramrods could not be held and bullets could not be seated, the powder that burned the eyes and the nostrils and scorched the tongue from biting cartridges open—Nathaniel had experienced all this at Brawner's Farm and South Mountain and Antietam Creek. But this time the odds were worse. His pocket watch had been smashed by a bullet at 3:27 p.m.—he had no idea how long ago 3:27 was or how much daylight remained. But the sun still seemed high to him and had no problem hurling its heat against combatants whose tongues were already swollen black from biting into the powder of their cartridges and whose mouths were parched and lips cracked and bleeding.

From the mist of light and smoke a man appeared in a black swallowtail coat. Long and dark as a fence rail he carried a musket almost as tall as he was. He seemed like a spirit who had materialized out of the ground. Nathaniel watched him aim and fire and reload. He glanced Nathaniel's way and spoke briefly.

"I fought the British invaders at Lundy's Lane in the War of 1812 when I was a young man like you. I have no intention of watching you boys defend my town from these Rebels and not lift a finger to help. I go by the name John Burns."

"Lieutenant Nathaniel King, Elizabethtown."

"That so? Good to have another Pennsylvanian beside me."

The smoke of the battle rolled over the old man as he aimed his musket a second time and Nathaniel did not see him again.

"There's dead secesh all over McPherson's Ridge and they still keep sending them up from those oat fields," Ham rumbled. "I haven't got bullets enough for them."

"Pick up cartridges from the dead and wounded," said Levi.

"I've tried that. There's nothing left. Maybe I should start pitching these fence rails on top of them Tar Heels."

"They're bound to run out of ammunition too, Corporal."

"Not soon enough for me. Plesko! You got any spare cartridges?"

Plesko tossed Ham three. "That's all. I need the other five rounds for myself."

"Didn't you fill your pockets when we left our packs this morning?"

"I did. But I've emptied them."

Hanson came up on foot, holding reins in his hand with no horse attached to them. "Ordnance wagons are rolling up behind us! They're throwing boxes of cartridges onto the ground! See 'em? Break 'em open, get your share, use every pocket you've got and every cartridge pouch you can get your hands on!"

The surviving troops from the four Iron Brigade regiments on the ridge crammed ammunition into their uniforms and returned to the fight. Muzzles continued to bark and flash. No sooner did a dozen North Carolina troops drop dead or wounded but another twelve took their place. Black Hats fell in the woods, on the open meadows between the clusters of trees, at the foot of the fence; they draped lifeless over the fence's top rails. Nathaniel was talking to Nicolson one moment and the next heard a thump as if a fence rail had been thrown to the ground—a ball had punctured Nicolson's heart and he lay dead on the ground. Ham was trying to work his musket with one arm broken. Levi had either opened his old head wound or taken a new one because his bandage was black with blood. Joshua had tied a tourniquet above his left knee and Plesko had wrapped a red handkerchief over a bleeding eye and another over a gash in his throat. Nathaniel counted heads and couldn't find Jones, finally spotting him sprawled next to the shattered boards of the ammo boxes, bullet holes in his head and chest and legs, no light in his open eyes.

"The brigade is falling back to Seminary Ridge!" Hanson shouted. "D'ye hear me? We're all pulling back to the Lutheran Seminary— you can see the top of it, can't ye? Make for that now! Keep firing at those gray devils and make your way off this ridge and onto the other! Hurry!" A ball struck him in the chest and he dropped.

Nathaniel quickly knelt by him. "How bad is it?" He saw the gaping wound. "I'll carry you."

"And get yourself shot or captured?" growled Hanson. "The boys need an officer to lead them. Long Sol's down. Williams is wounded. Nicolson's dead, God bless 'im. This isn't the end of it, Lieutenant. You'll make a stand at Seminary Ridge. You have to. The First and

Eleventh Corps are starting to fill the high ground but they're nowhere near enough. You've got to blunt the Confederate advance."

"Sir, there are only a few hundred of us left—"

Hanson heaved himself to his elbow. "Don't argue with me. We scooped up a couple of prisoners in the last half hour. From the 26th. They came against us with over eight hundred troops—the size of two of our regiments! And they're down to less than two-fifty, they reckon. They've been shot to ribbons. They'll not pursue you. Neither will the 11th North Carolina."

"The Rebs are sure to send somebody else."

"That's right. But they'll send them after *you*. They'll send them after Indiana and Michigan and Wisconsin. Not after the units of First Corps and Eleventh Corps that will dig in on Cemetery Ridge and Cemetery Hill. You'll buy the Army of the Potomac the night. Riders have been sent all over northern Maryland— *The enemy is at Gettysburg. Get there fast.* Those heights will be filled with tens of thousands of Union troops by dawn. They'll be spoiling for a fight. Lee won't break that line. I swear he won't break that line. After all, he couldn't break us, could he?" Hanson grasped the front of Nathaniel's coat. "Now go and lead. Make a stand. If the regiment has to die let them die with the fire in their eyes." He had trouble catching his breath and sank back. "The blood's coming out of me like Indiana's Big Blue River. Even your pretty wife couldn't fix me up now. Say a quick prayer in German and get over to the other ridge."

"Captain—"

"You're captain now. You have men to lead. Pray the prayer and go."

Musket fire was still crackling as the 24th Michigan marched past. Nathaniel took off his tall black hat and prayed in German for about a minute. He gripped Hanson's hand after he was done.

"Thank you, sir. For everything."

"It has been a grand ride, hasn't it? My best to the boys. Tell 'em I'm proud of 'em. No finer company. No finer platoon."

Nathaniel came to attention and saluted. "Go with God."

"I hope to. I may be a rough-and-ready type but I love him, I truly do."

Nathaniel picked up Groom's musket and began to run across the grass and through the trees to where he had tied Libby. He spotted the 19th regiment's standard and the Stars and Stripes of his own company in the marching columns between the ridges and could see his men were already close to the seminary. He leaped into the saddle and started down the slope as quickly as he could. Amid the yells and gunfire he heard Hanson calling after him a final time.

"By the by, it was the gunpowder. Raw gunpowder gave my coffee its bite."

27

Lyndel stood on the front porch of the seminary with a hand resting on one of the pillars and watched what was left of the Iron Brigade stream into a huge barricade of fence rails near the building. She knew she would eventually spot her husband and in time she did, as he rode his black mare down from McPherson's Ridge, crossed the valley, and came up the slope of Seminary Ridge in the midst of marching men in tall dark hats. He would see to his boys first, be sure his platoon and company were all right, talk with the other officers. Then he would come looking for her, hoping she would be there tending to the wounded.

She kept looking, watching, praying until she heard her name. "Lyndel!"

Nathaniel broke into a run as soon as he saw her at the front door of the tall brick building with its white windows and white cupola. She started to rush down the steps but he bounded up the stairs before she was halfway, his hat falling from his head, kissing her, holding her. He brought with him the smell of battle, of sulfur and fire and blood, but she didn't care. He was alive. She took his kisses and responded with her own. The wounded lying on the grass about the seminary watched and a few had the strength to smile.

"I love you." He brought her head into his chest.

"And I love you, Nathaniel—I prayed for you, I thank God he has spared you." Her tears came freely. "Hiram says your men have done more than anyone could have dreamed to slow the Rebel advance. He expects you to move into the high ground behind the Seminary now."

"The Confederate troops would just follow us there and storm the heights. They'd take them too—we don't have enough men to hold them."

Lyndel ran both her hands over his powder-dark face, a face nicked and cut and stained by blood. "You can't mean to stay in that flimsy barricade. I thought it was simply a place for the brigade to regroup."

"It's our last line of defense. We can't let them get to Cemetery Ridge, Lyndy. We have to wind down the clock here."

"Meade and the army will come."

"Not soon enough. We have to take as many hours of daylight from the Rebels as we can. Hit them so hard here that even if they overrun the brigade they won't be in the mood to try to take the heights." He smoothed back the loose strands of her hair with his palm. "We have to, my beauty. It comes down to this hour. We're going to need your prayers a while longer."

They both heard the drumming in the distance. It was coming from the west, where the sun was slowly dropping behind McPherson's Ridge. As they looked, the red and blue of the Confederate battle flag and its Southern Cross emerged over the crest from McPherson's Woods. Lines of soldiers in gray and butternut followed the flags over the top of the ridge and marched down the slope and into the valley behind them.

Lyndel's fingers went to her lips. "There are thousands and thousands. You are so few—so few, Nathaniel."

"We're not going to surrender America, Lyndel." He kissed her on the lips. "I must go."

He was running back to the barricade, where men were taking up their positions and aiming their long-barreled muskets. She quickly made a decision and went back inside. Hundreds of Union and Confederate wounded lay in the hallways and classrooms and offices. She stepped between them, longing to stop and continue helping them, but realizing she had to do something else first. She found one of the brigade doctors at the end of the main hall.

"I'm going up to the cupola for a few minutes," she told him. "I will be back shortly."

He stared at her. "Mrs. King, we need you here."

"I know that. I'm needed elsewhere as well. I won't be twenty minutes."

Suddenly the walls shook as Union cannon began to fire.

"What's going on?" demanded the doctor as Lyndel ran for the staircase.

"The Confederate army is attacking our ridge."

"Get back here, Mrs. King. A stray shot could easily find its way up there."

But she was gone up the staircase. When she opened the door to the cupola the advancing Rebel forces were spread out like an oil painting over acres of green grass, moving through golden shafts of sunlight toward them. Hiram was leaning out with his brass telescope and watching them come. She put her hand on his shoulder and he lifted his head.

"Lyndel! What are you doing up here? It's far too dangerous."

"You're here, Hiram."

"An occupational hazard. You must get back down."

"A stray shell could find me there just as easily."

"Really, I must insist—"

"Hiram." Her eyes became what Nathaniel called her gunmetal blue. "My husband is in that barricade. My brother is in that barricade. I'm a regimental nurse and my regiment is in that barricade. Right here is where I need to be."

The cannon roared again and smoke began to drift through the cupola. Hiram gave up the argument and returned to his telescope. "Just what do you hope to accomplish from up here? Have you turned into a sniper?"

"I'm going to pray."

He grunted.

"Do you think praying is a waste of time, Hiram?"

"On the contrary. Where the bloodiness of the war has turned some into unbelievers I find the miracles and mysteries of this conflict have worked upon me just the opposite effect. Your husband's brigade being a case in point. They cannot win yet they keep on winning."

"I would scarcely call the way they have been shot down today *winning*."

"Every minute they successfully resist a superior force they have won a battle." He handed her the telescope. "But I will be my usual realistic self and tell you they cannot possibly stand against the forces arrayed against them now."

Lyndel put the scope to her eye and the gray troops immediately jumped into focus. She saw faces and beards clearly and could see lips moving as men spoke to one another. She could count the stars on the battle flags and read the numbers on the regimental standards.

"How beautiful they look and how terrible," she said.

An explosion she couldn't hear suddenly appeared in the lens. Ten or twelve men she had been viewing vanished. She yanked the telescope away.

"How I hate war!"

Hiram took the telescope back. "And yet, at the present time, there seems to be no other means at hand to preserve the Republic, politics having been exhausted in 1860."

Lyndel clenched her fists. "There is the praying."

"Yes. Prayer and gunpowder."

Lyndel closed her eyes and prayed silently in German. As she prayed she could hear a single cannon booming in one ear and Hiram talking in the other.

"Now, do you see we have Rebels from Harry Heth's division and from the divisions of William Dorsey Pender and Robert Rodes converging on us? Alfred Scales's brigade of North Carolina regiments is advancing—North Carolina again!—there are the standards for Colonel Abner Perrin's four regiments from South Carolina—and yet more North Carolina regiments under General James Lane—I make out the 7th, 18th, the 37th, 28th and 33rd. The Army of Northern Virginia means to conclude business with the Iron Brigade this afternoon."

Eyes still closed, Lyndel spoke up. "What about Nathaniel?"

"Ah—your husband has with him the survivors of all the regiments save the 6th Wisconsin—they are outside the barricade and guarding six Napoleon cannon from Battery B—Old Jock, you know, James Stewart, he commands that battery—there are other guns—the Fifth Maine Battery—they are guarded by what's left of Biddle's brigade, who were on the 19th's left at Willoughby Run—there is artillery from the 1st Pennsylvania and from our fallen General Reynolds's New York batteries—I see troops from Colonel Stone's Pennsylvanians, the Bucktail Brigade—I hear they fought to the bone at the west end of McPherson's Ridge—those that are left are with Battery B—and aiming their muskets—here it comes—"

A shattering roar of muskets and cannon made the cupola shake and almost deafened Lyndel. She couldn't stop from opening her eyes. "What is it, Hiram?"

"The Rebel lines have reached a fence approximately two hundred yards from us. The Iron Brigade and its comrades in arms just loosed their first volley and all the cannon from all the batteries fired at the same time. The Confederates are falling like rain. It's as if a giant is gouging out the earth and tearing up life with great terrible fingers."

She closed her eyes and resumed praying as the explosion of thousands of muskets went on and on. Her words were words for the preservation of the nation and an end to slavery but they were also words for the sparing of husbands and fathers and sons and brothers, North and South...*Americans, Lord God, Americans.* She ached for the new battle to be quick and the South to be thrown back, though she knew there would be much more fighting to come, whatever transpired at the seminary gates.

"We have stopped their advance," said Hiram.

"Oh, Gott sei Dank."

"But they are reforming, closing in the huge gaps in their lines. They are coming. They are coming again."

"God help us," Lyndel whispered. "Please help us."

Cannons roared, muskets barked, the Rebels yelled, and the Union troops and cannoneers yelled back. She could hear men shrieking,

"Come on, Johnny, come on, Johnny!" and musket fire splitting the air in two. She could even make out officers screaming commands above the thunder of artillery and the crack of Enfields and Spring-fields. Then she imagined she heard Nathaniel's voice as clearly as if he were standing across from her in the cupola… *"Though I walk through the valley of the shadow of death, I will fear no evil: for thou art with me."*

She flew to the cupola rail. Cannons blazed white fire, dirty smoke covered the ridge like a fog, gray men marched up and up the slope and fell and died and other gray men marched up the slope in their place, muskets were like long black spears, flags collapsed, bayonets became bright-hot needles in the July sunlight.

"I can see Nathaniel."

Lyndel snatched the scope from Hiram's hands and pointed it at the barricade. After a moment she found her husband, standing while others knelt or crouched, shouting and clapping men on the back, once even standing on the rails and waving with his arm toward a line of charging, hollering Rebels.

Oh, Nathaniel, come down from that fence!

"Mrs. King! Mr. Wright!"

A doctor stood in the cupola in clothing that was red to his neck.

"We are sending three wagons of medical supplies to Cemetery Ridge as well as any of the wounded who can walk. The barricade will be overwhelmed in a matter of minutes. We desperately need you two and Miss David to drive the supplies."

"The barricade will not be overrun in minutes, doctor," Lyndel pro-tested.

"Minutes, half an hour, it doesn't matter, we need those supplies at Cemetery Ridge for a field hospital. A doctor is going with you. Any wounded who remain here will become prisoners of war. A number have already headed out across the fields. Try the Chambersburg Pike if it is still open. Go through town and get on the Taneytown Road. It runs behind Cemetery Ridge."

"Doctor—"

"Mrs. King!" The doctor's words became a plea. "Help us!"

Hiram's wagon rattled away from the seminary first, leaving from the back of the building. Morganne followed him and Lyndel was last. Several officers' mounts were tied at the rear of the seminary to keep them out of harm's way. Lyndel noticed Libby standing patiently and nuzzling another horse.

They went along wagon ruts in the high grass before getting on the road and heading into Gettysburg. Smoke boiled down the ridge after them and the shriek of the fighting seemed worse to her from this short distance than it had when she was right on top of it. She thought of Nathaniel and her brother and prayed for them and their men. She prayed for all of the men.

Nathaniel was grateful for the extra few minutes they were granted every time they knocked the Rebel lines off balance and forced them to regroup. The barricade flashed like forked lightning and rolls of smoke massed like thunderheads. Men dropped all around him, and he could see them dropping in the lines attacking their position. Despite the fever that came with the fighting, Nathaniel was staggered at the sight of the casualties. He hoped and prayed the Confederates would withdraw and the day would end. But the Army of Northern Virginia had no intention of drawing back from Seminary Ridge.

Levi seemed to be in a black uniform from neck to waist. He shot and reloaded and shot and reloaded as if he were a piece of farm equipment pulled by horses. Plesko wasn't quite as fast but was just as determined to stave off the Confederate forces, tearing his cartridges open, ramming the loads home, his eyes glittering in the strange colors created by the tumbling of sunlight, gun smoke, and muzzle fire. Nathaniel wasn't there when a Rebel bullet found him but once he discovered the young man's body, grief pierced his chest and he remembered what Plesko had told him before the attack—*When the war is finally won I, like Lincoln, will thank God for the chance to live in a world that is governed by the better angels of our nature. I know it must sound strange but one of the reasons I am fighting is so we can have that kind of country one day.*

Men in yellow and brown surged against the barricade and were hit with vicious volley fire. Those that made it to the rails were shot at five or ten paces by musket or pistol or clubbed down by gunstocks. Rebel charges were smashed by hundreds of balls, the strikes sounding to Levi like hail smacking the side of a barn, but a new charge always followed within moments. Union and Rebel standards were ripped by bursting shells or punctured by bullets. Color bearers were killed within seconds of lifting up the Southern Cross or the Stars and Stripes. Officers were blasted from their saddles or crushed beneath dying horses. Thick powder smoke blotted out faces and uniforms and the bodies strewn over miles of dandelions and grass and wildflowers. No matter how many times the Confederate army came shrieking at them, the Iron Brigade and their allies and artillery hurled them back with their own howls and screams.

Nathaniel saw men drop their muskets because they had become too hot from constant firing. They snatched up the Springfields of the dead and wounded and began to use them instead. A bearded giant, his left leg shredded by bullets and a tourniquet tight on his thigh, had a musket under one arm to prop him up and fired another musket at the Rebels. Wounded soldiers ordered into the seminary for treatment balked or pretended to go and then sneaked back without walking through the doors and returned to the barricade. The thin blue line bristled with musket barrels and bayonets and long flashes of orange flame. Firing and shouting encouragement and tying quick tourniquets on soldiers whose wounds were gushing blood, Nathaniel began to believe they could hold out on Seminary Ridge until nightfall and win the day from the Rebel brigades.

He often thought of Lyndel in the building and glanced over his shoulder frequently, afraid he might see her at a window cracked by a bullet or at an open door splintered by shellfire. *Stay back,* he would tell her in his head, *Stay well clear.* He noticed a man with a brass telescope in the cupola once but no woman and for that he was grateful.

He had dropped to his knees to search for extra cartridges in the pockets and cartridge boxes of the wounded and dead. Shot was slapping repeatedly into the fence rails close to his head, when Levi and Joshua gave a loud shout. He glanced up—they looked like ragmen with all the homemade bandages they had applied to different parts of their bodies. Levi caught Nathaniel's eye and pointed.

"The left flank is collapsing! The 1st South Carolina is pouring in even though Biddle's men are fighting like hornets!"

Nathaniel jumped up. "Hold! Hold!" He climbed the rail barricade again. "Maintain your line! Keep firing!" Bullets cut past his head but he grabbed an American flag, clambered up on the barricade as high as he could go, and waved it back and forth. "Stay on the barricade! Throw Johnny back! Do not break!"

But the gray and butternut troops were forcing their way in despite point-blank artillery fire and musket blasts. Attacking Rebels covered the slopes of the ridge, and more were ascending from the valley in long dark lines. Union officers behind him were ordering units to withdraw to Cemetery Ridge or Culp's Hill through the streets of Gettysburg and to do so as quickly as they could.

"Fall back!" It was Colonel Williams. "The 19th Indiana will fall back to Culp's Hill! Quickly, men, before the Chambersburg Pike into Gettysburg is cut off! You've stalled the Rebel assault, you've bought General Meade and the army all the time they need, now get to the heights and dig in!"

Nathaniel gathered his platoon and company as bodies swirled around them and muskets continued to bang and flash. He saw that the 7th Wisconsin were not withdrawing immediately and were covering the Iron Brigade's retreat—turning, firing, marching toward Gettysburg, turning and firing again as hundreds of soldiers streamed past them.

"We'll maintain a skirmisher's line on the 7th's left flank," Nathaniel said swiftly. "Pick a target, shoot, turn and march twenty paces, stop and pick a target, shoot. All the way down the ridge and into the town. What does your watch say, Sergeant?"

Ham pulled it from a pocket and snapped the lid open. "It's just coming on to 4:30, sir."

"The longer we keep at it and slow the Rebs, the more daylight we eat up. Then it gets less and less likely they'll charge Culp's Hill or

300 ~ Murray Pura

Cemetery Ridge. By tomorrow morning Meade and the army will have secured the heights. Are you with me?"

Ham nodded. "That's what we bought the tickets to the dance for. The final waltz with the prettiest gal."

The powder-blackened faces with the tall black hats grinned.

Nathaniel smiled back. "All right. God bless you boys. You've fought like lions. We'll talk again in Gettysburg."

"Amen," said Levi.

The group of Indiana men went twenty paces, Nathaniel shouting the count, and they aimed, fired, and walked off another twenty. The 7th Wisconsin was marching down the ridge into Gettysburg using their own rhythm—firing to the left, to the right, to the front. Screeching and shooting, the Rebels were coming after them but could never go too fast or get too far before Wisconsin bullets or the volley fire of Nathaniel's company slammed into them and brought them up short. They couldn't overwhelm the rearguard action of Union troops so they poured fire into them without letup.

Men fell in masses on both sides as the sun dropped in the sky, closer and closer to the fields and farms of Gettysburg. Nathaniel recited Psalm 23 to himself as his men fought their way from Seminary Ridge through the late-afternoon light that plated the tall grass, the Lutheran Seminary, the battling soldiers, and the small town in brass. The words of the Bible passage, he realized, made more sense to him in the middle of his men's desperate fight than they ever had in his life.

The Lord is my shepherd; I shall not want.

"One—two—three—four—five —six—"

He maketh me to lie down in green pastures: he leadeth me beside the still waters.

"Eighteen—nineteen—twenty—"

He restoreth my soul:

"Fire! Reload as we march!"

He leadeth me in the paths of righteousness for his name's sake.

"Seven—eight—nine—ten—"

Yea, though I walk through the valley of the shadow of death, I will fear no evil:

"Lieutenant, Nip is down, Lazarus is down!"

For thou art with me;

"Nineteen—twenty—turn, aim, fire!"

Thy rod and thy staff they comfort me.

"Reload as we march! One—two—three—four—"

Thou preparest a table before me in the presence of mine enemies:

"Joshua is down! Joshua is down, sir!"

Thou anointest my head with oil;

"Eleven—twelve—thirteen—fourteen—"

My cup runneth over.

"Fire!"

Surely goodness and mercy shall follow me all the days of my life:

"Levi!"

And I will dwell in the house of the Lord.

"Fifteen—sixteen—seventeen—eighteen—"

For ever.

When the shot hit him he thought he had been kicked by one of the Wisconsin officers' horses. He was spun in a full circle and thrown to the ground. Grass and dirt was jammed into his mouth and under his fingernails. He heard a sharp blast of volley fire. When the world stopped moving he stopped moving too. A monarch butterfly lighted on his arm and stayed there for an hour, unafraid, before making its way across Seminary Ridge to a cluster of wild roses.

28

The heavens opened and rain pounded like hammers on the canvas of the hospital tent. Hiram came riding up, his coat drenched, his hair plastered to his skull. He jumped off his horse and ran in.

"Davey! Lyndel!" He looked at them and looked at the doctors. "Lee is retreating! His troops have already withdrawn from the town and from Seminary Ridge!"

Lyndel put down the sponge she was using to clean a leg wound. "Are you certain?"

"I thought it was only a rumor and went to check for myself. They're leaving. Wagons with the wounded are at the front."

"All the wounded?"

"No. The townsfolk say the most severe cases have been left behind. And there is more news. General Grant is on the verge of capturing Vicksburg. It could have already surrendered."

"How can you know that?"

"I cabled my newspaper after I rode into town. They told me that dispatches had arrived that were dated July first. The word then was that the Confederate commander knew he could not fight his way free of the siege and would seek surrender terms. I would not be surprised if Vicksburg had surrendered by now, but we won't know for sure until the next steamer shows up in Washington with more dispatches."

"I've lost all track of time in here. Is it Saturday or Sunday? What is the hour?"

"Today is Saturday, July fourth, Lyndel. Independence Day. It's well after seven in the evening."

Lyndel threw a cape over her shoulders. "Doctor, may I take an ambulance?"

A nearby physician lifted his head from a Rebel corporal's shattered chest. "Go ahead, Mrs. King. Bring in all you can. Please stop by and see how the doctors are faring at the Lutheran Seminary."

"I will, sir. Davey, are you coming?"

Morganne was drying her hands on her apron. "Yes, of course."

"Mrs. King."

Lyndel stopped as she was about to leave the tent. "What is it, Doctor?"

"I hope you find your husband."

She nodded and put up the hood of her cape. "Thank you."

Hiram drove. Lyndel looked at the thousands of bodies as they rounded the back of Cemetery Ridge into the open. She had seen so much horror and killing that she thought she was past feeling anything, but the sight of so many dead in rain-black butternut and gray made her ill. She seized Morganne's hand.

"Too much…it's too much," she said.

Morganne put an arm around her. "I'm sorry."

Hiram flicked the reins. "George Pickett's disastrous charge yesterday afternoon. Terrible." He glanced at the two women. "You realize that with Vicksburg's fall and Lee's defeat here it changes everything about the war?"

The storm lashed the gray and green ridges and fields. The whole dark sky seemed to be sliding to earth. Horses lay dead beside the soldiers. Lyndel scanned the men they went by for signs of life. Most appeared beyond help, their heads and limbs shot open or crushed. Then an officer rolled painfully over onto his back and opened his mouth to try to take in some drops of rain.

"Stop!" cried Lyndel. "Hiram, stop the ambulance!"

"But Nathaniel would be near Seminary Ridge."

"There is a wounded man alive right here."

She climbed down and ran to the man, who was choking on the

rainwater. Lifting his head she helped him get his breath back before placing a canteen to his mouth.

"Drink this, Major."

"Thank you…God bless you…thank you." His eyes were swollen shut and oozing blood. "Can't see…can't see you…"

Morganne knelt by them. "You've been blinded."

"A shell knocked me down."

"It could be fragments, sir. A doctor might be able to get some of them out. We're getting you to a hospital."

"Thank you…thank you." His hand groped for Lyndel's hand. "I prayed someone would come for me."

Lyndel wiped his face with a cloth. "Can you walk, Major? There is an ambulance just here." As she cleaned away the last of the blood and dirt her hand stopped. "You're Nehemiah Hargrove."

He clutched her arm. "How did you know that?…Who are you?"

Morganne saw the look on Lyndel's face. "What is the matter?"

"He caught two men on our farm. Charlie Preston and Moses Gunnison. He lynched the one and forced the other back into slavery."

"You…you know about Charlie and Moses? You were on that farm?" He shrieked. "Have mercy! Don't leave me here! I want to see again! I'm sorry! I been baptized since!"

Lyndel stared down at him. Her husband was out in the same brutal rain somewhere. If he was not beyond help—no, she refused to think about that yet—he had been lying on the battlefield for three days. Why was she wasting time here when she needed to be saving him? She detested Hargrove and all he stood for and wished she had never asked Hiram to halt the wagon.

"For the love of God…for the love of Jesus…"

Lyndel bent and put one of his arms over her shoulder. "Can you stand up?"

"Yes, bless you…yes, I believe I can…"

Morganne got his other arm and they helped him to his feet. He staggered the few steps to the ambulance and crawled into the back. Lyndel sat down next to Hiram.

"He needs someone to look at his eyes," she said. "The sooner the better."

"The seminary is on our way."

"It's much shorter if we go back."

"Lyndel, your husband is out there."

She exploded into tears. "I know he's out there! I know he could be just barely hanging onto life! But we need to help this man! It's the road to Jericho and we need to help this man! Turn around!"

Lyndel gripped her hands together as they returned to the field hospital behind Cemetery Ridge. She stared straight ahead as Union soldiers helped Nehemiah Hargrove out of the ambulance and into the tent. When Hiram drove the wagon back to the battleground she shook her head.

"Why am I even bothering? I can't save anyone! I can't even save the man I love most! Look at the bodies! How many of them are wounded? There's only a handful of us! It's hopeless!"

"We save who we can," Morganne said softly.

"That's right. I rescue a slave driver while my husband dies! How wonderful is that?"

Hiram moved the wagon forward. "We're going to Seminary Ridge."

"Don't bother," Lyndel groaned. "It's been three days. None of his platoon made it to Culp's Hill. I have been praying day and night for a miracle...what sort of miracle do I expect? That I can still recognize his face and body after three days in the hot sun? Stay here, Hiram. The wounded from Pickett's charge have a better chance of surviving. Stop the ambulance."

"We're going to Seminary Ridge."

She struck him with her fists. "No! No! I don't want to see his body! Don't take me there!"

Morganne grabbed Lyndel's hands. "He could be alive."

"Not after all this time!"

"You don't know."

"I do know. We both know. You're just trying to be kind—"

"What is that line of wagons?" Hiram interrupted. "It's not the army."

The wagons were traveling the same track they were, the Emmitsburg Road, except they were coming from Gettysburg and heading toward them. Some were carriages. The sort of carriages Lyndel knew well.

How can this be?

"What is the matter?" asked Morganne as Lyndel strained forward to get a better look.

"I think…that man…in the first carriage…"

Suddenly she leaped from the ambulance, stumbled, fell, picked herself up, and ran through the mud and pools of water and the jagged streams of rain. "Papa! Papa!"

The driver of the first carriage reined in, applied the brake, and jumped down into the road. Lyndel threw her arms around him and kissed him on the cheek again and again. Hiram and Morganne saw that he began to weep as he held Lyndel in his arms.

"My girl—I feared you might have come to harm in the fighting—"

"What are you doing here? Who is with you?"

"Abraham Yoder is here. Adam King is here. Some of the women also came. Your mother is with the children but she sends her love and her prayers."

"But why? You said you would never come to a battlefield."

Her father's face was covered with rain. "*Then shall the King say unto them on his right hand, Come, ye blessed of my Father, inherit the kingdom prepared for you from the foundation of the world. For I was an hungred, and ye gave me meat: I was thirsty, and ye gave me drink: I was a stranger, and ye took me in: naked, and ye clothed me: I was sick, and ye visited me: I was in prison, and ye came unto me…Verily I say unto you, Inasmuch as ye have done it unto one of the least of these my brethren, ye have done it unto me.*" He placed his hand on her cheek. "We have come to bind up the wounds. The army let us through. Now tell us where to begin."

"Oh Papa, there are so many wounded everywhere. And I can't find him. I can't find Nathaniel. I can't find Levi. Or Joshua."

"Then we will make a start right here. I will tell our people to find the living and bind their wounds. Where is it they can take the soldiers after they have tended to them?"

Lyndel pointed. "Do you see that brick building on the ridge, Father? It's a seminary. There are surgeons inside taking care of the wounded."

"*Gut.*"

The men and women from the Amish church near Elizabethtown began to fan out over the slope of Cemetery Ridge, the women kneeling in their dresses, aprons, capes, and *kapps,* rolls of white cotton in their hands along with Canada wild ginger leaves for poultices, while the men began to carry wounded to the carriages and wagons and carts. Lyndel watched them a moment, feeling a love for them she had suppressed for a long time because of the shunning. Her father put a hand on her shoulder.

"Daughter, I and Mr. King and Pastor Yoder should like to help you find Nathaniel. Do you know if—" He stopped and took a breath. "Do you know if…Levi…and Joshua would have fallen in the same place as him?"

Shops and houses in Gettysburg were full of Union and Confederate wounded but they couldn't find the young Amish men there. The Lutheran Seminary was also full of men in pain. The blood left her father's face as he stood in the hall and saw the soldiers twisting and turning in agony on the floor. But Nathaniel wasn't there nor Levi or Joshua either. Nor any of the platoon. The barricade had long since been emptied of its wounded and only the dead lay quietly in the rain. They began to search the grounds but the grass too only held dead men. The light faded as they walked over Seminary Ridge. Now and then they passed horses, still saddled, standing alone with their backs to the storm.

"Someone should take care of them," Abraham Yoder said.

"They will," Lyndel responded.

"They are so attached to humans. So loyal to their masters." He pointed. "Do you see how that one will not leave her dead rider?"

Lyndel looked at the black mare in the downpour, its reins trailing on the ground, its head bent, now and then cropping grass, pausing to nuzzle the face of a soldier who lay unmoving. She watched for several moments. Then raced over the grass calling out to God and causing the horse to rear and skitter sideways.

"Nathaniel! Nathaniel!"

He didn't open his eyes but he managed a whisper. "I knew...my nurse would come...I hung on for my nurse..."

Lyndel gently hugged and kissed him while the others slowly gathered behind her. "I'm going to get you up to the seminary—where are you wounded?—here—I have a canteen—please take some water—"

"Libby has kept me alive on grass." He laughed quietly, his eyes still closed as he sipped water from the canteen she pressed to his mouth. "It was hot...lying here in the sun."

"I know. But that's over now, love, it's done." She looked at his shattered and swollen right arm. "Who put the tourniquet on?"

"Two Rebs. They argued about it. The one said he wouldn't do it, that I shouldn't be here...fighting for the slaves. The other reminded him they had both been baptized...at a revival meeting after Chancellorsville. Would leaving me to bleed to death...be what Jesus would want? So they tied on a pretty good tourniquet. But I know...I'm going to lose my arm."

"No, darling—"

"Lose my arm or lose my life. I've seen enough battlefield casualties."

"We're getting you to the surgeons right away."

He tried to lift his head. "Levi is nearby. And Joshua. Nip. Ham. Take care of them."

"Of course. I have others with me. They will find them. It's all right."

"Are they alive?"

"I don't know—yes, yes—I'm sure they are—we're going to move you now—"

"I don't even know what happened here. Did it matter?"

Lyndel wiped the rain from his eyes with her fingers. "Did what matter?"

"Did their…sacrifice make any difference…do we still have a country?"

But Lyndel couldn't respond. Her throat tightened and her eyes burned. Abraham Yoder and Adam King had left to hunt for Levi and Joshua, but Hiram and Morganne remained with her. Morganne wrapped Lyndel in her arms as Hiram dropped to one knee by his friend.

"Nathaniel. It's Hiram."

"Hiram…ah, Hiram. You would know what happened."

"I do know. The Army of the Potomac came in the night, Nathaniel, the night you fought to give them. They took the heights. Lee assailed them for two days and could not defeat them. Now he has retreated. You've won."

"I've won—"

"You've won. Your men have won. The Republic and the slaves have won."

"Thank God…my boys were so brave…and the Carolina boys coming against them were so brave…I pray we will be one nation…"

"It will come. Even I believe now it will come. Vicksburg will surrender any day now. That will make Grant a hero. I'm certain Lincoln will bring him east no matter what the naysayers do to block him. And Grant will run Lee to ground like a hound does a fox."

Nathaniel opened his eyes and took Hiram's hand in a grip like iron. "It mattered…the stand on McPherson's Ridge and Seminary Ridge…"

Hiram held the grip. "Yes, it mattered. A lot happened in the three days here, Nathaniel. Battles you never saw but I did. The South will never forget Pickett's charge on Friday. The North will never forget what happened at Little Round Top on Thursday. Both will honor the dead of Devil's Den and Emmitsburg Road and the peach orchard and the wheat field. And that's the way it should be. But I will write in my newspaper what I believe—the Battle of Gettysburg was won on the first day. By Buford, by Doubleday and the First Corps, by Howard and the Eleventh Corps, by cavalry, infantry, and artillery. By the grace of God the Battle of Gettysburg was won on the first day by the Iron Brigade. I will stand by that, my friend."

Nathaniel released Hiram's hand as they lifted him from the wet grass. He grimaced. "Thank you…thank you. But…where's my lady… where's my bride?"

Lyndel pulled away from Morganne and took Nathaniel's face in her hands as they carried him. "I'm here, my love. It's so good to see your green eyes."

"If I'm sent home after the amputation…your father will not receive me."

"He will receive you, Nathaniel. He is here now."

Bishop Keim had Nathaniel by the shoulders. "God bless you, young man."

"Bishop Keim…I never expected you to be on a battleground…"

"It was God's will we come to Gettysburg. To bring what healing we could to the wounded and the sick and the lame. Even your father is here."

"I'm sorry. For the problems we caused. But we had to…we had to fight…"

"The fight is past, Nathaniel. Perhaps it is we who should have forgiven and embraced you. It is we who have sinned in hardening our hearts. But God is the great forgiver. We begin anew. You are wounded. Let us care for you. Let us welcome you home. We wish to welcome home all our sons who felt, before the Lord God Almighty, that they had to wage war against slavery."

Nathaniel twisted his head and smiled up at Bishop Keim. "Home. I should like that."

His eyes returned to Lyndel. He reached up for a strand of her red hair and twisted it gently around his finger and his wedding ring, brushing the faint scar on her cheek as he did so. "Tomatoes…you are so beautiful."

Then his hand fell.

29

"He is almost gone. You know that."

"Yes, Doctor. I know."

"The amputation may not do any good at this point."

Lyndel straightened and wiped at her eyes with her fingers. "Please. Try."

"I will need your friends' help to hold him down."

"Of course."

Nathaniel's father, Bishop Keim, and Abraham Yoder gripped him by the legs and shoulders as the surgeon's saw bit into flesh and bone. Lyndel held a leather pad between his teeth as the pain made him arch his back off the table. He looked at her in anguish as sweat sprang out across his forehead and cheeks. She gripped his left hand, holding his gaze, moving her lips with the words *I love you.*

Then it was done and she was securing his wound and stanching the flow of blood. The men laid him in a room off the hallway that was filled with other soldiers recovering from amputations. On one side of him was a captain from Louisiana and on the other a private from Mississippi. Morganne knelt by Lyndel and Nathaniel.

"I'm sorry," she said, hugging her friend.

Lyndel hugged her back. "I just pray he will pull through."

"Of course he'll pull through. He wants to go home and live with his beautiful bride. Have babies. Raise a family. He'll pull through."

"I hope to our God you are right."

Morganne kissed Lyndel on the cheek. "He is resting now. The surgeons have asked for our help. There are so many wounded. Lee left his worst cases behind."

Lyndel passed both hands over her face and stood up. "Of course we must help. Where do they want us to start?"

"With the ones who are waiting for surgery. They need water badly and they need to have their wounds cleaned of corruption. We're losing too many of them."

Lyndel began to walk quickly along a hallway slippery with blood and urine, past the soldiers propped up against the walls. Morganne kept pace beside her.

"Is it all these men in the hall?" Lyndel asked.

"Yes. And out on the porch. And on the lawn."

"Where is my father? And Mr. King and Mr. Yoder?"

"They are out bringing in more wounded. And they are still looking for Joshua and Nip and your brother Levi. And Ham."

Lyndel suddenly bent down over a Confederate sergeant. "Let's start with this group here. Sergeant, I am Lyndel Keim. I will be your nurse. Have you had any water? Where are you wounded?"

"They...they won't give me water," rasped the sergeant. "On account I have a ball in my stomach."

Lyndel forced a smile and smoothed his brown hair back from his eyes. "Too much water is hard on a stomach wound. But I can give you a wet cloth and you can put that in your mouth. That won't do any harm and it will make you feel better. You'll be with the surgeons soon."

Lyndel and Morganne worked with the doctors and ambulance men through the evening and into the night. Lyndel was still awake when they brought Levi in and she gripped both his hands as a surgeon took off his left leg above the knee. She collapsed in a corner of the room for amputees at four in the morning on Sunday and did not wake for several hours, until a soldier's scream made her sit up with a start. Nathaniel and Levi were both fighting fevers and she spent several minutes bathing their faces and chests. Then she went looking for Morganne and found her asleep on the porch of the seminary by the dead body of a Union officer. She had been offering him water from a canteen that she still clutched in her hand. Lyndel let her sleep.

Nip and Joshua were both brought in that morning, Ham in the afternoon. Nip had an arm removed at the elbow and Joshua had both feet amputated. Ham was badly wounded at the throat and neck where two balls had torn open the flesh. All during the day she kept checking back on them as well as on Levi and Nathaniel. When others died in the amputee room she asked Hiram and her father to help move the four Amish boys together. Ham was on another floor.

By nightfall on Sunday she was certain she would wake to find Nathaniel dead—he was doing so poorly and his breathing was so rough. She fell asleep in Morganne's arms, her face streaked with the grime of tears and blood. In the morning, her husband was still alive, but Nip had contracted pneumonia. For the next two days he fought the illness. On Wednesday morning, Lyndel spoke with him, gave him some water, and went to get a fresh towel. When she returned she could see before she reached Nip's side that his gaze had become fixed. She scooped him up and hugged him to her and cried out his name, but his arms and head hung loose.

Hiram came running. "What is it? Is it Nathaniel?"

Lyndel was on her feet with her hand over her eyes. "I'm sorry…it's Nip…I didn't mean to shout like that…I'm sorry…"

Hiram dropped his gaze to the dead soldier. "You have nothing to apologize for. You must be exhausted. Who can blame you for grieving the loss of this fine young man?"

Lyndel stared out the window at the sun and clouds. Her lips were a straight line and the skin on her face was tight. "We need the burial detail now."

"Do you…do you want to pray over him?" Hiram asked.

"I have prayed over him!" she snapped. "Get someone to help you and get him out to the burial detail!"

"I do not need another's help."

Hiram lifted Nip gently in his arms and carried the small body down the hall and out the door. Lyndel suddenly placed one hand on the wall and another over her stomach. She began to groan and weep.

Her father found her. "Lyndy, what is this?" he asked. He looked anxiously down at Nathaniel but could see he was breathing deeply and naturally.

"Nothing. Nothing. It's just that…everything beautiful…ends in death…"

She collapsed against him and he held her tightly and kissed the top of her head. "Not everything. No, not everything. *In the world ye shall have tribulation: but be of good cheer; I have overcome the world.*"

"I wish I could believe that again, Papa. But…there has been so much death…"

"Death releases many to God. Still, it is no friend. It is an enemy. *The last enemy that shall be destroyed is death.* Remember our Lord, daughter. Remember his crucifixion and resurrection. Especially now and especially in this place and at this battlefield. *I am the resurrection, and the life: he that believeth in me, though he were dead, yet shall he live: and whosoever liveth and believeth in me shall never die. Believest thou this?*"

"I want to."

"My daughter, my daughter—*believest thou this?*"

Lyndel cried even harder. "Yes, yes—oh, yes!"

He continued to hold her. "You know how we tie a rope to the crossbeams when we work on the barn roof? So tie that in and tie it down, my girl. Make the knot strong. We need you. So many of us need you. Alive and strong and full of faith. For we are so weak."

Lyndel lifted her head from his chest and looked at him, her eyes wet. "Papa, how can you say that? I am completely undone."

"No. It is we who are undone. Only we hide it well. We need you. Make your knot to the crossbeams tight and help us."

Lyndel pulled away and straightened her back, one hand still on her father's arm. "I really don't know what good I have been when so many boys are under the ground but I will try, Papa, because you want me to. And because it is what Jesus would do. And because Nathaniel needs me."

Her father smiled. "That is a good way back."

"I must go find Davey. And talk to the surgeons." She glanced at

Nathaniel and Joshua and Levi. "The boys seem fine right now. Will you keep an eye on them until I return?"

"Of course."

"I must see how Ham is doing as well. He was one of their closest friends."

Lyndel started off. She was no more than halfway down the hall, when he watched her stop and bend over to help a man who was struggling with a canteen. Bishop Keim turned and knelt by the Amish soldiers and prayed. Then he went and knelt by each soldier in the room and prayed for them as well. When he was done he stood over Nathaniel, his broad-brimmed hat in his hands.

"*Komm zurück...komm zurück zu uns,*" he whispered. *Come back... come back to us.*

30

At one o'clock on Friday morning, Lyndel could go no further. She grabbed a clean blanket from a stack on a table and collapsed between Levi and Nathaniel, dropping into a deep sleep right away. Two hours later she emerged from a dream of baking bread in Elizabethtown to feel someone kissing and nuzzling her hair. She recoiled and sat up, pushing the person away.

"Excuse me, sir!" she spat out in a harsh voice. "Who are you and what do you think you are doing?"

A man laughed softly. "I am your husband, and your husband thinks he is kissing the woman he loves. The very beautiful woman he loves."

Lyndel gasped. "Nathaniel!" She swiftly ran her hands over his face in the dark. "Your fever has broken! I thank God!"

"I remember the amputation. I didn't think I'd find you lying beside me when I came back to my senses."

"Nathaniel—praise God, thank God!" She put her arms around him.

"I didn't think…when I felt the saw…I didn't think I would make it."

She kissed him on the mouth. "You had good nursing care. The best we could offer."

"I believe it."

"Levi is on the other side of me here," she whispered. "Oh, Nathaniel, *der Herr sei gelobt.*" *Praise the Lord.*

Nathaniel leaned over her to take a look. "How is he?"

"He's holding his own. So is Joshua."

"Thank you, Lord. I saw Joshua there next to me. He seemed to be breathing well." He stroked her hair. "Where's Nip? Where's Ham? In another room?"

"Ham is wounded at the neck. But every day he gets stronger. He is upstairs. Nip is…he is…" Lyndel let out her air quickly. "He's gone, Nathaniel."

"What?"

"An arm was amputated. Pneumonia set in. We buried him on Wednesday. Two days ago."

Nathaniel released her and lay back down. She waited a moment and joined him.

"Ah, Lord," he groaned. "It never stops. One after another after another."

"You're alive. And I believe Ham is going to make it. And Joshua and my brother."

"Do you honestly think so? Or is it just wishful thinking?"

"Pray with me."

"For what? The war to end? The killing to stop?"

"Yes. Yes. Why not? For the healing of the land and for the healing of Levi and Joshua and Ham."

"Haven't you and the others already been doing that?"

"But I haven't prayed with you. Not for weeks."

She could swear she suddenly heard him smile in the dark.

"Perhaps God can't deny us," he said. "Not two Kings."

She whispered her prayer in High German, her hand tight on his. When she stopped, he began. Once he'd finished, she prayed a second time. Then she grew quiet and he spoke the word *Amen.*

"Now I think I need to rest again," he mumbled.

"I will be right beside you, love."

"Yes, good, I was feeling chilled."

"I…I worried that you might be sullen. Angry. Depressed. You have lost an arm, Nathaniel."

"Believe me, I am grateful just to be alive. I have lost Nip and

Corinth. But I have you. And my friends. I don't know—perhaps I will be more upset about my arm later. But I have my left arm and it was always the stronger of the two."

She covered her mouth with her hand but the laugh came through just the same. "I wish—I hope—the others will have your way of looking at things…but I don't know…Joshua and Levi can both be so intense—"

"So pray about that too. Once I am asleep. I can't hold my eyes open any longer."

"I am not worried about Ham's disposition."

"Neither am I. I'm just worried my nurse will leave at any minute to take care of someone else."

She drew her army blanket over both of them and snuggled against his side. "No. Here I am."

Nathaniel was already breathing deeply. She wrapped her fingers around his. For half an hour she listened to him as well as to the gasps, whimpers, and moans of the men all about her. She realized they could not all live…not Levi and Joshua and Ham and everyone else as well. The world as it was, even with the possibility of miracles, could never offer that. But she prayed there would be more than a few. And fell asleep again, with her head on her husband's chest so she could hear the beating of his heart.

Three days later, on Monday afternoon, she helped her brother out the door of the seminary as he leaned on his crutch, while Nathaniel gave Joshua a hand as he maneuvered his way down the steps on two. They made their way to a cluster of trees and lay down in the shade as the sun gleamed all around them and the heat worked its way into their backs and shoulders.

"Ah, this is good, this is very good," sighed Joshua, leaning back against a tree trunk.

"It is better than good," responded Levi, settling himself with his sister's help. "We should be singing hymns. Don't you think so, Lyndy?"

Lyndel smiled and sat down facing the three men. "Sure, *ja*, hymns.

Hymns and prayers of thanks. If this were some Baptist Holy Ghost meeting we could even dance."

Nathaniel laughed. "The dancing Amish. How would that go over in Elizabethtown?"

"In Elizabethtown, I don't know," Lyndel replied. "But in heaven very well, I think."

"You are so sure?" asked Levi.

"*Ja.* So many people Jesus and the apostles healed in the Bible—did not some of them leap and dance for joy?"

"Yes, sister, they did. I have read it."

"So I am so grateful. So happy. It has been a long time since I have been this happy."

Nathaniel reached over and played with a strand of her red hair. "Back at the Fitzhugh House before we marched for Pennsylvania, maybe?"

"Maybe. But there was war waiting for us just through the forest. I could never forget that. Now our war is over. Even though we must pray for others while the fighting goes on."

Nathaniel nodded. "Yes. Our war is over." He looked around them at the wounded lying on the grass and the men and women giving them long drinks of water. "It is time to go home. Past time. But can they spare you here at the seminary?"

"Well. They will say they cannot. But they have plenty of help now. Plenty of volunteers, as you can see. Many, many soldiers. I will ask my father if we cannot hitch up the wagons. I know the women want to get back to their families." She smiled. "And to tell you the truth, though they will not complain, I think they are quite tired of army food."

"That must be an Amish thing," said Joshua, "because so am I."

"Is tomorrow or Wednesday too soon?" asked Nathaniel.

"Not for me," spoke up Levi. "I want to see how fast I can get chores done on the new leg they'll make for me once the stump is healed."

"What about Ham?" asked Levi.

"He is doing very well," Lyndel told them. "I am sure he will be able to walk outside to say goodbye."

Levi was startled. "Goodbye? No. I want him to come with us."

"To Elizabethtown? To our people? My brother, he is not Amish."

"He is not Amish but he can be our guest. For as long as he likes. He fought with us, Lyndel. He saved our lives and we saved his. I know he is an orphan. He has no home to speak of."

"Well, if he wants to, of course, no one would mind. But all four of you must be strong enough to travel—" Lyndel began.

Joshua waved his crutches in the air. "For me it is boots. Zook makes the best. The wooden feet they'll give me will never get tired and with new boots I will soon need two dairy herds and four hayfields and at least five crops to keep me busy. I will be tireless."

Lyndel shook her head. "How can you three be so cheerful when you have all been so badly wounded? Where is the anger I expected? Where is the bitterness?"

Levi put a hand on her shoulder. "Must we have that? Must you see that in us?"

"No, of course not, it's just…I don't understand how you men can be so hopeful when you have been through so much…when you have lost so much…war is a terrible darkness…"

Levi nodded. "But it is our bodies that are wounded, sister. Not our spirits."

The plans were made and the string of Amish wagons and buggies began to move away from the seminary and the battlefield early on Wednesday, July 15th. Ham was with them, his voice no more than a harsh whisper and his body thin, but he was eager to see his friends' houses and land. The four men lay or sat on mounds of hay as their wagon creaked along ruts of mud and rainwater. Bishop Keim glanced back at them, as did Lyndel, who was seated beside her father.

"I am going too fast? It is too rough?" he asked.

"It is fine, Father." Levi smiled. "The sooner we are back in Elizabethtown the better."

Hiram and Morganne walked beside the wagon. Nathaniel, who had been lying back, suddenly propped himself up on his elbow.

"Who is that?" he asked Hiram.

Hiram glanced over at a bearded man carrying a camera with a tripod on his shoulder. Several young men walked beside him, carrying all sorts of gear.

"Oh, that's Alex," Hiram replied. "Alex Gardner. Would you like me to introduce you?"

"What is he doing?"

"He's a photographer. Don't you remember his pictures of Antietam?"

Nathaniel frowned. "So he is here to take photographs of dead soldiers at Gettysburg?"

"Yes. He's been out on the battleground since just after the fighting ended."

"Who does he take pictures of dead people for? Who wants to see such things?"

"Well…the public, Nathaniel. The same people who buy newspapers to read my stories about the battles."

"So the war has become an entertainment, Hiram? Complete with photographs of corpses?"

"Not an entertainment, Nathaniel. But it's news. It's always been news. Now the pictures of the dead soldiers are news too."

Nathaniel sat up straight. "Stop the wagon."

Bishop Keim glanced back at him. "*Vas?*"

"Stop the wagon. *Bitte.*" *Please.*

Lyndel turned around in her seat as her father reined in the team. "What is it, Nathaniel? Is something wrong?"

"Are there clothes in one of the wagons or buggies, Lyndel? Bishop Keim? Clothes that would fit the three of us?"

Bishop Keim stared at him. "Sure. There are good plain shirts and trousers."

Nathaniel began to unbutton his uniform, a slower process with just one hand. "We have done our fight. Now we lay down our guns. And we will never take them up again. It is peace we return to. It is peace we pray for." He looked at Joshua and Levi. "It is time to become who we are once again."

Levi had watched as Gardner had set up his camera to photograph the rows of dead at the back of the seminary. He also began to unbutton the frock coat worn by the men of the Iron Brigade.

Joshua hesitated. "We needed to fight slavery," he protested quietly.

Nathaniel nodded. "Yes. We did. Now it is time to fight it in another way. And pray for the healing of the land. Have we not been part of enough death, Joshua? Let us be part of the other way now. Let us go home."

Joshua thought about it for a few more moments and slowly began to remove his coat, rolling it carefully into a bundle. Ham also began to tug off his.

"No," Nathaniel said to him. "It isn't necessary. You are not one of us."

"Of course I am one of you."

Nathaniel burrowed down into the hay so that he could remove his pants without being seen. Bishop Keim brought them four sets of clothes from another wagon.

"Thank you," Nathaniel said, taking shirt and pants and undergarments.

The bishop smiled. "It is I who thank you. It is good to have you back, Nathaniel. I brought clothing for your friend in case he also wishes to dress plainly for now."

"Yes. He has asked for a shirt and pants. *Das ist gut so, Bischof Keim.*"

Lyndel averted her eyes for several minutes. "May I look now?" she finally asked.

"Yes," responded Levi in his black shirt and coat and pants. He spread his arms. "What do you think?"

She smiled. "You are very plain again. It is very nice. And you also, Joshua. Perfect and simple."

"Does it work for me?" rasped Ham.

"Very much so. You look like one of our ministers. You are a natural."

"And I?" Nathaniel was placing a black hat on his head. "How is it with me?"

"All is well, *mein Mann.* Only one thing is not right."

"*Ja?* And what is that, *liebe Frau?*"

She stroked her chin. "There should be a beard. Or was that only a soldier's wedding, and are we not married among the Amish?"

"We are married among the Amish all right. I will get to work on the beard right away." He rubbed his jaw. "Only—I would have thought I would have more to show—for not having shaved since the end of June."

Morganne laughed. "A nurse did it. I saw her with the razor."

Lyndel looked away, covering her mouth with her hand. "I thought it would help you heal," she mumbled through her fingers, trying not to laugh along with her friend.

The wagon lurched and Nathaniel fell back into the hay. "It doesn't matter. I'm glad you gave me the last shave I'll ever have."

"So long," said Hiram, staying behind as the wagons continued east. "Read about me in the papers."

"Goodbye, Lyndel King." Morganne waved a hand. "I will write. And I will visit."

The wagons were not moving very quickly yet. Lyndel jumped down and ran back to her friend, throwing her arms around her.

"Of course you'll visit," Lyndel said. "And of course you'll be welcome. God bless you."

Morganne kissed her on the cheek. "When the war is over. Soon."

"Yes, soon. When the war is over." Lyndel extended a hand to Hiram. "Will it be soon?"

Hiram shrugged and took her hand. "If Meade had pursued Lee last week after the Army of Northern Virginia retreated. If he had attacked him when Lee could not cross the swollen rivers and streams and his men were trapped. But now it will go on."

Lyndel bit her lower lip. "Pictures for Mr. Alexander Garland."

Hiram looked down at the muddy road. "Yes. Too many pictures."

31

The war continued long after the wagons returned to the Amish community at Elizabethtown, long after the three soldiers learned how to chop wood, harness teams, nail boards, and thresh grain despite Nathaniel's loss of his arm, or Levi's loss of his leg, or Joshua's wooden feet tucked securely into two of Eli Zook's black leather boots. Battles raged from east to west, Grant was brought to Virginia to command the Union armies and pursued Lee south to Richmond, Sherman would capture Atlanta and march his way to Savannah and the sea, burning and destroying as he went.

But peace reigned among the Amish. Levi married and had a son, Ham learned how to work with dairy cattle, crops were harvested, hymns sung, and prayers offered to heaven for an end to the years of conflict.

Lyndel had twins in late March 1864. She gave birth in the house the Amish helped Nathaniel build after his return from Gettysburg. Lyndel's own mother, and Nathaniel's mother as well, were her midwives. Breads and soups and roasts came to the home in a steady stream for weeks afterward. The boy they named Corinth, the girl Lincoln. The year of 1864 was, Nathaniel declared in September, the happiest in his life.

"I have a whole family," he grinned, holding Lincoln while Lyndel fed Corinth. "A stunning wife. Two beautiful children. Why, I think we'll even get a couple of dogs and a cat."

"Slow down," laughed Lyndel. "Let the pair of them start walking first. Then we'll talk about pets."

"Oh, they'll be walking any day now. Kings don't wait for twelve months to slip by before they get in on that."

"Or Keims. Levi swears his boy will be on his feet by January."

"He was born before ours."

Yet other moods fastened themselves onto Nathaniel during the year. He fretted about the ongoing slaughter and the casualty lists that filled the newspapers. Refusing to view any photographs, he nevertheless read Hiram's accounts of the clashes, especially the ones the Iron Brigade and the 19th Indiana were involved in—the Wilderness, Spotsylvania Court House, Cold Harbor, and Petersburg. No, he did not want to take up arms again. He had sworn he would not. His weapons now were prayer and worship and faith. But he wished he could drive an ambulance or help carry wounded men off the field and out of harm's way.

"If you are thinking seriously of this," Lyndel said to him one afternoon in early October when both children were napping, "bear in mind they are not likely to take a man with one arm."

"I can drive a team better than most men with two hands!" Nathaniel said, his temper flaring.

"I know you can. But still they will not take you on."

He got out of his chair and paced the kitchen. For a moment he glanced out at the trees changing color near their barn. Then he said, "I could train as a surgeon. I only need one arm to administer medicines or ply a saw."

"I think you would be a wonderful surgeon. I am sure you could convince the teachers of your ability to do the tasks of a physician competently. But it will take you several years to complete medical training, Nathaniel. And then you would have another clash on your hands with my father and the ministers. The Amish do not become doctors."

Nathaniel leaned against the wall on his fist. "So I do nothing to save lives or hasten the war's end?"

"You and your men saved the country at Gettysburg. Sherman has captured Atlanta and Grant has Lee trapped in Richmond and

Petersburg. Everyone knows the conflict is coming to an end. Even Hiram writes that we are talking about months now and not years."

"Still."

Lyndel sat up in her chair. "Yes. Still. Lives are being lost that could be saved. And you can do nothing. But we are one flesh. I feel the same things you do. Only I am in a position to do something about them."

Nathaniel turned away from the wall and stared at her. "What do you mean?"

"The Lord knows I love being a wife to you and I adore being a mother to my children. But they need nurses at Petersburg. I have been reading about the battles at Peebles Farm and New Market Heights and Darbytown. I can make a difference to Grant's men."

"But you haven't nursed in over a year."

"The skills will come back quickly. You don't forget them any more than you forget how to bale hay or ride a horse."

"What about your father? Do you think he will still feel the way he did after Gettysburg?"

"I have spoken to him about it. Remember how he helped the surgeons at the seminary? He has changed forever, he says. He sees binding up the wounds as an act of Christ now."

"The children—"

"Lincoln and Corinth will miss me. I will pine after them. But their grandmothers will smother them in love. And they have a great father."

Nathaniel thrust his hand in his pocket and gave a low whistle. "So you have been thinking about this for some time. And your mind is made up."

She got out of her chair and came to him, resting both hands on his arm. "I think your mind is made up too. You want me to go, don't you?"

"No. Not at all. I don't want you to leave us."

"But you are grateful that one of us is going to do something to ease the suffering."

"You could be killed."

She shook her head. "I will be behind the lines. The wounded will come to us in minutes at Petersburg, not hours. I will be all right, love."

He narrowed his bright green eyes. "I could insist that you stay. The Keim and King families have seen enough war. I cannot bear to have you hurt."

She squeezed his arm. "But you won't insist. Because you know it is right we try to save the fallen. You know it is something holy, something sacred. Through me, we can do what so few others can—stop the flow of blood."

Nathaniel breathed out noisily. "Ah, it is difficult to argue with you. I have mixed feelings about this."

"You know it is right."

"Do I?" He brushed her cheek with his hand. "Have you thought about how you will get to the front?"

"The 19th Indiana is still with the Iron Brigade, isn't it? The Iron Brigade is at Petersburg. And I am a nurse of the 19th Indiana." She patted a pocket on her dress. "I still have a pass from the president of the United States."

Nathaniel cracked a smile. "You do beat all, Lyndel King. It's so easy to love you. Why, it's the easiest thing in the world." His strong arm pulled her into his chest. "I think I want to kiss this woman."

She tilted her head. "I think this woman wants you to go ahead."

Lyndel took the train in January, right after the Christmas and New Year's celebrations, with the blessings of her father and mother and the Amish community. The tears ran freely when she hugged Lincoln and Corinth but she turned quickly and stepped into the carriage driven by her brother Levi, who took her to the depot.

She had no trouble reaching the Union lines and was escorted with a military guard to a large field hospital. The 19th Indiana had amalgamated with the 20th Indiana in the fall and no one she asked knew where it was located on the line. Nor was the Iron Brigade anywhere in sight—but surgeons put her to work immediately regardless of the brigade's whereabouts. Along with the other nurses and volunteers she made sure the wounded were warm and fed and had their dressings changed regularly.

For the first few weeks the front was quiet but she was busy enough despite the lull in fighting. On February 5th and 6th Union cavalry and infantry clashed with Confederate forces at Hatcher's Run and the Union troops had extended their siege works and stranglehold on Petersburg by the time that fight was over. The casualties came pouring in with the ambulances and it reminded Lyndel immediately of Gettysburg and Antietam, though on a much smaller scale. She cabled Nathaniel and her father about dealing with the battle's wounded. They cabled back prayers and Bible verses and their love.

She wrote her friend, and Morganne came down to join her in March. She brought news from Hiram that with Sherman's march through Georgia before Christmas, much of the South was about ready to give up the fight. More Union troops were converging on Petersburg and Richmond and Grant would soon have enough to overwhelm Lee's dwindling army.

Morganne's return to nursing was as quiet as Lyndel's had been in January. They only dealt with a few soldiers who had been shot by snipers or who had come down with dysentery and other ailments. It gave them time to relax and talk. Hiram had asked Morganne to marry him as soon as the war was over and he was already planning on a spring wedding.

Lyndel laughed at that. "Oh, Hiram—always so confident about his predictions. Well, he has a lot riding on this one. The end of the war, a Union victory, and his marriage to Morganne David. Do you think the world will turn on the axis that Hiram plans?"

Morganne shrugged. "I've waited this long, Lyndy. Even if the war doesn't end until Thanksgiving, I plan on getting that man to the altar. You will be my matron of honor, won't you?"

"Matron. That makes me sound so old. But I'll stand with you. I'll be so happy to stand with you. So why isn't Hiram hanging around the camp with you here?"

"Oh, I expect him to pop in and out. But he's a big muckety-muck at the paper now—a lot of correspondents answer to him. He's in Boston and New York as much as he's here at the front."

Three days later, on March 25th, Confederate troops tried to break out of the Union encirclement and capture Fort Stedman behind

Union lines. The skies broke open as artillery shells streaked back and forth and Federal forces counterattacked. Once again the two nurses were dealing with Rebel officers and men as well as Union troops. The battle only lasted one day but other fights and skirmishes soon followed as Grant began to press in on Lee and Petersburg.

Lyndel saw the general himself ride up to the field hospital on the last day of March with his retinue. It was raining heavily and the horses splashed and slipped through puddles of mud. She and Morganne were working on five Confederate prisoners as the rain pelted their backs and the soldiers' faces. Grant called a captain to his side and pointed at the two nurses. The captain saluted, shouted for a number of his men nearby, and they went off at a brisk run, returning five minutes later with a tent, which they promptly began to erect right over the nurses and their patients, finally getting them out of the storm. When Lyndel realized what was happening she looked at Grant and lifted her hand in a small sign of thanks. He tugged on the brim of his hat and nodded and urged his horse forward. Lyndel wondered how he could keep his cigar lit in such weather but the trail of smoke he left behind him was obvious.

The next day a fierce fight at Five Forks between Philip Sheridan's bluecoats and George Pickett's men of butternut and gray kept the ambulances racing. From bits and pieces of information officers related to her and Morganne and the other nurses, Lyndel gathered that the South had suffered a severe blow when Sheridan led a charge that breached Pickett's left flank and won the battle. The Union victory had cut Lee off from his supply lines in Richmond.

As she worked through half the night it became clear from what she was told that Grant would launch an assault along the entire Rebel line in the morning. Anticipating a great run of casualties, Lyndel forced herself back to her tent, where she slept for five hours. When Morganne woke her the battle she'd expected had begun and the surgeon's probes and saws were already slick with flesh and blood. She lost track of all time, but she paused from bandaging a man's eye that evening to watch a cluster of Union soldiers outside the tent toss their caps in the air and shout.

"What is it?" asked the corporal she was nursing.

"I don't know," she replied. "Some sort of good news, I expect."

He forced himself up on his elbows. "What sort of good news? We been almost a whole year in this stinking mud. Find out what good news, ma'am. Please God, let it be that this siege is over."

Lyndel finished his bandage. "All right, Corporal. Sit here a moment."

She stepped to the opening of the tent. "What's is it, men?" she called out.

A young private grinned at her. "Why, Mrs. King, Lee is on the run west. The Army of Northern Virginia is whipped. Word is that tomorrow we will occupy Richmond and Petersburg."

Lyndel turned back to the corporal. Tears were flowing from his good eye. "I thank the Lord. It's over. It's pretty much over. I thank God I've made it through. I can go home soon, ma'am. Home to Illinois."

Lyndel wasn't sure what to say. "The South hasn't surrendered yet, soldier."

He laughed with his happiness and gripped her arm. "You'll see. Grant ain't no Hooker or Burnside or Meade. He'll go after Lee like a greyhound. It's all gonna happen fast now."

The next morning, April 3rd, with Lee's army gone, Richmond and Petersburg surrendered. The camp was a mass of running bodies and plunging horses and rattling artillery pieces as Grant prepared to go in pursuit. The Army of Northern Virginia was marching toward Confederate forces in North Carolina as fast as it could.

General Grant came galloping by the hospital tent with his cluster of officers. He meant to go past but suddenly reined up. He peered into the tent for a long minute. Then he spoke to an officer next to him. A major general dismounted. Lyndel and Morganne were working on a man who'd been shot through both lungs and was dying painfully. Lyndel could feel the major general's eyes on her and looked up. Grant and his attendants were only a few feet away, framed in the tent opening.

"Sir?" she asked, holding a bloody towel to her patient's mouth.

The officer's face and eyes were soft as he watched her nurse the soldier. His voice was quiet. "General Grant's compliments, ma'am. When you are finished with your patient, and the man is comfortable, he asks you both to attach yourself to one of the surgeons' units traveling with his army. I have asked one of my men to see to the arrangements. We are following Lee and General Grant very much wants you two working with our casualties."

"Of course, sir. I'm surprised the general could even think of the pair of us when so much is on his mind."

Grant spoke up as he sat on his horse outside the tent, a cigar stub burning out between his fingers. "It was always niggling away at the back of other matters and concerns after I saw you treating the Confederate prisoners in that rainstorm. I wanted to satisfy my memory and locate you."

"Thank you, General."

"May I have the honor of your names?"

"Why, sir, I am Mrs. King, Mrs. Lyndel King, and my friend and colleague here is Miss Morganne David."

Grant lifted his hat briefly. "Very good."

Once the major general had returned to his mount, Grant quickly rode off followed by his men. The soldier the two nurses were treating died five minutes later. The two washed their faces and hands and went back to their tent to fetch their clothing and bags. A half hour later a lieutenant tapped on the canvas flap. He told them his name was Carson and he was their escort. Tall and slender with a boyish face and a gentle voice, they trusted him from the start.

"Where's home, Lieutenant?" Morganne asked when he had them safely placed in a surgeon's wagon.

He rode a bay gelding beside the wagon. "New Hampshire, ma'am."

"I expect you are anxious for this war to end so that you can return to your family."

"I am. I hope it will be over before the month is out. I hope this pursuit of Lee will determine that."

"It seems to me your state is also the birthplace of the famous words of your Revolutionary War soldier," Lyndel spoke up. "My husband was with the Iron Brigade and he often quoted it to me."

"I hope he is well, Mrs.—?"

"King. Thank you, he is fine. He lost an arm at Gettysburg but he has readjusted to farm life regardless."

"I am heartily glad to hear it. Do you recall the quote, Mrs. King?"

"I do, but I do not remember the name of the man who said it. *Live free or die. Death is not the worst of evils.*"

Lieutenant Carson smiled. "I am honored that you and your husband know these words. It is from a toast by one of our soldiers of the Revolution, just as you surmised. General John Stark."

"Are they your sentiments, Lieutenant?"

"They are. And they would be even more so if I were one of our African soldiers. My Lord, just to take one lungful of air as a free man and not a slave I would willingly die a thousand deaths."

The women slept in their wagon of bandages and medicines as they rolled west with the army. Short, sharp battles occurred at places with names like Namozine Church, Amelia Springs, High Bridge, and Rice's Station. No matter how many casualties there were, Morganne and Lyndel always moved on the next day with several of the surgeons and ambulances. Lee's supply trains were captured and burned. His escape routes were cut off. At Sayler's Creek, he lost a quarter of his army as eight thousand men were trapped by Union troops and forced to surrender.

Lyndel held an image in her head—maybe she had dreamed it—of the white-bearded and distinguished Lee running desperately one way, only to turn and scramble in the opposite direction, seeking a route free of the many traps waiting for him. Sweat covered his elderly face. His horse, Traveler, was gone. His men were gone. Only the general was left and the forests, rocks, and rivers of Virginia were pressing in. Soon he was backed up against a gray mountain of stone and shale. His eyes were wild, frightened, in agony.

The image upset her. It returned to her mind again and again as she worked on Union and Confederate wounded and dying. Soldiers with gray or white beards took on Lee's features regardless of the color of their uniforms. In her mind she watched Lee die a dozen times. If he appeared at night he drew his sword from its long scabbard and lay it down on the dirt and grass, exhaustion and misery in the lines below and above his eyes.

"I'm sorry," she would whisper in her sleep.

The daily clashes went on for a week. After nursing for hours without a break, she would get out of sight with a cup of coffee for a few minutes and write letters to Nathaniel and Lincoln and Corinth. Once or twice letters from home caught up with her and she kept them in her pocket to read over and over again. Days and nights became one long streak of light and dark, of mangled bodies, of men's faces contorted by suffering. Then one morning they did not move forward. There had been a storm of musket fire at dawn but then nothing but the *pop-pop* of snipers and skirmishers. And silence. *Too much silence*, Lyndel thought. It made her twist her hands in her lap as she prayed her morning prayers. No thunder of cavalry. No artillery roar. No banks of white and gray smoke. But ambulances came in with wounded from the fight at sunrise and Lyndel rushed to the side of a Rebel officer who had been shot in the leg as they placed him carefully on the grass by the hospital tent.

"The day seems strange," she murmured, cutting off his pant leg below the knee and stanching the flow of blood. "What is going on, I wonder?"

"It's Palm Sunday, ma'am," the captain told her.

She bandaged his wound and then tugged a blanket over him. "Is it? I've lost all track of time and dates. Is that why there's no fighting?"

The captain did not respond to her question. "Thank you for the blanket. I'm not sure why I feel so cold on such a warm morning."

"You've lost a good deal of blood. But you will recover. The ball passed clean through and didn't hit any bones or arteries. You're a blessed man. Can I get you a hot coffee with sugar and cream?"

"Black is fine. I'm much obliged to you."

As Lyndel strode by the rows of wounded to get the coffee and move on to another patient she spotted Hiram and Morganne off behind a thick cluster of trees. She gave the captain his coffee then walked toward them, smiling at their love and passion as they kissed and hugged each other. Morganne opened her eyes and saw her friend and her face flushed with blood.

"Hiram. Stop. It's Lyndel."

Hiram broke off from kissing her neck and dropped his hands to his side. "Ah. Mrs. King."

Lyndel burst out laughing. "For heaven's sake, I haven't caught you two behind the schoolhouse, have I? You're courting, after all. And your marriage is only months away."

"Sooner than that," said Hiram. "Haven't you heard?"

"Heard what?"

"There was a brisk fight at Appomattox Court House at sunup."

"I know. We have the casualties now."

"Lee could not break through the Union lines. He's trapped for good. There's a cease-fire. He has asked for terms."

"For terms?" Lyndel looked at Hiram in surprise, her blue eyes lightening. "What do you mean? Is he—?"

"Lee is going to surrender the Army of Northern Virginia."

Lyndel gasped. The image of General Lee laying down his sword flashed into her mind and she felt tears start to flow down her cheeks and could hardly speak through the emotion. *So long it has been! So many lives…and is it now over?*

"But what…what about the other armies?" she whispered.

"That is up to their commanding officers. The general consensus is that once Lee's men lay down their arms, the rest of the Rebel armies will follow their lead."

A young man in a derby hat and dark suit came riding up.

"What have you found out, Sam?" Hiram asked.

"Lee is going to meet Grant at the village of Appomattox Court House. Grant let the Confederates choose the location."

"Well, which house is it? Or is it in the court house?"

"Not in the court house, sir. It's a home owned by a Wilmer McLean. They say he lived at Manassas Junction when the first battle took place there in '61. He headed down here to get away from the war."

"So he's in at the beginning and the end, eh? Write that up. Well done, Sam. Let's ride out that way and see how close we can get. What does the house look like?"

"Brick. Not that old. It was put up in '48."

Hiram's horse was cropping grass nearby. He kissed Morganne a final time and swung up into the saddle.

"I'll bring the news back with me when I return. Ladies." He touched his hat and he and Sam rode off across the field and into a line of trees thick with spring green.

Wounded from the dawn fight kept trickling in. The Confederate casualties were more subdued than the prisoners Morganne and Lyndel worked on usually were. Many would scarcely talk. At five-thirty that evening, while the two nurses took a break and sipped coffee with the ambulance drivers, Hiram came riding up with his assistant but did not dismount.

"The surrender is done. Grant's terms came from both himself and the president. They were gracious. Rebel officers keep their sidearms. All troops keep their horses and mules for spring planting. I will tell you more later. We must get to a telegraph station."

Lyndel stood up. "Hiram."

"What is it?"

"What about his sword?"

"Whose sword?"

"What did Lee do with his sword?"

"Why, he kept it. Grant let Lee keep his sword."

As Hiram and Sam rode off, Morganne stood up beside Lyndel and folded her arms over her chest.

"Now what?" she asked. "I feel we ought to do something. I ought to have brought my Martin on this campaign."

"There will still be wounded," Lyndel replied.

"Yes, the ones we have here. But no others. No others, I thank God." Morganne glanced around her. "How green the grass is. How blue the sky. Have you noticed?"

"I notice now."

That night they sat by a fire with one of the surgeons and watched the stars emerge from the darkness.

"How different it feels," Morganne continued to marvel. "Everything in nature feels different."

"The killing has stopped," Lyndel responded.

The next day at noon Lieutenant Carson, who had made sure they joined the surgeons at the beginning of the pursuit of Lee, appeared to escort them back to Richmond and Washington by rail. The two women had done enough, Carson said, and had rendered honorable service to the United States Army and the Republic. It was Easter week and they needed to return to their families. Regular army personnel would take care of what casualties remained.

"You have served our nation with distinction and you are here to witness that it has been made whole again. I am instructed to convey the heartfelt thanks of the Army of the Potomac and of General Grant in particular. Please fetch your belongings and I will see you safely to the capital of our united country."

"Our united country? But the other Confederate armies have not surrendered yet, Lieutenant," protested Lyndel.

"They will, ma'am. The rebellion is finished."

Lyndel assumed travel would be slow and the rail lines clogged with troop trains and freight. But the lieutenant took them on board an express that carried officers who had important dispatches for the secretary of war and the president. The locomotive and its two cars were waved through while other trains had to wait. When they entered Richmond, the city was somber and subdued, fresh ruins jagged and black in the pale April light.

"When the citizens found out Lee's army had abandoned them, they rioted and set those buildings on fire," Carson explained.

A few United States flags hung from charred beams and undamaged brick shops. Union troops were everywhere and Lyndel breathed in the heavy spirit of the defeated Confederacy. It wasn't until Washington that Lyndel caught a different spirit—of a war ended and a war won. The Stars and Stripes filled the air and flew from hundreds of buildings and homes, bands played "Dixie" and "The Battle Hymn of the Republic," couples danced in the parks and the streets. Once night fell hundreds of soldiers paraded with lit candles in the barrels of their muskets, the flames drifting up and down the broad avenues of the capital like feathers on fire.

Morganne still boarded at the Palmer house, and Lyndel and Lieutenant Carson stayed there overnight as guests. The jubilation in Washington and the North had infected the Palmer household too—red, white, and blue bunting decorated all the windows and doorframes, while several large flags draped the walls outside and in.

"The victory is a great relief," said Mr. Palmer as they dined that evening. "It is as if a crushing weight has been lifted off Washington's shoulders."

The lieutenant looked up from his plate. "And placed on Richmond and the South."

Mr. Palmer's face tightened and his wife gave him a worried look, opening her mouth to say something as he set down his fork and knife. But he simply looked out the window across the room from him at the darkness. "It will be so for some time."

Carson escorted Lyndel on the morning train as far as Harrisburg after she bid a long goodbye to Morganne at the depot. At Harrisburg the officer said his farewells and she carried on to Lancaster and Elizabethtown alone. Mr. Palmer had sent a cable on her behalf the night before and Nathaniel and the twins were at the station to meet her, as were her parents. Nathaniel laughed and shouted and lifted her off the ground with his arm. Lincoln and Corinth would not be separated from their mother and at home the three of them lay on the big bed and had a nap while Nathaniel smiled, sat in the rocking chair, and watched them sleep.

Lyndel had been gone for three months and many things had happened among the Amish in Elizabethtown while she had been away. Levi and his wife were expecting their second child. Ham was going to

take his baptismal vows on Easter Sunday and his wedding vows immediately afterward. On Good Friday evening the church would gather at
the Keim house to honor Christ's crucifixion with a singing of hymns.

Lyndel sat with the women that Good Friday, the twins quiet in her
lap, and thought how the Amish hymns that dwelt on suffering and
persecution suited Good Friday with their slow and darkly winding
words. Many times she sang and many times she closed her eyes and
listened to the others talk to God in the shadow of the Cross. When
they walked home from her parents' house, the home where she had
grown up, one part of the sky was completely black while the other
flashed with stars.

She had found it difficult to sleep the first nights back: Corinth
and Lincoln insisted on lying on either side of her and they kicked and
squirmed from dusk to dawn…a bed felt strange to her as did everything about the house and the Amish farming community…the shock
and carnage of battle followed her into the night and into the corners
of her room. But after the slowly moving river of singing on Friday she
slept with the children as if blessed while Nathaniel lay on the narrow
strip of bed and quilt that was left to him.

The knocking at the door of their house made her open her eyes.
The children did not stir but Nathaniel was no longer at her side. She
could see light beyond the shade of the window and wondered what
time it was. Certainly past six or seven. She wished Nathaniel would
stop letting her sleep in. It was time to get back into the daily routine
of an Amish wife and mother, and that meant getting up at five or five
thirty.

She heard her husband's voice thanking someone at the door. A
horse cantered out of their yard and out along the road. The floorboards creaked as Nathaniel took a few steps and stopped. There was a
rustle of paper. Silence.

He opened the bedroom door. There was a telegram in his hand.
She thought he seemed pale and decided it was the dimness of the
room. But his face was like stone.

"What is it?" she whispered. "What's wrong?"

"We have a cable from Hiram."

"Hiram? Is Davey all right? Is it about the wedding?" She sat up. "They're still going ahead with it, aren't they? Next week? I fear the twins will have to travel with us, they won't be parted from me again."

"The president's been shot."

Cold pierced through Lyndel's head and chest. "What? Shot? How could he be shot?" It felt as if a knife had gone into her throat. "They must get the surgeons. Stop the bleeding. Where was he hit? In the leg? In the arm? Someone must apply a tourniquet—"

"He was shot in the back of the head last night." Nathaniel's eyes were large and dark. "His heart stopped beating an hour ago, Lyndel. He's dead."

32

Lyndel stepped from the train and stood on the platform at Elizabethtown. People brushed past her to greet family and friends. A boy was selling newspapers and hollering at the top of his lungs.

"The Sunday edition for April 23rd, 1865! Lincoln's funeral train arrives in Harrisburg on Saturday! Moves on to Philadelphia! Lincoln placed in the east wing of Independence Hall where the Declaration of Independence was signed! Double line of mourners three miles long! Get your copy! This is history, folks!"

A lineup formed in front of him. Men and women had their coins ready. Lyndel stepped off the platform and looked toward the roadway. The sun was bright and she felt the warmth in her black dress.

"Lyndy!"

She turned. Nathaniel smiled and put his arm around her and hugged her tightly.

"How I missed you—even three days is too long! How we all missed you!"

She touched his face. "And I all of you. How are the children? How are you, my darling?"

"I'm well. Lincoln and Corinth have baked you a surprise cake with the help of half the Amish in Lancaster County. And, of course, their cousin, Levi's boy."

Lyndel laughed. "Nathaniel, all three are only a year old. What could they possibly do in the baking of a cake?"

"You can ask them—if you are able to understand their mix of

340

words and half-words you are better off than I am. However, the twins have an even bigger surprise than a cake."

"Oh, what could my sweet babes do that would be an even bigger surprise than a cake they baked?"

"Come home and you'll see."

She leaned against him. "Yes, please, take me home."

Good Boy pulled the carriage along the dirt road to the Amish farms. Lyndel rested her head against Nathaniel's right shoulder where the armless sleeve of his black coat had been pinned up. She closed her eyes a few minutes and listened to the hooves and wheels and the creak of the carriage. Finally she sat up.

"I want to tell you about the funeral procession," she said.

"I should like to hear about that."

"Not everything. Just what I think would have affected you the most."

"All right."

"The day was sunny—like today. African troops were at the front. After that came the funeral car and a horse without a rider. Those of us who wished marched behind."

"Did you?"

"Yes. And the most amazing thing happened. Soldiers poured out of the Washington hospitals and joined the procession. Nathaniel, they were all around me—still with bandages, some getting along as best they could on their crutches—several wore the black hats and uniforms of the Iron Brigade."

"No."

She smiled. "You would have been proud of them. How tall they looked. How brave."

A certain light came into his green eyes as she told him this. It was a light she didn't see often. Leaning forward she patted his knee.

"You knew the Iron Brigade was the honor guard."

His face lit up. "I didn't know that."

"And something else."

"What?"

"As I walked, hundreds—oh, no, thousands—of citizens, black

citizens, formed just ahead of me. They were in lines of forty from curb to curb—one hundred lines! They wore suits and tall black-silk hats and white gloves. They were holding hands as they marched."

"Thanks be to God."

"They laid him in the rotunda of the Capitol. I waited in line and paid my respects—our respects. I prayed."

"*Gut.*"

"I saw General Grant. And Lincoln's son Robert."

"How was…how was Lincoln's face?"

Lyndel brushed at her eyes. "Ah. He almost could have sat up and asked me how our family was. The same weariness. The same sadness. Very hard to see."

"But you're still glad you went."

"Yes, of course. And I believe his face is brighter now, Nathaniel. That he knows the joy that eluded him here."

"Amen to that."

They rounded a bend and the farms were suddenly very close. She could see people milling about in front of their house.

"What is this?" she asked.

"A homecoming."

"A homecoming? Nathaniel, I was only away three days."

"But it's also your birthday."

"Not until later in the week."

He shrugged and grinned. "Two birds with one stone."

She put her hand on the one arm left to him. "Slow down."

"What?"

"You must slow down so you can read something before we reach the house."

"Surely it can wait."

"No."

His left hand tightened on the reins. "Whoa then, Boy, whoa up, take it easy." Once the horse had slowed he looked at Lyndel. "So what is this thing that is so important I must read it immediately?"

She handed him an envelope she had already opened. It was addressed to them. He frowned as he looked down at it, examining it intently. "So this…this looks the same as the handwriting on the pass you took to Antietam."

"There is a reason for that."

He glanced at her then drew the letter from the envelope.

Maundy Thursday

April 13th

Dear Captain and Mrs. King:

There has been so much of a "to do" with General Lee's surrender of the Army of Northern Virginia it reminds me of an Illinois barn-raising, except we seem to be putting up a hundred barns at once with all the meals and celebrations that go with them. Yet I would be remiss if I did not mention several things: my gratitude, Mrs. King, for your volunteering to nurse in the recent Petersburg Campaign despite having two young children at home; the honor you both do me by naming your daughter after myself—daughters are wonderful gifts from our God and Mrs. Lincoln and I did not get our fair share; Captain King, recipient of the Medal of Honor, the thanks once again of a grateful president for the stand of the 19th Indiana and the Iron Brigade on July 1st, 1863, that helped bring our Republic to this glorious day. My speech at Gettysburg then was a simple thing, yet includes much of what I believe about America and the importance of that battle, so

I hope it may be taken as a token of my esteem for you and your men, living and dead.

I look forward to a grand celebration of God and the freedom he extends to us in Christ this Easter Sunday morning. While we venerate the Resurrection of our Lord I believe God will be gracious enough to permit me to also thank him for the resurrection of our nation.

Affectionately.

A. Lincoln

"That is...a great honor," said Nathaniel huskily, returning letter and envelope to Lyndel. "That goes in the family Bible."

"Thank you. I also think that is where we must place it."

"God bless the man."

She bowed her head a moment and nodded. "It was never mailed because of his death. Grant was asked to deliver the letter since he knew me from Petersburg."

"He gave it to you before the funeral?"

"*Ja.* Just hours before."

"Did he say anything?"

"He thanked me again for my nursing work at Petersburg. He also said the day of Lincoln's funeral was the saddest of his life."

Nathaniel thought for a few moments. "*Ja,*" he finally said.

Then he leaned over and kissed her on the cheek. "So. And now are you ready for your birthday party, old woman?"

She laughed. "Charge ahead. I am anxious to see what little Corinth and Lincoln have in store. You have piqued my curiosity, Nathaniel King."

"You won't have long to wait. Hey-yup, Boy, hey-yo!"

Good Boy surged ahead and brought them to the house and a yard overflowing with people in plain dresses and suits. There stood her father and mother and Nathaniel's as well. There was her brother Levi with his wife, Mary Yoder—now Mary Keim—Levi moving so vigorously when he tussled with his son, Nip, that no one could believe he had a wooden leg. Beside him was Ham, baptized into the Amish faith as Jacob, married to Lydia Fischer, and sporting a full beard that providentially masked the battle scars from Seminary Ridge on his jaw and throat. Joshua was close by with his crutches and the shining black Zook boots that came up to his knees. He pointed to a large white cake that took up most of a long table. Corinth and Lincoln shrieked and turned toward her.

Lyndel gasped. "They're on their feet!"

Both had been in their grandmothers' arms when Lyndel had left, both still crawling on the floor of the house and the grass in the yard. Now they stumbled and toddled toward their mother. Lyndel put her hands to her mouth.

"Oh, my heavens, Corinth King! Lincoln King! What a wonderful birthday present for your mother!"

"Lincoln started the day after you left," said Nathaniel. "Corinth walked the day after she did."

Lyndel jumped from the carriage, let her son and daughter fall down, one after the other, get up, and finally fall into her arms.

"Ma," said Corinth happily.

She hugged and kissed him. "Oh, thank you. Corinth King, you are so strong and such a good walker." Then she kissed Lincoln and held her close. "And you, my darling, I've never seen such a beautiful girl anywhere in my whole life. It looks like you've been on your feet for weeks."

Lincoln held a slightly crumpled card out to her.

"What now? My heart is full already."

Holding them to her she opened the card while everyone watched.

April 11, 1865

Dear Mrs. King:

For the assistance rendered at Petersburg that

saved so many wounded who, I am convinced,
would otherwise have perished, you have my
heartfelt thanks and a colt sired by Cincinnati
during an idle moment. My wife says horses
seem to understand me. I hope this colt will
understand you even if no one else is able to
do so.

Yours truly,

Ulysses S. Grant

After reading Grant's words about his gift Lyndel leaped up, a child in each arm, still clutching the note. "Where is he? Where is the colt?" She stared directly at her husband, who hadn't moved from his seat in the carriage, and tried to look fierce. "You knew all about this and said nothing?"

Nathaniel grinned and raised his hand to heaven. "Birthdays are for surprises, not proclamations."

"Come to the paddock behind our stable," laughed her father. "Come, come, bring young Corinth and Lincoln. The colt is waiting for you."

"Does it have a name, Papa?"

"Adam named the animals. You will have to name yours."

Lyndel half-ran to the Keim stable across the road, carrying her two children, greeting everyone as she hurried past. Most of the crowd left the cake and the food to follow, several women draping the heavily laden tables with sheets to keep off the flies.

Smiling, Nathaniel climbed down from the carriage and headed for the stable. There was no one else around so he lifted a corner of a sheet, scooped some icing onto his finger, and placed it in his mouth. Lyndel's shriek of delight upon seeing the colt, when it came, was so loud he was sure they could hear it all the way in the next county. He dropped the sheet back over her birthday cake and began to walk toward the Keim stables. He was certain she would have named the colt by the time he got there, and that it would be a good name that meant something— even if it might be different than one any other Amish horse had ever carried from the time their people had come to America.

Lyndel always ended her story with the naming of the colt "Galatia"—after what she considered was the cry of freedom in the Bible, the letter to the Galatians that Paul had written. Once her listeners left she sat and rocked while Nathaniel wound the clock and made tea. They would each drink a cup and he would tease her that she told the story differently each time—and that she always skipped something. What about how the other Amish communities looked down on her father for permitting soldiers to return to his church? How about the visit by Grant when he was President to see how Galatia, Cincinnati's colt, was faring as a full-grown mare? Why didn't she spend more time on their honeymoon in New York City? Then he would kiss the top of her head, play with a loose strand of hair that still had some red in it, and tell her to come to bed—he had many horses to shoe in the morning and needed a good night's rest.

"In a minute," she would always respond.

She didn't tell the story often. The Amish community didn't want to hear about the war, so the only ones who were interested were people from town or other counties.

All her children had listened to the story again and again. And every time Lyndel spoke about those years it stirred her own feelings and memories and lit a small fire inside.

When Nathaniel would leave her alone with the lamp afterward she would take down the plain wooden box from the mantel of the fireplace, a box that few noticed. Inside was his medal of honor, with its stars-and-stripes ribbon, its eagle, and its five-pointed star, which Abraham Lincoln had fastened to her husband's chest after Gettysburg. There was a slip of paper that spoke of his courage and gallantry in rallying his men at Seminary Ridge. A large gold button from a Union general's uniform also lay in the box. On its back was etched her name and the title *Nurse of the Army of the Potomac*. It had been presented to her after Petersburg. Another piece of paper had written on it the men of Nathaniel's company and platoon. Of course there was the pass to the battle lines that was written in President Lincoln's own hand. And underneath everything was a small envelope. Inside were the wedding rings Moses Gunnison had given them.

The Amish didn't wear wedding bands of any kind. Once they returned to the Amish community in Elizabethtown, Nathaniel and Lyndel had removed them. But the rings meant too much to hide away forever. So Nathaniel had built the box from wood he'd journeyed to Belle Plain to retrieve—in the fall of 1865—part of the log cabin that had been their first home was still standing—and into the box went their keepsakes from a war that had changed their country and changed their own lives and souls.

Lyndel would wear her ring again for a few minutes and turn Nathaniel's over in her hand in the lamplight. She would pray. She would thank God for all that had been, the hardships as well as the times of joy. She would remember that Moses' mother and father had worn the rings and defied the chains of men with their love.

Then in the quiet of her home she would speak softly the words from Galatians that Nathaniel had freely translated from Martin Luther's German, trying to get, he told her, not just the phrasing but the depth, the emotion, the force. It was these words they had spoken over Charlie's grave the day the war had ended, a soft rain on her shoulders and the shoulders of Nathaniel, Levi, Ham, and Joshua, the sun just beginning to make its way through the high pillars of cloud.

Stand fast therefore in the liberty wherewith Christ has made us free. Stand, I say, and do not submit again to a yoke of slavery. It is for this freedom that Christ has died. Do not lose it. Do not spurn it. Hold it to you, body and soul. For it is the gift of God to you through Jesus Christ our Lord.

Forever.

Acknowledgments

Historical fiction stands on two feet—the historical is about *what was* and the fiction is about *what might have been*. In order for *what might have been* to work well and tell a good story, *what was* must be as accurate and authentic as possible. For this I am grateful to my terrific editor at Harvest House, Nick Harrison, for his advice, insight, and support. I also wish to extend my thanks to those American Civil War scholars, living and dead, whose research has helped me to make *The Face of Heaven* as realistic and true-to-life as possible: Bruce Catton, Craig L. Dunn, Ernest B. Ferguson, Shelby Foote, Alan D. Gaff, Gary W. Gallagher, Warren W. Hassler Jr., Lance J. Herdegen, James O. Lehman, James M. McPherson, Mark E. Neely Jr., Alan T. Nolan, Steven M. Nolt, Stephen B. Oates, Stephen W. Sears, John Selby, Brooks D. Simpson, and Noah Andre Trudeau. I am also grateful for the published letters, journals, and diaries of the soldiers, surgeons, and nurses who lived and often died during that conflict. *Requiescat in pace.*

ABOUT MURRAY PURA...

Murray Pura earned his Master of Divinity degree from Acadia University in Wolfville, Nova Scotia, and his ThM degree in theology and interdisciplinary studies from Regent College in Vancouver, British Columbia. For more than twenty-five years, in addition to his writing, he has pastored churches in Nova Scotia, British Columbia, and Alberta. Murray's writings have been short-listed for the Dartmouth Book Award, the John Spencer Hill Literary Award, the Paraclete Fiction Award, and Toronto's Kobzar Literary Award. Murray pastors and writes in southern Alberta near the Rocky Mountains. He and his wife, Linda, have a son and a daughter.

Visit Murray's website at www.murraypura.com.

For more information about Harvest House books,
please visit our website at
harvesthousepublishers.com
and our Amish reader page at
www.amishreader.com

The Wings of Morning

Lovers of Amish fiction will quickly sign on as fans of award-winning author Murray Pura as they keep turning the pages of this exciting new historical romance set in 1917 during America's participation in World War I.

Jude Whetstone and Lyyndaya Kurtz, whose families are converts to the Amish faith, are slowly falling in love. Jude has also fallen in love with flying that newfangled invention, the aeroplane. Though the Amish communities have rejected the telephone and have forbidden motorcar ownership, they have not yet made a decision about electricity or aeroplanes.

Jude is exempt from military service on religious grounds but is manipulated by unscrupulous army officers into enlisting in order to protect several of his Amish friends. No one in the community understands Jude's sudden enlistment and so he is shunned. Lyyndaya's despair deepens at the reports that Jude has been shot down in France. In her grief, she turns to nursing Spanish flu victims in Philadelphia. After many months of caring for stricken soldiers, Lyyndaya is stunned when an emaciated Jude turns up in her ward.

Lyyndaya's joy at receiving Jude back from the dead is quickly diminished when the Amish leadership insists the shunning remain in force. How then can they marry without the blessing of their families? Will happiness elude them forever?